THE CUNNING KILLER
WHO FOOLED EVERYONE . . .
ALMOST!

It was no accident that Ed Post was named Realtor of the Year in the wealthy New Orleans neighborhood of Jefferson Parish. He was smiling, friendly, always "up." More than that, he was a model family man, with a lovely wife and two daughters whom he adored. Everyone who knew him, even his in-laws, considered him a truly great guy.

Certainly no one could ever think of him as a cold-blooded killer.

No one except the team of detectives who set about discovering who Ed Post really was and what he was capable of.

But even after they discovered the truth, with the aid of forensic evidence that became a legal landmark, the upholders of the law had an even more daunting task.

They had to convince a jury—in a trial that put justice itself in shocking jeopardy. . . .

EVIDENCE OF MURDER

EVIDENCE
OF
MURDER

Bill McClellan

AN ONYX BOOK

ONYX
Published by the Penguin Group
Penguin Books USA Inc., 375 Hudson Street,
New York, New York 10014, U.S.A.
Penguin Books Ltd, 27 Wrights Lane,
London W8 5TZ, England
Penguin Books Australia Ltd, Ringwood,
Victoria, Australia
Penguin Books Canada Ltd, 10 Alcorn Avenue,
Toronto, Ontario, Canada M4V 3B2
Penguin Books (N.Z.) Ltd, 182–190 Wairau Road,
Auckland 10, New Zealand

Penguin Books Ltd, Registered Offices:
Harmondsworth, Middlesex, England

First published by Onyx, an imprint of New American Library,
a division of Penguin Books USA Inc.

First Printing, February, 1993
10 9 8 7 6 5 4 3 2 1

REGISTERED TRADEMARK—MARCA REGISTRADA

PRINTED IN THE UNITED STATES OF AMERICA

Acknowledgments

During the course of researching this book, I spent an evening in the apartment of a newspaper columnist who had recently left the *New Orleans Times-Picayune*. We were talking about New Orleans and all the ways in which it differs from other American cities.

"Actually, it's like all other cities except more so," he said.

Much the same could be said about the case of Edward T. Post and its relationship to the criminal justice system.

Post, who is from New Orleans, has been convicted twice of murdering his wife, Julie, who drowned in a bathtub at the Omni Hotel in St. Louis on June 3, 1986. This book is a nonfiction account of that case. There were times during the writing when I wished it were not so.

Given a novelist's freedom, I would have produced a villain as horrible as his crime, and my criminal justice system would have been peopled by heroes and heroines of the highest moral order. Above all, there would have been no ambiguities.

But reality is never as clear as we would wish, and the people who operate within the criminal justice system are no more saintly than the rest of us. Consequently, in many ways Post emerges as a more likable character than the people who brought him to justice, including the chief detective who intuitively knew from the size of Post's feet that Post was guilty.

In this book, as in life, ambiguities abound. But with

that admission, let me thank the people who assisted in my effort to tell an honest story.

Many of the principal characters from St. Louis were already well known to me through my work as a columnist for the *St. Louis Post-Dispatch*. When Post went to trial, I became acquainted with many of the characters from New Orleans.

Later, in New Orleans, I visited again with many of these people and was introduced to many others. Their hospitality and their willingness to talk to me were, and are, much appreciated. Special thanks go to Bill and Judy Bethea and Dan and Martha Post.

In addition to benefiting from old and new friendships, I have been given, by both sides, access to whatever material I have requested—police reports, depositions, grand jury testimony, autopsy reports, military records, and private correspondence.

Attorneys from both sides have freely discussed trial strategy.

Needless to say, recollections sometimes vary. In places where this has occurred, either I have indicated that recollections vary, or, if the difference is insignificant, I have chosen to record the version I consider most credible.

It is especially difficult, of course, to re-create conversations that occurred months, and often years, earlier. When I have attempted to do so, I have tried to remain true to the participants' recollections of the context.

The exact language of those conversations is most often a mix of the participants' recollections and my own observations of a character's use of language.

Many people deserve mention. John McGuire, a fellow *Post-Dispatch* reporter, covered the first trial with me and accompanied me to New Orleans to do research. I am grateful to his wife, Lynn, who had doubts about two Irish newspaper guys going to New Orleans together, but for the most part kept those doubts to herself.

Michaela Hamilton, my editor, and Jim Stein, my

agent, deserve thanks—the latter for working with a writer who is accustomed to writing nothing longer than a newspaper column, the former for exhibiting great patience while the case took some unexpected turns.

And finally, I should thank Edward Post, who has been completely cooperative and unfailingly friendly. Whatever his sins may be, he is good company.

In fact, it is unnerving to visit him in prison, where he seems so obviously out of place. If his is the face of evil, it is a most affable one.

Prologue

Jury selection is a misnomer.

The process ought to be called juror elimination. What a lawyer really tries to do is weed out the people he doesn't want. And Ronnie Monroe, a criminal defense attorney who practiced his craft in Louisiana, knew he was in trouble.

He had already used all his strikes by the time he came to Juror 277. A plump and prosperous-looking man, Juror 277 clearly came from a world where cops are protectors, not predators.

Monroe knew the type. With a guy like this, Monroe's client was guilty until proved innocent.

The client was a young black man named Kelvin Gibson who had been charged with rape. The major part of the state's case came from the testimony of the victim.

Monroe's defense was going to be that old standby, reasonable doubt. Gibson had an alibi, and a clean record. What's more, cross-racial identification was a risky business.

With the right kind of jury, Monroe could win the case. He was sure of it. In fact, this was Gibson's second trial on the charge; the first had ended with a hung jury.

As the new trial began in a small, windowless courtroom on the first floor of the old courthouse—a three-story gray hulk built to WPA standards—Monroe argued reasonable doubt.

Years of trial experience at Tulane and Broad, the geographical location by which the Criminal District Court for the Parish of New Orleans was known, had given Monroe a sixth sense about jurors, and what he sensed now was that Juror 277 would become the foreman. Monroe could tell by the way the man carried himself that he was an executive, self-assured and accustomed to giving orders. In the parlance of the legal profession, he was a bull.

As the trial progressed, Monroe kept his eye on the bull, who was sitting in seat number six, front row, all the way to the right. He was the juror closest to the witness stand.

He was an attentive juror, practically leaning into the witness chair, but he seemed—if Monroe was reading things correctly—entirely too sympathetic toward the prosecution's witnesses.

Months later, Monroe would recall him.

"I could see him, sitting in the front row at the end of the jury box, with that round face of his, and I could tell all along that he wasn't buying anything I said."

Monroe's instincts were on target. When the case went to the jury, Juror 277 was selected foreman. The deliberations lasted less than two hours.

Gibson was convicted. He was eventually sentenced to life without the possibility of parole.

After the trial, the jury foreman confided to friends that the most remarkable aspect of the experience was the reluctance of some of the jurors to vote for a conviction, even with the victim's testimony.

He took full credit for swaying the holdouts.

Three months later, the bull took his wife to St. Louis.

Chapter One

The *Robert E. Lee* riverboat-restaurant swayed gently on its moorings along the west bank of the Mississippi River a block north of the Gateway Arch.

For an early summer evening in St. Louis, the weather was pleasant, warm but not too muggy. Inside the restaurant, the national advisory board of the Better Homes and Gardens real estate service (which is owned by the same corporation that publishes the magazine) was having dinner. The board's three-day meeting in St. Louis would end the next day.

Board members who had finished their three-year terms received plaques. The departing members were expected to say a few words.

Edward T. Post was one of the departing members. When it was his turn to speak, he got up with a smile and surveyed the room. Clearly, he was accustomed to speaking to groups.

"It's been a privilege and a pleasure to have worked with you," he began in a serious tone, and then he shook his head. "Let me get that straight. It's been a pleasure . . . and then a privilege. It's been fun."

Everybody laughed.

Post was forty-two years old. At five feet seven and 180 pounds, he was pudgy, and his round face suggested a man engaged in a lifelong struggle with his weight.

"The next time any of you get to New Orleans, I expect

you to call. Julie and I will show you some Southern hospitality," Post said.

Julie Thigpen Post, seated at her husband's side, looked around at the other tables and smiled. Dark-haired, fair-skinned, and slim, she was thirty-nine years old.

In the days to come, when the detectives would refer to the dinner as the Last Supper, her fellow partygoers would struggle to remember Julie's mood on what would be the final night of her life—a little quiet maybe, a little reserved.

Her husband's mood was easier to recall. Outgoing and friendly, Ed Post stood out even in a crowd of salesmen. He was always "on," always upbeat.

In the minds of some of his colleagues, his positive attitude bordered on the unnatural. Everybody knew that the economy in New Orleans was terrible. Even more than Texas and Oklahoma, Louisiana was geared to oil. In the spring of 1986, the domestic oil industry was suffering, and the real estate market was awful.

"Sure, the market is down," Ed would say, "but oil won't stay down forever, and the market will come back with it. Besides, there are opportunities in a down market."

For instance, Ed and his brother, a real estate attorney, had recently become general partners in a limited real estate partnership. If a listener wanted to know about the tax advantages of such a plan, Ed could knowledgeably discuss the intricacies of the tax code.

It wasn't only real estate or taxes he could talk about. He was a gourmet cook, a golfer, a wine connoisseur, a scuba diver, a photographer, a sky diver, an opera buff, a yachtsman, and, most recently, a jogger. In addition, he had been a Green Beret, and if anybody wanted to swap military stories, Ed loved to talk about a jungle training exercise in Panama during which he had been forced to eat snakes.

Often, it seemed, there wasn't a subject he couldn't discuss.

When the dinner party concluded shortly before midnight, the partygoers were ferried in a chartered bus back to their hotel.

Except for her husband, nobody ever saw Julie Post alive again.

At approximately 7:00 the next morning, Post emerged from the elevator into the lobby of the hotel.

He was wearing dark shorts, a white T-shirt, and expensive running shoes. As he crossed the lobby, he stopped briefly to speak to the concierge.

"I believe you're the one who told us about the Botanical Garden," Post said. "My wife finally got to see it yesterday. Spectacular. Just wonderful."

The concierge smiled.

"Well, if I'm going to run, I'd better get to it. I know I'll feel better when I stop!" said Post.

Flashing a grin at his own humor, Post continued on his way. When he reached the street, he spoke to the doorman.

"How you doing this morning? My name is Ed Post, and I'm a guest here. I'm going on a run this morning, and I expect to be gone about thirty minutes. Would you watch for me, please?"

"Yessir."

The Omni Hotel was located in Union Station about a mile and a half west of the Mississippi River.

As Post headed toward the river on this Tuesday morning, the city was beginning to come to life. Jogging east on Market Street, he passed the Municipal Courts Building, City Hall, the federal courthouse (the official name is the U.S. Courthouse and Custom House), and the Civil Courts Building. Then he was into the downtown business district. He headed toward the Gateway Arch, shimmering in the morning sun, but before reaching it, he veered to the south, toward Busch Stadium.

Then back west. As he approached Union Station, he angled north, cutting through the City Hall parking lot. Over his left shoulder was the downtown police station. Next to it was the city morgue. In front of him, as he cut through the lot, was City Jail, its small exercise yard bordered by a chain-link fence topped with concertina wire.

Turning the corner of City Hall, he ran past a man in a dark uniform. A cop, he thought. He noticed the man's name tag. Gay.

As he neared the end of his run, he saw an acquaintance from Better Homes and Gardens jogging away from the hotel.

"Have a good run!" Post called.

And then he was back in front of the hotel. To cool off, he walked an additional block, and then returned. He spoke to the doorman and entered the hotel. It was approximately 7:40 A.M.

Bette Schwent was working the switchboard at the main desk when the call came in at 7:43 A.M.

A voice she would remember as calm and unruffled announced an emergency in room 4063.

"My name is Edward Post, and I'm staying in room four zero six three. I found my wife in the bathtub, and she's not breathing. I need some help. Would you read that room number back to me so I know you have it right?"

"Yessir. That's four zero six three."

After telling her supervisor about the situation, Schwent called the security office to send help to the room. While she was on the phone, her supervisor called 911.

Two security officers from the hotel, a young man and woman, were the first to arrive at Post's room. The door was locked. They knocked, and a man wearing jogging clothes opened the door. He then ducked back into the bathroom, and proceeded to continue, or so they assumed, efforts to resuscitate the woman lying on the bathroom floor.

The woman was naked and lying on her back next to the tub. A towel had been thrown over her midsection.

Both of the security officers had been trained in CPR, but neither had actually performed it on anyone in an emergency situation.

Beverly Minor, the female security officer, took charge, squeezing past Post into the bathroom. She tilted the woman's head back, trying to clear the breathing passage, and then put her mouth to the woman's and attempted to blow air into her lungs. Post continued the chest compressions.

Minor's partner stood awkwardly. Uncertain of what to do, but wanting to help, he told Post that his hands were too low—"They're supposed to be on the chest, man." Then he made a halfhearted attempt to scoot Post away so he could take over, but Post and Minor had already achieved a rhythm, and it made no sense to interrupt it. There wasn't much room in the bathroom, so the young man backed away.

"Have you got an ambulance coming?" Post asked him.

That gave the young man something to do. He called the hotel dispatcher on his radio, and requested an ambulance. Then he went down to the lobby to await the EMS crew.

Actually, an EMS crew had already been notified by the 911 dispatcher. The closest ambulance, Medic 5, had been notified of a code 306—an unconscious person—at the Omni Hotel. But before the ambulance and paramedics arrived at 7:54, an EMS supervisor, who had been cruising around downtown, monitoring the radio, pulled up in front of the hotel. The security guard led him to room 4063.

Minor was more than happy to turn things over to a professional. Her efforts didn't seem to be working.

At one point, the man in the jogging outfit had stopped

the chest compressions. "We've been married for twenty years," he said, half-sobbing. Then he had resumed the chest compressions.

The EMS supervisor quickly went to work. He knelt next to the woman and turned her half over so he could get a hand under her back. He began rubbing his knuckles along her sternum.

These nerves are among the last a person loses as he or she slips into unconsciousness. When a sternal rub gets no reaction, it is a bad sign. This one got no reaction.

The supervisor also noted that the woman was not breathing. He felt for a pulse, and got none.

All this took only seconds.

He began CPR, using a demand valve, a plastic mask that fit over the patient's mouth and nose and, when manually compressed, inflated the patient's lungs.

Nothing.

Then the EMS crew arrived with more advanced equipment, and the supervisor stepped back.

Having a well-trained, fully equipped EMS crew at the scene was like bringing an emergency room to an accident. The paramedics came fully equipped with drugs, IVs, an EKG machine, a defibrillator to shock the heart, endotracheal tubes to clear the air passage, and Ambu bags, which are mask-like devices that connect to oxygen tanks, to provide high concentrations of oxygen to the lungs.

After moving Julie into the bedroom—they didn't want to work with the electrical equipment in the wet bathroom—the paramedics tried to bring her back to life.

Post called Minor into the bathroom.

"Look at that," he said pointing to the tub. "That must be what happened."

In the bottom of the tub was a towel ring.

Minor glanced up at the wall next to the tub where the towel ring should have been. The plate that attached to the wall was still there, but the towel ring itself had been yanked off.

"She must have slipped, and grabbed the ring to support herself," Post said.

Patrolman Timothy Kaelin had been at a convenience store getting a cup of coffee when the call came out: accident with injury at the Omni Hotel. By the time he got to room 4063, the EMS crew was already at work.

Kaelin had the boyish looks of a rookie but had actually been in the department for eleven years. He asked a member of the hotel staff if anybody knew what had happened, and the staff person pointed to Post.

"That's her husband."

Kaelin walked over to Post, who was intently watching the EMS crew. Kaelin asked Post what had happened.

"I went jogging, and came back and she was unconscious in the tub," Post said.

Kaelin watched the paramedics for a moment. They worked purposefully, quickly.

"I'm going to need to get a statement from you," Kaelin told Post. "I don't think there's anything we can do in here. Why don't we see if there's another room around here where we can talk."

The room next door was vacant, and Post and Kaelin went inside.

"If you would, start at the beginning," Kaelin said. "Who are you, who is she, and what happened?"

Post nodded, and began talking.

He said he was a real estate executive from New Orleans. The company that he partly owned was affiliated with the Better Homes and Gardens network. As a member of the national advisory board, he had to go to a lot of conventions. He and his wife were attending one in St. Louis.

Julie Post, his wife of twenty years, was the woman in the other room.

Kaelin asked what had happened that morning.

Post said he had been planning to go running before the

morning meeting. He had a wake-up call set for 6:30, but woke on his own at 6:25. He called the front desk and canceled the call. There was no sense disturbing Julie.

He then shaved before pouring a glass of water for his wife. He woke her, saying that as soon as he got back from his run, he'd have to wash up. If she wanted to eat with him before his meetings, as he knew she would, she ought to get up. This was the Posts' last day in St. Louis.

She was having her period, and when she complained about a pain in her back, he got out some oil they had gotten at a previous convention to give her a massage.

Then he drew her bath, and when the water was ready, he walked her into the bathroom. She said the water was too hot, so he added a little cold.

Post said he didn't actually see his wife get into the tub. She was standing next to it when he kissed her goodbye. As he left the hotel room to go running, he noticed the bathroom door was slightly ajar.

When he came back after his run, he expected to see his wife in the bedroom. She wasn't, so he called out her name. He wasn't panicked yet, just perplexed. He noticed the bathroom door was still slightly ajar.

He walked into the bathroom, almost slipping on some water. And there she was, lying facedown in the tub, her hair floating on the water.

"It was awful," Post said.

He managed to get her out of the tub, and then he called the front desk to ask for help.

Kaelin listened to the story without comment. Perhaps he raised his eyebrows a bit when Post was talking about the massage oil—that had a kinky ring to it—but otherwise, he didn't ask much. He simply jotted it all down. Later, he would think it had been an awfully detailed statement for such a stressful situation, but at the time he was too busy writing to notice.

"Let me show you something," Post said. "I think it explains everything."

They went back into room 4063, and Post led Kaelin into the bathroom. He pointed to the towel ring at the bottom of the tub.

"She must have slipped, and grabbed for the ring."

The conversation in the bathroom was interrupted by a flurry of activity in the next room. The EMS crew had decided to take Julie to the emergency room. She was, as she had been from the start, in full cardiac arrest.

"I'll drive you to the hospital," Kaelin said to Post.

As they started to leave, two other policemen arrived, a sergeant and a patrolman. "Better call homicide," Kaelin said as he walked out of the room.

The suggestion was not judgmental. In St. Louis, the homicide unit was called to the scene in cases of accidental or suspicious death. If the homicide detectives determined that no foul play was involved, they turned the case back to the district patrolmen.

Even though Kaelin didn't question Post's story, he had seen the EKG monitor. It was flat. This looked as if it was going to be more serious than an accident with an injury.

One of Post's friends from Better Homes and Gardens rode with Kaelin and Post to the hospital, where they were taken to a small waiting room next to the emergency room.

Kaelin walked over to a pay phone. He called his wife.

"Honey, you won't believe what happened to a woman this morning. It's really tragic."

A homicide crew, a plainclothes sergeant and two detectives, arrived at the hotel shortly after Kaelin and Post left. One of the detectives, Dan Nichols, walked into the bathroom. Without touching anything, Nichols leaned across the tub to study the wall plate that had once held the towel ring. Then he eyed the towel ring, which was still lying in the tub. Tempted to reach down and pick it up, he stopped himself. Better to let the evidence technicians gather the evidence. When a crime scene gets contaminated, the culprit is most often a curious cop.

Nichols estimated that there were about six or seven inches of water in the tub. He saw no sign of blood. He noticed that the shower curtain was inside the tub and the water spigot was turned all the way to hot.

Meanwhile, the homicide sergeant spoke briefly with the two officers in uniform. "The husband says he found her in the tub when he came back from his morning run," the uniformed sergeant said.

The homicide sergeant nodded. He walked into the bathroom and shut the door. A few minutes later, the toilet flushed and the homicide sergeant came out.

"Let's go," he said to his two detectives. "We're kicking it back to the district. Accident."

Nichols was flabbergasted.

"Let's not play this too cheap," said Nichols.

The detective sergeant gave him a quizzical look. "She probably had a heart attack. Let's go."

Nichols shrugged and shook his head. The uniformed sergeant from the district grinned at him.

A photographer from the evidence technicians unit, or ETU, had arrived to take pictures. Hearing that it was an accident, he turned to leave.

"Go ahead and take some for us," said the uniformed sergeant.

The photographer started into the bathroom, and then came back out. "We got to let this place air out," he said.

Everybody laughed. The homicide detectives were members of an elite, high-profile unit. It was good to have some fun at their expense.

Finally, the photographer went in and took his pictures. The cops left. The police investigation was over.

*   *   *

At the hospital, Ed Post still waited. A nun, whose job it was to comfort family members in time of crisis, had arrived from the hospital chapel.

She thought Post seemed nervous and upset. Neither emotion struck her as out of the ordinary.

At 9:03, the emergency room doctor pronounced Julie dead. The nun accompanied Post into the emergency room to see the body, and then she led him in the recitation of the Lord's Prayer.

"Would you like a few minutes alone with her?" the nun asked.

Post nodded. He seemed to be holding back tears.

When he returned to the waiting room, Lee Foster, the organ tissue coordinator for transplant services, approached him and began his "I'm very sorry but" speech.

"Whatever you can use I'll agree to," Post said.

He would later explain that he and Julie, a former president of the New Orleans Ladies Leukemia Society, were both strong believers in organ donations.

Shortly before leaving the hospital, Kaelin got a phone call from Joe Beffa, one of the homicide detectives.

"The sergeant says we're calling it an accidental death. What do you think, Tim?"

"Yeah, I think it's an accident," Kaelin said.

On the drive back to the hotel, Post brought up the towel ring again. He asked who was going to get it.

Kaelin promised that the police department would seize it as evidence. "You're going to have a hell of a lawsuit," he said. He couldn't help sympathizing with the bereaved widower.

They returned to the hotel, and on the elevator Post pulled out his wallet.

"I want to show you what she really looked like," he said. He pulled out a photograph of Julie.

Kaelin nodded. The woman in the photo was nice-looking.

Post's belongings had been moved to another room, and

one of his real estate associates led him away. Kaelin
proceeded to room 4063 to get the towel ring.

It was gone.

Maybe the homicide team, or the police photographer
from the evidence technicians unit, had already seized it,
Kaelin thought. But one of the hotel security guards who
had been watching the room said the police officers hadn't
taken anything, that the photographer had only shot a couple of pictures and then left.

The guard said that Gerald Arbini, the director of security for the hotel, had taken the ring. Kaelin went to
Arbini's office. His secretary told him Arbini wasn't in,
and she asked if she could help.

"I'm here to get the towel ring from room 4063," Kaelin said.

"It's on Mr. Arbini's desk," the secretary replied.

She walked over to the desk, picked up the towel ring,
and handed it to Kaelin.

As he would later testify, he would not even have
thought about the towel ring if Post had not mentioned it
on the way back from the hospital. At the time he retrieved
it from Arbini's office, he thought he was doing Post a
favor.

The mood in the hotel room where Post had been taken
was one of disbelief. People were coming to express their
sorrow. Many were crying. Post himself seemed to alternate between grief and shock.

During his lucid periods, he used the phone. From the
hospital, he had already called his brother, Dan, in New
Orleans. An attorney three years older than Ed, Dan made
plans to fly to St. Louis immediately.

Later from the hotel room, Post called Harby Kreeger,
a close friend, who then called Dalton Truax, Post's business partner, to let him know of the tragedy. Truax called
Post at the hotel and agreed to get the funeral arrangements
moving.

Post then called Ashton Phelps, Jr., the publisher of the *New Orleans Times-Picayune*, to inquire about an obituary.

And finally, Post called Kim Autin, Julie's best friend, who was vacationing in Florida.

Dan Post arrived in St. Louis shortly after noon. After a tearful embrace, the brothers discussed all the details that would have to be taken care of. Of foremost importance was how to break the news to Ed's teenage daughters. The brothers decided to fly home that evening and tell them.

They then discussed how to tell Julie's parents, Hollis and Etta Mae Thigpen, who lived in Poplarville, Mississippi. They felt somebody should tell them personally. Ed settled on Bill Bethea, a doctor who lived in New Orleans and had a summer home next to the Thigpens' home. Ed would call Bill and ask him to drive out and tell the Thigpens.

And then the brothers went to room 4063 to take pictures of the bathroom. They had a tape measure and a camera. Ed held the tape measure while Dan took the pictures.

It was going to be a hell of a lawsuit.

The first person other than Detective Nichols to feel a sense of unease about the death of Julie Post was Wanda Meyer, the nurse clinician for the hospital's orthopedic department.

She was a nightcrawler, as members of the bone-removal team called themselves, because ordinarily bone harvesting was done only at night, so as not to tie up the operating rooms. First priority went to the living.

But on the day of Julie's death, the nightcrawlers were given an operating room at 1:15 in the afternoon. The medical examiner's office had said that a funeral home in New Orleans wanted the body as quickly as possible, and the medical examiner wanted to expedite matters.

He would perform an autopsy in the morning, and then release the body. If the hospital wanted to remove the bones, it had better do so immediately.

As Meyer examined the body in preparation for the removal of the long bones, she was troubled, although she couldn't exactly say why.

In her examination, she found only two abnormalities— a soft area on the back of the skull, and an abrasion on the right temple. Otherwise, the body seemed to be in perfect condition. That in itself was unusual, but understandable, since this was a drowning victim rather than, as is much more common, a traffic-accident victim.

Unable to shake the sense that something was wrong, she called the medical examiner's office to make sure the ME would authorize a procedure as extensive as a bone harvesting before the autopsy.

The ME's office checked with the police department. The sergeant from homicide who had handled the case assured the medical examiner that this was an accidental death. So while state law still required an autopsy, the hospital could go ahead with its bone harvesting.

The nightcrawlers went to work. They removed the long bones from the body and inserted wooden dowels in their place. Julie's eyes were also removed.

Dr. Bill Bethea was nearly thirty years younger than Hollis Thigpen, and their relationship was closer to that of a father and son than of neighbors. They had met shortly after Bill and his wife, Judy, bought a weekend home in Poplarville. Hollis and Etta Mae Thigpen, who lived about a quarter of mile away down a dirt road, were their closest neighbors.

Although Thigpen had amassed a sizable fortune in the construction business, mostly working in and around New Orleans, he was a country man at heart. After selling his business, he returned to the small Mississippi town where he had been raised, the oldest boy in a family of five children. He bought 120 acres, and in the middle of it he built a modest house on a hill.

Thigpen had gone into construction while still a teenager. He had been working in Mobile, Alabama, when he met and married Etta Mae. He had joined the Marine Corps in World War II. On Iwo Jima, he was a quarter of a mile away from Mount Surabachi when the American flag was raised. After the war, he went back into construction. He moved to New Orleans in 1954, and twelve years later he founded his own construction business.

He was, he liked to say, a man who had started at the bottom of the ditch.

The Thigpens had four children, two sons and two daughters, and while Hollis loved all his children, he'd always had a special relationship with his oldest daughter, Julie.

From the time she could walk, Julie was always following her daddy. If Thigpen was digging in the front yard, Julie would be standing next to him.

"Child, you are in my hair all the time!" he would say in his very pronounced Mississippi drawl.

But if she wasn't standing next to him, he was sure to be looking around wondering where she was.

He had not been enthusiastic when Julie came home from college with a suitor, but his feelings had less to do with the particular suitor—Ed Post seemed like a nice enough young man—than with Julie's age. She was nineteen when she brought Ed home and announced her intention to marry him.

"You're just a child," Thigpen told her, but she was her father's daughter, and the same determination that had led Thigpen to success was evident in her eyes that night. Thigpen gave in to the inevitable.

Through the years, father and daughter had remained close. Julie and her family were frequent visitors to the Thigpens' home in Poplarville, and consequently Bill and Judy Bethea got to know the Posts well.

On the afternoon after Julie's death, Ed Post called Bethea. He briefly explained what had happened, and then he asked Bethea to go to Poplarville to break the news to Julie's parents.

Bethea was too stunned to do more than ask a couple of questions. "She drowned? In a bathtub?"

"Nobody's sure what happened yet, Bill. It looks like she fell and hit her head. She must have been knocked out," Post said, and then he repeated his request that Bethea go to Poplarville and tell the Thigpens.

"I think it would be best if somebody were with them. I don't think they should hear it over the phone, Bill, and I've got to tell my daughters tonight. Soonest I could get to Poplarville would be tomorrow, and that's too late."

"Of course we'll go," Bethea said.

Bill and Judy Bethea set off for Poplarville. It was only a little more than an hour's drive from New Orleans, but they must have gone through almost a pack of cigarettes in that hour.

They kept hoping that Post had called some other family members, and that maybe somebody else would already be at the Thigpens'. Bill and Judy Bethea didn't want to be the ones to tell them.

They arrived in Poplarville, drove through the town, and continued eight miles down Mississippi Route 26 before turning left onto the dirt road that led to the Thigpens'. To their dismay, they saw that nobody else was there.

Bethea pulled the car up to the house, and Bear, the Thigpens' old three-legged giant of a mutt, came hobbling over. Then the door opened, and Hollis Thigpen came out. He was of average height, and slender, and his eyes sparkled with an intelligence that age had not dimmed.

"Well, if this isn't a treat," he said. "Come on in and have a drink."

The Betheas followed Thigpen into the house. Mrs.

Thigpen was sitting at the kitchen table shucking corn. She looked up and smiled.

Thigpen walked over to the cabinet to get a bottle. Bethea stopped him.

"Hollis, please sit down," he said.

Thigpen sat down. His wife, suddenly wary, stared at Bill.

"Hollis, Etta Mae, I don't know any good way to tell you this, so I'm just going to say it. Julie's dead. She fell and hit her head, and drowned in a bathtub. I don't know any more about it, but she's dead. I'm sorry."

He waited for a reaction.

Etta Mae had gone back to shucking the corn. Hollis was staring straight ahead. Finally, he spoke.

"Dammit. She was just about to get married."

Bethea knew that this was wrong. Julie's younger sister, Joanne, was the one getting married.

"Hollis, I'm not talking about Joanne. I'm talking about Julie."

"Just about to get married," Hollis repeated, as if to himself.

Etta Mae continued to shuck the corn.

A couple of hours later, Ed and Dan Post arrived in New Orleans. Early in the flight, Ed had started to cry. The thought that he was leaving his wife's body in St. Louis alone, even for a night, was too much, he said. A stewardess came over and asked what the problem was. Dan explained that Ed's wife had just died in a terrible accident. The stewardess moved the brothers to the first-class section.

During a layover in Memphis, Ed called the Thigpens. The Betheas were still at their home. Ed told Hollis about the accident. He said he wasn't sure how it had happened, but apparently Julie had fallen in the tub.

When the plane arrived in New Orleans, Ed's partner,

Dalton Truax, and his friend Harby Kreeger were waiting, along with their wives. There was much crying.

Then Ed and Dan went to their parents' house, where the family had been assembled. Ed took his daughters upstairs and told them that their mother had fallen in the hotel bathtub, struck her head, lost consciousness, and drowned.

The girls took it hard, especially Stephanie, who at fifteen was the older by three years. She was small and pretty, and had light brown hair. She was also extremely emotional, and upon hearing of her mother's death, she became hysterical.

Her younger sister, Jennifer, similar in appearance but with lighter hair, took the news more calmly. The quieter of the two, and seemingly possessed of an inner strength that her sister lacked, she cried when she heard about her mother, but she didn't lose control.

At about the same time, Kim Autin was calling the real estate office where she and Julie had worked together.

One of the other agents, Katie Lehman, picked up the phone.

"Are you sitting down?" Kim asked her.

"Sure," said Katie, with a quick rush of anticipation. Kim was a beautiful young woman, and some of her older colleagues, like Katie, got a big kick out of her. People, especially men, always said the goofiest things to pretty women. Kim was a wonderful source of stories.

"I just can't believe this," said Kim, and there was something in her voice that made Katie understand that whatever she had to say was not going to be funny.

At this point, recollections vary. Kim recalls being emotionally distraught, and blurting out the news that Julie was dead.

Katie recalls it another way.

She remembers Kim telling her to sit down, and then hitting her with the news.

"I think Ed just killed Julie."

Chapter Two

"Will somebody tell me why in the hell this was kicked back to the district? Does anybody know why we let this guy get out of town without so much as questioning him?"

Lieutenant George Hollocher, deputy commander of homicide, stormed around the office, talking to nobody in particular. He was a big man, tall and husky, with hair slicked straight back in a style that had gone out with Elvis Presley.

Because there was no homicide report, Hollocher read from the incident report that Patrolman Kaelin had prepared the previous day.

"Listen to this. This is good. 'Edward Post stated that at approximately 6:25 A.M. he awoke from his sleep and prepared for his morning jog.' "

Hollocher looked around and took a drag from his unfiltered cigarette.

" 'His morning jog.' Isn't that nice?"

Some of the detectives exchanged grins.

"Let me keep reading. It only gets better. 'Post stated that prior to him leaving his room, he prepared the bathwater for his wife.' "

Hollocher took another drag from his cigarette and flicked the ashes on the linoleum floor.

"Nothing suspicious there. No reason to talk to the guy just because his wife ends up dead in the tub. After all, he was out *jogging* after he prepared her morning bath."

Muttering profanities, he walked over to the hot plate,

where two pots of coffee were keeping warm. "Regular" and "Decapitated," said the hand-lettered signs. He picked up the regular and poured himself a cup.

Hollocher looked like the kind of cop who enjoyed beating confessions out of people. The lieutenant did nothing to discourage those rumors. He was forty-six years old, and he belonged to the old school. He was not into sensitivity.

He had a huge, and mixed, reputation.

In one incident, a gunman was holding a woman hostage in the basement of a downtown building. Knowing that the woman had already been shot and was in need of medical attention, the cops sent a police dog down to try to flush the gunman out. When the dog was shot, Hollocher pulled out his gun and stormed into the basement alone. He killed the gunman and rescued the woman. It was like something out of the movies.

Another time he and his partner were interviewing a prisoner at City Jail when a riot broke out on another floor. To the astonishment of his partner, Hollocher marched up to the floor where the prisoners were out of their cells, roaming loose in the cellblock. From behind the cagelike cellblock door, Hollocher shouted at them.

"You've got ten seconds to get back in your cells, or I'm coming in," he announced.

There were more than two dozen prisoners, and at first, they laughed. But by the time Hollocher counted to nine, most had retreated into their cells. At the count of ten, Hollocher went in. He kicked one and slugged another, and the rest raced to their cells.

The Hollocher legend also had its flip side. There were stories about brutality, stories about favors for informants, and mostly there were stories about his tendency to exaggerate. Hollocher was, without doubt, the best storyteller in the department, but his sense of the dramatic outweighed his regard for the truth.

He had been off duty on the day of Julie Post's death.

Now he was letting everybody know that had he been in the office, the case would not have been kicked back to the district.

The detective sergeant who had handled—or mishandled—the case was not in the office as Hollocher stomped around, and none of the other detectives were at all cowed by Hollocher's behavior.

The jokes had started the day before with the story about the sergeant using the bathroom. Dark humor is common in a police department, and the humor is at its darkest in a homicide unit. "Our day begins when yours ends," said the sign in the section supervisor's office.

Normally, that's where the whole thing would have ended, with a little grousing and a few jokes.

But the spring of 1986 was not normal times. The new commander was from the new school. He was active in various civil rights groups, and he prided himself on his sensitivity. The sergeant who had blown this case was considered an ally of the commander. To show him up would be to show the commander up.

Hollocher would like nothing more.

After reading the incident report, Hollocher decided to go to the hotel and see if the security people there thought the death was an accident. He put on his fedora—the mark of an old-school detective—and drove to Union Station.

Union Station was a tribute to an age of optimism for the city of St. Louis. In 1891, the city fathers decided to build a monument to the future, something gaudy but practical. The decision was made to build the greatest railway station in the world.

The architectural plan borrowed heavily from the massive forms of the walled city of Carcassonne in southern France. The design came in three parts—the showplace headhouse or main building, with Romanesque arches and turrets; a 720-foot-long midway; and the train shed.

The structure was completed in 1894. Rising above this

limestone castle, with its turrets and its arches, was the design's signature—a 225-foot-tall clock tower.

But the station's most spectacular feature was its cavernous Grand Hall, an arching chamber with a sixty-foot vaulted ceiling covered with plaster moldings and sculptures, frescoes, elaborate light fixtures, and stained glass.

By the beginning of the century, more railroads converged at St. Louis than at any other point in the United States. But eventually, passenger traffic slowed, and the station's decline seemed to mirror the decline of the city it served. By the late 1970s, Union Station was deserted.

In the summer of 1985, after a rehab that cost $135 million, the station reopened. The old midway was lined with restaurants and shops. The train shed was a parking lot. The project was anchored by the Omni, a 550-room hotel located in the old headhouse. The Grand Hall served as its lobby.

From that lobby, Post had emerged for his morning jog.

Hollocher talked to Gerald Arbini, the security chief of the Omni Hotel. Arbini definitely thought something was wrong. He told Hollocher that the bathwater had been cool to the touch. He talked about Post's lawyer brother, who had been busy with his camera. And he told Hollocher about the towel ring. It looked as though it had been worked off the wall, he said.

The commander of homicide airily dismissed Hollocher's concerns, so Hollocher went over his boss's head.

He went to a major, another old-school cop, and received permission to go to New Orleans to talk to Post. Hollocher was authorized to take one man with him, and he chose Steve Jacobsmeyer, a sergeant and a veteran of the homicide unit. They decided to get to New Orleans in time for the funeral.

Before meeting with the major, Hollocher had gone downstairs to the fourth district station, which was housed in the downtown headquarters building, where the homicide division was also located.

Kaelin's report mentioned that the towel ring had been seized as evidence. Hollocher asked to see it, and a sergeant took it out of the evidence locker and handed it over.

Hollocher studied it, turning it over in his hand. He saw that the stem of the ring, the metal piece that attached to the plate on the wall, looked twisted.

"I suppose I can't sign this thing out, but I figure the ETU guys got some pictures. I want 'em," he said.

"Sure, Lieutenant. But the case is district-level, right?"

"Officially, yeah. Unofficially is something else again."

While Hollocher was at the police station, Dr. Michael Graham was busy conducting an autopsy on the body of Julie Post, which had arrived from the hospital the previous night.

Graham noted a small bruise on the right side of the head just above and in front of the ear, another on the bridge of the nose, two contusions on the left elbow, and a superficial scraping of the skin in the right temple area. When he opened the scalp to get into the skull, he found a two-inch bruise on the top right back of the head.

There were no skull fractures, nor was there any bleeding either on the surface of the brain or in the brain itself. In all probability, that meant that none of the head bruises would have rendered Julie unconscious.

All organs were normal. The stomach was virtually empty, so there was no way to determine the time of death. Toxicology tests showed no evidence of alcohol or drugs in the blood.

Graham certified drowning as the cause of death.

By law, he was required to classify the death. He had five choices: natural, suicide, accidental, undetermined, or homicide.

Natural, in this instance, would mean that some natural

disease had caused her to die. That seemed out of the question.

He saw no indication that this was a suicide. He felt uncomfortable calling it an accident. He felt equally uncomfortable calling it a homicide.

So he settled for undetermined.

The body of Julie Post was flown to New Orleans that afternoon.

Chapter Three

From the window of his office, Ben Matthews could see the traffic flowing along De Gaulle Drive. Storm clouds were rolling in from New Orleans across the river.

Slowly, painfully, he got up from his desk. The muscular dystrophy that had afflicted him in his adulthood was getting worse. Despite his medical problems, he was still a handsome man at forty-three, and looked younger than his years. He bore a slight resemblance—facially only—to Arnold Schwarzenegger.

Gripping the handles of his walker, he moved toward his door. "Storm's coming," he announced into the general office. "Looks like a big one."

Several of his agents sat at their desks, and upon his arrival, they looked up with affection. Matthews was a popular boss.

He returned to his office.

Julie's dead, he thought, sitting back in his chair. It was hard to believe.

As a high school chum of Ed's, and then a business associate for the past eighteen years, Matthews had known Julie very well.

In the early years, he had liked her, more than he had liked Ed, for that matter. Julie had seemed much more natural than Ed. Sometimes Ed's good spirits struck Matthews as forced, while Julie was always fresh, intelligent, spunky. Nothing seemed artificial about her.

But then, unfortunately, she had become a real estate

saleswoman. When Ed and Ben left one real estate agency to come to the Wagner-Truax agency, Julie joined Wagner-Truax, too. She had been assigned to the West Bank office, the office that Matthews managed.

In the very beginning, he had told her, kiddingly, that she posed a potential problem. Her husband, after all, was part-owner and general manager of the company.

"Don't ever forget the boss's wife syndrome," Matthews had said with a smile.

Forget the syndrome? It turned out Julie exemplified it.

She was impossible to get along with. She openly and repeatedly challenged Matthews's authority. She was critical of her coworkers and their working habits. She even ridiculed their clothes. It seemed as if she went out of her way to be spiteful.

When Ben would tell Ed of her disruptiveness, and he repeatedly did, Ed always downplayed the complaints. "I'm the boss. She's my wife. It's natural for the others to resent her."

Finally, early in 1986, Matthews called Ed and said things had gone too far. Other agents were threatening to leave the agency. Ed agreed to try to settle things, and he and Julie went to Ben's house for a big meeting.

Right in front of Julie, Ben told Ed the truth.

"The situation is completely out of hand," he said. "Julie is a negative force in the office. We're going to have a revolt. People are going to quit."

Ed turned to Julie.

"This is our company," he said. "We own part of it. You should be building people up instead of tearing them down."

The meeting ended with Julie accepting all the blame. She cried. She promised to be better.

Matthews felt like a heel. As an employee, Julie was an absolute headache. But Matthews knew the way she used to be, and he didn't believe that the office witch was the real Julie. So when she broke down, he felt more remorseful than triumphant.

She's under a lot of pressure, he thought. Maybe he was being too hard on her.

But three days later, Ben got called into the main office. Ed and Dalton Truax, the big boss, needed to see him.

"Your love life is getting out of hand," Ed told him. "Your office romance with one of the agents is unprofessional. It's a distraction to the other agents, and it's a disruptive influence in the office."

Ben was stunned. He'd made no secret of his involvement with one of the agents. Both he and the agent were divorced. What's more, she was popular with her coworkers, and the other agents approved of the romance. He was sure of that.

"We have a couple of options," Ed was saying. "We could let you go. We could let her go. We could let both of you go. But whatever we do, we've got to do something. We can't tolerate the present situation."

Inside, Ben was seething. He knew what this was about. Julie was getting even. And he was hardly the only person in the room whose actions bordered on unprofessional; after all, Ed slobbered over Kim Autin every time he came to the West Bank office.

But Ben swallowed his anger. He said he hadn't realized his conduct was bothering anybody, but if it was, then he'd put a stop to it. Immediately. No need to let anybody go. Just give him a chance. Please.

He was given a chance, and as soon as he got back to the West Bank office, he told the agent.

"Somebody has complained about us."

"*Somebody?*"

"Ed and Dalton just told me—really Ed, but Dalton was there—that our conduct is causing problems. Unprofessional. Disrupting the work force."

"Somebody has been saying that?"

When this news buzzed around the office, people were

livid. Ben had been right. The other agents did approve of his romance. Ben was a likable fellow. He was good at managing an office of women. He respected his agents and didn't patronize them. Although he generally left them alone, he was always there if somebody needed help.

When the other agents learned that somebody had complained that Ben's romance was disrupting the office, Julie was treated like a leper.

Her emotional storms came and went. Julie would be an absolute shrew for a couple of weeks, then she'd switch into a pleasant mood and could be a lot of fun. She'd join in the office camaraderie. "Here comes the Pillsbury Doughboy," she'd say when her husband pulled into the parking lot on one of his visits to the West Bank office.

Everybody would still be laughing when he came in the front door. He did look a little like the Pillsbury Doughboy, especially before his dramatic weight loss. In the months before Julie's death, he had lost approximately fifty pounds.

Strangely enough, Julie had been in one of her good periods before going to St. Louis. She was making an effort to get along with people. But still, nobody expected her pleasant demeanor to last forever. Around Julie, everybody walked on eggshells.

Then came the news that she was dead.

Despite her strained relationships in the office, Julie shared one trait with almost all the other agents—she was a mother. That bond canceled out a lot of misunderstandings.

One of the agents, Kim Howardton, reminded her coworkers that Julie was always at her best on those afternoons when she'd been able to go home for lunch to see her daughters. She just couldn't handle the pressures of work, somebody else said.

Along with sorrow, there was a strong current of disbelief. In their own way, the real estate agents were as cynical as Hollocher.

*   *   *

Even in the best of time, real estate was an uncertain business: no weekly paychecks, no health insurance, no expense accounts, no benefits. Because of the financial uncertainties, most of the agents were women.

In the industry, the agents were called "the producers." Most often, the men in the business were managers, helping and motivating the producers and constantly engaging in the recruitment of new agents.

Selling houses could sound so easy. After all, it wasn't going door to door trying to sell encyclopedias to people who might not want them. Agents dealt with people who wanted to buy, or sell, a house.

So said the men who did the recruiting.

Because it sounded so easy, new agents were constantly trying to cash in. Many of these women were intelligent and articulate. Many had college degrees that they'd never even used.

They took their real estate classes, paid their licensing fees, and were ready to go. In Louisiana in 1986, the classes lasted for two weeks, and the fee was $125.

The women quickly learned, however, that even if they put in the long hours necessary to become a producer, they were still a long way from getting rich. At Wagner-Truax, for example, when a producer sold a $100,000 house, the 6 percent commission was divided half to the listing agency, half to Wagner-Truax and the producer. Of the $3,000 that would go to Wagner-Truax and the producer, Wagner-Truax would get 60 percent. Another portion would go to the national office of Better Homes and Gardens. The remainder, not much more than $1,000, would go to the producer.

The average yearly earnings for a Million Dollar Club member were well under $20,000.

Still, some women persevered and succeeded. Those who did tended to be intelligent, self-confident, and assertive to the point of brassiness. These were not women to underestimate.

* * *

In the days between Julie's death and her funeral, Matthews could sense the uneasiness of his staff. Already, rumors were flying. There were raised eyebrows, knowing looks, a certain tone of voice when Julie's death was mentioned.

"Drowned in a bathtub. Ed called Kim."

It could have happened just the way Ed said, thought Matthews. He remembered the day Julie had hurt her back at the real estate office.

She had come to the front door carrying a box of papers. As she started to open the door, the box slipped. She tried to catch it, and she suddenly froze in pain.

Matthews had not witnessed the actual accident, but he had seen the aftermath. The other women helped Julie to the conference room and eased her to the floor. She lay there for a long time, apparently in agony.

So it was not farfetched to think that perhaps the same type of thing had happened in the bathtub. As she was getting into, or out of, the tub, she slipped, and her back went out.

But how did that translate into drowning?

The word was—and it was already being said rather snidely—that Ed was claiming that she must have hit her head and knocked herself out. To Matthews, that sounded unlikely, but it was possible.

The alternative was too terrible to contemplate.

Still, Matthews remembered a conversation with Post during one of Julie's bad times.

"You've just got to work it out, Ben," Post had said.

"Maybe Julie ought to quit for the good of the company."

"Oh, come on, Ben. I can't very well tell her to work for another company. I own part of this one. What do you want me to do? Kill her?"

But that had been said in jest.

Besides, as far as Matthews knew, Ed and Julie were

happily married; Ed had never said anything to the contrary. Then Matthews thought about the calls Post used to make on the days when he was visiting the West Bank office.

"Hey, Ben. I'm coming by today. Tell me what she's wearing. What have I got to look forward to?"

And Matthews would describe Kim Autin's outfit that day. Post had made no secret of his infatuation with Kim. It was so obvious, so comical, that it simply had to be innocent.

He'd always make a fuss over her. Sitting down beside her, studying whatever she was working on, he was like a lovesick high school kid. The other agents could barely contain themselves. Julie would ignore it.

Kim was a stunner, with long dark hair, big eyes, and a terrific figure. In looks, she was worlds above Ed Post, and she was married to a man with money. Nobody in the office seriously entertained the thought that Kim Autin would be interested in Ed Post.

On top of that, she was Julie's only friend, at least as far as the office was concerned. For that matter, Kim's husband, Bobby, was one of Ed's best friends.

The mood in the office had worsened after the release of Julie's obituary in the newspaper. The tone had been too heavy on her real estate accomplishments: "Mrs. Post was a member of the National Association of Realtors, the Louisiana Realtors Association and the Real Estate Board of New Orleans. She had also been a member of the Million Dollar Club, selling more than $1 million worth of property each year since 1982. She had already sold more than $1 million in real estate this year."

Her achievements were cited even before mention was made of her daughters.

Some of the agents thought the references to the Million Dollar Club and the amount of real estate she had already sold this year were in poor taste. Everybody

knew that the Million Dollar Club was mainly hype.
Julie had never even made $30,000 in a year.

While this storm of suspicion and mistrust was gathering, Ed Post remained in the eye of the hurricane.

Always a person of action, he had immersed himself
in the work created by the sudden death of a spouse.
The obituary, which he had written, was one of the
minor chores. Of far greater importance was arranging
the funeral. Post wanted it to be perfect.

The funeral director explained that one of the first
decisions had to do with flowers. Some families prefer
that instead of flowers, donations be made to a charity
in the name of the deceased. Post chose flowers.

He asked Harby Kreeger to compose and deliver the
eulogy. Kreeger's wife, Dianne, volunteered to contact
the caterer she had used just two weeks earlier when her
mother died. The caterer would handle the gathering at
the Post house following the funeral.

Despite the bone removal and the subsequent autopsy,
the funeral director assured Post that if he so desired,
the casket could be open.

Have it open, Post decided.

By all accounts, the funeral was a spectacular success.

The ornate funeral parlor on the grounds of historic
Metairie Cemetery was awash with flowers. In addition
to the flowers purchased by friends and business associates in New Orleans, colleagues from Better Homes and
Gardens offices all over the country had sent floral arrangements. The sheer amount of flowers, thousands and
thousands of dollars' worth, overwhelmed many of the
people who gathered to pay their final respects to Julie
Post.

As planned, Harby Kreeger delivered the eulogy.

"I was privileged to know Julie Post. I knew her
well. I knew her as a loving and devoted wife to my

dear friend Ed. I knew her as a caring and consummate mother to Jennifer and Stephanie. I knew her as a successful businesswoman, and as a charitable and outstanding citizen of this community, but most of all I knew her as a friend.''

The Kreegers and the Posts had met twelve years earlier through wine and gourmet food clubs. Eventually, the two couples became close. On occasion, they vacationed together on the Kreegers' boat. In fact, less than a year before Julie's death, the two couples had sailed to the Bahamas.

Yet, it was really Ed that the Kreegers knew. Julie could be outgoing, sometimes boisterous, and she was often quick with an opinion, but even her friends—and Dianne was certainly a friend—always had the sense that Julie held back a part of herself. It wasn't that she was quiet, or reserved, or shy. One simply had the sense that at her core, she was a private person.

Ed, on the other hand, was anything but private. He was always up, always chatty, always in charge.

Harby continued with his eulogy.

''It has been said before, but oh how true it is, that no book or manuscript is judged by its length, no work of art or painting is judged by its size. Our lives, like all things, are judged by their quality, not by their duration.

''Julie is gone now, and we will all miss her terribly, but her spirit and determination lives on. It has enriched my life and I hope yours as well. That is her legacy, and that is how I will always remember my friend Julie.''

Afterward, the crowd collected at the gravesite. The cemetery sat atop Metairie Ridge, a natural levee built by recurrent flooding, approximately four feet higher than the surrounding ground. During the Civil War, the site had been used temporarily as a Confederate camp until it was decided the place was too swampy.

Of course, what makes cemeteries in New Orleans distinct from cemeteries anywhere else in the country is the proliferation of above-ground tombs. Although they have become an art form, these tombs were originally crafted for utilitarian purposes. New Orleans is a sea-level city. Even on Metairie Ridge, most people opt for above-ground burial.

Ed Post, however, had decided on an in-ground burial for Julie.

In a cemetery as historic and ornate as Metairie, it would be impossible not to be near something dramatic, and the site Post purchased was in the shadow of granite column built as a memorial for David Hennessey, a New Orleans police chief assassinated in 1850.

It was near this monument that Jo Harsdorff, a colleague of Julie's from the West Bank office, saw a man she would have sworn was a policeman.

Married to a newspaperman, Harsdorff insisted that she could spot a detective in a crowd.

During the graveside ceremony, she saw a man who alerted her newshound instincts. A big man, rough-looking, he was smoking a cigarette and studying faces.

True to New Orleans tradition, the party afterward at the Post house was a splendid affair. The caterer recommended by Dianne Kreeger did a fine job. There was plenty to eat and drink.

Among the guests were Bill and Judy Bethea, who had not spoken with Ed since he had asked them to tell the Thigpens that Julie had died. But when they finally reached him in the receiving line, it was almost as if he didn't know who they were.

"Do you know who that is?" he said, pointing to an elderly woman who had preceded them into the living room. "That's Gertrude Gardner," he said, as if they should be impressed that the grande dame of New Orleans real estate had come to the house.

With that, he greeted the next visitors. Not a word was said about the heartbreaking task they had per-

formed earlier in the week. The absence of any acknowl-
edgment only added to the discomfort they already felt.

They had been among the last to leave the cemetery
parking lot, and they had witnessed a very strange
scene. From the front seat of their car, they had seen
Post come out of the funeral home. He started walking
to his car. His two daughters were a few feet in front
of him. Suddenly, inexplicably, he had begun to skip.

A couple of skips, and then he resumed walking.

The Betheas did not stay too long at the party. They
had already left when the doorbell rang. George Hollocher and Steve Jacobsmeyer were standing on the
porch.

Chapter Four

The two detectives had arrived the evening before on TWA Flight 371, nonstop from St. Louis.

As soon as they emerged into the airport, they put down their carry-on bags.

"Welcome to New Orleans, Jake," said Hollocher as he took a drag from his cigarette.

Jacobsmeyer smiled and lit a cigar. Like Hollocher, he was a big man. In his mid-thirties, he was about ten years younger than his colleague, but with much more experience in the homicide division.

Frankly, though, this trip had Jake puzzled.

Chances were slim that Post would agree to talk to them. Even the street criminals Jake dealt with in routine homicides generally knew enough not to talk to the cops. What chance would they have with Post?

First, he was a businessman. Surely he knew enough to keep his mouth shut. Secondly, his brother was a lawyer. Also, it was the day before the funeral. Post might be offended that they were intruding at such a sensitive time. He could even be too busy to see them right away. The major had authorized only a very short trip.

It was surprising, Jake thought, that the department had authorized even that. This was officially an accidental death. There were plenty of official homicides in St. Louis.

The two detectives rented a car and took Highway 10 in

toward town. They drove past Metairie Cemetery without paying it any attention.

Like a couple of tourists, they decided to stay in the French Quarter. The trip quickly took on a slightly farcical aspect. The first couple of hotels were filled. The next had a vacancy, but the price of a room was way over the limited budget the department had approved. Adding to the feeling that the trip was becoming a disaster was the oppressive heat.

"George, we'd better get out of the Quarter and look for a Motel Six or something," Jacobsmeyer said, as the two detectives, still wearing their sport jackets, sat dejectedly on a bench in Jackson Square.

All around them in the early evening was a whirl of tourists and French Quarter characters. A juggler casually tossed bowling pins into the air. Two preteens tap-danced. Sidewalk artists were everywhere, using the iron fence around the park as a display rack. In the midst of the carnival atmosphere, the detectives sat sweating, growing more morose by the minute.

"I've got an idea," said Hollocher. "Let me go call Arbini in St. Louis. He works for a hotel chain. Maybe he can get us something."

"I'll wait here," said Jacobsmeyer, and he pulled out a cigar.

Hollocher came back quickly with the good news.

"We got a hit!" he said. "We are guests of the Omni, at the Royal Hotel two short blocks from where you're sitting."

Neither man gave a thought to the fact that the Omni hotel chain was an interested party in Julie Post's death, and that someday Post's advocates could argue that the entire thing—the investigation, the indictment, the trial—had been a giant conspiracy designed not to promote the cause of justice, but to save the Omni from a multimillion-dollar lawsuit.

After taking a shower, Jacobsmeyer sat down by the

phone. From Kaelin's police report, he had Post's number. From the medical examiner's report, he had the Thigpens' number.

He decided to call the Thigpens first. Certainly if anybody was suspicious, it would be Julie's family.

When Jake called the Thigpens in Poplarville, a friend answered the phone and explained that Hollis and Etta Mae were in New Orleans for their daughter's funeral. The friend gave them the name of the hotel where the Thigpens were staying.

Jake called, and Hollis Thigpen agreed to meet the detectives for coffee the next morning at the Café du Monde.

The next morning the detectives left their hotel and walked toward the river. At night, the French Quarter had seemed like a string of nightclubs and T-shirt shops. But in the morning, it was obvious that the Quarter was also a residential neighborhood. The local inhabitants, seemingly invisible the night before, were now emerging from the apartments that lined the streets.

The detectives arrived at the riverfront with plenty of time to spare. They went to the Café du Monde and got the first table inside the door. They ordered coffee and awaited the Thigpens.

"How did the father sound when you talked to him last night?" Hollocher asked.

"Couldn't tell," said Jacobsmeyer. "He agreed to talk to us, but beyond that, I don't know."

"He's got to be suspicious. You know, before we left St. Louis I called the hotel association, the national association, and asked them how many people drown in hotel bathtubs every year. You know what the answer was?" Hollocher asked.

"Not many, I bet," said Jacobsmeyer.

"Try none. And you know one reason, something that's bothered me from the get-go. Women don't take baths in hotels. They shower. You know how women are. If they didn't scrub it, they won't sit in it. I know my wife is like that. You wouldn't find her taking a bath in a hotel."

"It's the part about drawing the bathwater that gets me," said Jacobsmeyer. "I can't imagine some guy doing that."

When the Thigpens arrived, they were easy to spot. They stood uncertainly by the door, an older couple, dressed up. An attractive young woman was with them.

"You must be Hollis Thigpen. I'm Sergeant Jacobsmeyer, and this is Lieutenant Hollocher."

Thigpen stood for a moment looking at the detectives. Then in a soft voice, heavy with a Mississippi drawl, he introduced his wife and daughter, Julie's sister, Joanne.

"We appreciate you seeing us," Jacobsmeyer said.

"What's all this about, Sergeant?"

"We have some questions as to whether your daughter's death was accidental," Jacobsmeyer said.

Hollis Thigpen was a composed man. During his years in the construction business, he had negotiated a great many deals. He liked to hear what the other side had to offer before he volunteered much.

"We know very little about what happened," he said.

"Your son-in-law says your daughter slipped in the tub," Hollocher said. "It never happens. We checked with the hotels. People don't just accidentally drown in bathtubs."

Thigpen remained silent.

"Do you know of any marital problems your daughter might have been having?" Jacobsmeyer asked.

"Julie had a real good marriage," Thigpen said, in his slow, even way. "Two fine children. Let me tell you something, Julie was a wife any man would be proud to have."

"Financial problems, maybe?" Jacobsmeyer asked.

"Julie was very good, you know, selling houses. Same with Ed. By the way, let me tell you fellows something else. I know my son-in-law, and I don't believe for one minute that he killed my daughter."

That was disappointing to hear.

"We're not saying he did, Mr. Thigpen. You've got to understand that in our business, we question everything. This is all routine procedure," said Jacobsmeyer. He regretted the words as soon as he'd said them. Thigpen was looking at him, taking his measure. Thigpen clearly didn't believe that there was anything routine about two St. Louis detectives flying to New Orleans.

"Let me rephrase that. This isn't exactly routine. We're not sure what happened with your daughter. We're not convinced it was an accident, and if it wasn't, well, we intend to find out," said Jacobsmeyer.

Thigpen gave the slightest of nods. It was impossible to tell if he was nodding to himself or acknowledging Jacobsmeyer's sideways apology.

"We need a little background information, family stuff," Jacobsmeyer said.

The detectives asked if Julie had any health problems, and Thigpen told them that she had a bad back. He wouldn't be surprised if that had something to do with her death.

In addition to the sister, Julie had two brothers. Neither would know much, Thigpen declared. The older brother still lived in Mississippi and didn't see much of Julie. The younger one, Robert, had his own problems. He drank a lot. It had been an ongoing thing since he came back from Vietnam.

"All the same, we'll probably want to talk to him," said Jacobsmeyer.

"Suit yourself," said Thigpen.

Jacobsmeyer scrawled down some family phone numbers, and thanked the Thigpens for their time.

"We'll probably be talking to you again," Jacobsmeyer said.

Thigpen nodded, and started to lead his family out, then stopped and came back to the table.

"I've already told you I don't believe my son-in-law killed my daughter," he said. "But if he did, I want you to get him."

"We will," said Hollocher. "We will."

* * *

The residents of New Orleans use uptown, downtown, lakeside, and riverside in lieu of east, west, north, and south, but perhaps the most confusing geographic designation is the West Bank. Actually, it lies to the south of the city proper. Snuggled against the Gulf, the West Bank is the heart of the oil industry.

The Park Timbers subdivision was developed in the early seventies to accommodate the oil yuppies. Its Tudor-style homes were designed and built for geologists, accountants, and other young professionals who worked for the companies that were exploring the Gulf and pumping the offshore wells.

The subdivision also became home to some of the professionals who serviced the oil company employees. Ed Post was in that category. He lived at 11 Glacier Court.

The house was crowded with visitors when the phone rang. Probably another message of condolence.

"Mr. Edward Post? I'm Sergeant Steve Jacobsmeyer from the St. Louis Police Department. I'm trying to close out our books on your wife's death. I've got a few questions, and I really don't need much of your time, but like I say, I've got a few questions before we can close this up."

"I'd be happy to answer any of your questions, Sergeant, but you've caught me at a very busy time. Perhaps if you could call back next week."

"I'd much rather do this in person, Mr. Post. If I could just come by for a few minutes, that would be all I'd need."

"Come by? You mean you're here? In N'Orlins?"

"Yes, right. I could drop by, and we'd be done with it."

"You mean come by right now?"

"And then we're done with it, Mr. Post."

"Well, sure. Come on."

* * *

Armed with a map and directions from hotel personnel, Hollocher and Jacobsmeyer crossed the Greater New Orleans Bridge. On the other side, they immediately saw rows and rows of public housing units.

"For the first time since we got here, I don't feel like a tourist," Jacobsmeyer said.

"Yeah, our element," said Hollocher.

They drove past the West Bank office of Wagner-Truax, and minutes later pulled into Park Timbers. Jacobsmeyer slowed the car down to a crawl as the detectives tried to get the feel of the place.

One detail jumped out at them: there were For Sale signs on every block.

"I wouldn't want to be selling houses around here," said Jacobsmeyer. "This looks like a disaster."

"Here it is," said Hollocher. "Glacier Court."

Parked cars, obviously belonging to Post's guests, lined the street. The detectives stopped down the block and walked to the house. A tall man in his forties, with dark hair and a thin face, answered the door. He held a drink. Judging by his eyes, it wasn't his first of the day.

"Yes?" he said.

"I'm Sergeant Jacobsmeyer. This is Lieutenant Hollocher. We're here to see Edward Post."

The man let them in and pulled out his wallet. He gave each of the detectives his business card: Daniel Post, attorney at law. He walked into the living room, and returned a moment later with a shorter man, who was plump and seemed to be alert and in control.

"I'm Ed Post. We can go into the study."

Before taking the detectives into the study, he spoke quickly to another man. "I'll be right back. A couple of men from the insurance company are here."

Ed, his brother, and the detectives walked into the study. Before the detectives could say anything, Ed spoke.

"I'd like to get your names."

Smart, thought Jacobsmeyer. Put us back on our heels

right away. Complain about us coming to his house in the middle of the funeral reception.

"I'd like to write your chief and tell him how thoughtful you guys are. I mean it. I know this is your job. But all of you guys have been really fantastic. Very professional. The young patrolman who was at the hotel, he was great, too. Actually, everybody in St. Louis has been fantastic. The emergency crew, the people at the hospital, the people at the morgue. You've all been great," he said enthusiastically. He stood for a minute, almost beaming, waiting for a response.

"Thanks a lot," said Jacobsmeyer.

"Even the stewardess on the airplane. When she saw how upset I was, she moved us to first class. At a time like this, these little courtesies mean so much. The only people I have any problem with are the hotel people. They didn't even offer me a glass of water. Even now, I haven't heard a thing from them. Not a call, not a card. Nothing. You know, I'm going to sue them for every penny they have."

"Well, sure," said Jacobsmeyer.

Dan Post and Hollocher were mute, each puffing a cigarette, warily eyeing the other, as if some silent alarm had gone off.

"You can see, I'm sure, that this is a very busy time for me," said Ed. "If you have some questions, go ahead. Let's get this over with. I have nothing to hide."

The only real questions the detectives had concerned insurance. How much did he have on Julie, and when had he gotten it? But hundreds of interviews had taught them that you never lead with the big questions.

"You say you were jogging? Why don't you just tell us what happened that morning," suggested Jacobsmeyer.

"Of course," said Ed.

He then recited to them what he had told Kaelin. He'd put in a wake-up call for 6:30, but he awakened at 6:25. He cleaned up, and got his wife a glass of water. When he woke her, she complained about her back, so he gave her a massage. Then he drew her bathwater and left.

Before leaving the hotel for his run, he had spoken to the concierge and the doorman. He ran toward the river, and on his way back, he saw another jogger just leaving the hotel. Yes, he'd been seen by that man. The detectives were welcome to verify his claim.

When he returned to the hotel, he found his wife in the bathtub. He also found a towel ring in the tub.

Finally, Ed finished his story.

"How 'bout insurance?" Jacobsmeyer asked. "This is something we can check on, you know."

"Of course Julie was insured," Ed said. "We have children. We believe in life insurance."

"Of course. I've got kids myself. How much insurance did you have on her?" Jacobsmeyer asked.

"Seven hundred thousand," said Post.

Jacobsmeyer resisted the urge to look at Hollocher.

"How long have you had the policy?" he asked.

"Actually, I have two policies. I got the last one, for an additional three hundred thousand, last month."

"I see," said Jacobsmeyer.

"There's nothing unusual about that, Sergeant. I'm constantly upgrading our insurance. I suggest you talk to Bob Masson. He's my agent. A very, very respected insurance man in this city."

"I'm sure," said Jacobsmeyer, and he wrote down Masson's number.

"Anything else?" Post asked.

"I've got something for you. I hope you don't mind taking a look at it," said Hollocher. As always, there was an undercurrent of menace in his voice. He asked a question as if he were hurling a challenge. "This is a picture of the towel ring you talked about. You can see how it's twisted. How do you think that happened?"

Post took the picture and briefly studied it.

"I doubt that my wife could have done that damage. Are you sure that's the right towel ring?"

"I'm sure," said Hollocher.

"I really don't know," said Post. He didn't seem bothered by it.

"For now, I guess that's about it," said Jacobsmeyer. "We'll be calling these people, checking things out. I'm sure you'll hear from us again."

Post led them to the door and stepped out on to the porch with the detectives.

"I want you to look around and tell me if you notice anything unusual," he said.

The two detectives looked around.

"The azaleas!" said Post, pointing to some flowers in the yard. "Did you see any other azaleas in the neighborhood?"

"Not that I noticed," said Jacobsmeyer.

"These are the only ones that are blooming," said Post. "Julie planted them, and they're blooming today, the day of her funeral. It's a miracle!"

The two detectives looked at the flowers.

Already, they felt disoriented. Post was so cheerful and forthcoming. The interview was like no other either of them had ever conducted.

As they started to leave, Post hugged Jacobsmeyer. The detective was caught completely off guard. He didn't know what to do with his hands. Finally, awkwardly, he patted Post on the back.

Hollocher stared. Then Post released Jacobsmeyer, and before Hollocher could step away, Post was embracing him. Hollocher only stood there, hands at his side.

"I want to thank you both for coming," Post said.

"Yeah, sure," said Jacobsmeyer.

When they got back to the car, they looked at each other.

"He's guilty," said Hollocher.

Jacobsmeyer was from a St. Louis police family, the son of a colonel. His uncle had been the homicide division commander for twelve years. He'd grown up hearing stories about bizarre cases.

When he first joined the department, he'd worked in narcotics. An informant had told him that a drug dealer named Willie McCurrie was getting ready to move a large shipment of heroin. Jake and his partner, Marvin Allen, went to McCurrie's house. When the drug dealer answered the door, the detectives said they wanted to buy some heroin.

McCurrie left them on the porch, and when he came back a minute later, he held a gun. He shot Jake in the neck. Allen took a round in the chest.

McCurrie later alleged that he had been beaten after his arrest. From his prison cell, he sued the two detectives, despite the fact that both of them had been in the hospital recovering from their wounds at the time of the alleged beating.

By the time the lawsuit got to court, Allen was doing time in the same prison as McCurrie. It seemed that armed robbery was his hobby when he was away from the police station. It was deduced, but never proved, that McCurrie shot the two cops because he recognized Allen as the man who was knocking over dope houses in the area.

For the lawsuit, McCurrie and Allen were brought to court in St. Louis in the same van from the prison in Jefferson City. So Jake had seen some weird things. But still, he had never heard of a suspect hugging his inquisitors.

Meanwhile, Post was back at the party. In a move he would later regret, he called Bobby Autin, Kim's husband, off to the side.

"I know Kim's got a twin sister, Bobby. Maybe when all this is over, you could fix me up with her."

Chapter Five

When the detectives returned to St. Louis, Hollocher reported to the major who had authorized the trip.

"I was right. He did it," said Hollocher. "He thinks this is some backwater Dodge City, and he can come here and do his wife. Like we're too damn stupid to catch him."

The major listened. The big news, as far as the investigation was concerned, was the insurance. But Hollocher's feelings were important, as well.

He was profane and blustery, but everyone knew his instincts were good—even if it was widely understood that Hollocher was too much the storyteller to take literally. Already, in the homicide squad room, his flair for the dramatic had begun to outdistance the facts.

"So I said to him, 'How much insurance did you have on her?' and he says, 'A little bit.' I say, 'How much is a little bit?' and he repeats himself, 'A little bit.' So I poke my finger in his chest, and raise my voice, and say, 'How much is a little bit?' and he says, 'Seven hundred and fifty thousand.' "

A pause, then, for the listeners to absorb the figure.

"So then I say, 'How long did you have it?' and he says, 'A little while.' I say, 'What's a little while?' and he says, 'A little while.' So again, I go through the routine, raise my voice, and say, 'What's a little while?' and he says, 'Less than a month.' "

Another pause.

"So I hear that, and I say to him, 'You're going to jail!' His eyes got real big. He nearly passed out."

Maybe it didn't happen exactly like that, but the major knew that the insurance angle was an important development. And if there was going to be a full investigation—an expensive cross-country one—he wanted some backup.

"Go talk to Peach," the major said. "See if you can get him on board."

George Peach was the circuit attorney, the head of the prosecutor's office for the city of St. Louis.

The outer rooms of the circuit attorney's office were of the same design as the homicide squad room—government functional. The inner sanctum of the circuit attorney's office was much nicer, with a carpet, a conference table, bookcases lining the walls, and a large desk faced by three chairs.

Hollocher sat down in one of the chairs and lit a cigarette. "The major suggested I talk to you, George, about a case I'm working."

"And what case would that be?"

"Ed Post, businessman from New Orleans. Murdered his wife over at the Omni."

Peach had a good, if somewhat fragile, relationship with the police department. On one hand, he was a law-and-order conservative. He feuded with the liberal judges and the liberal newspaper.

On the other hand, his office often found itself at odds with the cops. Most often, this opposition concerned the issuance of warrants.

When the police arrest a suspect, that suspect is not officially charged until the circuit attorney's office issues a warrant.

The key statistic for the circuit attorney's office is the conviction rate, the percentage of cases that result in convictions or guilty pleas. The only cases that count are those in which warrants have been issued.

The police department produces its own statistics, with the key statistic being the arrest rate. For the department's purposes, a case is cleared as soon as an arrest is made.

Consequently, you can have a situation in which the police can claim an arrest rate of 70 percent, and the circuit attorney can claim a conviction rate of 85 percent, and the reality is that most criminals get away.

Like much in the criminal justice system, the statistics are all smoke and mirrors, part of an effort to convince the public that the forces of good are at least gaining a draw.

Although the debate seldom goes public, the cops sometimes accuse the circuit attorney's office of inflating its stats by refusing to issue warrants on tough, but makable, cases. The circuit attorney's office sometimes accuses the cops of making "paper" arrests, arrests without sufficient evidence, in an effort to inflate their stats.

"The Omni case," said Peach. "That would be the woman in the tub." He spoke in measured tones.

Hollocher smiled. The newspapers had carried stories about the "accident" at the Omni the morning after Julie's death. Peach must have read about it.

"What have you got on it, George?" asked Peach.

"Post had seven hundred thousand dollars of life insurance on his wife. Bought a good chunk of it last month."

"Who told you that?"

"He did. Me and Jacobsmeyer just got back last night. We talked to him. Let me tell you about this guy."

As Hollocher talked, Peach asked few questions. Hollocher repeated what Arbini, the hotel security manager, had told him. On the day of the death, Dan Post had flown in from New Orleans, and the two men had taken pictures in the bathroom.

Such callousness offended Peach. His entire adult life had been spent in the muck of the system. He'd seen plenty of different reactions to the death of a loved one, but this was a new twist—preparing a lawsuit before the body was even cold. The insurance situation interested Peach, as well.

Hollocher also went on at some length about Post's character. He obviously did not like the man. Then again, thought Peach, Hollocher doesn't like a lot of people.

When Hollocher finished his presentation, Peach nodded.

"Sounds like you could have something there. I appreciate your coming to see me. This sounds like something we might want to get involved with early. I'll get back to you."

"Let's not let this one get away," said Hollocher.

Peach thought of Dee Vossmeyer.

As a trial lawyer, she had a sense of what would be needed, and what could be used, if the Post case was ever to get to court. What's more, Peach was concerned about Hollocher's running this investigation. He had a tendency to come on strong.

If a couple of eighteen-year-olds were picked up for shooting somebody over a dope deal, Hollocher was great. There was nobody better at getting one guy to talk by telling him that his pal had just confessed and fingered him as the trigger man.

But these people were probably more sophisticated. It would be wise to have somebody a little smoother go down to New Orleans. Vossmeyer would be good. For that matter, so would her former investigator, Gary Hayes.

Peach buzzed Vossmeyer.

"Do you remember the woman who drowned at the Omni last week?"

When she said that she did, he continued, "Call George Hollocher at homicide, Dee. Tell him you're on it."

Vossmeyer called Hollocher, who told her that he and Jacobsmeyer were going to have lunch with Arbini at the Omni. She agreed to meet them.

*   *   *

Dee Vossmeyer was thirty-nine years old, the same age as Julie Post. Like the dead woman, she was dark-haired, and slender. And like Julie, she was a Southern girl.

Raised in a small town in Virginia, Vossmeyer had gone to college in Williamsburg, Virginia. After graduating with a degree in government, she went to work in Washington, D.C., where she met her husband. Soon after their marriage, they moved to his hometown of St. Louis.

She had been out of school for nine years when she started law school at St. Louis University. She graduated in the spring of 1980, had a baby that winter, and went to work in the circuit attorney's office the following year.

In 1984, she and her husband divorced. By the spring of 1986, she was living with Gary Hayes, the detective who had formerly been assigned to her as a pretrial investigator. The two were planning an August wedding.

She remembered reading the newspaper account of Julie's death.

"No husband draws his wife's bathwater," she had said to Gary.

At lunch, Hollocher entertained Vossmeyer and Arbini with tales of New Orleans. One of his favorite stories had to do with the morning the two detectives had met the Thigpens. Before entering the café, Jacobsmeyer had his shoes shined.

"So Jake's sitting there, not paying any attention, right? I say to him, 'Hey! He just spit on your shoes!' and Jake hauls off and slugs the kid!"

Jacobsmeyer shook his head, and laughed. "Just for the record, that story's not true," he said.

Vossmeyer had not met Hollocher before, and she was a little worried about his obvious penchant for stretching the truth.

The most serious discussion centered on the towel ring. Hollocher said he'd done a lot of kitchen and bathroom work, and he didn't believe a woman slipping in the tub could have yanked it off the wall. Arbini said the hotel people didn't believe it, either.

In preparation for the lawsuit that was surely coming, the hotel was preparing a battery of engineering tests.

"You're welcome to observe, of course," said Arbini.

After lunch, Vossmeyer reported to Peach that the woman's death seemed awfully suspicious.

"How would you like to go to New Orleans? You could take Hayes with you," Peach asked.

Vossmeyer was definitely excited. She had never been involved in a case before an arrest. Besides, this seemed like a case out of a movie. Most murder cases in the city were mind-numbingly similar. The victims and the defendants were generally young and black, and drugs were somehow involved.

"I'll ask Gary," she said.

Gary Hayes had retired from the police department with a non-service-connected disability from an old back injury. He was working as a private investigator.

The next day, Hayes called Peach.

"I know you're in practice for yourself now," Peach told him, "but all I can give you is expenses. Still, if this works out, you can put it in your résumé."

The assignment was simple: talk to as many people as possible, family, friends, business associates; get a feel for the situation; research the details on the insurance; and check with the doctor about Julie's back. Did she have a history of fainting? Was it likely she'd passed out?

Hayes said he would start making arrangements.

The same day that Hayes talked with Peach, Hollocher received a call in his office.

"Homicide. Hollocher."

"Yessir. My name is Robert Thigpen. I'm Julie Post's brother. I understand you were down here talking to my folks, and my other sister. There's some stuff I know you'd probably want to know. None of them know it.''

So this was the alcoholic brother, Hollocher thought. The stressed-out war veteran. But so what? Information is the coin of the realm, and it matters not where you get it.

"What do you know, Robert?"

"Ed Post killed my sister."

"How do you know that?"

"She told me."

"She tell you that before or after she was murdered, Robert?"

"Before. She told me that he tried to kill her once before, and she was afraid he'd try again. She said that if anything ever happened to her, she wanted somebody to know."

Hollocher asked for details.

Robert claimed to have had this discussion with Julie while she was in the hospital last year for her back. She had been heavily sedated, and maybe that's why she was being honest, he said.

"Julie told everybody that she'd hurt her back gardening, but she wanted me to know the truth," Robert said. "She hurt her back when Ed knocked her down in the bathroom during a violent argument. She felt lucky to be alive, and she said she was sure he was going to try to kill her again."

Hollocher didn't know what a lawyer would think of Robert's story, but if Robert was telling the truth, this was dynamite.

"Robert, if we were to fly you up here, would you be willing to take a lie detector test on this?"

"Yessir. I'm telling the truth."

"Give me your number. I'm gonna get back to you."

After Hollocher hung up, he sat at his desk for a long time. He felt good.

Meanwhile, Jimmy Holloran, a St. Louis personal injury lawyer, was also getting a long-distance phone call.

A lawyer who handled real estate work for Gordon Gundaker, the real estate man who owned the Better Homes and Gardens affiliate in St. Louis, had spoken to Holloran earlier and told him to expect a call from Ed Post.

"Remember that story in the paper about the woman drowning at the Omni last week?" the real estate lawyer had said.

"You bet," said Holloran. Like most lawyers who specialized in personal injury lawsuits, Holloran paid particular attention to accident stories.

"This guy Post, the husband, got in touch with Gordon and wanted the name of a lawyer who does personal injury work. Gordon asked me, and I gave him your name."

So when Post called, Holloran was ready. He listened to Post for a while, and he knew he had a hell of a case.

The accident victim was a thirty-nine-year-old career woman, a loving mother of two, a devoted wife.

A towel ring had come out of the wall. When Holloran was in college, he had worked summers installing bathroom fixtures. He knew how shoddily they could be mounted.

An expensive hotel, part of an international chain, would have very deep pockets.

"The police haven't finished their investigation, but I believe they're almost done," Post said.

"Let's not do anything until they complete it, and then I'll look at their report," said Holloran.

When he hung up the phone, he was as excited as Hollocher.

Chapter Six

Before Vossmeyer and Hayes went to New Orleans, Jacobsmeyer phoned Post. He said he wanted to tape Post's statement.

"My notes aren't good enough," Jacobsmeyer explained.

Frankly, the interview in New Orleans had caught Jacobsmeyer by surprise. Post had simply started talking, and the detective hadn't even tried to take it all down.

Better to tape it, he thought.

It turned out to be an important decision, not so much for the information, but for something quite different, a turn of phrase that had nothing to do with innocence or guilt, but was, much later, seized upon by a jury.

That's something a detective learns early. In a sense, an investigator is like a fossil hunter. He picks up everything he can. A bit of bone, seemingly insignificant, might prove to be the missing link—at least in the minds of a jury.

When Post returned the detective's call, the widower was chatty, and upbeat. He began the conversation by complimenting Jacobsmeyer on the police department's phone system. He liked the fact that when a caller was put on hold, there was music.

He cheerfully talked about the insurance, and said he had routinely increased coverage as his station in life changed. The coverage also reflected his family's lifestyle, which was filled with activities like traveling, snorkeling, and diving.

His insurance agent, "one of the most respected agents in town," would be happy to supply their insurance history, Post said, while Julie's medical records could be supplied by her doctor, "one of the most prominent surgeons" in New Orleans.

Post talked about what a great honor it had been to serve on the advisory board for Better Homes and Gardens. At the riverboat dinner, he had sat at the table with the host.

Then Jacobsmeyer asked about the morning of Julie's death.

Post went into the events of that morning—waking up at 6:25, canceling the 6:30 wake-up call so it wouldn't disturb his sleeping wife, cleaning up in the bathroom and the rest of the now familiar story.

He decided to wake his wife, he said, because he knew she wanted to have breakfast with him on what would be their last day in St. Louis.

"So I woke her up," he said. "This was at about seven. I got some fresh water to bring over to give her. Fresh water that had not been sitting out all night."

"Did she ask you for the water?" Jacobsmeyer inquired.

"Oh no. I brought that to her voluntarily. And then at that point, she said, 'Hey, you know my back is really kind of bothering me this morning from the cramps,' and I said, 'Fine let me give you a massage.'

"She then went to the bathroom to, you know, just to urinate, to relieve herself in the morning, as we all do, and came back to bed and she took her gown off and I had some massage oil that we had gotten together in a previous trip."

After the massage, Post filled the tub.

"Did she ask you to fill the bathtub?" the detective inquired.

"Oh no. I do that for her quite routinely at home. We're very close," Post responded.

"Hot water, cold water, medium?" asked Jacobsmeyer.

"Tepid," said Post. "In other words, what you would

want when you stepped in. Then I came back and got her and brought her into the bathroom, and she put her foot in the water and sad, 'Gee, that's fine,' and at that point she turned around and I kissed her and said, 'Look, I'll see ya in a few minutes,' and I left the room and that was it.''

"You followed her into the bathroom? Why would you do that?''

"Well, just to say goodbye, that I was gonna go run. That's a routine thing,'' Post said.

He said his wife left the bathroom door slightly ajar.

At Jacobsmeyer's request, Post launched into a detailed description of the route of his jog, starting with the hallway outside the room, then the lobby.

"I said something kind of half-ass cute to the concierge, because we had been talking,'' Post added.

After chatting with the bellhop, he started his run, going past a Brooks Brothers store, which was on the right, before veering toward Busch Stadium. On his return trip, as he cut through the parking lot of City Hall, he saw a policeman named Gay.

"How was it that you caught his name?'' asked Jacobsmeyer.

"Well, I almost ran into him,'' laughed Post. "So I just happened to notice it. I'm a very observant individual. You don't know me, but any of my friends would tell you that. And Gay is kind of an unusual name.''

"Sure.''

Back at the hotel, Post saw another advisory board member just beginning his morning jog. He then described his cool-down routine, and his subsequent conversation with the bellhop.

Post said he opened his door with his key, walked in, and called out his wife's name. He wasn't particularly alarmed when she didn't answer, and then he noticed the bathroom door was in the same position it had been in when he left, open only about an inch.

"I walked in and almost immediately slipped and fell, because there was water on the floor and I had my jogging shoes on, which are, you know, not boat shoes."

He said he was horrified to see his wife in the tub. Her face was completely underwater, and she was lying on her left side, with her hair floating on the water.

"This is going to be difficult," Post said. "You have to understand that."

"Hey. Far be it from me to question a man that's just lost his wife. Then you pulled her out of the tub, or what?" asked Jacobsmeyer.

"For a couple of seconds, I was in pure shock, and then the first thing I did was, yes, I pulled her out of the tub. With, I must tell you, with great difficulty," Post said.

"I struggled. It was really very difficult to get her out of the water. She was very flaccid, if you know what the word means. Since she was obviously unconscious and God forbid, I mean, it just hurt me that much more, but her head hit the floor as I was trying to get her out of the bathtub. All I could do is barely just drag her over the side of the bath.

"I couldn't pick her up because of the angle, and being wet. It was, if you can understand the physics of the situation, difficult to try to bend over and pick up a dead— you know, no pun intended—but a dead weight," said Post.

He said that as he tried to drag her out of the tub, she slipped two or three times.

"It was an ordeal," Post said.

"What part of her head did she hit?" Jacobsmeyer asked.

"Well, she was facedown at that point, because I was dragging her out over her stomach. It probably would have been the right front side of her head. I'm just guessing, but I would think it was somewhere on the front of her head that definitely hit the floor pretty hard as she came over the bathtub.''

Post described the bathroom, and how he decided to move Julie's body so that when the door opened, her feet wouldn't get in the way. Then he decided to cover her with towels around the midsection, for dignity's sake.

After that, he called the switchboard and reported an emergency.

He talked at length about his efforts to revive Julie, the help from EMS staff, and his time at the hospital.

Jacobsmeyer asked if Post had noticed any bruises on Julie.

Not a bruise, but a scrape on the right forehead, said Post. He'd noticed it at the hospital, and also at the funeral home. It probably came from hitting her head when he dropped her as he was lifting her out of the tub, he suggested.

"Okay. Now Ed, it's difficult for me to ask you this question, but just on the surface, you know, if the case seems strange, suspicious, would you be willing to take a lie detector test at some point in time, if we deem it necessary?'' asked Jacobsmeyer.

Post hesitated, and then said he didn't know. At the moment, he was too emotional, he said.

"Well, it doesn't have to be now, or this week, or even this month, but you know, somewhere down the road,'' suggested Jacobsmeyer.

Post said he had nothing to hide, and that he had cooperated in every possible way, but he just wasn't sure about a lie detector test.

Then he added that he knew the police had been at the funeral. When Jacobsmeyer denied it, Post launched into a story about the funeral home. It was the premier mortuary in New Orleans, and the staff had told him that there had been only one other funeral with as many flowers.

"We were very important people in this community. We had a very, very important marriage. Anybody that you would talk to would give you complete testimony on that. So many people in their prayers and their written word say that they wish they could just model their lives after the way we led our married life.''

Then, with no prompting from Jacobsmeyer, Post said that lie detector tests were not admissible in court, and even though he had absolutely nothing to hide, he didn't see any reason to take one.

''I'm devastated by the whole situation as it is,'' he concluded.

After a pause, Post continued, ''I understand the reason that you need to do this and I'm not being offended by anything yet. I do, however, want to make one statement at this point that I think is very important. My father-in-law is very upset about something that George Hollocher said, and I'm going to handle that at a separate point, but he made a direct accusation to my father-in-law that he thought I killed my wife. That is the most inappropriate remark I can imagine under the circumstances, and it will be handled, and dealt with later.''

''Okay,'' said Jacobsmeyer. ''Last question. Your marriage, no problem whatsoever. Is that correct?''

''Absolutely correct,'' said Post. ''I would like to send you a copy of the eulogy that my very best friend delivered. It was two pages long. He knew me better than my brother and he knew Julie like a sister, and I think that that would be something meaningful for you. And from the very beginning I've told you this: you don't know anything about us, you don't know who we are.''

''That's true,'' said the detective.

''There are some circumstantial . . . Very honestly, I'm concerned about the insurance thing because of the timing, but . . . godammit, you know, I didn't control what happened. My insurance man will tell you that we reviewed our insurance on an annual basis.''

Post then repeated that he'd send the detective a copy of the eulogy.

"Gordon Gundaker's attorney is getting us an attorney up there, and they have both requested that when I talked to you today I find out the date that they will be able to receive the police report, because they need that very badly to start what they need to do," Post said.

Jacobsmeyer said he couldn't give a firm date, but he expected it would be soon, probably within the next couple of weeks.

Post asked if Jacobsmeyer had any more questions. The detective said he didn't.

"Well, I'm very devastated by this entire thing. That's all I can tell you," said Post.

With that, the conversation, which had lasted more than an hour, ended.

Jacobsmeyer hung up the phone.

It's too bad we don't have any evidence, he thought. Otherwise, this guy could talk himself right into jail.

What kind of guy are we dealing with? wondered Jacobsmeyer.

Chapter Seven

Edward Post felt good about the phone call. It was important that the police know that he was very upset about Hollocher's statements to Hollis, just as it was important for them to know they weren't dealing with a nobody.

Post was an important figure in the New Orleans real estate community, a man newspaper reporters would call when they wanted a quote about the business. As vice chairman of the legislative committee for the state Realtors' committee, he had led the fight to defeat a property transfer tax in 1984. The following year, he had been named Realtor of the Year in Jefferson Parish. In early 1986, he had gone to Washington to lobby Congress as a member of the legislative committee for the National Association of Realtors.

He was active in gourmet food and wine clubs. He had owned one of the largest private wine collections in the city until he sold it to the world-class Windsor Court Hotel. The collection had fetched more than $30,000.

Although not a member of high society—New Orleans had a caste system only slightly less rigid than that of old India—he ran with a prosperous crowd. His social circle consisted of doctors, lawyers, and businessmen.

He had a big house, an attractive wife, and two lovely daughters.

On the surface, he was the picture of success.

*　　*　　*

Born on Christmas Eve in 1943, Post grew up in post-war America, where upward mobility was the only constant.

His father, Al, managed a Woolworth's on Canal Street at the edge of the French Quarter. His mother, Ann, was a homemaker. Ed was the younger of two boys. Dan was three years his senior.

When Ed was five, his father was transferred to Austin, Texas, and the family remained there for the next eight years. During that period, his father quit Woolworth's and opened several general stores of his own.

Ed was a well-adjusted, well-rounded kid. The Posts' house was on the edge of town, and the brothers spent a lot of time in the country. They rode their bikes and hunted in the west Texas hills.

Although the brothers spent much time together, they were very different. Dan was a loner; Ed was outgoing. Dan was neat; Ed was disorganized.

Whenever the family went out together, Ed was the last to be ready. He'd come running out of the house buttoning his shirt as he ran.

"Cow's tail," his mother called him. "Always the last thing out the door."

His mother was the stronger of the two parents. As a child of the Depression, she had not gone to college, but she considered herself a lady. She was determined that her sons would grow up cultured. Under her aegis, both boys took piano lessons. Ed had a real aptitude for it, and finished second in a state competition. Naturally, it was simply assumed that both boys would go to college. Ed was going to be a doctor.

In 1957, the family moved back to New Orleans, and Al opened a toy store. Both boys worked there on weekends.

When the store faltered, Al turned its management over to his wife. He got a job as a real estate salesman. It turned out to be a wonderful move. He got in at the beginning of the boom.

Ed went to Fortier High School. Although the best schools were all private—and in New Orleans, where you went to high school meant a lot—Fortier was considered the ritziest of the public schools. In order for Ed to attend that school, he registered under the address of the toy store. It was his mother's idea.

Like the more exclusive private schools, Fortier had fraternities. Ed was a member of Phi Kappa, the number-one frat. In a scene out of *American Graffiti*, he and his friends would cruise down St. Charles Avenue, zipping along in someone's convertible, racing the streetcar, honking and waving, intoxicated with life. Most nights they'd end up at the College Inn restaurant near Tulane University, where they'd eat shrimp poor boys and mingle with kids from the private schools.

In a sense, Ed was on the fringe of the group. He didn't have a car, and he wasn't much of a jock. His parents were not nearly as well off as most of the kids' parents.

But even then, Ed had a way of making people feel important. He was ingratiating, some might say. Kinder ones might just call him a people person. At any rate, he was accepted.

Ed graduated in 1961. He started his freshman year in premed at New Orleans University. But something happened to his attitude that first year in college.

He spent too much time in the Student Union, playing chess and engaging in philosophical conversations. He drank too much beer. And he flunked out of school. For a youth unaccustomed to failure, it was truly awful. He felt he'd let his mother down.

In an effort to find himself, Ed enlisted in the Army Reserve in August of 1962. He would spend six months on active duty and would be trained as a medical specialist.

Ed liked the Army, its discipline and its camaraderie. By the time he was given leave in November, he felt like a success again. He reveled in the realization that he had regained his parents' approval.

There was something else, too. A rite of passage. He felt he had become a man.

During this first leave, he visited his brother, who was newly married and attending Tulane Law School. While Dan was in the backyard working at the barbecue, Ed went into the kitchen and got a butcher knife. Returning to the yard, he handed the knife to Dan.

"Attack me," he said to his older and taller brother.

"I don't want to attack you," said Dan.

"Just try," said Ed.

So in slow motion, Dan raised the knife and brought it down toward Ed. Quick as a wink, Ed grabbed Dan's arm, twisted his butt into Dan's midsection, and threw him on the ground.

Ed stood there beaming.

When he returned to Fort Sam Houston in Texas, he wrote his parents: "I really enjoyed talking with you on Sunday. I think we understand each other much better now. We never have talked this way before, although you and Dannie have several times. I think it was about time that we had this kind of talk and I am looking forward to more like it."

The letters that followed were like portraits of a young man feeling better and better about himself. He was at the top of his class in medical training. He was proving he could make it as a doctor.

While undergoing this training, Ed met a number of airborne volunteers whose gung-ho spirit infected him. He briefly thought about enlisting in the Regular Army and going into Special Forces. But then he learned of another option. The Louisiana National Guard had a Special Forces unit.

When his six-month-tour was up in February 1963, he transferred from the Army Reserve into the Louisiana National Guard unit. That summer, he was sent to Fort Benning for the three-week airborne course. He had never been as proud of anything as he was of his jump wings.

As a jump school graduate, he was a bona fide member of the airborne reserve unit. He was a medic with Company D of the 1st Special Forces Group in the Louisiana National Guard. He was a Green Beret.

Within a couple of years, as the war in Vietnam heated up and the National Guard became a haven for kids who didn't want to fight, the idea of an elite unit of weekend warriors would seem ridiculous. In truth, there were a number of such outfits.

In the late fifties, when Senator John Kennedy realized that he ought to own, in a political sense, some military specialty, he decided to become patron of a super antiguerrilla force. These soldiers would be extremely well trained, so it made little sense to lose their services completely when their enlistments ran out. Organizing Guard units would ensure that they could return to active duty at a moment's notice.

In 1963, the men of Company D were gung-ho. They regarded themselves as authentic special forces, and their annual training exercises were indeed rigid, including night parachute drops and jungle training.

Years later, the whole experience would still be central to Ed's identity. He wore a Special Forces ring. Sometimes he'd wear his fatigues with his jump wings. Like so many veterans, Ed began to enhance his military career.

In his case, he didn't like to mention that his service had been spent in the National Guard. Perhaps he felt, and justifiably so, that this own service was unfairly tainted by public awareness of what the Guard had been during Vietnam—a haven where the sons of privilege could sit out the war after their student deferments ran out.

On his résumés, he made it seem that he'd been an active-duty soldier for three years.

By the fall of 1963, when Ed started college for the second time, he had decided to make his father's business his own. After all, real estate was a good career for a people person.

He enrolled at the University of Southern Mississippi in Hattiesburg, which was an afternoon's drive from New Orleans. Unlike his first try at college, this one he took seriously. Rather than pledging a social fraternity, he joined Delta Sigma Pi, which was a business club. He also joined Collegiate Civitan, the collegiate version of Kiwanis.

Still, the focal point of his identity was his status as a Green Beret. In November 1965, playing his role of veteran to the hilt, Ed organized a blood drive to aid the troops in Vietnam.

He was sitting at the sign-up table outside the student union when a slender, dark-haired young woman signed up to give blood. Her name was Julie Thigpen.

She fainted when the nurse put the needle in her arm, and Ed rushed over, a Green Beret medic coming to her rescue.

They began dating, and the next spring, at the business fraternity's formal dance, Ed and Julie were engaged. They were married in January 1967.

The union did not meet with Ann Post's approval. By that time, Al had risen to a management job with the largest real estate company in New Orleans. After meeting the plainspoken Thigpens, Ann decided that Ed was marrying beneath his station.

Ed and Julie moved back to New Orleans and rented a second-story apartment across from City Park. From their balcony, they could see the huge oak trees dripping with Spanish moss. Ed began his career as a salesman with Gertrude Gardner Inc. Realtors, the company for which his father worked. Julie, who had dropped out of college to marry, got a secretarial job at Tulane Medical School.

During those early days of married life, Julie was the main breadwinner. She didn't make much money, but they lived cheaply. Rent was low, and entertainment generally consisted of having friends over for hamburgers.

Julie and Martha, Dan's wife, became good friends. Among the interests they shared was a fascination with extrasensory perception. Julie told Martha of a friend who could make her husband do things just by thinking about them. She was also convinced that her long-deceased grandfather visited the apartment late at night. The two young women felt that they could sometimes read each other's minds. When one would telephone, the other would remark that she had been thinking of calling at the very instant the phone had rung.

Within a couple of years, Ed's career had progressed to the point where he and Julie could leave the apartment for their first home, a small tract house in Metairie. At about the same time, Ed and Dan took a wine-tasting course, and Ed discovered he had a remarkable ability to differentiate various wines. In blind tastings, he could tell one vintner's product from another.

As he began to take wine more seriously, he took up gourmet cooking. His interests, fortunately enough, coincided with a rise in his income.

When Ed and Julie moved from their tract house to a new development on Colony Road, he insisted on building a wine cellar—complete with air conditioning—in the garage. Julie made no secret of the fact that she would have preferred to spend the money on furniture.

In fact, the couple seemed to make no secret of any of their disagreements. In that way, they were strange. Sometimes they would act like lovesick high school kids. Other times—and often in the same evening—they would argue loudly in front of their friends. Dinner parties could be embarrassing for the guests.

If Julie was chopping something in the kitchen, Ed was likely to correct her, and then she'd challenge *him*, saying that maybe he ought to do it himself. In a loud voice, he'd announce that he would do just that, and then he'd banish her from the kitchen.

The Bickersons, people sometimes called them. It was almost amusing. Ed and Julie were two strong-willed people who knew exactly what buttons to push to aggravate each other.

That was in public. In the privacy of their own home, they'd sometimes scream and hurl dishes at each other. Even more ominous was the fact that Julie told close friends that Ed beat her.

Still, they stayed married. And despite the picture the state of Missouri would eventually paint, the fights were not a constant thing.

Ed and Julie had two daughters. Stephanie was born in August 1970, and Jennifer was born three years later.

The younger girl was quiet and withdrawn, but Stephanie was an exaggerated version of her mother—highstrung and theatrical. By the age of eleven, she was in therapy.

"Life at Ed's house is like driving through a parking lot filled with speed bumps," his brother once said.

The adolescent problems that drove Stephanie to therapy only worsened as she hit her early teen years. By thirteen, she was drinking and getting kicked out of school. When she was fourteen, she tried to commit suicide.

By the fall of 1985, she was completely out of control. Ed and Julie took her to a clinical psychologist. She went wild in the office, screaming, cursing, calling her parents names. At the psychologist's recommendation, Stephanie was hospitalized for several weeks.

In the fall of 1985, Julie confided to a friend that she was considering a divorce.

If Ed's home life was becoming increasingly stressful, his professional life was no less so.

By 1976, he had moved into a management job at Gardner. Eventually, he allowed himself to get drawn into a family fight—one of the Gardners was going to be ousted in a palace coup, and Ed was to be his replacement—and when the coup failed, Ed was in disfavor with the man he had been slated to replace.

In 1983, he left his job with Gardner to buy a 10 percent interest in a new real estate company. His timing was terrible. Oil prices collapsed, and the Louisiana economy, dependent on oil, was shattered. The real estate market fell through the floor.

As a 10 percent owner of the new company, he was entitled not only to his salary, but to 10 percent of the company's profits. Unfortunately, there weren't any. Post was forced to contribute money to cover 10 percent of the losses. His share had come to more than $20,000 so far. He had had to borrow money and sell assets to make those payments. Among the assets had been his prized wine collection.

By the spring of 1986, he had no more assets to sell—except for his new house on the West Bank.

Nevertheless, he persevered. In fact, he seemed almost to thrive. In the spring of 1986, he was the guest of honor at a real estate banquet at which he received the Realtor of the Year award for 1985.

Furthermore, he was in the midst of a weight-loss program which had helped him shed more than fifty pounds.

His family continued its visits with the psychologist who had been treating Stephanie. The psychologist thought the family was making great strides. Another thing she noted—Ed and Julie were not bored with each other.

"I would have described their relationship as being one of high energy, in that this was a couple that argued a lot, yet seemed to have a very intense bond," she later said. "There was definitely a lot of energy between these two people. They were not parents who were drifting apart."

The family was under a lot of pressure, the psychologist added, but Ed and Julie seemed to be handling it.

If the constant speed bumps were causing Ed to lose control of the wheel in the spring of 1986, nobody noticed.

*   *   *

The day after he spoke with Jacobsmeyer, Post took his daughters to a world-class resort in California. Dustin Hoffman was in a room down the hall.

Post called the owner of a very fashionable restaurant in Los Angeles. Introducing himself as an officer in the New Orleans chapter of *Chaîne de Rôtisseurs* and a member of *L'Ordre Mondial,* he was able to get reservations. When he and his daughters arrived, he was pleased to see that they were put in front with the celebrities, not in the back with the tourists.

Stephanie and Jennifer were extremely impressed when rock star John Paul Jones was seated at the next table. Post noticed that Jones ordered a bottle of Château Beychevelle, which was "companion wine" to the bottle of Château Léoville-Las-Cases that Post was drinking. That is, the wines were produced in adjacent vineyards in the town of St.-Julien in the Bordeaux region of France. Using their similarities in taste as an entrée, Post struck up a conversation with the rock star.

During the course of the conversation, Post explained that he was a widower and had brought his two daughters to California to help ease their grief over their mother's untimely death. Jones was touched, and moved his chair over to the Posts' table. The next morning, Post sent him three expensive bottles of wine as a thank-you.

He also explained to his daughters that they might soon be leaving New Orleans. Post was thinking of California or Florida.

Chapter Eight

Vossmeyer and Hayes arrived at the airport a little late, missed their flight, and had to wait an hour for the next one.

Not a great start, but it added to Dee's feeling that this case was like a movie—William Powell and Myrna Loy running through the airport. She had to laugh.

Hayes was less excited. A free trip to New Orleans sounded good, but he had been a cop for eighteen years before he retired in 1985, and he didn't see how they would ever make a case. What's more, he knew Hollocher, and he didn't trust him much.

Hayes had joined the department in 1967, during the days of "flower power." Being a cop was like being a knight on a white horse. He had hoped to make a difference.

But there had been little chance of that. In reality, the cops swept the streets. It always bothered Hayes that some cops enjoyed doing it roughly.

He'd gotten his big break—a transfer to the circuit attorney's office—after he'd rescued a retarded girl who had been raped by two guys inspired by repeated viewings of *Texas Chainsaw Massacre*.

Peach had personally handled the case, and was impressed with Hayes, who seemed too soft-spoken and gentle to be a cop. Peach had pulled the right strings, and Hayes had been transferred. He had been assigned to work for Vossmeyer. Once her marriage broke up, he was there for her. A nice-looking, street-smart cop, but still soft-spoken, Hayes actually believed in the Bill of Rights.

On the flight, he read the transcript of the tape.

Vossmeyer had read it the night before, and she had already picked up on the phrase that would come back to haunt Post.

"Did you see what he called her?" she asked, as Hayes finished.

As a matter of fact, he hadn't. He had been struck, however, by the wealth of detail. The cop named Gay— maybe that was explainable, it was a strange name. And Post remembered the name of the store he'd jogged past— Brooks Brothers. Well, maybe he shopped at one.

But all the other stuff—the little details, precise times, filling forty-one pages of transcript. No wonder Post had told Jacobsmeyer that his friends would say he was observant. In Hayes's experience, most people couldn't remember the color of their best friend's eyes.

"You didn't notice what he called her?" Vossmeyer asked again.

"No."

"Dead weight. 'No pun intended, but she was dead weight.' "

When they got to New Orleans, they rented a car and headed to the French Quarter. Arbini, the security chief at the St. Louis Omni, had called his counterpart in New Orleans. There was a room with a garret window overlooking the roofs of the French Quarter waiting at the Royal Hotel.

They spent the first afternoon on the telephone, trying to set up appointments for the next day.

Neither the suspect nor the chief accuser was on the list of people to talk with; that would be a waste of time. Post had already given his version of events, and Bobby Thigpen was going to be brought to St. Louis. They wanted to talk to the people on the periphery of the investigation and get a feel for the situation.

They called the real estate office and lined up an interview with the first person they talked to. They arranged to see Julie's doctor, the insurance man, and the Thigpens. They got a number for Kim Autin, who was in Florida, and Vossmeyer left her name and number on the answering machine.

Before they went out to dinner, they stopped at the desk and asked to see the security chief. They wanted to thank him for arranging the room.

Arbini had mentioned the man was an ex-cop, and Gary was expecting someone completely different from the sophisticate in a tuxedo who came up and introduced himself.

The three went into the bar and ordered drinks. "Yes, Arbini has told me a little about the case," the security chief said. "Please tell me more."

Dee and Gary described the towel ring, and the suspicion that it had been twisted off the wall. They told him about the insurance.

He smiled.

"Cherchez la femme," he said.

Later, when the St. Louisans went out into the Quarter to have dinner, Gary asked what "shashay la fahm" meant.

" 'Look for the woman,' " said Dee.

That evening, when they were back in the hotel room, the phone rang, and Dee answered. She listened for a second, then said, "Oh, Kim Autin. I appreciate your returning my call."

Gary went quickly into the bathroom and picked up the extension. He held his hand over the mouthpiece and listened.

Dee explained again that she was from the circuit attor-

ney's office in St. Louis. Because of the unusual circumstances of Julie Post's death, the office wanted to confirm
Ed's general statements, she said.

Kim asked what Post had said.

"Oh, mostly what a happy marriage he and his wife
had," Dee said. "He went on and on about that."

Kim gave a short, derisive laugh.

"You might have a hard time confirming that," she
said. "Look, I was probably Julie's best friend. It was
not a happy marriage."

Kim went on to talk about a recent trip to San Francisco
that she and her husband, Bobby, had taken with Ed and
Julie.

The Posts had fought the whole time. One morning,
Kim and Julie had gone shopping. Kim was in the changing room when Julie undressed.

"Julie was really embarrassed," Kim said. "She was
all bruised up. She didn't want to talk about it, but it was
obvious what had happened."

Vossmeyer and Kim talked for a long time. The general
thrust was that Ed and Julie were under financial strain.
The real estate business was bad. The marriage wasn't
going well, either.

Dee asked if there was another woman.

"I don't know anything about that," Kim said.

When the conversation finally ended, Dee thanked her
and said that she'd be back in touch.

When Gary heard the connection broken, he hung up
and walked into the main room.

"Sounds like our 'important marriage' wasn't so healthy,"
said Dee.

"She sounded scared," said Gary.

"I thought so, too," said Dee. "What she'd be scared
of, though, I don't know."

"We ought to get some sleep," said Gary. "We've got
to shashay our fahm tomorrow."

Through the open window, the sounds of the French Quarter floated into the room.

The next morning they crossed to the West Bank and went to the real estate office. At the front desk, in a voice even softer than normal, Gary introduced himself.

An agent was already coming over. In her late twenties or early thirties, she was an attractive, flashy-looking young woman with long blond hair and a colorful dress.

She said she had been expecting them. She obviously wasn't concerned with being discreet. "We can walk across the lot to Denny's, and talk there," she said.

When they got to Denny's, Dee went through her routine about wanting to confirm some of Ed's statements. The agent nodded, as if to say, Sure, sure.

"Do you mind if I tape our conversation?" Gary asked.

The agent shook her head, and Gary brought out the tape recorder.

"Nobody thinks it was an accident," the agent said.

She told them about an incident a month earlier.

"It was the Million Dollar Club banquet. An annual event to honor the producers. Everybody in the business goes, everybody. Always a big blowout, you know. Dress to kill, and go out and party.

"If ever there was a year that deserved a blowout, this last year was it. Business was horrible. The oil, you know.

"This year's dinner, April 18th, was held in the Grand Ballroom of the Intercontinental Hotel on St. Charles. Very ritzy.

"Ed was peaking. You've got to understand that. The week before, at a different banquet, he'd been given the Realtor of the Year award for Jefferson Parish."

"Jefferson Parish?" asked Gary.

"It's what you'd call a county. It's the parish just west of the city. The suburbs. Real-estate-wise, this is a funny town. The city is mostly very rich or very poor. The pretty rich are in the suburbs. Some of the very rich, too, of course, but if you want upper middle class, you go outside the city.

"Jefferson Parish is some prime country. Take Metairie, for instance. Twenty-five years ago it was farm country. Then when the city started going bad, it's where everybody ran. Now, of course, it's all developed. So to be Realtor of the Year in Jefferson Parish is a pretty big deal. Even in a year like we had.

"Ed and Julie and Kim and Bobby Autin sat together at a table at the Million Dollar Club banquet. Bobby's a big drinker, and Ed was apparently keeping right up. This was unusual, because Ed had been on a health kick. Jogging, diet, the whole thing, I guess. And he'd lost a lot of weight, too.

"Then again, don't get the idea that Ed and Bobby were the only ones doing any drinking. This is a big party. There are several hundred people there. It's a long, long program. Awards, introductions, and so on.

"This banquet was the New Orleans dinner, and Ed was on the board of directors for New Orleans, just as he was for Jefferson Parish. That's Ed for you. Very active. So he got introduced as 'our own Ed Post, Realtor of the Year in Jefferson Parish.'

"After the banquet, a number of us decided to go to Lenfant's, a very hot club out on Metairie Road. Right by Metairie Cemetery, actually. Bobby and Kim had had some kind of drunken argument on the way to the club, and Bobby just dropped her off and went home. Then Ed and Julie arrived.

"Remember, everybody's already been drinking pretty heavily. And at the club, they just kept going.

"Then Ed invited Kim to dance. Well, nothing wrong with that, you know. But one dance, two dances, three dances. They just stayed out there on the dance floor. Finally, we all see Ed give Kim this really big kiss.

"Julie stormed out on the dance floor and grabbed Kim. I mean, it was a scene.

"None of us were crazy about Julie. That's something you ought to understand, but still, I think we all sympathized with her. It had to be humiliating. In fact, after the fight, she walked out of the club. Not long after, everybody left. Everybody but Ed. I understand he took a cab home."

"What about Kim Autin? What does everybody think about her?" Gary asked.

"Oh, you have to know Kim. She's beautiful, of course, and she knows it. She's also the world's biggest flirt. But that's just Kim. She's really a good person."

"Might she have had something going with Ed?" Gary asked.

"Oh, no. Like I said, you have to know her to appreciate the situation. I'm not saying she wouldn't encourage him. At least she wouldn't do anything to discourage him, but would Kim have had anything *going* with Ed? No, I couldn't see that.

"In fact, the story she tells is that later that night, after the scene at Lenfant's, Ed went over to her house. They're neighbors, you know.

"Bobby was passed out on the couch, and Ed came in. Remember, Ed and Kim were both pretty drunk themselves. And anyway, Ed talked to her for a while, apologized for Julie's behavior—can you imagine that!—and then as he started to leave, he grabbed her and kissed her again.

"Now, if they had something going, Kim wouldn't be telling that story, would she?"

Other agents confirmed, and expanded upon, the general themes: Julie was unpopular; Ed was infatuated with Kim.

"Chocolate would melt if you looked at it the way he looked at her," Jo Harsdorff said.

According to one of the agents, Julie complained about having to go to St. Louis, but Ed insisted.

The agents also confided that the word had been spreading that Dalton Truax, their boss, was not happy with Ed's performance. Ed was always running around like a hotshot, going to Washington with a delegation to lobby for this or that, spending a day at the state capitol in Baton Rouge for something else.

Dalton thought of Ed as a manager, but Ed thought of himself as an owner. The situation had gotten so bad that when Ed won his Realtor of the Year award, he managed to aggravate Dalton even further. In his acceptance speech, he said he wanted to give special thanks to his partner, Dalton Truax.

Dalton owned the whole parent company, and 90 percent of the subsidiary of which Ed owned 10 percent. He did not think of Ed as a partner.

By the time they left the real estate office, Dee's heart was pounding. She was sure they were on to something.

Gary wasn't convinced. An office full of women could be a catty place. Then you had to throw in all the subplots about the boss's wife, and how unpopular she was. Maybe some of the current strong feelings had to do with the guilt everybody felt for having disliked her so much while she was alive.

Circumstances looked bad for Post, but that was all they had—circumstances.

There were an awful lot of men in this world who, if their wives were to die suddenly, could be made to look bad, Gary thought.

Dalton Truax, in his headquarters in Metairie, was much more circumspect than the agents in his West Bank office.

He and Ed had had some philosophical differences regarding management style. It was true that he wanted Ed to be more of a hands-on manager, doing a little more work in the trenches, so to speak. But Truax had every expectation that the differences could be resolved. Truax acted like a man talking to a newspaper reporter, courteous but cautious.

Only at the end of the conversation, as he walked Gary and Dee to the door of his office, did he give a glimpse of any personal feelings.

"I'm sure you two know what you're doing, but if you proceed with this thing, you'd better have your ducks lined up," he said. "Julie hurt her back at the office one time. The wind pulled the door out of her hand, or she dropped something. At any rate, she wrenched her back.

"A few days later, Ed indicated he'd like to sue. Didn't say he would. Just that he'd like to. 'Sue the insurance company' is the way he put it, but what he was talking about, of course, was suing the damn company. The company he owns ten percent of!"

Naturally, Truax discouraged the idea.

"But don't think for a moment that Ed Post won't sue you," Truax warned. "You'd better know what you're doing."

Bob Masson, the insurance agent, said he had known Ed Post since college. In fact, Ed was just a year out of college when he bought his first policy, valued at $10,000. Within a year or so, he had upped it to $20,000. After another couple of years, he boosted it to $35,000.

"Very unusual for a young man to be insurance-conscious, but smart," Masson said. "Very smart."

By 1979, Ed had $300,000 on himself and $100,000 on Julie. Three years later, Ed went to $500,000 and Julie to $250,000.

"And so it went," said Masson. "Periodic checkups, you might say. These checkups continued all the way to this spring."

Gary said that people had been talking about the economy crashing because of the oil. Wasn't it unusual for a person to take on more debt during hard times?

Masson explained the vagaries of the insurance business. Term insurance always starts with a relatively low premium. The premium increases, sometimes dramatically, in future years. Consequently, a person company-hops. You buy a policy, hold on to it for a couple of years, and then hop to a different company to take advantage of the low initial premiums. It's often possible to increase your coverage while lowering your premiums. Further, the more coverage you buy, the cheaper it is per unit of insurance.

Was that the situation this spring? Were Ed and Julie lowering their premiums when they each increased their coverage?

"No, actually these were separate policies," Masson said. "These were in addition to their old policies. Each of them got an additional three-hundred-thousand-dollar policy."

Ed's new policy cost about forty-five bucks a month. Julie's was less than thirty-five a month.

Masson went on to say that he had recommended the new policies. And there was certainly nothing unusual about Ed's upgrading his insurance.

As the St. Louisans started to leave, Dee stopped.

"Ed says their combined income was in the eighty-five-thousand-dollar range. They had a million seven hundred thousand worth of coverage. Doesn't that seem excessive?"

A trace of smile crossed Masson's face.

"Miss Vossmeyer, they weren't even near their limits."

If that round had gone to Ed Post, the one with the doctor was a draw.

Yes, Julie had a back problem, the doctor said. It seemed to be under control, but back problems tend to be chronic. One never knows.

Dee and Gary wondered if the back problem could have caused Julie to black out.

"That's hard to know," the doctor replied. "Is that what Ed is saying?"

"Well, no. He's not saying that. He's suggesting that she must have fallen and hit her head. We were just thinking that maybe she blacked out before she fell."

"Highly unlikely," said the doctor. "On the other hand, could sudden back pain cause a person to lose his or her balance? Certainly."

The Thigpens were next. Hollocher and Jacobsmeyer had thought that their interview had gone well, but when Post had talked to Jacobsmeyer over the phone, he had made the remark about his father-in-law's being upset with something Hollocher said.

Dee really didn't know Hollocher as Gary did. Given Hollocher's style, which was short on subtlety, it was possible, even likely, that he had communicated his true feelings to the Thigpens.

Still, you couldn't be mad at George. He was, after all, the guy who was pushing this whole thing. Gary knew the system from inside. He'd been a cop. The responsibility for pushing the investigation belonged to the cops. They could have circled the wagons after the first homicide sergeant had summarily dismissed the case.

It was early evening when the St. Louisans got to the house outside Poplarville. Heading up the long dirt driveway, they were surprised by the modesty of the house. It was really no more than a bungalow on a red clay hill. A big dog came running up to the car.

"Bear!" The word came out in two syllables. Bay-er.

Dee, born and raised in Virginia, finally felt at home. New Orleans was not quite a southern city. It was too cosmopolitan.

The man who came out after the dog introduced himself.

"Hollis Thigpen. I'm Julie's daddy."

Again, Dee heard the South, where there are no fathers or dads, just daddies.

Thigpen led Dee and Gary into the living room, where Etta Mae, Julie's mother, and Joanne, Julie's sister, waited.

"Now, you're from what office up in St. Louis?" Thigpen asked.

"The circuit attorney's office," said Dee. "I'm an attorney, and Gary's an investigator."

"The circuit attorney's office. Is that the same thing as a prosecutor?"

"Yes, it is, but we're not prosecuting anybody right now," said Dee.

"Uh huh. You know, I suppose, that two of your homicide men were down here. I guess they were just looking into it, too."

"Just because homicide is investigating doesn't mean it's a homicide, Mr. Thigpen. Part of their job is to investigate what we call 'suspicious deaths,' " Dee said.

Thigpen didn't seem unfriendly, just disbelieving.

"Well, you tell me something. You're the ones who've been investigating. Do you think it's a murder?"

Gary didn't miss a beat.

"I don't know," he said.

Dee asked about the relationship between Julie and Ed. As far as anybody knew, it was fine.

What about Julie's back? Had anybody ever seen her black out from the pain?

"No, not exactly black out," Thigpen said. "But there was one time when she was up here—she used to come up here quite a bit—when she was loading the dishwasher, and her back went out. She was in terrible pain. She just froze. The pain was so bad she could have blacked out, if there hadn't been people around to help her."

How about finances?

"Overall, Ed and Julie were doing pretty well. But business had been so damn bad everywhere in Louisiana because of the oil that maybe they weren't doing as well as they had been before. But that's only natural."

Did they ever ask to borrow money?

"Not in a long while. They borrowed some money back in '83, but that was for Ed to buy into a company. It wasn't like they needed the money to live on. It was a business opportunity."

Was this a loan or a gift?

"A loan. Fifteen thousand."

Have they been making payments?

"They've been paying interest on the loan. It was a three-year loan, you see. They were going to pay the principal back this August."

Is that still on?

Thigpen hesitated.

"Sure, I guess," he said. "Look, this wasn't a high-pressure thing. You like to see your children do well. If you have a chance to help one, you're happy to do it. Julie knew, Ed too for that matter, that if for some reason they weren't able to pay it back, I'd have given them more time."

Vossmeyer brought up Bobby Thigpen's telephone call.

"Bobby called you?" Thigpen asked.

Vossmeyer told Thigpen the general outline of what Bobby had told Hollocher.

Thigpen shook his head.

"Bobby's got his own problems," he said. "He wouldn't intentionally lie, but sometimes I don't think he remembers what the truth is."

"Been like that since he came back from the war," said Mrs. Thigpen.

Vossmeyer asked about bruises on Julie's body. Had they ever noticed any?

"If you're trying to ask if Ed ever beat Julie, I'd say the answer is no," said Thigpen.

Joanne spoke. She said she'd been down visiting the week before Julie went to St. Louis. Julie had been here, too. They all went swimming at a nearby pond. Julie was wearing her bathing suit, and she didn't have any bruises.

Thigpen walked the investigators to their car. The sky

was filled with stars. Whippoorwills and crickets cried into the darkness.

"I don't think you got it right," said Thigpen. "If it was murder, I'd like to know. But I don't believe it was."

On the way back to New Orleans, Dee and Gary talked about communication within families.

"We've both been through divorces, Gary, and you know that you just don't tell your parents when things are starting to get rocky. Just because the Thigpens thought everything was fine doesn't mean that everything was fine."

On that point, Gary had to admit she was right. Besides, it was easier to believe your daughter died accidentally. It would be much harder to make yourself believe she'd been murdered.

Especially by her husband of almost twenty years, the father of your grandchildren.

Dee and Gary got back to New Orleans and went out for a late dinner in the French Quarter. When they got back to the hotel, they found they had a message.

Jo Harsdorff, one of the West Bank agents, wanted them to call.

"I thought of something after you left," she said. "I know a young girl who's friends with Stephanie, Ed and Julie's oldest, and she told me that Stephanie had told her that Ed and Julie were going to get a divorce. This girl would be willing to talk to you."

Dee called and spoke to the girl. Her information had been secondhand, she said. She gave Dee the number of the girl who had told her.

Dee called the second girl, who said that yes, she'd be willing to talk to the investigators.

"We can come by tomorrow," Dee said.

A few minutes later, the girl's father called. Dee explained who she was, and said that she was just trying to talk to as many people as she could. After a slight hesitation, the man agreed.

The next morning, Dee and Gary visited the teenager. The girl's mother was present during the interview. The girl said that Stephanie had come over one night and said her folks had been in an argument, her dad had hit her, and her folks had decided to get a divorce. Apparently it was a very emotional night, the girl said.

The mother confirmed the story to some extent. While her daughter never mentioned any beatings, she did tell her that Stephanie's parents were going to get divorced.

"When I saw Stephanie next, I told her I was very sorry about her parents," the woman said. "Stephanie told me they had decided to stay together."

"When was this?" Dee asked.

"Last fall. Maybe September."

After that interview, Dee and Gary flew back to St. Louis. Dee was really pumped up, while Gary was still skeptical.

The next morning, the two of them went in to see George Peach. Dee told the circuit attorney that the picture Post had painted of himself was not accurate.

"The people down there think he killed her. She was a real bitch in the office, George. And Ed had the hots for somebody else, the woman he called from the hotel. And Julie's back wasn't so bad that she would have fainted, either."

"Did you confirm that Post increased the coverage on his wife shortly before they came here?"

"You bet."

Dee gave him a quick rundown. She said that Bobby Thigpen would be coming to town soon and would be interviewed. He had already agreed to take a lie detector test.

Peach nodded.

He hoped that Bobby Thigpen would work out. His

testimony might be crucial. What else was there except a towel ring that looked as if it had been twisted off the wall, some people saying that the marriage hadn't been a happy one, and an insurance policy that had been purchased just before Julie's death?

A defense attorney could chew that evidence up and spit it out.

Bobby's recollection of what he alleged Julie had told him—this message from the grave—might put the case over the top.

Chapter Nine

Detective Mike McCraw, an Irishman with blond hair and blue eyes, was sitting at his desk in the homicide office when Lieutenant Hollocher came up to him.

"I need a scribe," Hollocher said.

There was no police report from the trip Hollocher and Jacobsmeyer had taken to New Orleans. Jake had taken some notes, but had not yet translated them into a report.

Intrigued by the news from his own investigators, Peach had called the major and announced that the case called for further investigation. He had suggested that McCraw be assigned to the case.

McCraw was a twenty-year veteran of the department and had the reputation of being a solid and thorough investigator. On the sensitivity meter, he ranked somewhere between Hollocher and Hayes.

Hollocher gave McCraw the transcript of Post's statement. It contained a wealth of details that needed to be run down. Hollocher told McCraw to check with Jacobsmeyer and get his notes.

"There's something that won't be in the notes, McCraw. But something you ought to know. This guy's got little feet. In all the years I've been doing this, that's something I learned. If he's got little feet, he did it."

As was often the case with Hollocher, it was hard to tell if he was kidding.

* * *

Bobby Thigpen had the look of a casualty from Woodstock. He appeared unnatural in his coat and tie, like a little boy who had been forced to go to church. But what really bothered Vossmeyer was the vacant look in his eyes. He sat in one of the two homicide interview rooms to tell his story. Hollocher, McCraw, and Vossmeyer sat across the table from him.

"Julie was in the hospital," he said. "This was last year. She was heavily sedated, and that's probably why she talked to me. Of course, we were once real close. We're less than a year apart in age. Lately, though, these last few years, we haven't been so close.

"She was in for her back. You probably know she had a bad back. She'd told everybody that she'd hurt herself gardening, but now she was telling me it was really from Ed. They'd had a fight in the bathroom. She thought he was going to try to drown her in the tub, but it didn't get that far. But he knocked her down, and that's how she really got hurt.

"She told me she thought he was going to try to kill her someday. She said she was afraid it would be on a trip. She said if anything ever happened to her, she wanted somebody to know it wasn't an accident."

Vossmeyer was worried. Dynamite stuff if it was true, but frankly, Bobby didn't look like a reliable witness. Besides, there'd be all kind of admissibility problems in court. Still, if even a few sentences could be salvaged . . .

McCraw took Bobby to the small, windowless room on the third floor where polygraph tests were administered. The walls were painted light green and the lighting was recessed.

Bob Meyers, the polygraph operator, had already been briefed. With almost ten years experience on the polygraph and a total of twenty-two years in the police department, Meyers was a cross between a cop and a scientist.

Although he seldom mentioned it to the other cops— there were enough skeptics already—he was convinced that he could usually determine a subject's truthfulness before he even turned on his machine.

With Bobby, though, he just wasn't sure.

Because he was a potential witness rather than a potential defendant, Bobby was not an ideal subject for a polygraph. He had less to fear, and fear, in the form of adrenaline, is what a polygraph measures.

As was his habit, Meyers first explained the "lie box" to Bobby. It was a fascinating piece of machinery, with a console that had eighteen control dials and six stylus pins poised over the graph paper. It measured the response of the body's involuntary nervous system by charting the rates of blood pressure, perspiration, and pulse.

After explaining his machine, Meyers hooked Bobby up and prepared to begin the examination. It's not like the movies—the questions are not simple, simple, simple, and then boom: "Did you kill her?"

If a person is asked no-stress questions—Is your name John Smith? Are you a white male?—his readings are going to show no signs of stress. If he is then asked a stressful question, his involuntary nervous system will heat up regardless of whether he is telling the truth or not.

So even the "innocent" questions, the control questions, are designed to produce stress. For Bobby, Meyers had prepared a standard examination. He would ask Bobby seven or eight questions. The first would be an ice-breaker to make sure the machine was functioning properly, followed by a couple of stressful control questions. Finally, he'd get into the relevant questions. The whole series would take only a couple of minutes.

Then there would be a 'fifteen-minute break, and the exact pattern would be repeated. The break allows a person to replenish his adrenaline.

"Do you live in the United States?" Meyers asked, his eyes on the console in front of him.

"Yes."

The styluses started scribbling. The machine was working.

"Are you a habitual liar?"

"No."

"Do you sometimes lie?"

A hesitation.

"Answer, please. Do you sometimes lie?"

"Yes."

"Do you lie when it suits your purposes?"

"No."

"Did you visit your sister Julie in the hospital last year?"

"Yes."

"Did she tell you that her back was injured in a fight with her husband, Ed?"

"Yes."

"Did she tell you that she was concerned that Ed was going to try to kill her?"

"Yes."

"Let's take a break, Bobby."

As Bobby sat there, Meyers studied the graph paper.

Fifteen minutes later, they repeated the process.

"How'd I do?" Bobby asked, as Meyers unhooked him.

"I'll need to study the graph," Meyers said, but he had already reached a firm conclusion.

McCraw took Bobby back to the interview room in the homicide division, then went back to confer with Meyers.

"How'd he do, Bob?"

"He's not telling the truth about his conversation with his sister. My guess is he believes she was murdered, and he wants to point us in the right direction, but he's making up the stuff about the conversation in the hospital."

"You're not saying inconclusive, Bob? You're saying he definitely failed?"

"Definitely failed."

McCraw went back to homicide with the bad news. Hollocher smashed his fist against the wall.

"I ought to go in there and get the truth from that

asshole,'' he said. Then he shrugged. ''His heart's in the right place. Send him home.''

When McCraw called Vossmeyer with the news, she wasn't too disappointed. She didn't even want to think what a defense attorney could do to a witness like Bobby.

McCraw returned to the routine investigative work. He went over the hotel's records. He called the people who had stayed in the room next to the Posts. The man said that they had awakened that morning at about 7:00, and hadn't heard a thing.

McCraw talked to the concierge. She vaguely recalled speaking with Post. McCraw questioned the maid who had cleaned the Posts' room the previous day. She said she didn't remember specifically, but she routinely polished the towel rings before hanging the clean towels. If she had noticed that the ring was loose, she would have reported it, she said.

McCraw called the people who had stayed in the room the day before the Posts checked in. They didn't recall that the towel ring was loose.

So it went. McCraw talked to everybody at the hotel who had been mentioned in Post's detailed account of the morning.

Post's story seemed to have no holes. McCraw was becoming convinced that there would never be an indictment, let alone a conviction. All the state had was a twisted towel ring, a lot of insurance, and an unhappy marriage.

And one other thing that Hollocher constantly harped on—a suspect with little feet.

A Great White Defendant gets everybody's blood coursing. Tom Dittmeier, the U.S. attorney for the Eastern District of Missouri, had seen the newspaper story the day after Julie's death.

After her husband prepared her bath, she had drowned while he was jogging.

In a pig's eye! thought Dittmeier.

He had been a Golden Gloves boxer in his youth, and even at the age of forty-seven, he had the look of a pug, with rough features, broad shoulders, and shortish hair slicked unfashionably to the side. A picture of John Wayne was on the wall. A life-size porcelain statue of a bulldog, realistic enough to make a visitor flinch, stood next to his desk.

He had called Peach on that first day, just to chat about the case. He said that it reminded him of a case he had handled back when he was a prosecutor for the county—the Pickle Barrel Case.

A twenty-three-year-old man was charged with drowning his estranged wife three days before their divorce was to become final. The body was discovered by the victim's sister, who had arrived at the house just as her brother-in-law, the accused killer, was leaving. He was pushing a large pickle barrel down the stairs.

Authorities always believed that the pickle barrel must have contained the body of the victim's mother. At any rate, the man's estranged wife was found in the tub, her skull crushed. The man's mother-in-law was never seen again. Dittmeier was forced to settle for one murder conviction.

He had been unable to shake the Omni tub case from his mind. So he called Peach again.

"George, how you guys doing on that Omni thing?"

"We're looking into it, Tom, making some progress. Exactly where it's going to take us, I don't know."

"Let me make an offer to you, George. We could do an Englemann on this thing."

Englemann was a dentist who had committed a series of murders a few years earlier. He would befriend women, and then murder their husbands for a share of the life insurance. Because insurance forms are sent through the mail, the feds had investigated Engelmann for mail fraud.

"You see what I mean, George? If this Omni guy murdered his wife, we could do a mail fraud on him."

Federal agencies have better access to financial records, especially tax records, than local authorities have. Also, if the feds were to investigate, the feds could bring the New Orleans people to St. Louis for a federal grand jury.

The power of the federal government was massive. If the feds wanted a witness to appear in St. Louis, they had only to order the person to appear. When the locals, like Peach, wanted to subpoena out-of-state witnesses, they had to go through the interstate witness compact, which could mean court hearings on somebody else's territory.

In addition to making things easier, a federal investigation would mean a huge savings for the circuit attorney's office. The feds would be picking up a lot of the expenses.

"Of course I'm agreeable to it, Tom. In fact, I appreciate it," said Peach.

"Great. Who's handling it on your end?"

"Dee Vossmeyer."

"Tell her to expect a call from Dean Hoag."

Chapter Ten

Three weeks after Julie Post died and just a few days after Bobby Thigpen failed his lie detector test, their sister, Joanne, was married in Poplarville. It's what Julie would have wanted, everybody agreed.

Ed Post was very much involved in the festivities. For one thing, he brought the liquor for the reception. Poplarville was in a dry county.

On the morning of the wedding, he and Bobby Thigpen were assigned to set up the reception at the Poplarville Country Club. They had to cart everything to the country club—hard liquor, champagne, soft drinks, champagne glasses, regular glasses. A ton of stuff.

They spent about two hours setting everything up. By the time the caterer arrived, they had finished their work. All that was left was to get some ice from the golf pro shop and carry it over to the reception hall.

Ed and Bobby were not good friends. Once, several years earlier, there had been a very ugly incident between the two.

Ed and Hollis were out hunting quail. When they returned, Etta Mae, Joanne, Julie, and the two girls were playing Scrabble at the kitchen table. Bobby, who had dropped in unexpectedly, was standing in the kitchen watching the game.

Ed had not had a successful hunt, and Bobby began to tease him, noting that Ed was wearing jungle fatigues, his

Special Forces insignia on the left shoulder of his camou-
flaged jacket.

While Ed was extremely proud of being a Green Beret,
it was Bobby who had spent two tours in Vietnam. It
bothered him that Ed, a former weekend warrior, carried
on so much about the Special Forces, and even chided
him, Bobby, about not "going airborne."

So Bobby started riding Ed about not having a good hunt.

"Don't they teach you reservists how to shoot?" he
asked, with a hard edge in his voice.

Ed ignored him, and Bobby got angrier.

"Who do you think you're impressing with this soldier
bullshit? You think you're fooling my father? You think
you're fooling me? If you wanted to be a real soldier, why
didn't you join the real Army? Were you afraid of the
war, Ed? Is that it? Were you afraid of the war?"

Ed continued to ignore him. Finally, after a few minutes
of extremely abusive talk, Bobby walked over to Ed and
pulled the Special Forces insignia off his jacket.

"Green Beret! Bullshit! You don't deserve to wear this!"

The women hollered at Bobby to cut it out. Hollis announced that he would have peace in the house, and if
Bobby couldn't behave, he'd have to leave.

The truth was, Hollis didn't think much of either man's
service. As far as he was concerned, Ed had never really
been in the military, and maybe that was for the best,
because he'd probably be insufferable if he had.

And since Hollis considered Vietnam a "scratch scrim-
mage," which almost didn't count as a war, Bobby didn't
deserve much praise, either. Additionally, Bobby had
served with an engineer outfit.

Neither man could carry the bags for a Marine rifleman,
Hollis thought.

After tearing off Ed's insignia, Bobby left, and on future occasions when they would see each other at family
gatherings, neither man mentioned the incident. But it was
always there, hanging between them.

On the morning of Joanne's wedding, they worked side by side. Though Ed was cheerful and chatty, Bobby didn't say too much.

The wedding went very well. Joanne was a beautiful bride. Stephanie, who always reminded people of her mother, was a lovely bridesmaid.

Ed shot rolls and rolls of film at the reception.

When the reception ended, members of the wedding party and a few close friends went to the Thigpens' house for more champagne, food, and photographs.

Finally, Joanne and her husband left.

Ed approached Bobby and asked if he'd step outside for a minute. Bobby figured Ed knew that he'd been talking to the police. Ed probably didn't know that Bobby had gone to St. Louis, because he hadn't told anybody. But the family knew Bobby had called the cops.

Outside, the two men stood under an oak tree. From inside the house came the sound of laughter.

Several years earlier, Bobby had been looking for a condo. He'd been going through a period when he was trying to pull his life together. But a combination of high interest rates and an unsteady work record had doomed his effort to be a homeowner.

"Bobby, I remember when you were looking for a condo. Julie was really pulling for you. So was I. You might not believe that, but I was.

"Right now is the time for you. Because of the oil, prices are down. Interest rates are down too. It's a buyer's market, Bobby. It's sort of a window of opportunity, if you know what I mean."

Bobby stood there, drink in his hand. In the darkness, his face was hidden. He said nothing, so Ed continued.

"Julie was really hoping you'd buy that condo. Or a house. She thought homeownership would be good for you. Well, Julie's not here anymore, but I'm dedicated to following up on her dreams.

"Your sister had a large life insurance policy, and I

expect the insurance company will be settling the claim in a few weeks. I want you to know that when that happens, I'll be in a position to help you get that house, Bobby.''

Bobby exploded.

"You think you can buy me off with your filthy insurance money? You killed my sister. You murdered her. You think you can buy me off with a house?''

Ed was stunned. This was not the reaction he had been expecting. Later, he would say it was as if a rattlesnake had jumped out of the brush and bitten him.

Bobby told Ed that Julie had talked to him last year in the hospital. "I know why her back was hurt, man. She told me. She told me you were going to try to kill her. I know, man, I know. And you think you can offer me some of the insurance money. You're just unbelievable.''

Ed had been sure that Bobby would gratefully accept financial help. He couldn't believe what he was hearing.

"Let me tell you something else, man. You're in big trouble. You think you're gonna get that insurance, huh? Well, it's too late for you. I've already talked to the cops. A matter of fact, I'm pretty close to the center of the investigation. And I can tell you this. You're not fooling anybody. The cops know exactly what happened up there. The big guy, Hollocher, he wants you, Ed. I just talked to him this week. I went up to see him. He said he'd get you.''

For Ed, it was like an out-of-body experience. Behind him were lights and laughter. In front of him were only darkness, a shadowy figure, and these awful words.

"You couldn't possibly mean what you're saying,'' Ed finally said.

"Every word.''

"You're sick, Bobby. Just stay away from me, and stay away from my daughters. I never want to talk to you again.''

Ed turned and walked back toward the house. He went into the den, where people were talking and laughing.

Bobby followed him, walked over to the bar, and picked up an unopened bottle of whiskey. He mumbled something and then walked out. Ed heard the sound of a car door slamming, then an engine starting. Bobby had gone.

Ed pulled Etta Mae aside and said he had to talk to her. They went into the living room.

"Where's Hollis?" Ed asked.

"He's in bed. The long day has worn him out," Etta Mae said.

"Just as well," said Ed. "I don't want him to know about this. Not with his bad heart."

Ed told Etta Mae that Bobby had accused him of killing Julie.

Etta Mae patted Ed on the arm.

"Surely he didn't mean what he said, Ed. When Bobby drinks too much, he gets all mixed up. What with that Vietnam stress he's got, and drugs from over there, when he drinks a lot he's just crazy. He doesn't even know what he's saying."

"You're right, of course," Ed said. "But there's more. He said he's gone to the St. Louis police. He says they believe him. Remember that Hollocher guy?"

Etta Mae nodded.

"Bobby said Hollocher is going to arrest me."

Etta Mae remembered Hollocher. Hollis hadn't liked him. Meanwhile, Ed was still talking. Etta Mae tried to concentrate on his words, but it had been such a long day. Her baby had finally gotten married. She'd been trying to stay happy for Joanne's sake, and yet Julie's absence had been so pronounced. Etta Mae had tried to will her mind away from sadness. Now this happened.

"What scares me, Etta Mae, is that the police don't know Bobby like you and I do, and if they believe him, well, there's no telling what might happen. I can just imagine huge legal fees to straighten this out, and all because of these crazy false accusations."

Finally, Ed seemed to wear himself out. He asked Etta Mae, once again, please not to tell Hollis.

"It'll only upset him," he said.

Early the next week, George Leggio visited Ed Post. Leggio explained that he was an investigator for Equifax, a company that did investigations for several insurance companies.

"Basically, we obtain information which allows them to settle their claims. What I need from you, Mr. Post, is a health history of your late wife. What her physical condition was, any health problems she may have had, what doctors have treated her. That sort of thing. At this time, we're not interested in the circumstances of her death, other than very generally."

Post nodded.

"Let me tell you what happened," he said.

Then, to Leggio's surprise, Post went into the entire story. He woke up at 6:25. He went to the bathroom and cleaned up, then he woke his wife. He gave her a back rub, and ran the water for her bubble bath, and escorted her into the bathroom.

Leggio reminded him that he didn't really need the details of her death—interesting though they were, thought Leggio—but Post continued.

He went jogging for about thirty minutes. When he came back he found her facedown in the tub. He tried to get her out, but because of the bubble bath, she was slippery. As he tried to pick her up she slipped back into the water. Finally, he got her out, but in the process her head, probably the temple area, hit the floor.

He told Leggio that he had administered CPR, and using a phone in the bathroom, had summoned help. The paramedics had been unable to resuscitate Julie, and she was pronounced dead at the hospital. He then authorized the donating of several of her organs and the removal of her bone marrow for transplant.

Later, the police had notified him that a towel ring had been found in the tub, Post said.

He added that investigators from St. Louis had already been down to New Orleans to interview people, and had later called him to say that it looked like an accident.

Leggio wrote down the information.

Later that same week, the last week in June, Dalton Truax called Post into his office.

Post's annual employment contract ran from September 1. A clause in the contract stipulated that if Truax wanted to terminate the relationship, Post was to receive sixty days' notice.

"This is very difficult for me to do, Ed," Truax said. He handed Post a letter.

Post looked at it with a sinking feeling. He tried to argue that the problems with the company had to do with the market, not with the management.

Truax shook his head.

"Ed, we've been through this before. We have philosophical differences about your role with the company. I know the economy is a problem, but that doesn't take away our differences."

Truax hated to be causing another problem for Post right then, but he had been unhappy with Post for a long time. In fact, he had intended to deliver the letter as soon as Post returned from St. Louis, but after Julie's death, he hadn't been able to bring himself to do it.

But he had only until July 1, or he'd have to wait an entire year. Bad timing or not, it had to be done now.

"I'm sorry about this, Ed," Truax said.

Post was stunned. But still, he thought, it wasn't final. It was a notice. That was all. It wasn't termination. He had sixty days to change Dalton's mind.

Besides, losing a job was the least of his worries. Bobby had been talking to the St. Louis cops.

"The big guy, Hollocher, he wants you, Ed."

Chapter Eleven

Dean Hoag was thirty-eight years old, and an unlikely assistant U.S. attorney. Compared to the state courts, federal court is a genteel place. There was nothing genteel about Hoag.

He was five feet seven and stocky, and he wore his hair short enough that he didn't have to comb it. When people found out that he had played semipro baseball as a catcher, they'd nod in understanding. He had the short, squat look of a catcher. His nickname had been "Stump."

Emotionally, he was tightly wound, always intense, a volcano ready to explode. His mother described him as "spit on a hot griddle."

He could be a fury in a courtroom, the kind of prosecutor who takes things personally. To hell with the theory about hating the sin and forgiving the sinner. Hoag was an avenging angel.

He had to remind himself constantly to tone it down. If a prosecutor came on too strong, juries could feel sorry for the defendant. So he learned to tread the fine line— just enough disgust in his voice, just enough sarcasm to his questions, just enough distaste in the glare he would direct at the defendant.

Given his style, Hoag seemed more comfortable in the "dirty building," which is what the lawyers called the Municipal Courts Building, where crimes against the state were tried in St. Louis.

State crime is about evil. Federal crime is about greed.

Besides, state crime is where the challenge is. Federal juries are predisposed to conviction, partly because of the majesty of the federal government, partly because federal juries are more affluent than those at state trials. In the dirty building, only city residents can be called to duty. A great number of those citizens are poor, and many are members of minority groups who view the city police through glasses shaded by years of mistrust.

Federal juries, on the other hand, view the FBI with undisguised awe.

As a prosecutor, then, it meant a lot to bring home a victory in the dirty building, where Hoag had started his career.

While working for the circuit attorney's office, he went to trial seventy-seven times and won sixty. He was twelve and two in murder trials. Then he came over to the U.S. Attorney's office and won his first forty-five cases, including one of the rare murder cases handled by the feds, one involving a man who had been accused of drowning his wife and teenage daughter on an Ozark river that was part of the federal river system.

When Dittmeier told Hoag to check with Vossmeyer on the Omni case and start a mail fraud investigation to run parallel with the state's murder investigation, Hoag was delighted.

It was good to be fighting evil again.

In her cubicle at work, Dee Vossmeyer considered herself on hold as far as the Post case was concerned. An industrial testing lab was scheduled to run some tests on towel rings from the Omni. The hotel would pay for the testing. The police and the circuit attorney's office would be allowed to observe.

McCraw was still interviewing people.

Hoag was preparing to subpoena financial records.

For the moment, Dee would be spending her time on

other cases. Her thoughts, however, often drifted back to the Post case. She and Gary talked about it a lot at home.

Gary was still skeptical. As far as he was concerned, the insurance angle had not checked out. It would be one thing, Gary argued, if all the insurance had been newly purchased. But Post was apparently a guy who believed— you could say overbelieved—in life insurance. He had a pattern of upgrading his life insurance and Julie's as well. The timing could be completely coincidental.

He also doubted the unhappy marriage stuff. Ed and Julie had stayed married for almost twenty years without even a trial separation. The problems at work could be overblown. Whenever you have a boss's wife in the office, you've got problems.

Nor did the towel ring impress Gary. First of all, there wasn't yet any proof that the towel ring really hadn't come off in a slip and fall.

There were explanations for everything.

Dee, however, had a feeling about this case. Even though she hadn't been able to get a real fix on Julie— Julie was, and would always remain, a mystery to the people in St. Louis—Dee felt a kinship with her.

Having met Julie's parents, Dee had deduced that Julie's childhood probably had resembled her own. Growing up in the South, in the fifties and early sixties, they probably had shared the same experiences.

Both had gone to good, solid Southern colleges, but then, of course, their paths diverged. Julie married young and dropped out of school. Dee got her diploma and went out into the work world before she met her first husband. That gave her a great deal more freedom. Dee had never been financially dependent.

Then, too, as Dee saw it, Julie's situation had been further complicated, her independence further constrained, by the presence of the two girls. Dee had not had her first child until after she had passed the bar exam.

Despite dropping out of school and having two kids,

Julie had ended up a professional. Like the smart, tough woman that Dee imagined her to be, Julie had joined Dee in the company of career women who were juggling families and careers.

They could have been friends. Maybe good friends.

At the Thigpens' house, Dee had seen a photograph of Julie. She had been a very attractive woman, no question about that.

For Dee, the real mystery character was Ed Post. He seemed so self-important. Julie had called him the Pillsbury Doughboy.

Why had Julie stayed with him? Had it been for the girls? Had it been inertia? Had she been so swamped with other things that she had just given up on the relationship, dismissed it as unimportant? Or perhaps Gary was right— maybe the marriage had been more solid than it had seemed in the office.

Dee had little time to ponder the Post situation. She was reading a police report regarding another case when the phone rang.

"Mrs. Vossmeyer? This is Ed Post. From New Orleans. I've been told you were down here, talking to people. Judging from the people you spoke with, it sounds like you're doing a very thorough job."

Was this sarcastic or sincere? Dee wasn't quite sure how to respond. Ed quickly filled the silence.

"So I just thought I'd call to see if there's anything I can do. You probably know, I'm sure you know, that I talked to Steve Jacobsmeyer and, uh, Lieutenant Hollocher when they came down. I'm doing whatever I can to cooperate."

Not sarcastic. Sincere. Or at least attempting to seem that way.

"As I'm sure you've been told, Mr. Post, there was nothing secretive about the trip," Dee said. "We're basically running a background check, trying to verify the things you told Jacobsmeyer."

"Of course, of course. I have no problems with that. At any rate, the reason I called is to see if there's anything I can help you with. Maybe you have some questions you want to ask me."

Why did you call Julie dead weight?

"Well, thank you, Mr. Post. I can't think of anything specific as far as what we've done. The one area we still need to look into, would like to look into anyway, is your finances. We'd like to have some kind of picture of your overall situation."

"I have no problem with that."

Ed suggested she call his banker. He gave her the banker's name and number.

"How about credit cards?" he asked. "I suppose they're part of my overall situation."

"Sure," said Dee.

"Let me pull my wallet out and I'll read you my card numbers," said Ed.

He had all the impressive ones. As he read the numbers, he'd say, "This one's a gold card. Do you need to know that?"

"Sure," Dee would say.

"That's the last one," he finally said. "I hope it helps. I really want to get this behind me. People keep telling me that it's going to get better, but it just keeps getting worse. We were married for almost twenty years, you know. We raised two wonderful daughters together."

"I feel very bad for you," Dee said.

"Well, thank you. I don't mean to cry on your shoulder. I just want to help any way I can. And I hope I have. If you have any more questions, please feel free to call."

"I'm sure I will," Dee said.

Dee called the U.S. attorney's office and left all the numbers for Dean Hoag. Maybe they'd be of some help with the subpoenas.

*   *   *

In early July 1986, George Peach called a meeting of everyone involved in the Ed Post investigation.

Hollocher and McCraw from the police department were there. Vossmeyer and Hayes represented the circuit attorney's office. Hoag was there on behalf of the U.S. attorney's office.

"Where are we?" asked Peach.

McCraw gave a status report on his investigation. "Arrangements are being made to test the towel ring," he said.

Vossmeyer reported the results of her and Hayes's trip to New Orleans. "The marriage seemed to be in trouble," she said. "You already know about the insurance."

Hoag gave a brief report on the financial records he had so far obtained.

"Where do we go from here?" asked Peach.

"I've got a thought," said Hoag. "I handled a drowning on the Jacks Fork a couple of years ago. Water retards bruising."

"What are you saying, Dean?" somebody asked.

"I say we dig her up. Take another look at her."

Two years before Julie Post died, David Rothgeb, his wife, April, and their fifteen-year-old daughter, Windy, went canoeing on the Upper Jacks Fork River in Shannon County, Missouri.

David was thirty-five, a driver for United Parcel Service. He also dabbled in hypnosis. April was thirty-four.

The Rothgebs floated until noon, ate lunch, and then resumed the trip. They made camp near a swimming spot called Black Hollow Hole.

According to David, they swam awhile, ate dinner, swam some more, and then decided to change into dry clothes for the night. David said he left the camp to look for firewood. When he came back thirty minutes later, his wife and daughter were gone.

He built the fire and waited for them to return. Finally,

he took a flashlight and headed upstream for help. Shortly after midnight, he stumbled into a campsite at the Bunker Hill Ranch.

At 1:15 A.M. the water patrol began its search. Five hours later, one mile downstream from the Rothgeb campsite, April's body was found in thirty-two inches of water. She had a laceration on her right forehead and a cut on her lip.

A couple of hours later, Windy's body was found face-down in an eddy, approximately three hundred yards downstream from the Rothgeb campsite.

About two hundred yards from her body was another campsite where five young men, aged twenty-one to twenty-five, were staying.

The highway patrol was called. One of the young men had a conviction for burglary. Another had been arrested for robbery.

The prosecutor in Shannon County was a young woman who had never tried a felony. Because that particular section of the river was in the Ozark National Scenic Riverways system, the young prosecutor was able to ask the feds for help. Hoag, who had joined the U.S. attorney's office the previous year, was assigned the case.

He had a gut feeling that the five young men weren't involved. Their statements seemed to be consistent, and they did not strike Hoag as the kind of guys who could get together on a story and then hang tough.

Furthermore, neither April nor Windy had been sexually molested.

Finally, if the young men had murdered the women, why in the world would they still be hanging around their campsite at 10:00 the next morning?

About a week into the case, Hoag got a call from an attorney in Alabama. The attorney said he was inquiring about the Rothgeb case on behalf of Kitty Eldridge.

Who is that? Hoag asked.

David's fiancé, the attorney said.

Rothgeb had a secret life. He had met Kitty the previous fall at a hypnosis convention. Kitty knew that David was married, but he had assured her he was about to get a divorce. He and his daughter would be moving to North Carolina.

The subsequent investigation turned up 166 telephone calls and twelve love letters. David had recently taken out a $100,000 life insurance policy on his wife.

The case went to trial in March 1985.

Hoag argued that Rothgeb had originally intended only to murder his wife, but must have been caught by his daughter. Consequently, he had been forced to kill her, too.

Both women had been good swimmers, he told the jury. Somebody had had to murder them. And all the evidence was that only one person stood to gain by their death.

The jury convicted Rothgeb of first-degree murder for the death of his wife, and second-degree murder for the death of his daughter. Rothgeb was sentenced to life in prison.

In addition to delivering a closing argument that he would later, with small revisions, deliver again, Hoag had learned something about medicine during the investigation.

On the day the bodies of April and Windy were discovered—Father's Day—a highway patrolman photographed the bodies. He took more pictures the next day at the funeral home.

Hoag had studied both sets of pictures, and had noticed a difference. The bruises in the second set were more pronounced. He took the photographs to Dr. Mary Case, the assistant medical examiner in the city.

Easy to explain, she said. In the first place, bruises don't always show up right away. More important, water retards the bruising process. It's like when you bang your finger and put it under cold water. The bruising process gets slowed up.

That was a piece of information Hoag had tucked away.

And now it seemed to have a special relevance to the Post case.

It was agreed. There would be another trip to New Orleans. This would be the big one. McCraw, Hollocher, Vossmeyer, and Hayes would all go.

They would talk to everyone except Ed. His statement was already on tape. But they would contact everybody else—family, friends, work associates, even the people at the newspaper who got the call about the obituary.

There was still some thought, a hope actually, that Ed had dictated the obituary too soon. Could he possibly have written it before Julie was dead?

Chapter Twelve

Dee Vossmeyer was sitting in Jack Peeples's office. The first assistant district attorney for the Parish of Orleans was an older man, courtly and gracious, who spoke with a soft Southern accent.

"As you're probably aware, Miss Vossmeyer, our system down here is a little different. Perhaps antiquated, some might say."

Dee nodded. "You operate under the Napoleonic Code," she said.

"Just so," said Peeples. "A concession to our heritage."

"It's my understanding, Mr. Peeples, that your office will guide me through the code so we can exhume the body."

"Oh, absolutely, Miss Vossmeyer. I anticipate no problems with that."

"Very good. Where do we start?"

"The first thing we must do, Miss Vossmeyer, is put together an affidavit of probable cause showing exactly why you want to exhume the body. Then we present that affidavit to the coroner. We have no medical examiner, you see. A quirk of our laws. We still have an elected coroner, and it's up to him to approve or disapprove your request."

"I hope he won't be a problem," said Dee.

Peeples smiled. "This office has an excellent relationship with Dr. Minyard. By the way, have you heard of him?"

Dee shook her head.

Peeples smiled again. "You're in for a treat, Miss Vossmeyer."

While Dee met with Peeples, Hollocher and Hayes visited the *New Orleans Times-Picayune* to learn what they could about the phone call Post had placed to publisher Ashton Phelps, Jr., on the morning of Julie's death.

The *Pick,* as it was called, represented an unfortunate geographical trend in newspapers. Once, all newspapers had been located in the heart of the city, walking distance from the courts and City Hall.

But as the old buildings wore out and the value of downtown real estate increased, publishers began putting up their replacement buildings in low-rent industrial zones.

And so the *Pick* sat on Howard Avenue, next to a cement factory, a chain-link fence separating it from the railroad tracks. With its signature spire resembling a watchtower, the *Pick* exuded all the charm of a medium-security prison.

Hollocher asked the receptionist for Ashton Phelps, but was told the publisher wasn't in.

"We'll see the deputy publisher then," said Hollocher.

Eventually, they were escorted to the office of Fritz Harsdorff, the paper's associate editor.

Harsdorff was a longtime newspaperman, accustomed to dealing with police officers. But Hollocher was unlike any cop Harsdorff had ever run across. The big detective made no secret of the fact that he was convinced that Ed Post had murdered his wife. Actually, he presented it as a fact. Post did it, and Hollocher was going to get him.

He wanted to know if there was a record of Post's call to Phelps. What time had he called, and what kind of information had he called with?

"We think he might have had the obituary already written," explained Hollocher.

Calls to Mr. Phelps were, in fact, logged in, but the records had been misplaced.

At any rate, the publisher would not have taken dictation. Had Post called in with the obituary already written, Phelps would simply have referred him to the city desk. (Later, they would find out that Post did not have the obituary already written. He was instead asking what information would be needed.)

But it wasn't the questions that struck Harsdorff as odd. It was the manner in which they were asked. Harsdorff was accustomed to detectives who played their cards close to their vest.

He was from that school himself. He didn't say that his wife, Jo, worked in the West Bank office of Wagner-Truax.

The next morning, the four St. Louisans gathered to discuss strategy in one of their two rooms at the Royal Hotel.

The rooms were compliments of the Omni, but the meals were not on the house. McCraw ordered a pot of coffee, and when he signed for it, he saw the charge was fourteen bucks. They're going to kill me back in St. Louis, he thought.

Actually, expenses were the least of his problems. He was not only the group's scribe, he was already settling into the role of peacemaker.

Hollocher didn't think much of Hayes or Vossmeyer. They were far too cautious for his taste. As far as he was concerned, the idea of having a lawyer along was nonsense. The best way to handle this investigation would be to go confront Ed Post. Why come all the way to New Orleans and not at least talk to the guy? It made no sense.

McCraw tended to think Vossmeyer was right. On the other hand, Hollocher was his boss.

The only thing everybody agreed on was that there was plenty of work to do.

In addition to checking in again with Peeples, which was Vossmeyer's job, somebody had to talk to Post's good friend Harby Kreeger. Also, Bobby Autin and Dan Post needed to be interviewed.

Vossmeyer had already made arrangements to have lunch with Kim Autin.

"Count me in on that," said Hollocher. "Hayes and McCraw can go ahead and talk to this Harby Kreeger."

Dee thought she might have better luck with Kim alone, woman to woman. But Hollocher really wanted to go, so Dee relented.

Harby Kreeger had inherited a chain of upscale clothing stores for women, specializing in furs. The business had been unable to survive the economic downturn. Bankruptcy proceedings had already started.

Hayes and McCraw found the Kreegers at the main store in New Orleans. Harby Kreeger agreed to talk to them, but on one condition. Ed was his best friend, he said, and he didn't want Ed to know that he had spoken with the authorities.

No problem, said Hayes.

Kreeger took the men into his office. His wife, Dianne, followed.

"You mind if we tape this?" asked Hayes.

"No, no, go ahead," said Kreeger. "First of all, let me say that I consider Ed Post to be my best friend, and I do not believe that he killed Julie."

A pause.

"Do you have any questions?"

"Sure we do," said Hayes.

But the interview did not go well. The Kreegers were very supportive of Ed.

Hayes probed. Politely.

"We've heard that the marriage wasn't so good. We've been told about a very public fight, and some people have suggested that maybe that was just the tip of the iceberg."

"Oh, come on now," said Kreeger good-naturedly. "All married people argue. I would say that Ed and Julie were a demonstrative couple. They fought hard, and they loved hard."

"They were both strong-willed people," said Dianne Kreeger, "and of course they had disagreements. But that's natural. I wouldn't try to stretch an argument into an unhappy relationship."

And so on.

At the end of this unproductive session, Kreeger again sought assurance that Post wouldn't learn about the interview.

After leaving the store, Hayes and McCraw decided to grab a sandwich. There was a restaurant half a block away. They sat at a booth and ordered lunch.

A couple of minutes later, Kreeger came in with another man. They didn't see Hayes and McCraw, and went directly to a booth. Kreeger talked, while his companion, a short, round-faced, fortyish fellow, listened. Occasionally he'd ask a question.

It came to the two detectives at the same moment that Kreeger's companion must be Ed Post.

"Kreeger must have called him the minute we left," said McCraw.

" 'Don't tell him I talked to you,' " said Hayes, mimicking Harby.

The detectives finished their sandwiches and left.

Vossmeyer and Hollocher met Kim Autin at a steak-and-ale restaurant on the West Bank.

Kim looked stunning. Even at noon, she was dressed in expensive clothes and was heavily made up.

Hollocher was not intimidated. He was his usual blustery self. Kim seemed to get a kick out of him.

"So tell me, did you ever fool around with this guy?" he asked her.

"I'm a married woman, Lieutenant."

"I didn't ask if you were married, I asked if you ever fooled around with this guy."

"No," she said with a laugh.

Mostly, though, Dee handled the interview.

Kim talked about the incident at the nightclub after the Million Dollar Club banquet. She said that Ed had come over later that night. Kim's husband, Bobby, had passed out on the couch. After apologizing for Julie's actions at the nightclub, Ed started to leave.

"Then he grabbed me," Kim said, "and kissed me. It was more than a friendly kiss."

"Have you had much contact with Ed since Julie's death?" Dee asked.

"Hardly any," said Kim. She explained that her own personal life was in a state of flux. After Julie's funeral, Kim had returned to Florida. She'd heard from a friend that Bobby was cheating on her. Ed and Bobby were great friends, and she called Ed, who confirmed that, yes, Bobby was running around. She had come home and confronted Bobby.

"At any rate, that's been the extent of my contact with Ed since Julie's death," she said.

Dee repeated questions they had discussed on the phone. What about the fights between Ed and Julie?

"Early this spring, February or March, Bobby and I went to San Francisco with Ed and Julie," Kim said. "It was a nightmare. They fought all the time."

One morning, Kim said, Julie had told her that they had had such a loud fight in their room that she honestly thought somebody was going to call hotel security.

Dee asked about the bruises.

"Oh sure," Kim said. "On this same trip, Julie and I went shopping, and when Julie was trying on some clothes, I noticed two large bruises on her left arm and left hip. Julie said Ed had knocked her down."

As Dee listened, she kept imagining Kim on the witness stand.

She'd be dynamite, Dee thought. She was articulate and intelligent, and best of all, just looking at her you could see why Ed was lusting after her.

In that sense, the interview went well. Part of this whole process was figuring out who would testify if there was a trial. But as far as gathering new information was concerned, the interview wasn't so successful.

Until the very end. Then Kim remembered something she hadn't already mentioned.

"One time back when Ed was first starting to lose weight, he and Julie had a big argument and I was there to hear it," Kim said. "Ed told Julie that as soon as he lost forty pounds, he was going to leave her."

"And how much weight has he lost by now?" Dee asked.

Kim shrugged.

"At least forty pounds," she said.

Late that afternoon, Hollocher and Vossmeyer visited Marianne Mautner, a friend of Julie's and one of the last people to have seen her before she went to St. Louis. Dee wanted to learn if Julie had seemed reluctant about the trip to St. Louis, but Hollocher seemed more interested in convincing Mrs. Mautner that Julie's death was a murder.

"How does somebody drown in a bathtub with only three inches of water in it?" he asked.

He's making that up, Dee realized, but she didn't want to get in an argument in front of a potential witness.

Mautner was noncommittal. She said she didn't recall any reluctance on Julie's part about the trip to St. Louis, and she certainly didn't have any explanation about the drowning.

Throughout the interview, Mautner was distracted. Her German shepherd, Lagniappe, was sitting a few feet from Hollocher, growling ever so slightly. She had never heard the dog growl at anybody. In fact, its too-friendly disposition was a joke among her friends.

When the investigators left, Mautner called her next-door neighbor to tell her of the interview and of the dog's strange behavior. She knew her neighbor would be interested. After all, it was because of her that Mautner knew Julie.

Mautner lived next door to Dan and Martha Post.

That evening, Bobby Autin came to the hotel to see the investigators. He was short and dark and wore casual but expensive clothes. A lounge lizard, a fast-laner, Hollocher thought.

Autin said Ed had called him the day of Julie's death. He hadn't been in, so Ed had left a message. When he returned the call, probably right after lunch, Ed told him Julie had drowned. Ed had gone into the whole story about jogging and fixing Julie's bath.

Also, Ed had wanted him to call Kim in Florida. Apparently, Ed had tried and she wasn't in. A few days earlier, the day the Posts had left for St. Louis, Ed had called and asked for the phone number of the Autins' condo in Florida.

"You think Ed was fooling around with your wife?" Hollocher asked.

Bobby shook his head. He said he couldn't imagine that.

He also told the detectives about the party after Julie's funeral.

"Ed came up to me and asked if I could fix him up with my wife's twin sister," Bobby said.

Later, McCraw and Hollocher went looking for Bobby Thigpen.

They'd tried calling him earlier, but his phone was disconnected. They did, however, have an address. Finally, after asking strangers for directions half a dozen times, they found the place. It was a little two-story apartment building near an overnight market in a rough part of town.

There were no lights on, and no answer when Hollocher knocked. He knocked on the other apartment's door. A neighbor told Hollocher he hadn't seen Bobby in a couple of days.

While Hollocher and McCraw were looking for Bobby Thigpen, Gary Hayes got a phone call at the hotel.

"There's something you need to know," said an older woman's voice. "Harby and Dianne Kreeger know more than they told you."

"Who is this?" Hayes asked.

"It doesn't matter," said the voice.

And then the phone went dead.

Chapter Thirteen

The next morning, Hollocher was furious when he learned about the anonymous phone call. He complained bitterly to McCraw.

"Now we've got an old lady telling us we're too soft, and the damn thing is, she's right. If this were strictly a police investigation, which it ought to be, we wouldn't be pussyfooting around. The very first thing we should do this morning is go confront Post. We got more than enough from this Autin woman. He was trying to come on to her," Hollocher said.

"Vossmeyer thinks it's a bad idea," said McGraw.

"Bullshit! We're the ones who know how to run an investigation, and let me tell you something. Little Feet is a talker. I told Jake that the first time we met him, I said his alligator mouth was going to get him in trouble. And it would. If Vossmeyer would let him talk, that is."

McGraw shrugged. There was some sense in Hollocher's idea. The more somebody talked, the more trouble he could get into.

"Look where we're at now. Anonymous phone calls from old ladies who want to tell us we're getting smoked. Me and you are going to visit the Kreegers tonight, and they won't blow smoke at us. That's a promise."

But first, they drove to the Thigpens' in Poplarville. There would be two very different versions of this visit.

The police version went like this:

Thigpen was gracious, inviting them inside, where the three men were joined by Mrs. Thigpen. They sat in the living room.

The talk first turned to finances. Thigpen explained that he had lent Ed and Julie $15,000 three years before at 12 percent interest. As per the agreement, Ed was making interest payments only. The balance was due next month.

"By the way," Thigpen said, "it was Julie who asked for the loan." That seemed to bother him. The detectives sensed that he was not the kind of man who would ever have sent his wife to ask anybody for money.

Mrs. Thigpen then added that Ed spent all the money he and Julie made. "They don't even own a car anymore. They lease," Etta Mae said.

The detectives asked if the Thigpens knew of any instances of physical abuse in their daughter's marriage. Thigpen said he was unaware of any. He added that even though he and Julie had been very close, he could understand why Julie wouldn't have confided in him about abuse.

"She'd know I'd kick his ass," Hollis said.

Mrs. Thigpen sat silent for a minute, and then said that she did know of one instance of physical abuse.

Once, several years ago, maybe nine years ago, Julie had called and said she was hiding in a closet because Ed was trying to beat her up. The next day, Mrs. Thigpen and Julie had talked again, and Julie had told her that she had called Dan, Ed's brother, and he had come over and straightened things out. Julie blamed the incident on the fact that Ed was drunk.

It was never spoken of again, Mrs. Thigpen said.

The Thigpens then told the detectives about the incident the night of Joanne's wedding. Ed offered to buy Bobby a house, and Bobby just blew up.

McCraw, who was taking notes, thought he sensed a strong note of disapproval. It bothered the Thigpens that Ed would make that kind of an offer, an obvious bribe.

Thigpen then asked the detectives why they were investigating this as a murder case.

The interview was going well, and the detectives laid their cards on the table. They told the couple that the towel ring appeared to have been twisted off the wall, and that the timing of the new insurance policy seemed suspicious.

"What new policy?" asked Thigpen.

The detectives explained that Ed had upped Julie's insurance by $300,000 shortly before the trip to St. Louis.

Thigpen stood up. "I knew that son of a bitch did it," he said, more to himself than to the detectives, and he walked into the kitchen. He stood with his back to the table, obviously struggling with his self-control. After two or three minutes, he returned to the table, and the interview continued.

He told the detectives that on the day of the funeral, an attractive young woman came up to him and told him that Julie shouldn't have died. The woman's name was Kim.

When the detectives left, they were sure that Thigpen was on their side. Hollocher, in particular, felt a kinship with the tough old man. They were two of a kind, he thought. No nonsense. No pretense.

As McCraw steered the car down the driveway, he said to Hollocher, "George, we've got him. He's on our side."

Hollocher lit a cigarette.

"If Ed were to come here right now, we wouldn't need a trial."

The Thigpens would recall the meeting differently.

Yes, they sat in the living room, and talked about finances, and Etta Mae revealed the long-ago incident of abuse, if you could call it that. A drunken argument from years ago.

Yes, there was talk about the incident on the night of Joanne's wedding.

But the tone was entirely different.

Hollis remembered Hollocher running down Julie's marriage. The big detective claimed to have some kind of a source, a woman who knew Julie and who apparently had been feeding Hollocher stories about Ed's infidelity.

Then Hollocher said that Bobby was missing, and he was afraid that Ed had something to do with it.

Hollis thought this was nonsense. Bobby disappeared a lot, and furthermore, it was ludicrous to think that Ed would have something to do with it.

By the time the interview was over, Hollis was very much against the detectives. His initial impression of Hollocher had been reinforced. The big detective was not an honest man.

Vossmeyer and Hayes took their affidavit of probable cause to the coroner's office in the basement of the courthouse. On a wall in the outer office was a crocheted sign, in the style of "Home Sweet Home." It read, "Where death delights to serve the living."

The inner office looked like some kind of offbeat Jazz Hall of Fame. On one wall there was a stylized portrait of a trumpet player, a companion piece to the posters the coroner handed out to visitors. In these posters, the coroner, dressed all in white, stood on the banks of the river blowing his horn. At the top of the poster was the name to which the coroner most often answered—Dr. Jazz.

The other walls were lined with autographed celebrity pictures, from Admiral Zumwalt to Billy Martin to Al Hirt.

Frank Minyard, a lifelong resident of the French Quarter, sat at his desk. The duly elected coroner was not even a pathologist. He was an obstetrician.

In the criminal justice system, it is axiomatic that the people in the "dead business" tend to be slightly odd, but Dr. Jazz seemed weird even by the standards of his profession.

On his desk were figurines of Louis Armstrong, Al Hirt,

and Pete Fountain. The books on his desk, titles facing
the visitors, were further expressions of his eclectic tastes:
Sherlock Holmes mysteries sat next to the collected writ-
ings of Sigmund Freud.

"I understand you need a body," Dr. Jazz said.

He was in his late fifties, but affected a much younger
persona. He was dressed casually, and the top couple of
buttons of his shirt remained undone.

Vossmeyer handed him the affidavit. The doctor mused
aloud while he read it.

"So many people think the coroner system is out-
dated," he said, "and yet here we have a jurisdiction with
a medical examiner, and a very good one, coming to see
a coroner for assistance. How very strange."

To Vossmeyer, Minyard seemed like a character from
Alice in Wonderland.

"There are, of course, a couple of problems," Dr. Jazz
said cheerfully.

"You mean you're not going to authorize this?" Vossmeyer asked.

"Oh, I'll authorize it," said Dr. Jazz. "That's not what
I mean. I mean, problems with your case. Just last year
we had a similar case. Husband, wife. It was murder dis-
guised as suicide."

"Jack Peeples mentioned that," Vossmeyer said. "He
said the state got clobbered."

"Indeed they did," said Dr. Jazz. "The husband had
unlimited resources, so he brought in all kinds of expert
witnesses who, for a fee, would say anything. It muddied
the waters."

"Well, we're not even sure what we have yet," said
Vossmeyer.

"That's your second problem, your big problem. This
woman," and he tapped the affidavit, "has been buried
for six weeks. Buried. This is a sea-level town. Eighty-
five percent of our burials are above-ground. This, obviously, is in the fifteen percent that isn't."

"Meaning what?" said Vossmeyer.

"The likelihood of the body still being in good shape is very low."

Nevertheless, he signed the affidavit.

"I'll also be assigning a pathologist to this case," Dr. Jazz explained. "We dig it up, we do the autopsy."

"That's fine," Vossmeyer said. "Our medical examiner is prepared to fly in to observe."

"Very well," said Dr. Jazz. "You're extremely fortunate, Miss Vossmeyer. This is a particularly difficult case, and you're going to get our very best—Dr. Paul McGarry."

Like Dr. Jazz, McGarry was also best known by a nickname. He was called Dr. Death.

He had a reputation around the courthouse for siding with the prosecution. No question about it, Dr. Jazz was doing the St. Louisans a favor by assigning the case to Dr. Death.

With Minyard's order in hand, Vossmeyer and Hayes returned to Peeple's office. He notified the cemetery, and Charles Gonano, the director of the cemetery, called Ed Post.

In a state of shock, Post called his brother. From the reports the brothers had been getting from the people who had been interviewed, both men had assumed that the investigation was going nowhere. Neither had suspected that an exhumation was in the offing.

"What should I do?" Ed asked Dan.

Dan knew he was in way over his head.

"Little brother, you don't need a real estate lawyer any more. You need a criminal lawyer. Let me make a couple of phone calls, and I'll get right back to you."

A few minutes later, Dan called Ed back.

"I talked to a couple of people, and I got the name of a top criminal lawyer. I just called him, and we're supposed to be at his office in half an hour. The guy's name is Ralph Whalen, and his office is in the Quarter on Exchange Alley. I'll meet you outside.''

After hanging up the phone, Dan sat for a moment at his desk. He knew that his brother's marriage had been, at times, a violent one. Julie had called him not once but several times to ask him to intercede.

On the day of the funeral, when Dan viewed Julie's body, an unwelcome thought had come into his head:

''Ed is going to pay for this.''

A block and a half from Bourbon Street is the colorful Exchange Alley. On this day, the sun was out and a strong breeze moved the wooden sign for the American Café. Two couples sat at the café's outdoor tables as Ed and Dan Post hurried past to the next door.

Once inside the door, the brothers found themselves in a small hallway that led to an elevator, located next to the café's kitchen.

A plaque near the elevator notified visitors that they were in the Edgar Degas House. ''The house was bequeathed to the artist and his sister by their maternal uncle, Michael Uneson. Degas sold the house in 1866. It was declared a national landmark in 1978.''

When the elevator opened on the second floor, the brothers saw a receptionist seated behind a desk.

''We're here to see Ralph Whalen,'' Dan said. ''He's expecting us. Ed and Dan Post.''

She picked up the phone, pushed a button, and announced their arrival.

A moment later, Whalen came down the hallway. He was tall, thin, and elegantly dressed, with a wispy, silver-streaked beard that gave him the look of a swashbuckler. Introducing himself with a warm smile, he radiated confidence.

''Come on back to my office,'' he said, leading the way.

Certificates and diplomas hung on the hallway wall outside of Whalen's office. A framed certificate attesting to Whalen's appearance before the United States Supreme Court rested on the floor. In the space where it had been was a diploma crediting Whalen with completion of a prenatal training course.

"Changing priorities," he said with a grin, when he noticed one of his visitors reading it.

Whalen was in his early forties. He had grown up poor, and his childhood had been spent in a string of small towns throughout the South. He had gone to college on a scholarship. Student loans had gotten him through law school.

He had joined the district attorney's office back when the DA was Jim Garrison, who became something of a national celebrity with his investigation of the Kennedy assassination. In fact, Whalen achieved the status of historical footnote when he was delegated to perform the final official act in Garrison's efforts to uncover a conspiracy. When Garrison finally threw in the towel, it was Whalen who filed a dismissal against an alleged conspirator.

But Whalen had made his real reputation as a prosecutor in murder cases. In an office where Won and Lost records were prominently displayed like baseball standings, Whalen was the star. The press loved him. His aggressive manner in the courtroom had earned him a nickname—Ralph the Whacker.

In cross-examination, he would get right in the defendant's face. He would wave the grisly photographs of the homicide scene. He was, in short, an avenging angel.

As he ushered the Post brothers into the office, however, he was calm and courtly. Unlike the building in which it was located, his private office was modern, up-to-date, and classy.

He settled into the chair behind his desk.

"Now, what's this about an exhumation?" he asked.

Ed explained the little he knew. Investigators were looking into his wife's death, he said. She had died in a terrible accident in St. Louis; she had fallen and drowned in a tub.

"Other than the unusual circumstances of her death, is there anything that would make the authorities suspicious?" Whalen asked.

"One thing," said Ed. "It's a coincidence, but it looks bad. I purchased a three-hundred-thousand-dollar life insurance policy on Julie about a month before she died."

Ed then launched into his insurance history. It could easily be checked out, he said. At the same time he'd purchased Julie's additional insurance, he had bought an identical policy for himself. That brought his coverage up to $1 million, Julie's up to $700,000.

Whalen nodded. No wonder the authorities were suspicious.

"It's extremely difficult to stop an exhumation," he said to the brothers. "I think our next step should be to get a pathologist of our own in here to observe the autopsy. Is there any reason you can think of why we shouldn't go along with the exhumation?"

Ed shook his head.

"I've got nothing to hide," he said.

"Very good," said Whalen. In truth, it was almost impossible to stop an exhumation. Whalen knew that firsthand. As a prosecutor, he had once exhumed a woman's body. The exhumation had led to a murder conviction. The motive had been life insurance.

"Ed, let's go to the district attorney's office and meet these people from St. Louis," he said.

Post was not what Dee had been expecting. She had seen pictures of Julie, who was a very pretty woman. She had met Kim Autin, who was also attractive. She knew that Post had been a Green Beret, and she associated him with Jeffrey MacDonald, the Green Beret doctor who had been convicted of killing his wife and daughters.

From the pictures she had seen, MacDonald had been

a hunk. Post was round-faced, short, and a little over-weight. He was wearing a dynamite suit, though, and a very large ring.

Because of Hollocher's constant talk, both Vossmeyer and Hayes checked out Post's feet. They were indeed small.

Whalen looked dapper and very composed. "What's all this about?" he asked.

Whalen sat across from Vossmeyer. Post was to one side, and she could feel his eyes boring into her. She addressed all her comments to Whalen.

The case was unusual, Vossmeyer explained. There were many oddities: the circumstances of Julie's death, the timing of the purchase of new life insurance. Additionally, some of Ed's statements seemed to be at variance with what other people were saying. The first autopsy had been done hurriedly, and only after the police had assured the pathologist that the death was accidental. The new information made that original finding less certain. Therefore, to clear everything up, a new autopsy would be necessary.

Whalen studied the affidavit. The exhumation would be tomorrow, the autopsy the following day.

"My client wants to cooperate," Whalen said. "His only concern is that Julie's body be treated with respect. We will, of course, have our own pathologist present. By the way, who's going to be doing this second autopsy?"

"A Dr. Paul McGarry," Vossmeyer said.

Whalen nodded. Dr. Death. Thanks for nothing, Dr. Jazz.

As Vossmeyer and Hayes left Peeples's office, a man stopped them.

"Are you the people from St. Louis?" he asked.

"Yes," said Vossmeyer, puzzled.

"I'm a reporter from the *Times-Picayune*," he said. "Do you have any comment about the exhumation?"

Vossmeyer shook her head. At this point of the investigation, she didn't want to deal with the press. But it seemed, and not for the first time, that everybody knew what was going on regarding the investigation.

The whole trip had been like that. Whenever she talked to somebody, she had the feeling that the person had already been briefed. Everybody was friendly, but could anyone be trusted?

She wondered if Peeples, or one of his staff, had called the reporter. It was bad enough that she had to keep Hollocher on a short lease. He made no secret of his hostility.

And now somebody had called the press.

Whalen and Post returned to Whalen's office.

"Run through everything, Ed. Start with why you were in St. Louis in the first place," Whalen said.

Post explained that he had gone to St. Louis because he was on the national advisory board of Better Homes and Gardens. That was a great honor, he told Whalen. Then he recited his story about the morning of Julie's death—waking up at 6:25, drawing Julie's bath, and so on.

Whalen listened intently. Then he asked about the insurance, and if any medical problems could explain why Julie might have fallen in the tub.

The insurance history could be verified by Bob Masson, one of the most respected agents in New Orleans, Post said. The fall might have been caused by mitral valve prolapse, a heart condition, Post said. That condition could be confirmed by Julie's doctor, who was a personal friend as well as one of the top cardiologists in town, Post assured Whalen.

Whalen nodded. He had a vague sinking feeling. "Have you talked to the police yet, Ed?" he asked.

"I've been very cooperative," Post said.

"Well, that's fine. I understand completely, Ed. But in the future, if anybody from St. Louis has any more questions, call me, and we can talk to them together. I'm not suggesting you don't cooperate. I'm suggesting we be very careful."

After Post left, Whalen went downstairs and had a glass of iced tea at the café. He had been struck with how hard Ed had tried to impress him. Most likely he had tried the same thing with the cops. Probably he thought that if he came across like a big deal, they'd back off.

Whalen knew better. He understood the mentality in the system. That kind of talk would only get everybody aroused.

And what a talker he was, thought Whalen. If you asked him what time it was, he told you how to build a clock.

That night, Hollocher and McCraw paid a visit to the Kreegers. They lived in Metairie, near Lake Pontchartrain.

"Hello, Harby," Hollocher said. "I'm Lieutenant Hollocher. I'm in charge of the investigation concerning Julie Post's death."

Kreeger invited the detectives into the house. The three men went into Kreeger's study.

"We're not gonna record this conversation, Harby. Just a little honest talk. Nothing recorded," said Hollocher. "McCraw, take your tape recorder out and put it on the table here. I want Harby to see that we're being straight with him."

McCraw put his recorder on the table.

Bang! Hollocher hammered his fist on the table.

Kreeger jumped.

"Let's talk," Hollocher said.

Kreeger did.

He said that he had not wanted to hurt his friend, but the truth was, Ed and Julie did indeed have some loud, explosive arguments.

As far as physical abuse is concerned, Kreeger claimed to know of only one incident. Several years ago, the Kreegers had had a party, and Ed had got very drunk.

Later that night, Julie had called Dianne Kreeger and said that Ed had struck her.

"I don't know of any other time he hit her," Kreeger said, "but I sometimes had the impression that maybe he did. One time I was telling him about problems I was having with Dianne, and he told me that sometimes you just need to put women in their place. Well, I tried, but I've got the wrong bride for that, if you know what I mean."

"What about other women?" Hollocher asked. "Does Post ever talk about women to you?"

"Oh sure," said Kreeger. "He talks about sex a lot."

Hollocher was pushing on. "Are we talking about other women?"

"Hookers. You know, prostitutes," Kreeger said.

"What does he say about them? Is he a regular customer?"

"Not regular, no," said Kreeger. "But when he's on trips, he goes to prostitutes."

"Did he ever say anything about a woman named Kim Autin?" Hollocher asked.

"He's infatuated with her," said Kreeger. "I don't think he's ever done anything with her, because I'm sure he would have told me about it."

During the interview, Dianne Kreeger had come home. She had not seemed surprised to see the detectives. She told them she hadn't lied to them the previous day, but she and her husband had not been as forthcoming as they could have been.

She claimed to know of only one definite instance in which Ed had struck Julie, the same one Harby had already mentioned.

"Julie also told me that after that fight, she and Ed were seeing a marriage counselor," Dianne said.

Although she knew of only that one incident, Dianne said she too sometimes suspected that maybe there was something more.

"Why? Did you ever see her bruised?" asked Hollocher.

"No, but not long ago there was a story in the paper about abuse," she said, "and Julie and I were talking about it. I told her that one time, Harby had struck me, but I gave him so much hell that he never laid another hand on me. I said it kind of jokingly.

"But Julie took it very seriously. She told me that I didn't understand brutality, and that just because Harby hit me once didn't make him a violent person. She told me a brutal man says he'll quit, but he never does. Julie was so serious about the whole thing that it made me wonder," Dianne said.

On the way back to the hotel, Hollocher felt vindicated. Nobody dared blow smoke at him.

Chapter Fourteen

As the St. Louisans arrived at the cemetery for the exhumation the next morning, Vossmeyer felt somehow disoriented. She was still feeling emotionally drained. Now she wondered if they were doing the right thing. It seemed almost obscene to be disturbing the dead woman's peace.

The cemetery itself was strange, with its mausoleums, tombs, and cenotaphs. Some of the tombs looked like castles. The monuments to the Confederate dead struck Vossmeyer the most. That's what she felt like—a soldier of a lost cause.

The men didn't help, either, talking about the way the body was going to stink. Even Gary seemed caught up in the macho atmosphere of dark humor.

The cemetery director had closed off the section where Julie was buried, and by the time the St. Louisans arrived at the gravesite, the cemetery workers were ready to go.

One worker sat on a backhoe. Two others in hip boots stood nearby with shovels.

The backhoe scraped into the ground and came up with a load of dirt. The crane swung to the side, deposited the dirt, and swung back again for another load.

Almost immediately, the hole began to fill up with water. The workers obviously had been expecting that. The laborers put down their shovels and stepped into the muck with hoses that were attached to a couple of gasoline-powered pumps. They stepped back out and turned on the pumps, which noisily spewed black fumes into the air. Water came spurting out of the hoses.

The backhoe continue to scoop. It seemed that the water filled in as quickly as it was being pumped out.

"We're wasting our time, Dee," Hayes said softly to Vossmeyer.

She felt sick.

Now and then, the diggers would hop into the deepening hole, probe around with their shovels, and then climb back out again.

Vossmeyer turned and walked away. For some reason, she thought of her mother back in Virginia. She wouldn't believe this, Dee thought.

Now and then, Gary would walk over and give her a progress report. The search was not going well. Dee started thinking they wouldn't find anything, that the casket had drifted away.

"Here it is!" shouted a voice from the hole.

Gary rushed back. Dee started walking away. She wasn't quite ready for this. When she heard footsteps behind her, she turned and saw Hollocher.

"Hey, you okay, babe?" he said, putting his arm around her shoulders.

He doesn't want to be there either, she realized.

McCraw and Hayes stood at the edge of the hole. The backhoe had temporarily stopped. The pumps continued to spew out their fumes, and the hoses seemed to be making headway.

Inside the hole, the two diggers, up to their knees in water, were trying to get their shovels under what must be the casket.

Finally, they had it. The casket had settled in at an angle and was tilted head-up. The lid was partially crushed. The workers raised the casket until it finally rested uneasily on the mud. Hayes and McCraw stared down.

"Take the lid off?" one of the workers asked.

McCraw nodded.

The worker pried at the lid with his shovel. Suddenly it popped off.

Julie's body was awash in the water and mud that had seeped into the casket. Only her white face remained untouched, staring up from the sea of mud. Even from the top of the hole, McCraw and Hayes could see the bruises.

The two men stood still for a moment, speechless.

Then Hayes turned and rushed over to Hollocher and Vossmeyer. He put his hands on Dee's shoulders.

"We did the right thing," he said.

The body was taken to the funeral home on the cemetery grounds. The four St. Louisans watched as the body was put on a table and hosed down.

One eye was blackened. There was a nasty bruise on the temple.

Michael Graham, the St. Louis medical examiner, flew in that night. After dinner, the St. Louisans gathered on the roof of the hotel for drinks. The mood was upbeat.

For the first time on the trip, they felt a sense of camaraderie. Hollocher's report of the interview with the Kreegers seemed to be good news, strong stuff from Post's best friends. Most important, the bruises on the body had been readily apparent.

The four investigators felt a bit sorry for Graham. They all respected him, even Hollocher. They all thought that he must feel slightly chagrined. After all, he had conducted the first autopsy.

But he didn't seem to be put out by the whole affair. He was his usual self—good-humored, calm, a little withdrawn.

For a guy in the dead business, he was actually pretty normal.

The next morning, Dr. Paul McGarry conducted the autopsy.

EVIDENCE OF MURDER   147

A graduate of Temple Medical School in 1954 and an employee of the Orleans Parish coroner's office for eleven years, McGarry had personally conducted more than six thousand autopsies and had participated in more than ten thousand others.

He was balding, and his dark eyebrows seemed to jump out from his long thin face. He spoke slowly in a deep monotone. The sound of that emotionless voice combined with the antiquated facilities in the basement of the court-house to lend a strange Frankenstein air to the proceedings.

Present for the autopsy were Dr. Graham, Detective McCraw, and Dr. Roger Fossum from Dallas, who had been hired by Whalen to observe the proceedings.

Graham and Fossum knew each other by reputation. Both were considered leading members in the new generation of pathologists. The yuppies of the dead business, they were more scientists than cops.

McGarry announced his ground rules. This was his autopsy, and he would do it alone. He would dictate his findings as he proceeded. Graham and Fossum could take notes, but could not voice any opinions.

Later, they would each get typed copies of the report he would be dictating in their presence. In addition, he would be taking samples of tissue for microscopic examination. When taking these specimens, he would take two from each area of interest. One he would keep. The other would go to Graham and Fossum, who could make whatever arrangements for sharing they desired.

Although Graham and Fossum were representing different sides in this particular case, they agreed to confer as to the objective findings. If one man thought an area of discoloration was a bruise and the other thought it wasn't, they would discuss their differences and, if possible, come to a mutually agreeable conclusion. As far as interpretation was concerned, each man would work independently.

Actually, most of the interpretive work would not be

done at the autopsy itself. It would require laboratory analysis. For instance, in Julie Post's case, the key fact about a bruise would be when the injury had occurred in relation to her death.

Within minutes after a bruising occurs, the body begins to respond to its injury. Inflammation occurs. The area becomes swollen. The blood in the tissue changes. Inflammatory cells come into the area. This process stops at the moment of death.

A pathologist can put a sliver of bruised tissue under a microscope and, depending upon the degree of inflammation, determine the age of the bruise. Of course, such determinations are not quite exact, and that's where interpretation comes in.

McCraw looked at the body on the table and thought back to the first autopsy he had watched, almost twenty years ago, as a cadet in the police academy. Nearly sick, he had left the room that day.

Now, here he was, fascinated, eager for McGarry to get started.

"I begin with an external examination of the body," McGarry dictated. "The body is that of a young woman, already embalmed, measuring five feet three inches long, having dark brown hair. Her eyes have been removed. Her teeth are in good condition."

So was the body, for that matter. A credit, thought Graham, to the embalmer.

McGarry noted the incision from the first autopsy. It extended from the tips of the shoulders to the breastbone and then down past the belly button, allowing access to the chest, the abdominal cavity, and the pelvic area.

He noted the incision on the head. As is customary, it extended from behind each ear across the scalp.

Then he began recording the bruises.

Although McGarry had made it clear that he did not want to be interrupted, McCraw figured the rule was aimed at the other doctors. Being a cop meant you could always ask questions.

"How come some of these bruises seem milky-colored?" he asked.

McGarry stopped. For a second, McCraw thought he might be upset with the interruption, but then McGarry seemed almost pleased, the way a teacher might be if a slow student asked an intelligent question.

"It has to do with circulation. The whitish bruises are postmortem," he said.

McCraw nodded. McGarry continued.

Graham and Fossum took notes as McGarry continued his dictation.

McGarry noted a bruise above the bridge of the nose, a bruise on the right lower eyelid, a bruise on the right forehead, and a bruise on the right temple. He noted a large bruise on the right side of the back of the head.

As he formally noted each bruise, he measured it. Then he would slice two slivers of tissue from the area of the bruise and put each piece in a small plastic vial filled with formaldehyde. Each tube would then be marked with a number corresponding to the location of the bruise.

McGarry worked his way down the body. A bruise on the right front of the chest. A bruise on the left side of the chest. A large bruise on the lower back.

A bruise on the right shoulder. A bruise on the right forearm. Two bruises on the left shoulder. Bruises on both elbows. A bruise on the back of the right hand.

A bruise on the right knee. A bruise on the right leg.

A bruise in the groin area.

Graham dutifully took notes, but to this point, he had seen nothing that would justify this second autopsy. The bruising he had noted in his first autopsy was certainly more pronounced than it had been six weeks ago, but these additional bruises could be easily explained. Many of them seemed to correspond to areas that had been damaged during the bone removal and the subsequent procedure in which wooden dowels had been inserted in place of the long bones.

After finishing his external examination—he had noted thirty-six areas of bruising—McGarry proceeded to open the abdominal cavity by tracing the cut from Graham's first autopsy.

McCraw, drawn by a morbid fascination, edged next to McGarry to peer into the body.

It seemed to be a blue-and-white checkered pattern!

McGarry pulled on this pattern, and out came a hospital gown. There was nothing else inside. The embalmer had obviously removed the bag of organs Graham had placed inside the cavity after the first autopsy.

This emptiness surprised only McCraw. At that moment, as he stared into the hollow cavity, McCraw decided that when his turn came, he would donate his body to science. After all, there was nothing left anyway.

McGarry noted that the breastbone was broken. The third, fourth, and fifth ribs were fractured.

With this part of the examination concluded, McGarry moved to the skull. He had now been working, methodically dictating, measuring, and cutting, for more than two hours.

Graham had not been surprised about the breastbone, or the ribs. The breastbone could have been fractured during the first autopsy. The injuries to the ribs could have been caused during the resuscitative efforts.

McGarry traced the ear-to-ear cut from the first autopsy. He lifted the skin of the scalp forward. Nothing. He pulled the scalp back toward the neck.

He pulled it down beyond the point Graham had pulled it during the first autopsy.

A little bit above where the neck merges into the back of the head, two distinct bruises came into view. One was on the left side, the other on the right side.

McCraw stared.

It was like a handprint, he thought. The thumb on one side, the fingers on the other.

Chapter Fifteen

For the past two days, the *Times-Picayune* had carried stories about the investigation: "ST. LOUIS OFFICIALS TO EXHUME BODY OF N.O. WOMAN" was the headline of the first story, and "BODY OF WOMAN WHO DROWNED IN ST. LOUIS DUG UP" announced the second.

These articles were unsettling to Dee Vossmeyer, mostly because the information seemed to have come from somebody inside the investigation. Not that any of it was confidential; it just added to her general feeling of unease. Nobody could be trusted.

Post, of course, found the stories even more unnerving. He valued his position in the community. The thought that people now realized he was being investigated for the possible murder of his wife was difficult to handle.

On the morning the first story came out, Dalton Truax came rushing into Post's office.

"What in God's name is going on, Ed?" he asked.

"It's unfortunate it's in the paper, but I tell you, it's routine. It's just a normal part of what the authorities do when there's an accident like this," Post said.

Truax looked disbelieving.

"Ed, this doesn't sound like anything routine," he said.

Truax left, and Post picked up the newspaper again. He reread his quote.

"It is my understanding and they've also told numerous friends of mine that this is a routine investigation."

He wondered how many people believed that.

* * *

Although the bruises on the back of the head were troublesome, they were not necessarily damning to Post's case.

That was Fossum's feeling, anyway.

After the autopsy was concluded, he returned to the law office in Exchange Alley, where Post and Whalen awaited him.

"Good news," Fossum reported. "There's nothing to indicate homicide. All the injuries could be consistent with a finding of accidental death. The only new bruises were on the back of the head, and could be consistent with a fall. Or they could have occurred when Ed dropped her as he pulled her out of the tub. Frankly, as is the case with most bruises, they could be consistent with a dozen different scenarios."

Including murder, thought Whalen.

He knew McGarry well enough to know what kind of scenario he'd find most plausible.

"Exactly where are these bruises?" Whalen asked.

"Back here," said Fossum, turning his head and fingering the area where the bruises were found. "A large one over here, a smaller one over here."

Whalen closed his eyes and thought like a prosecutor. Fingers and thumb, he said to himself. Consistent with a hand holding her down.

Of course McGarry would say that.

Post thought the news sounded great. Nothing indicated homicide. His ordeal was over.

"What does the St. Louis guy think?" Whalen asked Fossum.

"We didn't talk about conclusions, not at any length, anyway," said Fossum. "But, as you know, I've reviewed his initial findings, and I'm quite sure there was nothing today to make him change from an 'undetermined' finding."

"You don't think he could be pressured on this? He'd

probably be a popular guy if he changed his mind,'' said Whalen.

"I wouldn't worry about that," said Fossum. "He's a very good doctor."

If it's two to one, thought Whalen, they have no case.

That night, Ed Post composed a letter to Bill Bethea, the doctor who had delivered the bad news to the Thigpens.

With the letter, Post included a copy of the autopsy report.

After dismissing the investigation as "insane accusations, none of which have been substantiated by anyone in New Orleans," Post blamed his problems on Bobby, Julie's brother, and then predicted that the end was in sight.

"Until then, we must all suffer from this, which delays the ever-important grieving-healing process that should be taking place at this time.

"I can never thank you or Judy enough for the support you've given to me, Stephanie, Jennifer, Hollis and Etta. You are the type and quality of friend any man is lucky enough to have once in a lifetime. I've been lucky twice— you and Harby Kreeger."

Bethea was a bit taken aback when he got the letter. Although he was indeed good friends with Hollis, he hardly knew Post. It seemed as if Post, aware of his friendship with Hollis, was lobbying him.

Besides, he couldn't forget the sight of Post leaving the funeral home, skipping like a little kid.

With the conceit of a biographer who believes he can conjure up a flesh-and-blood person from a cardboard box of old letters, Dean Hoag was imaging Ed Post from his financial records.

The first thing that struck Hoag was that Post was not nearly as important as he pretended to be—at least not if money translated into importance. Income-wise, he wasn't any more important than Hoag.

Post made $50,000 a year. Throw in benefits and expense accounts and he pulled in about $60,000. His deal with Truax wasn't really so sweet after all.

Wagner-Truax had been a three-pronged operation— property management, commercial real estate, and residential real estate. In September 1983, Truax had bought his partner out and reorganized the business. Essentially, he had set up a subsidiary to handle the residential real estate business.

Post had put up $10,000 for a 10 percent share of the subsidiary. In addition to his salary, he would receive 10 percent of the profits.

Instead, the subsidiary had lost almost $250,000. Post was responsible for picking up 10 percent of the losses. So far, he had been forced to kick in approximately $23,000.

These losses did not seem to be reflected in his lifestyle. According to the statements from his three bank accounts, Post had spent almost $50,000 in the first five months of 1986. That did not count the $10,000 he had borrowed to pay for Julie's funeral.

Hoag looked at the banking records for the previous year. Post had spent $114,000.

The tax records showed that Ed and Julie had not made anywhere near that kind of money. Julie's gross income in 1985 had been $28,000. When her expenses were itemized out, she had a taxable income of $12,000. Ed's taxable income, after deductions, had been $7,361.

Hoag looked at those figures and shrugged. Creative bookkeeping, maybe. Should he have an IRS guy look at them? The damn tax codes were too complicated for a normal person to understand.

Surprisingly, Post had prepared the returns himself, which impressed Hoag. A return like this could easily get audited. To claim as many deductions as Post did, you'd have to have a lot of confidence in yourself. You'd also need to keep immaculate records.

He's a detail guy, thought Hoag.

One of the chief deductions was interest payments, which in 1985 totaled more than $25,000. That's a profile of a guy in hock up to his neck, Hoag thought.

In February 1986, Post had gotten $12,000 from the refinancing of an office building he and his brother had invested in. In April, he had borrowed $2,000 from that partnership.

He owed the bank almost $30,000.

On a financial statement, he had listed his 10 percent holdings in the Wagner-Truax subsidiary as being worth $30,000.

That's got to be creative accounting, Hoag thought. He bought in for $10,000, the company has done nothing but lose money, and he's figuring that the worth of his stock has tripled.

The financial records seemed to show a steady selling off of assets. Post had sold a wine collection in 1984, as well as some stock. More stock, maybe the last of it, had been sold in 1985.

Hoag started thumbing through the canceled checks.

The Posts spent more money on clothes in five months than Hoag and his wife, a schoolteacher, spent in five years, and yet the Hoags' combined income was about the same as the Posts' had been.

This got to Hoag on a gut level. Hoag was not a fancy character. He dressed nicely for court, but he tried to buy his clothes on sale. He was as conservative in his finances as he was in his politics. He lived within his means.

Hoag and his wife were expecting their first child in early July. He was already thinking about starting a college fund.

At the moment, his financial strategy, if you could call it that, had to do with IRAs. Put two grand in every year, and you'll have something for retirement. As he studied

Post's records, he realized he was dealing with somebody who was almost his polar opposite.

Post spent more than he made. He bought expensive clothes. He collected wine. He had nothing put away for a rainy day.

Except the life insurance.

Oddly enough, he had borrowed $2,000 on the very day he purchased the additional life insurance.

Chapter Sixteen

On July 21, Hollocher, McCraw, Vossmeyer, and Hayes went to Industrial Testing Laboratories, Inc., in south St. Louis.

At the behest of the Omni Hotel, the laboratory was ready to test towel rings that had been removed from the hotel. The purpose of the tests was to determine if 130 pounds of pressure—Julie had weighed 128—could cause a towel ring to pull away from the wall bracket.

Towel rings and brackets had been mounted on boards to simulate the ring and bracket from room 4063 of the hotel. The tests were videotaped by technicians from the police department.

In the first test, 200 pounds of pressure was applied to duplicate a sudden downward pull. In the second test, 130 pounds of pressure was applied at a forty-five-degree angle to simulate an angled pull. In the third test, the same towel ring that had been used in the first test was subjected to 200 pounds of pressure applied at a horizontal angle. In the fourth test, 200 pounds of pressure was applied at a forty-five-degree angle.

Then 130 pounds of lead shot was suspended by a rope. The rope was cut and the lead shot fell eight inches before being stopped by a chain attached to the towel ring.

Finally, Vossmeyer, who weighed 129 pounds, hung from a towel ring. Then Hayes, who weighed 190, hung from the same ring and pulled himself up.

None of the rings pulled away from the wall brackets.

When the rings and brackets were removed, none of the rings showed the type of deformation present in the ring from room 4063.

Next, a technician pulled and twisted two towel rings from their wall brackets. In each instance, the rings exhibited deformation similar to the deformation found in the ring from room 4063.

The night after the testing, Kim Autin called Vossmeyer and Hayes at home. She seemed upset and excited.

Hayes kept his tape recorder in a kitchen drawer, so he quickly pulled it out and attached the telephone recording device to the earphone.

"Ed's been here," Kim said. "I hope I'm not bothering you, but you told me to call if anything happened."

"Sure. What happened?" Gary asked.

"He came over with Stephanie. He'd obviously been drinking. We talked for a little bit, and then he said, 'You know, our friendship is more than business.' I didn't know what to say, it was so spooky. I think he's been watching the house, because every time Bobby leaves, he calls. So I didn't say anything, and then he said, 'I'm in love with you, Kim.' Then Stephanie got up and said, 'God, I don't want to hear this,' and she got up and ran out. Ed followed her out. I'm freaked out."

Gary and Kim talked for a few more minutes. Dee got on the other phone. Finally, Kim seemed to calm down.

"We'll be back in touch," Dee said. "And, of course, call us again if he comes back. Call us anytime."

The more Dee thought about it, the more an idea took root.

Maybe Post's daughters knew something. Maybe they suspected their father. It might be a good idea to go back to New Orleans one more time—this time to talk to the girls.

Meanwhile, at the police department, McCraw put the finishing touches on a sixty-nine-page police report.

"It is respectfully requested that this incident be reclassified to a Suspicious Death with a further investigation continuing. It should also be noted that the facts surrounding this case will be submitted to the August Term Grand Jury."

Hollocher read the final paragraph and grinned. Then he routed it to the commander of the homicide unit, the new-school officer who had been so uninterested in pursuing the case.

Like General Custer cheerily planning his march toward the Little Big Horn, the investigators plotted their next trip to New Orleans.

When Vossmeyer broached the suggestion that they try to talk to the girls, Hollocher enthusiastically endorsed it. Because it was already believed—quite erroneously—that Hollocher had established a rapport with Hollis Thigpen, Vossmeyer agreed that Hollocher should accompany her and Hayes on the trip.

Besides, this was still a police department investigation, which meant it was Hollocher's baby. The circuit attorney's office was merely cooperating.

Kim Autin volunteered her help. She told Vossmeyer that she would let the investigators use her house for the interview. The familiar surroundings might make the girls more comfortable.

Vossmeyer was aware, of course, that Stephanie had experienced emotional problems in the past. Earlier in the investigation, with Post's consent, Vossmeyer had called Stephanie's psychologist, Barbara Hardin, who said that Stephanie was "stabilized."

So back to New Orleans they went. Vossmeyer was filled with hope. If the girls suspected their father or could document abuse against their mother or themselves, the case against Post would be that much stronger.

Hollocher brought his wife and was calmer than he had been on the last trip. This time, there would be no arguments about confronting Post. The plan was to contact the girls, meet them at Kim's house, do the interview, and leave.

From the hotel, Hollocher called Post's house and left a message for Stephanie. The investigators waited for her to call back.

Finally, Hollocher called again, and reached her. He did more listening than talking. When he hung up, he said that she'd told him she couldn't meet with him.

It was his sense, he said, that she really wanted to.

When the investigators came back from dinner, there was a message from Whalen. "Do not try to talk to the girls!"

Vossmeyer was furious. "We have a right to try to talk to anybody we want to talk to," she announced.

The next morning, she went to the district attorney's office. As she had done for the exhumation, she asked for help.

A young female attorney was assigned to help Vossmeyer. As for the exhumation, an affidavit would be required.

"You know, of course, that a judge can't order the girls to talk to you. The best we can hope for is that the judge will order Post to bring the girls here, where they will have the opportunity to talk to you."

"That's all I want," Vossmeyer said.

In filling out the affidavit, Vossmeyer stated that there had been allegations that Post had physically abused at least one of the girls in the past, and that there was a likelihood that the children were frightened of him.

Vossmeyer felt justified in making the allegation. After all, she had been told as much by one of Stephanie's friends. In truth, though, Vossmeyer was uncomfortable with the whole procedure. She knew nothing about juvenile law. Furthermore, she was accustomed to the more casual atmosphere of criminal court, where an attorney can walk into the judge's chambers and explain things.

In this courtroom, she was not allowed to talk informally with the judge. Her communication was limited to the affidavit, which was presented to the judge by the attorney from the DA's office. It all seemed too sterile.

But the judge, a young woman with a reputation for brooking no nonsense, granted a motion for a writ of habeas corpus ad testificatum. In other words, Post was to produce the girls and give Vossmeyer an opportunity to talk to them, and he was to do so that very afternoon.

With two policemen assigned to the district attorney's office, Leon Flott and Napoleon Williams, the St. Louisans headed to the West Bank to serve the legal papers on Post. When they arrived at his house, they were met by a squad car and two uniformed policemen.

Al Post, Ed's father, was with the girls that afternoon. He was in the back room, reading a book, when the policemen knocked on the door.

One of the girls answered the door, then ran into the back room, screaming that there were policemen on the porch.

Al went to the door and looked out. He saw two men in civilian clothes and another man in a police uniform, and then, also on the porch but to the side, he saw Hollocher.

Instantly, he recognized Hollocher as the big, heavyset, menacing-looking man his son had described, the man Robert Thigpen had talked to.

Al opened the door.

"What do you want?" he said to Hollocher.

One of the other men handed Al a piece of paper.

"We're here for the girls," he said.

Al took the piece of paper. It was official-looking. He didn't know what to do.

"You're serving this on the wrong person. I'm the grandfather," Al replied.

"We came for Jennifer and Stephanie," said the man.

"I'll call their father," Al said. He stepped back inside and quickly closed the door.

He called Ed's office, but Ed wasn't in. He looked outside and saw that another squad car had arrived. He opened the front door again. The porch seemed to be filled with policemen.

"You'll just have to wait while I try to reach my son," he said. But this time when he tried to close the door, he couldn't. One of the uniformed cops had put his foot in it.

"Please, I'm going to close the door while I try to reach my son," he said.

"You don't want me to break the door down, do you?" the cop asked.

Al left the door open and went back inside. He called his other son, Dan. He explained that the police and the St. Louis people were there with some kind of subpoena for the girls. What should he do?

Dan told him to calm down. If they have a subpoena, he said, you'll have to let the girls go. Go with them and I'll meet you at court, Dan said. He immediately called Whalen.

Meanwhile, a sense of panic pervaded the house. The girls were crying. The policemen were rapping on the open door.

The phone rang. It was Ed. His father explained what was happening as best he could, and what Dan had said.

"I'll meet you at court," Ed said.

The girls, still crying, were led to a police car.

By now, Vossmeyer and Hayes, who were standing at the side of the house, realized that the whole thing had turned into a disaster.

Things got even worse at juvenile court. The St. Louisans were standing in the hallway when the girls were led past. Stephanie stopped crying long enough to look hatefully at them.

A female deputy briefly interviewed the girls. Both denied that their father had ever abused them. Both denied that they wanted to talk to the St. Louis investigators.

In the courtroom, Whalen was furious, accusing Vossmeyer of lying in the affidavit. He told the judge that Stephanie was unstable and had once tried to commit suicide, and that, more important, Vossmeyer knew about Stephanie's delicate emotional condition.

"I know she's aware of that, your honor, because my client gave Stephanie's psychologist authorization to talk to Vossmeyer. We've done everything we could to cooperate, and now they do this!"

The judge became enraged. The people from St. Louis had made no mention of any emotional problems, she said. If they had thought that they could come to New Orleans and mislead the judiciary, they were about to learn differently!

Vossmeyer felt as if she'd been hit in the stomach.

When Whalen demanded a hearing the next day, Vossmeyer hardly heard what he was saying. Something about probable cause. He said he was going to have the psychologist testify.

Enough, thought Vossmeyer. The girls obviously don't want to talk to us. We're going to get slaughtered at a hearing.

"Judge, I withdraw the request."

"This matter is concluded, then," said the judge.

When she left the courtroom, she met Hollocher in the hallway. He said he'd scuffled with Dan Post.

"He stuck a finger in my chest," said Hollocher. "I don't take that shit."

Oh, fine, thought Vossmeyer. An assault charge.

The three St. Louisans left the courthouse. The beautiful day had turned ugly. Rain was pouring down.

They ran through the storm to their rented car. Somebody had taken a sharp object, maybe a key, and had raked the side of the car.

Perfect, thought Vossmeyer.

"Back to the hotel, I presume," said Hayes, as he climbed into the driver's seat.

"No. I want to go talk to that psychologist who told me that Stephanie was okay. I want to find out what's going on," said Vossmeyer.

She fished the letter out of her briefcase. They stopped at a gas station and got directions to an office in the Garden District, not far from the Civil Courthouse.

Because it was raining and they were dropping in unannounced, Hayes suggested that Vossmeyer stay in the car while he made sure the psychologist would see them.

He dashed off into the rain. Vossmeyer sat in the car, still fuming. Minutes later, Hayes came back and gave Vossmeyer a rueful smile. He slid into the driver's seat.

"What's the matter? Isn't she in? Won't she talk to us?" Vossmeyer asked.

"She's in, and she'll talk to us, but she's with her attorney, and she wants him present for the interview," said Hayes.

"I've got no problem with that," said Vossmeyer.

"Her attorney is Dan Post."

"Screw 'em all!" said Vossmeyer. "They can all come to the grand jury."

Chapter Seventeen

After the disastrous trip to New Orleans, Hollocher complained to Dittmeier, the U.S. attorney. The two were friends from Dittmeier's days as a prosecutor in the city.

"We've got to talk to those girls, Tom," he said. "We've got a girlfriend of the daughter telling us that she complained about being abused. We've got this woman calling us saying that Post put the moves on her in front of his daughter. These girls can tell us something."

"Hoag is working the insurance angle on the case. I'll tell him," Dittmeier said.

That suited Hollocher fine. He knew Hoag from the prosecutor's days in the dirty building.

Hoag called Whalen.

"Ralph, this is Dean Hoag from the U.S. attorney's office in St. Louis. I'm looking into mail fraud on the life insurance Edward T. Post had on his wife."

Mail fraud? This was new to Whalen. Criminal defense work was somewhat reactive, but still, you hate to be surprised.

"I appreciate the call, Dean. I'm not aware of any allegations of fraud. What's your concern?"

"A couple of different fronts," Hoag said. He talked in rapid, staccato bursts. "There seems to be a question about income levels on the application."

Income levels? This could be good news. Maybe the

murder investigation has petered out and this is the best the St. Louisans can do.

"Look, Dean. I'm talking off the top of my head here. Like I say, this is the first I've heard about this. I'll have to talk to my client, of course, but if you give me some specifics, I'll give him a call and see if we can answer your questions."

"First off, I want to talk to the girls."

Ahh. As if the girls would know about income levels. So this is the kind of insurance fraud he's investigating.

"I don't know if the girls would be much help with income levels, Dean. You're aware, I'm sure, that we just had a real problem with people coming down to try to talk to the girls."

"Look. I'm going to talk to those girls, okay?"

Hoag said it as if it weren't a question. Then he hurtled on.

"Now we can do it in one of two ways. I can come down there, sit in your office or anywhere it's convenient, interview the girls alone, tape the conversation, and give you a copy of the tape. Or I can send a federal marshal, a female, who will accompany them to St. Louis, sit with them in the hotel, and bring them to the grand jury the next morning, and they're going to talk to me then. Now, one way or the other, I'm going to talk to them, okay?"

Again, it wasn't a question.

Whalen couldn't help but smile.

"Why do I get the impression my arm is being twisted?" he asked.

"Because it is. The long and short of it is I'm going to talk to these girls alone, without you or anybody else present," said Hoag, and then his tone softened. "Look, I'm not going after these girls. I'm not going to be a bad guy with them."

"When do you want to come down?" Whalen asked.

*   *   *

Whalen called Post into his office to give him the news.

"The U.S. attorney's office, a very powerful entity, is now involved. They're talking about insurance fraud and income levels on applications," Whalen said. "We're going to have to go over your insurance applications. The chief one, I suppose, will be the last one you took out on Julie."

Post took the news calmly, almost cheerfully.

"We have no problems, Ralph. I've been with Bob Masson for years. He knows me well. I'd say he's one of the best, most respected insurance men in the area."

Whalen nodded. How typical of Post. Once again, the attorney tried to imagine the conversations Post had had with the St. Louis cops.

"Ed, let me explain a couple of things to you. I want you to listen closely, too. First of all, I'm not entirely convinced that the U.S. attorney is interested in the kind of fraud they're talking about. Technically, in this instance, murder could be construed as fraud."

Post's face went from cheery to startled.

"Now, that's for me to worry about. I'm your lawyer. Nothing you can do about their suspicions. But here's the important thing I want you to understand. It's something you can do."

Post looked at Whalen expectantly.

"I wish I knew a nicer way to say this, Ed, but I don't. I am absolutely convinced you're innocent, but dammit, you hurt your case every time you say something. You've got to keep your damn mouth shut!"

For weeks, Hoag had been imagining Edward T. Post. Finally, he met him in Whalen's law office on Exchange Alley.

When Whalen made the introductions, Hoag stared intently, but briefly, at the man he felt he already knew.

"Pleased to meet you," said Post.

"Yeah," said Hoag.

Hoag, short and stocky and rumpled, was brisk and businesslike. Whalen, with an easygoing elegance, was his opposite.

He tried to engage Hoag in conversation about the nature of the investigation. After all, any information he could elicit would be information he didn't have.

"I hope you're going to be in town long enough to enjoy your visit," Whalen said.

"The girls are here?" Hoag asked in a tone that made it clear that he had not come to New Orleans for idle talk.

"In my office," said Whalen.

"I'll make two copies of the tape. I'll give you one before I leave," said Hoag.

Hoag interviewed each girl separately. The older daughter, Stephanie, was the one he was most interested in. She was very polite, but also extremely defensive of her father.

She said her parents had a wonderful marriage and that she was not aware of any financial difficulties in the family. She had never told anybody that her father had abused her, nor did she know anything about her father professing his love to Kim Autin.

Hoag didn't push her on anything.

The younger daughter was less animated, but also described her parents' relationship as very good.

Hoag was gentle with her, too.

After the interviews, Hoag went back to the hotel and met Hollocher. Part one of the job was over. Now came part two, delivering subpoenas for the federal grand jury.

Hoag could have had the federal marshals deliver them, but he wanted to do it himself. He wanted to explain to people how this was going to work.

"We're trying to make this as convenient as possible. There are two grand juries considering this case. A federal grand jury, which I'm in charge of, is looking at a possible fraud violation. A second grand jury, a state grand jury, is investigating the circumstances of Julie Post's death.

Rather than force anybody to come to St. Louis twice, we're going to serve you with this federal subpoena. After you testify at the federal grand jury, you'll be served a subpoena to testify the same day at the state grand jury. They're a block apart. We will, of course, provide transportation to St. Louis and back, accommodations for a night in St. Louis, and meal money.''

On the way from the hotel to Metairie, Hollocher asked Hoag if he had noticed anything unusual about Post.

"I hardly talked to him," Hoag said.

"Did you see his feet?" Hollocher asked.

"His feet?"

"Yeah, they're real small, Dean. That's how I first knew he did it," said Hollocher.

When they delivered the subpoenas to the Kreegers, Harby Kreeger greeted Hollocher like an old friend and invited them into the house. Rather odd behavior, thought Hoag, for the guy who was supposed to be Post's closest friend.

"This guy's the best," Hollocher told Kreeger, pointing to Hoag. "This guy hasn't lost in forty-five trials, and he's not gonna lose this one. Eddie's going to jail."

Kreeger nodded.

"You understand, of course, that Ed is a very good friend of mine," he said.

Dan Post took his subpoena without a word.

Back in St. Louis, Hollocher told people he had stuck the subpoena to Dan's forehead.

Chapter Eighteen

"My name is Dee Vossmeyer. I'm an assistant circuit attorney, and while you'll be hearing about a lot of cases from the prosecutor assigned to you, I'll be presenting witnesses concerning only one case. It involves the death of a thirty-nine-year-old woman. Her name was Julie Post. She drowned in a bathtub at the Omni Hotel."

The room in the St. Louis Municipal Courts Building resembled a small classroom. There was no judge and no spectators, only twelve jurors who sat at individual desks arranged in a U. In the center of the U, a chair had been placed for the witness. On the wall hung travel posters.

The grand jury proceedings would be informal, with the prosecutor asking a few questions and then turning the witness over to the jurors. After the witness had been excused, the grand jurors would be expected and, in fact, encouraged to discuss the case as the evidence unfolded.

Despite the informality, the jurors took their work seriously. They were all volunteers. In St. Louis, a person has to be recommended, most often by a judge, to serve on the grand jury. Thus they tended to be respectful of authority—according to some critics, too much so.

The grand jury that convened in August 1986 consisted of seven women and five men. Their duty was to hear evidence for the next three months and determine, in each case, if the evidence was sufficient to warrant a trial. Unlike a regular jury, the grand jury did not require unanimity. Under Missouri law, if nine of the twelve jurors agreed to indict, the charge was issued.

The jurors would hear evidence in hundreds of cases involving drugs, robbery, murder, mayhem—the dark side of life in the city.

For the most part, the grand jurors would deal with a single prosecutor. On occasion, however, and only for the most serious of offenses, a particular prosecutor was assigned a case before an indictment. In those cases, that prosecutor would present evidence.

"You will hear that Julie's husband, Ed Post, has said he went jogging the morning of her death. The last time he saw Julie alive, he says, is when he ran her bathwater and then walked her into the bathroom," said Vossmeyer.

A couple of the grand jurors exchanged looks. As older, married women, they found the husband's story a bit hard to take, unless, of course, this was a honeymoon.

"How long were they married?" one of the women asked.

"More than nineteen years," answered Dee.

More knowing looks.

The first witnesses were from St. Louis. The paramedics testified, as did the people from the hospital and the hotel.

McCraw testified about the investigation. He figured to be a better witness than Hollocher, who had a tendency to overstate things. McCraw had an easy manner and a quick smile, and he didn't seem to take himself, or the police department, too seriously. He readily told the grand jurors that the initial investigation had been botched.

"Until I got into it, that is," he said.

Everybody laughed.

If this had been a movie, he would have made an ideal hero, with his blond hair, blue eyes, and charming, boyish grin.

"How did you get into the case?" a grand juror asked.

"We needed a scribe," he said. "I can spell."

More laughter.

On a more serious note, the grand jurors were shown the videotapes from Industrial Testing Laboratories.

Late in August, shortly after the grand jury convened, Vossmeyer and Hayes were married. They had almost one hundred people to their home for the reception. Nobody from the Post investigation was invited.

Mae Pelafigue had spent more than forty years working with the elderly for a religious order when she answered the ad that Post put in the newspaper after Julie's death.

He needed live-in help.

He was such a sad man. Often she had heard him sobbing in the middle of the night. Sometimes early in the evening when he was barbecuing their dinner in the backyard, she'd hear him, too. She'd go outside. The steak would be burning, and he'd be sitting in a chair, crying and crying.

One evening she was passing his bedroom and looked in. He was standing by his wife's closet, as if trying to work up the nerve to open the door. She said nothing, but the next day, she looked in, and saw that the clothes were undisturbed.

A second time, she saw him standing in front of the closet. Again the next day she checked. The clothes were undisturbed.

The third time, he noticed her watching. He called to her for help, and together the two of them cleaned the closet. Most of the clothes they packed in boxes for the poor. A few things he kept. Two or three dresses he gave her for her daughters.

And the whole time, he was sobbing like a child.

For the people at work, Post had a braver face.

As the grand jury summons had made it apparent that the investigation was anything but a routine look into an accidental death, he seemed almost to revel in his role, ridiculing Hollocher to the real estate agents, joking about the "Keystone cops" who were trying to get him.

He was acting, the agents said to each other, as if he thought the whole thing was fun.

To his closer friends and family, he dismissed the investigation as a conspiracy put forward by the Omni Hotel, which would go to any lengths to fight the inevitable lawsuit. Hollocher's behavior lent credence to that theory. Most of Post's friends who had met the lieutenant distrusted him.

In September, Truax exercised his option to terminate Post. A little more than sixty days had elapsed since Truax had given Post his sixty days' notice, so Truax figured the termination would not come as a complete shock. To his amazement, Post acted stunned.

He tried to argue with Truax. None of the problems were his fault, Post said. He shouldn't be forced to take the blame for the economy.

"We've been over this before," Truax said. "We could sit here and discuss this till hell freezes over, and my mind would still be made up."

Post started to cry.

Truax didn't know how to react.

"I don't want to put you out on the street in a bad position," he finally said. "I'll buy back your stock for what you paid for it, and I'll pay you through October. What's more, you can keep the car till then, too."

It was, Truax thought, a most generous proposal.

Near the end of October, people from New Orleans started coming to St. Louis to testify.

The women from the real estate office made it clear that Julie was very unpopular. There was also a feeling among these women that Julie had not wanted to come to St. Louis.

To some of the grand jurors, this seemed immensely significant.

Vossmeyer asked Truax if Post had known before coming to St. Louis that his job was in jeopardy.

"He knew I was dissatisfied. I'm not sure he knew to what extent I was dissatisfied."

"And your dissatisfaction had actually reached the point where if Julie hadn't died here in St. Louis, you would have terminated his position?"

"Yes."

"You had not told him?"

"No. Ed did not know that I had intended to not renew his contract. He did not know that until I handed him that written notice sixty days prior to September 1."

If Truax struck some of the grand jurors as a bit of a cold fish, Ben Matthews, the manager of the West Bank office, made an entirely different impression. He was something like McCraw, likable and boyish-looking.

Julie was a fine agent, he said.

He was asked if he perceived Julie as being a person who was under a lot of pressure.

"Definitely. Julie had a lot of problems in the office. She was extremely hard to get along with. She was a critical individual—very critical—of everyone. Our office is made up of independent contractors. People in that position don't have to put up with disparaging remarks, and they didn't. They fought her constantly. Julie lived a miserable existence in the office. She was constantly in turmoil."

Kim Autin looked as if she had stepped out of the pages of a fashion magazine. She was wearing an expensive suede suit, and when she sat down and took her jacket off, the jurors could see the designer label.

Diamonds sparkled from her watch. She wore a lot of makeup.

Kim described the relationship of Julie and Ed as "tension-filled." She said they argued a lot.

She was asked if she had ever had any indication that Ed had been violent with Julie.

"In San Francisco, Julie and I were trying on clothes in one of the main department stores—Saks, I think—and I saw a bruise on her thigh that was very, very big. It was almost yellowish at the time. I asked her about it and said, 'What happened?' And she said that Ed had pushed her. She didn't go into any other details about it."

Kim also told the jurors about the fight at the nightclub after the Million Dollar Club banquet, and how Ed had come over to her house and suddenly kissed her. She said that after that, she had been uncomfortable around him. She felt he was attracted to her.

"How do you mean?" Dee asked.

"I don't know, Dee. It's just a feeling I have, and I'm usually not wrong about it."

"Did it ever cross your mind that he killed her?" Dee asked.

"Yes, it did."

"At what point?"

"Immediately."

Robert Masson told the grand jurors more than they wanted to know about life insurance.

But the salient points were these:

Ed Post had a consistent track record of increasing life insurance on himself and Julie.

There had been absolutely no fraud regarding income levels.

Julie had no serious medical problems as far as the insurance company knew.

The Posts were paying monthly premiums of $246.77 for life insurance at the time of Julie's death.

The premiums would have accelerated in the future.

*   *   *

Dee did not know what to expect from Harby Kreeger. He was the only person in the world who was pals with both Ed Post and George Hollocher. Now he was ready to testify, and there was no telling whose side he'd be rooting for on this particular day.

For the most part, he straddled the fence. While not recanting anything he had told the investigators, he leaned toward the side of his old friend.

"Yes, it was a stormy relationship, but what's the sense in getting married if you can't fight with each other?"

He had one new bit of information. He had come to St. Louis with Dan Post, he said. And last night, Dan had pulled a towel ring off the wall.

From the very beginning, Dan Post had tried to submerge all doubts about his brother's innocence, but the suspicions refused to go away. Still, for every question, Dan was able to manufacture an answer, or at least a less compromising question.

Yes, he knew that Ed's relationship with Julie had been violent, but they had stayed married for almost twenty years, hadn't they? Yes, a fatal accident in a tub seemed bizarre, but had there been a life-and-death struggle, wouldn't someone have heard it?

There were questions, however, that Dan tried not to think about. For instance, on the flight back to New Orleans on the day of Julie's death, Ed had been massaging his right hand. How had he injured it?

And what about the towel ring that the prosecution considered so crucial?

Immediately upon checking into his room at the Omni the night before he was scheduled to testify at the grand jury, Dan went into the bathroom to inspect the towel ring. It did not appear to be substantial. He noticed that the setscrew that attached the ring to the wall plate seemed loose. He worked at it with his fingers and loosened it further.

Made for each other: Julie Thigpen and Ed Post, in the spring of 1966, during their college formal engagement weekend.

Julie's newspaper
engagement picture,
winter of 1966.
BELOW: Her Million Dollar
Club awards photo, 1986.

Ed and Julie's wedding with (from left) Hollis and Etta Mae Thigpen and (from right) Al and Ann Post.
BELOW: Ed and Julie with daughters Stephanie (left) and Jennifer, Mother's Day, 1978.

(From left) Ed and
Julie with
Ben Matthews.

Julie (right) with
Kim and Bobby Autin
and Mary Schulte.
BELOW: Ed and Julie's
home.

Photographs of the crime scene taken by the police evidence technician unit on June 3, 1986, the day of Julie's death.

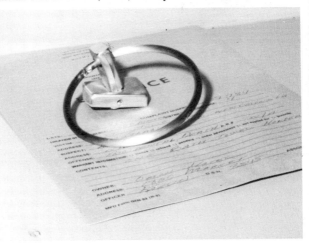

Accident or murder? Homicide investigators Mike McCraw (left) and George Hollocher were determined to find the truth. (Scott Dine)

BELOW: Ed Post, in January 1987, being led down the steps of the police station by Hollocher. (*St. Louis Post-Dispatch*)

Art Margulis (left) with co-counsel Ralph Whalen outside the courthouse during the 1989 murder trial. (Scott Dine—*St. Louis Post-Dispatch*)

LEFT: Investigators Gary and Dee Hayes. (Scott Dine)

BELOW: Dean Hoag being interviewed in 1992, after jury convicted Post a second time. (Wayne Crosslin—*St. Louis Post-Dispatch*)

Dan and Ed Post during a break in the trial (Scott Dine—*St. Louis Post-Dispatch*)
BELOW: Ed with daughters Stephanie (left) and Jennifer. (Scott Dine—*St. Louis Post-Dispatch*)

Finally, he knew he could pull it out.

He went next door to the Kreegers' room. "Harby, come to my room for a minute."

The two men knew each other only through Ed, and were acquaintances rather than friends. As far as each knew, the other harbored no doubts about Ed's innocence.

Dan led Harby into his bathroom and pointed out the towel ring. "That looks about as solid as a pop top on a beer," Dan said. He reached over, grabbed the ring, and pulled it off the wall plate.

"Some case they have," Dan said.

But even if the demonstration bolstered Kreeger's faith, Dan knew it proved nothing. The towel ring that was in evidence supposedly showed a great deal of deformation. The ring in Dan's hand showed none.

The next morning, after Dan testified at the federal grand jury, he approached Dean Hoag in the hallway.

"Dean, I'd like to suggest a scenario. Let's say my brother is telling the truth about finding Julie in the tub. But maybe he panicked and was afraid he'd be blamed, and so he pulled the towel ring off the wall. Or maybe it's more sinister. Maybe he was thinking about suing the hotel, and that's why he pulled it out. If that second version is true, then we're talking about fraud, not murder. Right?"

He tried to offer the notion casually, lawyer to lawyer, the way an attorney in a civil case might broach a possible settlement offer.

But with Hoag, such an approach was useless. Hoag did not believe in any brotherhood of lawyers. To him, the practice of law was adversarial.

"Look, I don't know what you're trying to pull, okay? But if you have some knowledge of this, then you'd better get your ass back in the grand jury room and come clean. If you and your brother think you can pull this stunt in a trial, you're dead wrong."

He gave Dan a withering look and walked away.

Later that day, Dan testified in front of the state grand jury. Determined to help his brother but equally determined not to lie, he was responsive, but vague. He suggested that Ed and Julie had had a good marriage. No marriage is perfect, he said.

"Have you ever known of any incidents of domestic violence in the household?" Vossmeyer asked.

"Julie complained to me a couple of times that Ed had punched her. She called me one night and said, 'Come over. Ed's kind of rowdy.' I got over there and both of them had been out that night drinking, I think excessively. Then there was a squabble, and Julie said, 'Come over here, calm your brother down.' That was it. That happened about eight years ago."

Vossmeyer asked if he had ever witnessed any violence.

"No, no, no," Dan said.

As far as Vossmeyer was concerned, the most pleasant development was the testimony of Dianne Kreeger. She testified that Julie had talked about getting a divorce less than six months before her death. It was the first time Dee had heard that.

The case was still incomplete when the grand jury's term expired in November. The term was extended for the Post case.

In December, Boulter Kelsey, an accident reconstructionist, testified. His testimony included videotapes of his work.

In one videotape, a woman the same height and weight as Julie Post was unable to pull a towel ring out of the wall.

Most important, he said, even if a person was able to pull a towel ring off its wall mount, the deformation of the metal would be entirely different from the deformation present on the ring from room 4063.

He gave the opinion that the deformation on the ring in question was caused by someone pulling it to the left, and twisting it out of the wall.

A week before Christmas, the Thigpens arrived in St. Louis to testify.

When they arrived at the courthouse, Dee had them wait in the victim's assistance office rather than in the hallway in front of the grand jury room. Etta Mae was silent and withdrawn. Hollis seemed almost overcome with sadness.

Before he went into the grand jury room, Hollis told Dee she was making a terrible mistake.

"Ed Post did not kill my daughter," he said. "You people up here didn't even know my daughter. You don't know Ed. I don't understand why you're doing this."

Hollis was polite and reserved in his testimony.

"Mr. Thigpen, you're here, of course, because you were subpoenaed here, but you have also come up because Mr. Post's attorney wishes you to be here. Now, you have expressed to me your belief that Ed Post couldn't possibly have murdered your daughter, and I would like you to tell this jury how you feel. Tell them anything that you think is important for them to know."

For a long moment, Hollis was silent. Then, in his slow, heavy drawl, he began.

"I just don't believe it could happen. I don't believe that. I basically don't."

He halted, searching for words.

"There's little conflicts. There's no question about it. I have conflicts with my wife after fifty years, but that don't mean that we don't love each other. I was close enough to my daughter. Me and her were real close. If there had been anything between Ed Post and Julie Thigpen Post, my daughter would have told me. I can't believe, never will be able to believe, that Ed Post could have killed my daughter. I can't help it, but I just can't believe it."

One of the grand jurors told Hollis that she had a thirty-eight-year-old daughter who was as close to her father as a daughter could be. The daughter had once been engaged to a man who beat her, and she'd never told her father.

Very softly, Hollis began to cry.

Dee asked if he still saw much of Ed.

"Yes, he brings the girls all the time. We love our granddaughters. We love them to death. The oldest one's so much like Julie, when you talk to her on the phone you can't help but cry. It's been a miserable time. No way in the world Ed Post could do it. I know he didn't do it. I know it."

The grand jury reconvened one last time in January to consider the Post case. On the day before what would have been the Posts' twentieth wedding anniversary, the grand jury voted eleven to one to indict Edward T. Post for first-degree murder in the death of his wife.

According to the laws of Missouri, conviction on such a charge carries one of two penalties—death, or life without the possibility of parole.

The U.S. attorney's office immediately dropped its fraud investigation.

In February, Dee told Peach that she had decided to look for a job in private practice.

When Hoag heard this, he asked Dittmeier if the U.S. attorney's office could lend him to the circuit attorney's office to try the Post murder case. Dittmeier consented.

Hoag called Peach with the offer. Peach gladly accepted.

A short time later, Kitty Eldridge's ex-husband called Hoag, as he had once or twice a year since the Rothgeb case—just wanted to chat, he said.

Hoag told him about the Post case.

A couple of days later, the ex-husband called again.

"Thought you might enjoy this, Deano. I saw Kitty,

and told her that old Deano had another drowning case, some old boy from down South who came up to St. Louis and drowned his wife. She said, 'I hope the old boy did it, because if Deano's after him, he's going to jail.' "

Hoag laughed.

Chapter Nineteen

On a cold, snowy late afternoon in January, Arthur Margulis was reviewing some paperwork in his law office in Clayton, a suburb just west of St. Louis, when he received a telephone call.

Ralph Whalen was on the line.

"I represent a man named Ed Post," said Whalen.

Ed Post. The name rang a bell. Like most criminal defense attorneys, Margulis read the newspaper thoroughly, paying especially close attention to crime stories.

"Ed's charged with murder, Art. His wife, Julie, drowned in a bathtub at the Omni Hotel," Whalen said.

Of course, thought Margulis. He remembered the case now. On the morning after Julie's death, Art's wife, Joyce, had been reading the paper at the breakfast table.

"He drew his wife's bath," Joyce had said with disbelief in her voice.

"I remember the case," Margulis told Whalen. "Post was from out of state."

"That's right. New Orleans."

"What can I do for you, Ralph?"

"I've decided to get a St. Louis lawyer as cocounsel. You're one of several lawyers who've been recommended. I'd like to talk with you."

"Of course," said Margulis.

Sometimes he was amazed at how many high-profile cases ended up in his office. Not that he took all of them.

Still, it surprised him how many people came in, and he could say, "Yes, I've read about it."

In January 1987, Arthur Margulis was fifty-three years old. A handsome man, he bore a slight resemblance to Walter Mondale, and whenever anybody described him, the first thing mentioned was his piercing blue eyes.

As in any city, there were four or five lawyers who were considered the best in the business. Margulis was first among equals in that elite group.

He was a former FBI agent, and although he had earned several commendations during his three and a half years in the bureau, it was typical of Margulis that the story he most liked to tell was about one of his failures.

He had been poolside at a fancy resort, posing as a sunbather while keeping track of a reputed mobster. The bureau had equipped him with the latest high-tech equipment, a radio transmitter that looked like a book.

Suddenly, from across the pool, a voice rang out.

"Art Margulis!"

With a sense of dread, Margulis looked across the pool and saw a high school classmate.

"What are you doing here, Art? Last I heard, you were in the FBI!"

After leaving the bureau, Margulis returned to St. Louis to establish a law practice. In doing so, of course, he switched sides. Because of his law enforcement background, he became a criminal defense attorney.

That was more than twenty years ago. Now he was at the top of his profession. Any doubt about his status had been removed when the chief judge of the federal court hired Margulis to represent his son. The youth had murdered a former girlfriend with an ax. In a nonjury trial, Margulis got the young man declared innocent by reason of insanity.

"I'd like to come over now, if I could," said Whalen. "I'm in town with Ed's brother."

Margulis suggested they get together the next morning.

He had only come into the office to look at some papers before going cross-country skiing in Forest Park. He was dressed casually, and such attire in the office was not the Margulis style.

But Whalen insisted, saying he was on a tight schedule, and that everything would be easier if they could meet that afternoon.

So Margulis relented, and within the hour, Dan Post and Whalen arrived at the building where Margulis had his office. Whalen looked at the register on the wall. Margulis was on the thirteenth floor. Whalen liked that hint of theatrics.

Margulis led the men into his private office. The large window to the west offered a spectacular sunset.

They talked briefly about the case. Margulis, aware that they already knew of his reputation, didn't feel compelled to sell himself. He already knew a little about the case, and he asked sharp, perceptive questions. Both Whalen and Post were impressed.

Whalen sensed from the very first that Margulis was a man he could work with. Margulis did not seem overbearing. That attitude can be a problem when you're seeking a top gun to copilot a case.

Originally, Whalen had thought he would get a lesser figure. He didn't really need a copilot, just somebody who could monitor the local scene.

But his client had thought otherwise. Let's get the best lawyer we can, Ed Post had said.

So Whalen called people and tried to get a feel for exactly who was the best lawyer in St. Louis. Margulis was on everybody's short list. He lived up to his billing, as far as Whalen was concerned.

Dan Post was impressed, too. When Dan and Whalen left Margulis's office, they turned to each other and simultaneously gave each other a thumb's-up sign. They went back inside immediately and retained Margulis as cocounsel.

That evening, Margulis talked to his wife. Joyce had

been his high school sweetheart. Together they had successfully raised four sons. Only the youngest, sixteen, was still at home.

Margulis long ago had understood the wisdom of listening to his wife. She thought like a juror rather than a lawyer.

"I'm going to represent Ed Post," Margulis said. "He's the man from New Orleans who's accused of murdering his wife at the Omni."

Joyce nodded. *"He drew her bathwater,"* she said.

Dean Hoag was happy to be working on a murder case again.

Although the indictment had been won, a lot of work remained to be done. The state had convinced a grand jury that the evidence warranted a trial, but Hoag knew he was a long way from being able to prove to a trial jury that it was sufficient for a conviction.

When he asked Peach for assistance, the circuit attorney suggested a young prosecutor Hoag hardly knew.

"He could learn a lot from being second chair on this one," Peach said.

Hoag shook his head. "George, he's new! I haven't been over here in three years. I need somebody who knows the law, somebody who knows the judges."

Peach shrugged.

"Who do you want, Dean?"

"Steve Moore."

Moore was the yin to Hoag's yang. Where Hoag nearly vibrated with energy, Moore was quiet, laid-back, and sleepy-eyed. He was short, a little plump, and he looked and acted more like a friar than a big-city prosecutor. At forty, he was still single. He lived in the same quiet neighborhood in which he had grown up.

Originally, he was going to be a scientist. He had studied chemistry at college, and now in an office of liberal arts graduates he was something of an oddity. He actually knew something about math and science.

He was an able prosecutor, very organized and matter-of-fact—definitely not an avenging angel. Moore had backseated for Hoag during a high-profile murder case several years earlier. A court reporter was raped and murdered in her apartment. A man confessed, and then recanted. The first trial ended in a hung jury. The second resulted in a conviction.

Besides recalling their previous work together, Hoag was thinking of something else. This case would lean heavily on science. The towel ring would play a crucial role.

Everything else they had could backfire. Hoag was convinced that the Posts had a history of violence, but the state had uncovered very little of that. Furthermore, Julie's coworkers described her as an aggressive, demanding person—not exactly the profile of an abused wife.

Julie was killed, Hoag felt, partly because Post lusted after another woman, but that theory too could blow up in the courtroom. There was nothing to prove an affair, and, in fact, all the evidence—and especially the testimony of the ''other woman''—indicated there had not been one.

That left the second autopsy, and the towel ring.

Hoag was comfortable with this. He didn't need the other woman, and he didn't need the violence. The nice thing about circumstantial evidence is that the other side can't cross-examine it.

So when Peach consented to let Moore second-chair the case, Hoag told Moore the towel ring would be key.

''So far, the testing that's been done has shown what didn't happen. A sudden yank did not produce the distortion we've got on the ring. Now we've got to take it the other direction. We've got to show what did cause it,'' Hoag said.

Because of his scientific bent, that part of the case would go to Moore.

Hoag would do the medical stuff.
And he would handle Ed Post.

Whalen briefed Margulis on the strengths and weaknesses of the case.

The two men had similar professional backgrounds. Both had done their hitch on society's side in the war on crime. Now they looked at the war from the other side, where the issue was not about predators attacking society, but about individuals fighting the massive power of the state.

This particular case offered the greatest of challenges: the charge of first-degree murder. The state's case did not look overwhelming. If things went right, their client could walk. Although it didn't really matter, there was even a chance that he was innocent.

One of the biggest strengths in the case was the support of Julie's family. Her parents and her sister were strongly behind Post. They would help dispel any questions about the marriage.

Another strength was the medical evidence. The pathologists seemed to be split two to one in favor of the defense. Fossum said Julie's injuries could be consistent with Post's version of events. Graham had initially ruled undetermined, and, according to Fossum, still seemed to be of that opinion. McGarry, of course, was already screaming homicide.

On the problem side of the ledger, you could start off with insurance, but that could be minimized by Post's history, and the fact that Masson would testify that Post could have bought a larger policy for Julie.

Still, the case would be tried in the city. Since most of the upper middle class had long since fled to the suburbs, the jury panel would most likely consist of people who were not affluent, and they would be awfully skeptical about $700,000 worth of life insurance.

And last there was the towel ring. The state would

surely have experts saying it was not yanked off the wall in a slip-and-fall accident.

But perhaps other experts could be found to contradict the state's experts. Additionally, the state would have a problem with the chain of evidence. The staff of the hotel had had possession of the towel ring before the police got it.

Suppose you were working at the hotel, and you heard that a woman had just died after pulling a towel ring out of the wall. Maybe you would go to a vacant room and see how easily the ring came off. Suppose you gave it a yank and loosened it, but it didn't come all the way off. You couldn't leave it half on, so you'd twist the darn thing off.

Maybe it was this second ring that the cops later picked up. At least this was a scenario that could muddy the water.

The outcome of the trial might well hinge on Ed Post himself.

On one hand, he was an articulate fellow. On the other hand, he talked too much.

That reality sank into Margulis in the first days of the discovery process, when the state provided its evidence to the defense. Everything had to be turned over. Among the items was the transcript of the Jacobsmeyer tape.

Margulis was not a demonstrative man. As he read the transcript, he said, very softly, "Oh shit."

It wasn't really so much what Post said as that he felt compelled to answer at such length.

Margulis knew Jacobsmeyer. Years ago, when the federal government had been providing grant money to send police officers to classes on law enforcement at local community colleges, Margulis, with his FBI background, had taught some of the classes. Jacobsmeyer had been one of his students.

Margulis read the transcript and he thought of Jacobsmeyer.

A smart cop. He must have been amazed, too, by Post's volubility.

As America evolved into a lawsuit-happy country, "expert testimony" became a growth industry. You could find an expert for anything.

Hoag called a college friend who had a successful practice in civil law on the East Coast. The prosecutor described the towel ring that appeared to have been twisted off the wall.

"Where would you get an expert witness for something like this?" Hoag asked.

The friend recommended Skinner & Sherman Laboratories, just outside of Boston.

Hoag called the firm, explained his problem to a receptionist, and was directed to David Colling, who had a Ph.D. in metallurgy from the Massachusetts Institute of Technology. Colling said he could examine a towel ring and conduct experiments to reproduce whatever deformation was present on the original ring.

In early February, Hoag flew to Boston to deliver his prime exhibit, along with several other towel rings and wall plates that the hotel had provided.

Hoag received a written report in late spring. Colling had inadvertently conducted his experiments with the towel ring installed upside down.

"Don't worry," Colling said when Hoag called. "It doesn't matter whether it was upside down."

Hoag was furious. "Maybe it doesn't matter to a professor from Harvard with an IQ of a hundred and sixty who understands the physics involved, okay? But to an average juror, who's going to have an IQ of a hundred and five, it's going to matter. You think I'm going to stand in front of a jury and tell them that it doesn't matter if my expert did his testing with the thing upside down? It doesn't matter?"

Furthermore, Colling had used nuts, fastened from behind, to attach the plates to a wallboard. That was not the way the plates had been attached to the wall in the hotel.

In July, Hoag and Moore flew to Boston to talk to the metallurgist. Colling agreed to redo his tests, but to Hoag, the misgivings he'd been having ever since the upside-down report were reinforced when Colling said his tests, which he still insisted were valid, led him to believe the towel ring had been subjected to simultaneous forces from two people—one standing outside the tub, and one standing inside the tub. Colling suggested the test results could indicate a death struggle.

Hoag didn't want speculation about the events leading to Julie's death. He wanted scientific facts. He wanted to know exactly what forces had caused the deformation of the towel ring.

After leaving Colling, Hoag and Moore drove north to see Roger Fossum, who had left Texas to become the medical examiner for the state of New Hampshire.

During the drive, Hoag complained about Colling.

"Is this the way you engineers operate?" Hoag asked Moore. "Upside down but it doesn't matter? You know how a guy like that is going to look on the witness stand?"

Had Moore not known Hoag better, he might have reminded him who it was that had found the guy. But Moore understood that Hoag wasn't blaming him. He was just thinking out loud.

And this was a blow. Two facts, that's all they needed. Injuries too extensive to have come from a single fall, and a towel ring twisted and pulled off the wall.

The towel ring testimony had to be clear, because the medical evidence could get muddied. The defense had had a pathologist at the second autopsy, and expert witnesses had a habit of seeing things the way their paying client wanted things seen.

The unhappy experience with Colling did lead to one

decision. From now on, the two prosecutors decided, there would be no more written reports on experiments. All experts would deliver status reports informally, by phone, to Moore.

In a criminal case, the prosecution is obliged to turn over all evidence to the defense. So Colling's written report about the two forces acting simultaneously would have to go to the defense. The state would be giving the defense the very mud with which it could discredit the towel ring.

Fossum, the potential problem, was a pleasant surprise.

He did not seem committed to the cause of the defense. In fact, he seemed to be aligned with Graham—not quite comfortable declaring with certainty that Julie's death was a homicide, but ready to say that the injuries could be explained by a homicide.

That would be good enough. McGarry could say it was definitely a homicide, and Graham and Fossum could say it possibly was a homicide.

On the drive back to Boston, Hoag was more cheerful. He talked about throwing the defense a curve, and calling Fossum as a state's witness. He imagined putting Fossum on the stand.

''Who hired you to attend that autopsy, Dr. Graham?''

''Ralph Whalen did. On behalf of Ed Post.''

That would be a good one.

That night, Hoag and Moore went to Fenway Park to see the Red Sox. Hoag was a real student of the game. He had loved being a catcher. When you're behind the plate, you're in charge. You call the pitches, and try to stay a step ahead of the batter.

Hoag had been very good at that part of the game. If he could have hit just a little better—the fastball on his hands and the slider away were his undoing—he could have made it a career.

This game promised to be a treat. Roger Clemens, the best pitcher in baseball, was pitching for the Red Sox.

He got knocked out early. Sometimes you never can tell.

Chapter Twenty

At about the same time Hoag was preparing to go to Boston to confront Colling about the upside-down experiments, Whalen filed a lawsuit against Vossmeyer, the circuit attorney's office in St. Louis, and the New Orleans police department.

He alleged that Vossmeyer had misrepresented facts to the juvenile court when she had Post's daughters brought to juvenile court in August of the previous year. He sought damages of $300,000 for each girl.

To George Peach, the circuit attorney, the suit was just a reminder of how expensive this case was. The feds had paid for the witnesses during the grand jury proceedings, but now the whole expense fell on Peach's office. Hoag had already gone to Boston for one expert and clearly wasn't completely happy with the guy. That meant there'd be more experts.

And now a lawyer.

Peach called his counterpart in New Orleans.

"I need the name of a good lawyer in private practice. I'm being sued," he said.

The first trial date in the fall of 1987 was waived. Neither side was ready.

In March 1988, Whalen flew to Boston to take Colling's deposition. Hoag and Moore also were present.

The deposition was taken in an office in the laboratory. Whalen was, as usual, warm and cordial and ready to engage in the sort of pregame chitchat that makes the practice of law such a cordial business. Hoag was, as usual, very brusque.

So Whalen got to work.

"Could you state your name for the record, please."

"David Allen Colling."

"And are you addressed as Dr. Colling?"

"It works."

Whalen smiled. Hoag didn't. His impression of Colling was going down further.

When asked about the deformation, Colling said, "There was only a minor distortion in a vertical plane, which would have been more of a torsional effect. It had to come after the distortion in the horizontal plane."

"Why is that?" asked Whalen.

"In order to have it that way," said Colling.

Hoag tried very hard not to wince.

Colling also affirmed his belief that two people had acted together to remove the towel ring.

The deposition lasted only forty-five minutes.

Hoag and Moore both had the feeling that Whalen could hardly wait to get Colling on the stand. Cross-examining him would be fun.

As the three lawyers left the building, Whalen couldn't help himself. "So this is what you've got, huh, Dean?"

Hoag didn't reply, but as soon as he was alone with Moore, he blew up. "Jesus Christ! 'Why do you say the vertical distortion came before the horizontal distortion, Dr. Colling?' 'In order to have it that way,' " Hoag mimicked. "If that's the way you engineers testify, Steve, you're going to get your ass eaten on the stand," Hoag said.

Moore wasn't so worried. The towel ring was already in the hands of another expert.

His name was William Weins, and he was a professor of mechanical engineering at the University of Nebraska.

He had been recommended by Boulter Kelsey, the accident reconstructionist from St. Louis.

Hoag and Moore had flown to Nebraska in January. They had met Weins for a drink. He had seemed genuinely excited as the prosecutors spelled out their problem.

He believed he could examine the towel ring and determine what forces had created the deformation of the metal.

The thought of Weins offered some solace as Hoag and Moore left Colling's office after the deposition.

In August, more than two years after Julie's death, Margulis met with Whalen in the law office on Exchange Alley.

Whalen had located a metallurgy expert in Illinois who was willing to testify that the damage to the towel ring could have been caused earlier. That is, a previous guest could have twisted the ring almost off the wall, and the deformation would have been present *before* Julie grabbed it and yanked it off the wall. Unless the state could prove that the damage had not been present, the defense had a chance of establishing reasonable doubt.

The medical evidence still appeared to be a wash. Fossum was prepared to say that Julie's injuries could be consistent with Ed's story. Graham was still undetermined. McGarry was for homicide.

The workload had already been divided, of course. Whalen would handle the towel-ring testimony and the medical evidence. He would also handle the cross-examination of the real estate people and the Thigpens. Oddly enough, it turned out he knew Julie's parents. The Whalens and the Betheas were close friends. Bill Bethea had delivered Whalen's daughter.

Margulis would handle the opening statement and the closing argument and would present the defense case. He would also cross-examine the Kreegers.

Harby Kreeger, Ed's best friend, was a mystery. Among the evidence the state had turned over in discovery was the long and detailed police report from Detective McCraw.

Margulis, who had read the report by the time he met Harby, was far too scrupulous an attorney to suggest that a witness shade the truth, but he still had to wonder what kind of best friend volunteers incriminating information from the distant past.

Well, that was Harby Kreeger. Maybe he was too eager to please; maybe he was simply too honest.

Kreeger's latest stance was that the police report was riddled with errors and lies. The Thigpens were saying the same thing. But the stuff about the long-ago violence and the prostitutes—well, no way could the cops have made that up.

Still, Kreeger wouldn't be a problem. He might say one thing to the prosecution and another thing to the defense, but in a courtroom, with both sides present, he would be for Ed.

The real problem was Kim Autin.

The two lawyers had read the report about her calling Gary Hayes the night shortly after Julie's death when Ed had allegedly professed his love to her. They had reviewed her grand jury testimony, which had been handed over as part of discovery.

The other-woman angle was damning.

To really complicate matters, she was refusing to talk to the defense attorneys. She was in the midst of what appeared to be a nasty divorce.

Margulis and Whalen had to figure out what to do about Kim.

"What do we know about her?" Margulis asked.

Whalen shrugged.

"Art, the best description I've got on her comes from somebody else. 'She's the kind of girl who when you see her, bad thoughts come to your mind.' If she testifies that Ed was chasing her, the jury is going to believe her."

"Is she going to testify to that?"

Whalen shrugged.

Because she was refusing to meet informally with either of the defense lawyers, they had only two options.

The first was to do nothing.

The second was to subpoena her and take her deposition. But that would mean putting her under oath, and whatever she said would become part of the official record. Without having any idea what she was going to say, that seemed foolhardy. She might just bury them.

Her soon-to-be-ex-husband was another problem. According to McCraw's police report, Ed had asked him, on the night of Julie's funeral, if it might be possible to get fixed up with Kim's twin sister.

Whalen was not so concerned about Bobby. He would be easy to take apart in cross-examination. Fast-laners always are.

Circumstances had made Whalen a defense attorney, but in his heart, he was still an avenging angel. If the state decided to put Bobby Autin on the witness stand, Whalen would handle the cross-examination.

Chapter Twenty-one

Ed Post was becoming increasingly restless. Efforts to find a job had come to naught. His parents were supporting him. He was playing golf several times a week, and had pretty much decided that his next venture would be to sell golf-course homes. That would mean leaving New Orleans, of course.

He was ready for that. He wanted to go someplace where the population was growing and the real estate market was vibrant. He still thought about California or Florida.

Besides, going where he wasn't known might be a good thing. The indictment and the impending trial had cast a cloud over his reputation. Being charged with murder was like having a fatal disease. Although few people dared to ask about it, almost everybody wanted to hear about it.

That was fine with Ed. He was a natural salesman.

The cheerful contempt for the St. Louis cops that had marked his attitude in the days of the investigation had been replaced by a sense of disbelief.

"This is absolutely crazy," he'd tell people. "It's preposterous. They're doing this to protect their new hotel. We'd increased our insurance, both of us, shortly before her accident, so that's what they're basing my 'guilt' on. I can hardly wait for the trial—they keep postponing it—so I can try to get on with my life."

His closest friends had rallied around him. They exchanged St. Louis stories. Dianne Kreeger thought it was ridiculous that the investigators were trying to make a big deal out of the catered party at Post's house on the night of Julie's funeral. Funeral parties were a New Orleans tradition. Martha Post thought it was comical the way the St. Louis people tried to put a sinister spin on Julie's being buried in the ground, as if her body might have washed out to sea.

And Hollocher was capable of anything, most everybody agreed.

But outside this circle of close friends, Post's support wasn't so strong.

The real estate community was especially rife with suspicions. The women still working at the West Bank office often discussed the case. Male menopause, one suggested. The sudden emphasis on the body as seen in the crash weight-loss program was discussed, as well as his romantic interest in a younger woman. The women agreed that Post showed the classic symptoms of a mid-life crisis.

In the fall of 1988, with the trial looming, Post attended a national convention in Hawaii. Ostensibly, he was still looking for work. But even those in the industry who didn't know Ed knew who he was and what he was accused of.

When Ed came into the lobby of the hotel, several other agents spotted him with an attractive young woman.

"I don't believe it," one of the men said.

"He's got nerve," said another.

About that time, Ed noticed them, and came over.

"I want you to meet my daughter, Stephanie," he said.

The men who had made the remarks felt awful.

But if Ed sensed anything, he didn't let on. He seemed the same upbeat guy they had always known.

Shortly before the trial was supposed to begin, Whalen's two brothers-in-law were involved in a terrible car accident. One was fatally injured.

The trial was rescheduled for the spring of 1989.

*   *   *

In January 1989, Post saw a help-wanted ad that sounded intriguing. It was from Emerald Seas Yacht Sales.

Post's interest in boats dated back to high school, when his father had bought a sixteen-footer. More recently, Ed had spent countless hours on Harby Kreeger's forty-six-foot sport fishing boat. If anybody could sell boats, it was Ed Post.

He drove to the marina where the Emerald Seas office was located, but at the last moment, he didn't go in.

Later that same week, Post went to the wedding of a neighbor's child. He drank some champagne, and left the celebration to drive Jennifer to a friend's house. After dropping off his daughter, he stopped at Lenfant's, the trendy bar where Julie and Kim had fought almost three years earlier.

After ordering a glass of champagne, he noticed an attractive woman. She seemed to be looking at him, so he went over to her table.

He talked and he talked, mostly chattering about boats. She seemed to find him fascinating. Finally, after about forty-five minutes, he realized he had been doing all the talking and had not asked her anything about herself.

"What do you do?" he asked.

"I'm a yacht broker," she said with a smile. "And you do know about boats."

She worked, oddly enough, for Emerald Seas. Her name was Toni, and she was thirty-three years old and single.

When it was time for her to leave, Post walked with her to the front door. He took her keys and handed them to the parking lot attendant. Toni noticed that he tipped the young man five dollars.

When she drove away, she looked in the rearview mirror. Sure enough, he was watching.

Charming, she thought to herself. You don't find many men that considerate anymore. She was glad she had given him her number.

*   *   *

The next morning, Post was on the golf course, but he couldn't concentrate on his game. After nine holes, he decided to quit and call Toni. This is strange, she said when he identified himself. I was just thinking about you, too.

They went out that night to a sushi bar. Right from the start, they hit it off again. Toni had to admit to herself she was interested in this guy.

Abruptly, in the middle of some light banter, he turned serious.

"Toni, before we go much farther, and I say this because I think we can go much farther, there's something you have the right to know," he said.

She held her breath. He had told her the previous night that he was a widower. Now she wondered if he was going to tell her that he was actually married.

"Let me tell you the way my wife died."

He told her he had gone jogging, and when he had returned, his wife was unconscious in the tub. She had apparently fallen down and hit her head.

"What you have to know is this: the St. Louis police have the ridiculous idea that I killed her. It's absolutely crazy. I loved my wife. But we had increased our life insurance, both of us, shortly before we went to St. Louis. That's why, I guess, they think I did it."

Toni was staring at him.

He misread her stare.

"I didn't kill her," he said. "Eventually, soon, this will be over. They'll either drop the charges or I'll go to trial and be acquitted."

"I've heard the story," Toni said. "Do you know a man named Bobby Autin?"

Now it was her turn to talk.

She told Ed that two months earlier, she had gotten a call from a potential buyer. It was Bobby. She showed him some boats, and then he invited her out for a drink.

During the course of their conversation, the subject shifted from boats to Bobby's personal life, she told Ed. Bobby drank more and more and started talking about his divorce. He blamed his problems on a friend who had told his wife about some affairs.

"He said he was going to get even with his friend," Toni said. "He told me he was going to testify against him in a murder trial. He told me the guy's wife had drowned in a hotel bathtub in St. Louis."

The news didn't surprise Ed. He had long since read McGraw's police report, which included Bobby's statement that on the night of the funeral, Ed had asked to get fixed up with Kim's sister.

So when Toni told him about Bobby's statement to her, he merely shrugged.

"It's crazy. He blames me for his divorce. I'm sorry he's so bitter, but I know what he's talking about. Shortly after Julie died, we were drinking, and I was taking Valium on my doctor's advice—I was pretty badly shaken, and this was *before* any investigation—and I mentioned that maybe, some time in the future, we could have dinner. Him and his wife, and his wife has a sister, and I thought maybe we could all go out some time. I guess he wants to testify that I was in love with his wife's sister, who, incidentally, I think I've met once."

"He said he's going to make sure you're convicted," Toni said.

Ed shook his head.

"Well, he can try, but I can't see a jury convicting me because of his testimony. As crazy as it must sound, I still have faith in the system. If you didn't do something, they can't prove that you did."

Despite this bizarre turn of events, Toni had to admit she was still very interested in this man.

A few days later, they met for lunch.

"Will it ruin you for the rest of the day if we have some wine with lunch?" Ed asked.

She shook her head.

Ed studied the wine list, making comments about the various choices. Obviously, he knew a lot about wine.

Over lunch, Ed was upbeat again, charming, interested in her. His problems would be resolved. The situation was so crazy, it wasn't even worth talking about, he said.

So they talked about other things.

"I very much enjoyed being married, Toni. I know you've never been married, and maybe for you, that's the best way to go through life."

It's just that I'm picky, and I've never met the right person before, she thought.

"For me, though, married life is exactly right," Ed continued. "It probably sounds corny, and maybe I'm hopelessly square, but I'm a one-woman man. Someday, when all this craziness is over and life is normal again, I hope to focus my life again on one woman, and marriage."

She and Ed began to see each other on a daily basis.

In February, he invited her home to meet his daughters. On that day, he picked her up at her place. They stopped at a grocery store to buy food. Ed was enthusiastic about cooking dinner. While they were shopping, Ed bought a bouquet of flowers. Toni thought they were for her.

"There's something I have to do," Ed said when they got back to the car.

He drove to the Metairie Cemetery.

"Would you come with me?" he asked.

Of course, Toni murmured. She followed Ed to Julie's grave. A vase was propped up against the headstone. Ed took the old flowers out of the vase and replaced them with the new bouquet.

He began to pray. Abruptly, he began to cry.

"Julie, you must understand that I have to get on with the rest of my life," he said. "What I want you to know is I've found someone you would approve of."

Afterward, they drove to Ed's house.

The older daughter, Stephanie, seemed vivacious. The younger daughter, Jennifer, was quiet.

While the dinner cooked, Ed gave Toni a tour of the house. Pictures of Julie were everywhere. Her cosmetics were still in the bathroom. Ed pointed out that her wedding gown was hanging in the closet next to his wedding tuxedo.

Toni saw these mementoes of Julie and was even more convinced that this was not the house of a man who had murdered his wife.

After dinner, Ed played some music on the stereo.

"Somewhere in Time" came on, and Ed started to cry.

"I'm sorry, but this was Julie's favorite song," he said.

The moment was so emotional that Toni began to cry, too. So did Stephanie.

In March, Ed and Toni became engaged. They set a wedding date of June 24. Ed's trial was due to begin in mid-April.

Shortly before the trial, Ed called Toni at work. He seemed devastated. Could she come over at once? he asked.

She rushed over.

Stephanie had accidentally crushed Rambo, the family cat, in the automatic garage door. When Toni arrived, Ed was in tears. He had put the cat in a small box. He had partly covered its body with a pillowcase. He had put flowers at its head.

He dug a grave, and marked the grave with a small cross.

Toni was enchanted. She recalled the moment in a letter she later wrote to the judge.

"How could a man grieve so much over his dead pet and still be the 'cold-blooded murderer' he was described to be in closing arguments by the prosecution?"

Chapter Twenty-two

On a warm Monday morning in mid-April, with a wind from the north blowing thunderclouds across the river from the Illinois prairie, sixty-seven citizens marched into a St. Louis courtroom to audition, for the most part reluctantly, for the role of juror in the state of Missouri's first-degree murder case against Edward T. Post, businessman from New Orleans.

Judge Thomas C. Mummert greeted the veniremen, as potential jurors are called, with a nod. The judge was thirty-seven years old, but looked much younger and bore a striking resemblance to Bob Costas, the sports announcer and television talk-show host.

"Good morning, ladies and gentlemen. Welcome to Division Six," Mummert said, and then he grinned.

Everybody knew this trial would not be good duty. Not only would the jurors have to wrestle with a first-degree murder charge, they would be sequestered. The three men sitting at the defense table—Margulis, Whalen, and Post—shared a chuckle with the jurors over the judge's ironic welcome.

It was impossible to tell which of the three was the defendant. All were dressed impeccably. All had legal pads in front of them. All were trying to look friendly and open, making eye contact with the veniremen, but not staring.

At the state's table, Hoag was wearing his game face, a scowl. He wasn't interested in establishing rapport with the veniremen. Moore, being a team player, maintained a somber expression.

So far, things had gone well for the state. It had prevailed in the pretrial battles over admissibility of evidence, particularly with the towel ring. The defense had argued that because the police had not seized it at once, the chain of evidence had been broken. Mummert had disagreed.

In terms of legal philosophy, Mummert described himself as a kitchen-sinker. Within reason, he felt, the jury should see and hear as much as possible.

The potential jurors were seated in the spectators' benches in the courtroom. As Whalen studied them, he fingered the rose in his lapel. He realized how right Margulis had been when discussing the probable venire, or jury pool. The veniremen were middle-income to poor, with most somewhere in the middle of that range.

Oddly enough, the mix was fine with the defense lawyers. They weren't looking for a jury of Post's peers. They especially didn't want a single peer—a strong-minded juror who could impose his will on the others.

With a reasonable-doubt defense, the whole idea was to cloud things up. The defense could not afford to let a bull knock away the ambiguities.

Although generally ignored by Hollywood, the process of jury selection can be the most pivotal part of a trial. More art than science, it involves figuring out what kind of juror will be the most susceptible to the kind of case you intend to present.

Of even greater importance is determining what kind of person should not be on the jury. In addition to wanting no bulls, the defense wanted no youngish career women who could identify with Julie.

Joyce Margulis had suggested to her husband that it also would be advisable to eliminate any older people who might identify Julie with their own daughters.

That might be true, the lawyers decided, but still, you had to end up with somebody. Each side, the defense and the state, could disqualify only seven veniremen purely on instinct.

Hoag had not given much thought to his "ideal juror." He was concerned with discovering who among the veniremen nurtured a vendetta against the system. These snakes in the woodpile were an avenging angel's nightmare. Often they wanted to be on juries, so they would hide their true feelings. Hoag's job would be to unmask them.

Mummert read the first instruction that the jury would have to follow. The defendant is presumed innocent until proved guilty. Was there anybody who couldn't follow that?

Several hands went up.

Mummert called on one woman.

"I'm not sure, 'cause I'm not sure what the case is, and—"

"We don't want you to know anything about the case right now," the judge said, adding that he'd get back to her concerns in voir dire, when each venireman would be questioned individually by the opposing lawyers.

The judge recognized four other veniremen who said they would be unable to follow the innocent-until-proved-guilty rule.

Then after introducing Post, Margulis, and Whalen and Hoag and Moore, the judge gave the veniremen the standard pep talk.

"This is the only country in the world that has the type of system that we have," Mummert said. "It's certainly got its problems. There are some imperfections in any system, but this is the best system we have. And the only reason it works is because you all come down here and volunteer. Quote, volunteer. You know you get a summons. It's like joining the Army, huh?"

He assured the veniremen of two things. First, the state was not asking for the death penalty. Second, the hotel in which the jury would be sequestered was a good one, and nobody would have to share a room.

Referring to the fact that there had been quite a number of sequestered jury trials in recent months, the judge made a remark rich with an irony no one could yet appreciate.

"We're getting good at this," he said.

The veniremen began the process of disqualifying themselves. The first was a Jehovah's Witness who claimed she would be unable to judge another person. She cited a Biblical passage.

The judge dismissed her.

The next man said his wife had died twelve days ago, and he was too busy dealing with the aftermath of her death to sit on a sequestered jury.

The judge dismissed him.

The next man said he was in poor health and wasn't supposed to be under stress.

The judge dismissed him.

A woman said she was living in a shelter for abused women, was suffering emotional distress, and had mental disabilities.

The judge dismissed her.

The process continued. Thirteen veniremen complained of poor health, five had ill spouses, three had sick mothers, one had a sick aunt, five were single parents who couldn't leave their children unattended, one was unemployed and had a job interview, two couldn't serve for religious reasons, and several others cited assorted personal calamities that would preclude them from serving on a sequestered jury.

Each side listened closely as the judge questioned the veniremen who were seeking to be excused. The judge's dismissals would not eat up any of either side's strikes.

The woman who had earlier said she didn't know anything about the case repeated that even now, even after being in the courtroom, she still didn't know enough about the case to render a good verdict.

"That's good. We haven't told you anything about it

yet. We don't want you to know anything about it yet,"
said the judge.

"Plus I'm a very weak and nervous person and I'm just
confused and I just don't feel that I'm qualified and that
I'll make the right decision," she said.

"Why is that?" asked the judge.

"It's just something that bothers me."

"Is there something about your religion that would keep
you from doing that? Is it a moral issue?" asked the judge.

"Yeah, it is, it is."

"Or do you feel confused?"

"I just don't feel like I would make the right decision,"
she stammered.

"Let me ask you something, and I don't mean to pry,
but you're not being treated for any mental disorder or
anything like that, are you?" asked the judge.

No, she said. But in response to a question about
whether she would be able to follow the judge's instructions, she said, "That's what I'm afraid of. I wouldn't be
able to do that. I just don't know."

The judge wavered.

Margulis indicated that in his opinion, she'd be a fine
juror. Hoag disagreed.

"She's indicated she's not very healthy. She's indicated
she is confused. She's indicated that she doesn't really
know whether she could follow the Court's instructions,
and she's indicated a problem with the concept of reasonable doubt. I don't think she's qualified."

To the pleasure of the defense, the judge refused to
dismiss her. If Hoag didn't want her on the jury, he would
have to use one of his strikes.

Later that afternoon, voir dire began.

Just as there are baseball fans who enjoy watching bat-
ting practice, there are courtroom observers who find voir
dire fascinating.

These observers compare it to being on a bus, when

you look at your fellow riders and try to guess at the details of their private lives. Are they married or single? What kind of jobs do they have? What kind of horrors has life visited upon them? These are the very things you learn about strangers in voir dire.

Hoag went first. He asked if anyone had served on a jury before. To those who replied affirmatively, he asked more questions.

Civil or criminal? Had the jury reached a verdict?

He was most interested in the replies of those who had served on a criminal jury. To reach a decision in a criminal trial, a unanimous verdict is required. A single person can hang a jury. Hoag would have great reservations about anybody who had served on a hung jury.

Margulis, meanwhile, didn't want anybody who had served on a criminal jury at all. Veniremen who had served on a jury that convicted were convictors. Those who had served on a jury that acquitted probably felt duped. Service on a hung jury produced the same feelings of having been cheated. He wanted virgins.

After going through jury experience, Hoag asked who on the panel had a close friend or relative who had been the victim of violent crime.

Several had.

Had anybody been arrested for the crime? Hoag asked. If so, what eventually happened?

He listened closely to the answers while Moore and the defense attorneys scribbled notes on their pads to discuss later.

The confused woman had a friend who had been beaten to death. Nobody was arrested, as far as she knew.

Another woman's sister-in-law had been murdered. The victim's husband had done it. He had shot her, and he had been convicted of second-degree murder, the woman said. She was a black woman, quiet, matter-of-fact.

The lawyers thought even as they scribbled. This one was a wild card. Angry at the system, maybe? Her relative gets murdered, and it's second-degree. A white woman from New Orleans gets murdered, and it's first-degree. Or would she be bonded into the sisterhood? Hateful of men who hurt women, ready to accept the notion that this plump white man in his business suit had drowned his wife?

Down the line it went. Hoag would ask what had happened, and the lawyers would try to figure out how the potential jurors' experiences would play to the stories that they would soon spin.

Hoag continued with the question that always sounds so prying.

"The next question, and that is, have you yourself, a close friend, or a relative ever been charged with or convicted of a crime?"

Polite but stern, Hoag was not a man to lie to.

"And I'm not getting nitpicky again, but I'm excluding traffic offenses and stuff like that, okay? I'm talking about something you can spend some time in jail with, so let's deal with that. Anybody in the back row?"

A woman's stepbrother had done time on burglary.

"The question I really have, have you formed an opinion one way or another as to whether or not you think he was treated fairly or unfairly by the criminal justice system?" Hoag asked.

"I've not formed any opinion," said the woman.

A man had been convicted of fradulent use of a credit card, but had been given a suspended sentence. He announced emphatically that he had been treated fairly by the system.

Clearly, he was ready to serve. Could he be a born-again law-and-order guy? Or a snake?

The lawyers scribbled their notes.

Next, Hoag talked about life without parole.

"Now is there anyone of you here who feel that perhaps you wouldn't be able to do that, feel that you would not be able to follow that instruction either because you don't believe in that type of punishment?''

The confused woman raised her hand.

"I just don't feel I'm qualified to do that," she said.

Hoag nodded. As far as he was concerned, he had been down to six strikes even before she raised her hand.

But that was okay. He was about to call for the fastball in on the hands, a pitch that was going to be unhittable.

"You're going to hear evidence of an insurance policy, a policy that the defendant or that Mrs. Post had on her. And I'm interested in whether any one of you has policies on themselves, life insurance policies on themselves, or their spouse," he said.

The judge asked everybody to speak up. The acoustics aren't as good as they should be, he said.

So loud and clear, the potential jurors began shouting out how much life insurance they and their spouses had.

Three thousand on me, four thousand on my husband, the first lady said.

Three thousand on my wife, eight thousand on myself, the next man said.

I'd say about ten thousand on my husband and five thousand on myself, said the next woman.

Five thousand on myself, said the next woman.

I have two thousand, said the next man.

I don't really know, said the next woman.

"Do you think you have life insurance?" said Hoag.

"I don't think so. I'm not sure," she said.

And so it went. Some had none. Most had a little.

Ten thousand on the wife and a hundred thousand on myself, announced one of the last veniremen.

When he stated that last figure, somebody whistled in awe. Everybody laughed but Hoag.

Despite his grim demeanor, he was very pleased. These figures were even lower than he had expected. And now everybody would remember these low figures when Post's insurance policies came up.

Margulis and Whalen exchanged glances. To most of these people, $700,000 in life insurance would sound like a motive.

Hoag glanced triumphantly at the defense table as he sat down.

Jury selection was completed the next morning. The group included nine women and three men; six whites and six blacks. Two women and a man were chosen as alternates. Among the jurors was the woman whose son had been shot, the woman whose stepbrother had done time for burglary, and the woman who wasn't sure whether or not she had insurance.

The judge had dismissed the wild-card lady because she was attending school. Actually, Hoag had been going to strike her, anyway. The judge had also dismissed the confused woman.

It was a working-class jury, and although it was hardly a jury of his peers, Post was pleased.

As far as he could tell, this was exactly the jury his team had wanted. The previous afternoon, he had written a favorable note about one of the prospective jurors, the most affluent man on the panel, a management-type guy.

He'd passed the note to Whalen, who then whispered in his ear, "He reminds you of yourself. Do you really want Ed Post on this jury?"

Margulis had used one of his strikes to knock the guy off the panel.

Ten of the twelve jurors were married. Post figured that was good, too. The state was going to try to say he and Julie had not had a good marriage, but married people knew that all marriages had their ups and downs.

The judge was explaining what it would be like to be sequestered. One of the men said he had a problem.

"My wife doesn't believe this sequester business. She thinks I'm just saying it to stay out all night, and play cards."

Everybody laughed, including the judge.

"I'll have a deputy go over to your house and explain that we're making you do this," the judge said.

The judge instructed the jurors to bring their suitcases with them in the morning. Everybody could have the rest of the afternoon off, and the trial would start in the morning.

Post felt exhilarated. He could hardly wait to go back to the hotel and talk to Toni.

Bringing her had been the source of an argument with his lawyers. They had argued that it didn't look right for a grieving husband to bring his girlfriend to St. Louis when standing trial for the murder of his wife.

But Post was adamant. Finally, a compromise was reached. Toni could come to St. Louis, but she would have to stay away from the courtroom.

Post was mildly disappointed that the local media hardly noticed his trial. Most of the attention in the courthouse was being directed to a different courtroom where two young men were being tried for the murders of six people in a grocery store. What made that case particularly interesting was that two other young men had confessed to the murders, but later it turned out that one of them had been in Michigan at the time of the crime. Both young men recanted their confessions and were released. They claimed the police had beaten them.

Chapter Twenty-three

In Hoag's opening statement, he formally recited the facts of the case—"The evidence will show that on the morning of June 3, 1986, at the Omni Hotel in St. Louis, Missouri, at approximately 7:30 A.M. in the morning, a telephone operator received a phone call from room 4063"—and he ended with the pathologist from New Orleans.

"He will tell you that the patterns of bruising are consistent with defensive wounds and are inconsistent with the pattern of bruises you would find in a fall."

While Hoag generally looked as if he'd slept in his clothes, Margulis was immaculate, and the defense attorney's manner, as well as his attire, presented a sharp contrast with that of the prosecutor. Hoag had been matter-of-fact in his opening statement; Margulis was emotional.

He waved away the state's case. He said what was being done to Ed Post, his family, and Julie's family wasn't right. He talked about the relationship Ed had with his in-laws.

"And Hollis, Hollis Thigpen, will tell you this, because he's already testified to it in an earlier proceeding in this trial. 'How could a family with so much love have been hung out to dry like this?' And that's the question you're going to have to answer when you eventually go to deliberate.

"Ladies and gentlemen, I believe when you've heard all of the evidence in this case, the flimsy evidence, the vague evidence, the inconsistent evidence, the circumstantial evidence, and the total lack of evidence, you're going to find that you'll put this tragedy behind these people, find Ed Post innocent, and let these people .get on with their lives.''

As Margulis sat down, Post squeezed his arm.

The rest of the day was uneventful. The maid, a nervous young black woman, testified that she had cleaned the room the day before Julie's death and had not noticed anything wrong with the towel ring.

One of the jurors, a young woman who had once worked at a White Castle hamburger restaurant, found the maid's testimony unconvincing. Nobody ''always'' cleans everything, the juror thought.

Sure enough, Whalen was on the juror's wavelength. Tall and slender, with his neatly trimmed beard and his courtly manner, he approached the witness and gently reminded her that in a previous interview, she had said she didn't ''always'' clean the towel rings.

At first, she said she didn't remember saying that, but when Whalen produced a transcript of a taped interview with McCraw, the maid remembered. She had said she didn't always clean the towel rings.

Whalen was gracious. The interview had been conducted almost two years earlier, he said.

Under further questioning, the maid said that if she had cleaned the towel ring, she would only have wiped it off. She certainly wouldn't have inspected it.

A couple from a nearby room testified that they had not heard any strange noises from the Posts' room.

The switchboard operator said she remembered the voice on the phone as being calm, but when Whalen crossexamined her, she admitted that the man had talked for only a moment.

At the end of the day, the judge admonished the jurors not to discuss the case, and he then turned them over to the sheriff's deputies.

The deputies escorted the jurors to a Holiday Inn, where both jurors and deputies would be staying.

When the jurors gathered for dinner in the hotel restaurant, Deputy Scotty Lammert explained that there would be no unsupervised contact with the outside world, including television. The televisions had been removed from the jurors' rooms. If any of them wanted to watch television, they would have to go a deputy's room.

After dinner, Deputy Kurt Steffen met his pal, Deputy Johnny Molina, in the hotel lounge. Molina was not assigned to the sequestered jury. His job was to guard the empty courthouse at night. So the hotel, just a couple of blocks from the courthouse, was a convenient spot for their nightly rendezvous.

The second day of the trial was a wash.

Two of the paramedics testified about their efforts to revive Julie. The former maintenance director of the hotel testified that there had been no problems with the towel rings prior to Julie's death.

The organ procurement coordinator from the hospital testified that Post had been unemotional—"Whatever you can use I'll agree to"—when asked about organ or tissue donations.

Whalen handled that well in cross-examination.

"You don't know what prior discussions Mr. Post and his wife may have had about organ donations, do you?"

"No sir, I do not," said the witness.

The doctor who performed the bone removal and the nurse who assisted him testified about the procedure.

Post was excused during this graphic testimony.

At about the same time, the agents from the West Bank real estate office flew into St. Louis in preparation for testifying the next morning.

The state sent a police van used to transport prisoners

to the airport to pick them up. To the women, the transportation seemed appropriately tacky.

The whole investigation seemed like something out of a B movie—the overzealous cops, the rumpled prosecutor who always seemed about to explode. No wonder Post had maintained such a scoffing attitude during the investigation.

On the way in from the airport, one of the women pointed out a highway billboard. On the billboard was the smiling face of the Pillsbury Doughboy, Julie's nickname for her husband.

Kim Autin arrived the same day. She flew in with her lawyer and her new boyfriend. Her lawyer had made it very clear to Hoag that Kim was not going to be portrayed as "the other woman."

She had just undergone a very messy divorce.

The next morning was overcast and cool, and the Civil Courts Building, where the trial was being held, looked even more forbidding than usual. Originally, the building had been intended to house civil trials only, but crime had long since outpaced the designers' intent and now the building took care of the overflow from the Municipal Courts Building a block west.

Built in the late 1920s, the structure ran over twenty stories, some measured in half-floors. It was topped off by two sphinxes crouched on the ridge of a penthouse temple set off by Ionic columns. The temple looked as if it had been designed for human sacrifices.

In 1939, Frank Lloyd Wright took one look at the squat high rise and said: "I neither like it nor dislike it. I deplore it."

Ralph Whalen was up early. It would be his task to cross-examine Kim. Because the defense had opted not to depose her, what she was going to say was a mystery.

She was staying with her boyfriend at the Omni Hotel. On her way to the elevator, she walked past room 4063. It gave her the shivers.

The day's first witness was an emergency room physician, Dr. Laurence Lewis. He testified about the futile efforts to resuscitate Julie.

Whalen asked only a couple of questions in cross-examination. The fact that Julie had died was not an issue.

Then Kim Autin came into the courtroom, with her lawyer and her boyfriend. She marched to the witness stand without looking at Post. He stared at her.

Hoag got up slowly.

"State your name for the record, please."

"Kim Autin."

She said she had known Julie socially and professionally. She lived a block from the Posts' house, and she had worked as a real estate agent with Julie.

In addition, she and her husband—her ex-husband now, she said hastily—used to have dinner with Ed and Julie two or three times a month.

"Where did you go to dinner, what kind of places?" Hoag asked.

"Nice restaurants. Expensive."

Hoag asked if Kim had been in Florida at the time of Julie's death, and she said she had been.

"Okay. And did you receive any phone calls on Tuesday, June the 3rd?"

"I received a phone call from Ed Post. I was on the beach. It was about twelve noon, and I didn't return the call," Kim said. She still had not looked at Post.

"And subsequently did you receive another phone call?"

"I had another message when I got back to the condo that he had called again, and it said, 'An emergency, please try calling,' so I tried calling the number and I couldn't get an answer, and I decided to wait to hear from him," Kim said.

"And when did you hear from him?"

"Probably right after I hung up the phone after calling him in St. Louis."

"Okay. And did you go on trips with Mr. and Mrs. Post?"

Whalen felt as if somebody had lobbed a grenade into his foxhole. Hoag had assured the defense attorneys that he did not intend to go into the "other woman" or "battered wife" allegations, but Hoag was an avenging angel, and Whalen knew the type. He had once been one himself.

"Only a trip to San Francisco," said Kim.

Whalen waited for the next question, the explosive question about the bruises Kim had seen, or maybe about the constant fighting on the trip. She had testified to both before the grand jury.

"All right," said Hoag. "And what kind of clothes did Julie wear?"

"Nice clothes. Not terribly expensive, but not cheap."

"Designer clothes?" asked Hoag.

"Some of them," said Kim.

"No further questions," said Hoag.

For a moment, Whalen just sat there. The grenade had not gone off. Hoag had not pulled the pin.

Then Whalen stood up, anxious to get Kim out of the courtroom.

"Miss Autin, did Julie have a better friend than you at the time of her death?"

"I don't think so," said Kim.

"Thank you, ma'am. That's all I have."

As Kim started out of the witness chair, Whalen sat down. It was over.

Hoag was on his feet, motioning Kim back into the witness chair.

"I'm sorry. There was one other area I wanted to get into. I think I forgot."

Whalen leaped to his feet.

"I object," he said.

Mummert called the lawyers to the bench.

Hoag spoke first.

"I wanted to ask her about the work situation and whether Julie caused a problem, and I apologize to the Court, but I forgot and I'm asking leave of Court to reopen, okay?"

Mummert overruled Whalen's objection, although, really, the work situation didn't bother Whalen at all. Everybody was going to testify that Julie was a problem at work.

Hoag asked about Julie's conduct and attitude at the office.

Kim testified that Julie was a "pretty big problem" at work and that Julie had "an opinion about everything, and whether it was wanted or not, she gave it."

Whalen didn't bother to cross-examine her again. The grenade still hadn't gone off.

But still, he was upset by Hoag's tactics—that business about "forgetting" had been done just to annoy him—and things got worse during the testimony of the next witness, Gerald Arbini.

When Arbini said that he no longer worked for the Omni Hotel and had turned down a transfer, Hoag asked, "Your roots are in St. Louis, and you intend to stay here, is that correct?"

"That's correct," said Arbini.

Whalen objected to the leading form of the question.

Before the judge could rule, Hoag was asking something else and smirking at Whalen.

Whalen asked for a conference at the bench.

"Judge, I don't want to be a horse's rear end about this leading-question business, but what I resent is when I object to a question of his, and then he asks a fairly proper question, and gives me a look in front of the jury like 'Is that okay?' You know, a look of disgust."

"Well, let me say this—" Hoag started saying to the judge.

"Just don't look at me!" said Whalen.

Mummert nodded. Lawyers can be like children.

"I haven't noticed the looks, but if you're doing it, Dean, stop."

"There's only been one," said Hoag.

As he walked back to continue questioning Arbini, he was tempted to look at Whalen, but he didn't.

Arbini testified that the temperature of the water had not been hot when he picked up the towel ring. In fact, it had been almost cold.

After lunch, Arbini's secretary testified that no one had gone into Arbini's office from the time he returned with the towel ring from room 4063 until the time Officer Tim Kaelin came to pick it up.

Kaelin was the next witness. Medium height with a muscular build, he walked with a slight swagger, as if to overcome the discomfort he felt about the testimony he was going to give. He considered himself street-smart. He had recently been transferred to a detective division, and he was embarrassed that he had been fooled by Post's story. But he was a good witness, and calmly answered Hoag's questions about the morning of Julie's death.

Margulis handled the cross-examination and went right to the chain-of-evidence question.

"How do you know that the towel ring in the bottom of the bathtub is the same towel ring that you picked up off the desk in Mr. Arbini's office?"

"Other than what I was told, I have no way of knowing," said Kaelin.

"So other than the fact that somebody may have told you that it was the same towel ring, the truth is you don't know?"

"That's correct," said Kaelin.

Calm and matter-of-fact, Kaelin was wise enough to know that if he tried to pretend a knowledge he didn't have, Margulis would hammer him.

"Did you have a conversation with Detective Beffa later on?" Margulis asked.

This was the question Kaelin had been dreading.

"Yes sir."

"Did you tell him you thought it was an accident?"

"Yes sir."

"I have nothing further," said Margulis.

Still outwardly composed, but inwardly seething, Kaelin left the witness stand. Post gave him a friendly nod as he walked out.

After Kaelin left the courtroom, he exploded. "That guilty little sleazeball!" he said.

The agents from New Orleans and Dianne Kreeger were sitting on a bench outside the courtroom. They couldn't help but hear Kaelin's comment.

A few minutes later, the judge called a short recess, and when Post went into the hallway, he smiled and went over to the women.

"It's going great," he said. "There hasn't been a single witness who's said anything bad. Even that young policeman is on my side. He knows I'm innocent."

Dianne Kreeger took Post by the arm and told him that the young policeman most certainly did not believe that he was innocent, but Post just smiled as if he didn't hear her.

Harby Kreeger was the next witness.

"What kind of a person is Ed?" asked Hoag.

"I would say he has a zest and love for life common to few," said Kreeger, not confused at all about his loyalty. "He has been an absolutely marvelous friend to me in times that I needed him, and I think he has that reputation with all his friends. He is obviously bright and has a tremendous outlook on life that has stood him in stead in times that have been hard for him, certainly not the least of which is the last two or three years which is the result of this court."

"Is he a person who is prone to detail or one that is not so prone to detail?"

"Meticulous," boomed Kreeger.

"What was the word?" asked Hoag.

"Meticulous," repeated Kreeger.

He was almost as effusive about Julie.

"Julie was very frank. I admired that in her. She's the kind of person to tell you exactly . . . you knew where you stood with her. That frankness and that honesty probably at times was hard on some people. A lot of us maybe like to hear what we want to hear rather than what the truth is."

What kind of family life did the Posts have?

"Absolutely normal!" declared Kreeger.

He seemed a strange state's witness, and when he left the stand, he stopped for a moment to put his hand on Post's shoulder.

The real estate people followed in quick order.

Ben Matthews testified that Julie had caused problems at the office, but he also said that the situation had improved before the trip to St. Louis.

Jo Harsdorff said that Julie was "abrasive and arrogant, but an excellent agent."

The other producers weren't as strong. Julie did cause problems, they said, but she was not unbearable.

At the end of the day, Post had reason to feel good.

One spectator did not share his good feelings. One of the grand jurors, an older well-to-do woman who had become absolutely immersed in the case, felt awful. All of the details that had seemed so important to her were being omitted. The people from New Orleans had been so much more effective in front of the grand jury. Kim had been a thousand times stronger. The grand juror was very disappointed.

"They'll never convict him if they don't know the truth about that marriage," she said.

When a reporter mentioned to Whalen that the first couple of days had gone pretty well for the defense, Whalen smiled and told a story about a case in which he'd defended a jockey who was accused of throwing a race.

"Everybody said things were going great—and then the jury convicted him," Whalen said.

The same reporter tried to talk to Hoag, but the prosecutor had nothing to say.

That night, after dinner, Deputy Lammert hosted a card game with beer and liquor in his hotel room. Several deputies not assigned to the case dropped by. Two or three of the jurors came, as well.

Chapter Twenty-four

Steve Jacobsmeyer was the first witness on Saturday morning.

Hoag asked him if he had taped an interview with Post, and Jacobsmeyer said he had.

The tape was then played for the jury. The part in which Jacobsmeyer asked Post if he would consent to a lie detector test had been deleted. Just as a lie detector test is inadmissible in court, the jury is not allowed to know if a defendant refused to take one.

While the tape played, the defense lawyers carefully studied the jurors. None of the jurors displayed any emotion when Post described his wife as "dead weight."

In cross-examination, Whalen asked if the Omni Hotel had paid for the rooms in New Orleans in which Jacobsmeyer and Hollocher had stayed.

Jacobsmeyer said the police department had paid for the rooms.

"You're sure of that?" Whalen asked.

"Yes sir," said the detective.

The next witness was Bob Masson, Post's insurance agent.

He was firmly in Post's corner. He explained that Ed and Julie Post had a long history of updating their life insurance, and he vigorously defended the decision to provide Julie with $700,000 of life insurance despite the fact that her income was only $28,000.

She was a lovely individual, he said.

"Well, I might think my wife is worth fifty million dollars, okay, but that doesn't mean I go out and insure her for fifty million," Hoag said, arguing with his own witness.

When Hoag turned him over to Margulis for cross-examination, Masson cheerfully volunteered that it had been his idea, not Ed's, to increase the Posts' life insurance, and furthermore, he had suggested insuring Julie for a million. Ed had turned the idea down.

The final witness of the day was George Leggio, the man from Equifax. He explained that his job involved obtaining information for insurance companies before claims are paid.

In this instance, he said, he went to talk to Ed Post about Julie's health history.

The back rub, drawing the bath, kissing goodbye, the whole story started spilling out, Leggio said.

"I mentioned two or three times that all of the specific details weren't really necessary, because we were not looking into the circumstances of her death, only the health history. But he volunteered, you know, all these other details.

"He said he returned about thirty minutes later and found her facedown in the bathtub, and that he had tried to get her out of the tub two or three times, but because of the bubble bath, it was slippery and in the process of trying to pick her up, he said she fell back into the tub and finally he was able to get her up on the edge of the tub, and then out of the tub—at which time she again slipped and slid across the floor and her temple hit either a pipe or the base part of the lavatory.

"He said that later, the police had notified him that a towel ring was found in the bottom of the bathtub."

Hoag stood with his arms folded across his chest and pretended to look puzzled.

"The police had notified him about that?"

"Yes," said Leggio.

To Hoag, this was an important moment. According to Beverly Minor, Post had shown *her* the towel ring before the police even arrived. Kaelin had testified that Post had shown him the towel ring and had offered it as an explanation for Julie's accident. In very few instances was Hoag able to show that Post had lied.

That night, with no court scheduled for the next morning, there was another party in Deputy Lammert's room. Other deputies came, and again a couple of jurors.

One of the jurors drank too much, and Deputy Johnny Molina, who was visiting his pal Deputy Kurt Steffen, cheerfully led the juror back to his room.

As far as the lawyers on both sides were concerned, the first week had been a good one for the defense. One part of the state's case, the insurance angle, had been largely discredited. In addition, the state's witnesses from New Orleans seemed to be, for the most part, on Post's side.

But what was going on under the surface was, as always, much harder to figure.

Had Hoag convinced the jury that Julie was a bitch? Did the tape make Ed sound like a guy who was trying to cooperate with the investigation? Or did he come off as a man trying to buffalo the cops?

The first three witnesses Monday morning had nothing significant to say. A real estate conventioneer who had had the room down the hall said he had heard nothing unusual from the Posts' room. A paramedic testified about the efforts to resuscitate Julie. The emergency room nurse testified about similar efforts at the hospital.

Then came Charles Gay, the fire fighter whom Post had noticed during his early-morning jog.

Technically, Gay's testimony was absolutely meaningless. He testified that he worked at City Hall and would have been arriving at work at approximately the time Post claimed to have seen him.

But at a deeper level, he was considered an important witness. Hoag was convinced that a normal person jogging through a strange city would not have paid attention to a name tag on a uniform. Only if a person was trying to establish an alibi would he note such a detail.

To remind the jurors that Post had paid attention to a name tag, Hoag had called Gay as a witness—even though Gay's testimony actually corroborated Post's story.

Whalen stood up to cross-examine Gay.

"I don't want to make you mad, but do people ever pick on you about your last name?" Whalen asked.

"As far back as I can remember," said Gay.

With a smile to the jury, Whalen sat down.

Dalton Truax was the first important witness of the day. The state needed to portray Post as a man beset with financial problems. Truax's testimony was to be a big part of that portrait.

Truax nodded at Post as he settled into the witness chair.

He said he had been in the real estate business for thirty-one years. He and a partner had established a brokerage in 1960—residential, commercial, and property management.

In 1983, he reorganized the business and split the residential part of the company from the commercial and property management. That's when Post joined him, he testified.

"He was a branch manager for one of my competitors, and he was very successful at what he was doing. He had an excellent reputation in the community, and was very active in many facets of the business. He came to me when he realized that I had bought my former partner out," Truax said.

He explained that Post had paid $10,000 for 10 percent of the company, and was therefore entitled to 10 percent of the profits—except there had not been any.

Instead, the company had lost more than $200,000. Post

had been responsible for 10 percent of that loss. He had
kicked in more than $20,000 in two years.

And what was his salary? Hoag asked.

"Mr. Post had a base salary of fifty thousand dollars.
In addition to that, we had an automobile allowance of
six thousand dollars, an entertainment allowance of three
thousand dollars, and hospital and life insurance benefits
totaling another two thousand dollars. Finally, an allowance for trips and miscellaneous business for two thousand
dollars."

A total package, then, of $63,000.

Asked to describe his decision to terminate Post's contract, Truax seemed to address Post almost apologetically.

"Ed has a tremendous amount of ability. He really
does. I have no problems with that. I just felt like I needed
someone who was really going to grab the people on a
one-on-one basis a little more, and spend more time at
that level."

Whalen handled the cross-examination.

He approached Truax in a friendly manner, as if he
considered the realtor to be another witness for the state
who was really sympathetic to the defense.

Wasn't Ed named Realtor of the Year in 1985, and
hadn't he received that award shortly before going to St.
Louis?

Yes, Truax said.

"If I understood your testimony correctly, you never
told Ed Post that you intended to end this partnership prior
to June the 3rd of 1986?"

No, said Truax.

Whalen then turned to the matter of the business losing
money.

"While all this is going on, while Ed's contributing
twenty thousand dollars or so, are you having to make
your ninety percent contribution and therefore putting in
about two hundred thousand dollars?"

Absolutely, Truax said.

"Intending no disrespect, Dalton, but did you ever plot to kill your wife during that period?"

Of course not, said Truax.

The final witness of the day was Mike McCraw. Like most homicide detectives, he was an experienced witness. He appeared relaxed and composed as he took the stand.

Steve Moore handled the questioning for the state. The questions pertained to the towel ring and the chain of evidence. Had the towel ring ever left the property room of the police department without McCraw's authorization?

No, at least not until it was signed over to the circuit attorney's office for use in that office's testing, McCraw said.

Moore asked no questions about McCraw's trip to New Orleans.

Whalen stood up slowly for cross-examination. So far in the trial, the jurors had heard no references to any allegations of police misconduct. Several people, most notably Harby Kreeger and Hollis Thigpen, claimed that Hollocher had lied and bullied his way around in New Orleans. They also claimed that the police report, authored by McCraw, had misrepresented their statements.

It was clear the state had no intention of calling Hollocher to the stand. The defense lawyers had toyed with the idea of calling him themselves. But he was too unpredictable, and whatever he said would be negative toward the defense.

Even though the lawyers were sure they could make Hollocher look bad, he'd certainly get in a few knocks of his own.

That left McCraw, and unfortunately, he was a much more difficult target.

"You called this investigation 'kind of botched from the beginning,' didn't you?" asked Whalen, referring to McGraw's testimony in front of the grand jury.

"Yes, I did make that statement," answered McCraw, "not referring to my own investigation, sir."

"With regard to your own investigation," said Whalen, "did you ever direct the evidence technician to take any fingerprints in that room?"

"No, I did not," said McCraw.

"Did you ever direct him to take any fingerprints from the towel ring?"

"No, I did not."

"Did you ever ask him to check the tub or the edge of the tub for any scrapings of skin, hair, fibers, et cetera?"

"I did not give those directions," said McCraw casually.

He's doing fine, thought Hoag.

"You've told the ladies and gentlemen of the jury that State's Exhibit 1 is, in fact, the towel ring from room 4063, haven't you?" Whalen asked.

"Yes, I have," said McCraw.

"You don't know that, though, do you?"

"I believe it is, yes," said McCraw.

"You *believe* it," said Whalen. "Do you *know* it?"

"Yes, I do know it."

Whalen stepped back, puzzled.

"You do know it?"

"Yes," said McCraw.

Whalen nodded. This was to his liking. A small matter perhaps to the spectators, but to a defense attorney, this kind of exchange could plant the seed in a juror's mind. The cops are lying.

"You took it out of room 4063?" asked Whalen.

"No, I did not," said McCraw, still casual, unperturbed.

"When did you first lay eyes on it?"

"I first laid eyes on it on June 17th," said McCraw.

"That's two weeks after the incident occurred?" asked Whalen.

"That's correct," said McCraw, a little uneasily.

"But you *know absolutely* as a *matter of fact* that that's the same towel ring?"

"Yes," said McCraw. In for a dime, in for a dollar.

"Okay," said Whalen, turning toward the jury. "And how do you know?"

"Chain of custody through the police department," said McCraw.

"But all that assumes that the towel ring that Officer Kaelin picked up was the towel ring from 4063, and Officer Kaelin didn't take it from 4063, did he?"

"No, he did not," said McCraw.

"And you don't know what happened to it before it got on Jerry Arbini's desk, do you?"

"No, I don't," admitted McCraw.

"Do you *know* that's the towel ring from 4063?"

"No," said McCraw.

And with that, Monday's testimony concluded.

The towel rings used at the Omni Hotel were two-piece. A baseplate attached to the wall, and the second piece, the towel ring assembly, was attached to it. The towel ring assembly included a bracket that screwed into the baseplate. Welded to the bracket was a post. The circular towel ring fitted through a hole in the post.

The entire towel ring assembly had been found in the bathtub. The baseplate had remained securely attached to the wall.

Tuesday, the state began presenting its evidence concerning the towel ring. The owner and the manager of Industrial Testing Laboratories testified first.

Static load, dynamic force, kinetic energy. The words seemed to run together. Moore asked the questions for the state. Whalen conducted the cross-examination for the defense.

The basic message from the state was that a 130-pound woman could not have caused the towel ring to come off the wall in a slip-and-fall accident.

In the afternoon, a videotape of the testing procedures was shown.

In the hot, stuffy courtroom—the St. Louis weather, always unpredictable, had turned unseasonably warm, and the old window air conditioner was too loud to be run constantly—the videotape seemed to run on and on.

Even the judge grew bored, and finally he called the lawyers to the bench and directed that the tape be fast-forwarded.

"I understand you've got to show your testimony, but this is out of hand," he said. "There's no need to watch them prepare for the tests. Let's just show the actual tests."

Hoag sulked back to his chair.

Finally, the tape was over, and Whalen rose for cross-examination.

"Are you aware that one of the experts hired by the prosecution referred to these tests that we've seen today as, quote, *terrible*?" he asked.

It seemed a fitting way to end the day.

Wednesday had more promise, Michael Graham, the pathologist who had conducted the initial autopsy, was scheduled to testify.

The first witness of the day, though, was like a mystery guest on a television show.

Ashton Phelps, Jr., the publisher of the *New Orleans Times-Picayune*, was known to his irreverent staff as "Half Ash." He looked at Hoag with obvious distaste, as if he couldn't figure out why he had been summoned to St. Louis.

He testified that he knew Post only slightly from attending real estate functions. He said it in a way that implied the two were from different levels of society. He recalled Post calling him on the day of Julie's death to inquire about an obituary.

"And did you write one?" Hoag asked.

Phelps shook his head. "I'm what you would call the 'nonworking press,' " he said.

Phelps was followed by Boulter Kelsey, the accident reconstruction engineer.

"It's my opinion that this was removed from the wall in a deliberate fashion by an individual standing outside the tub. The individual that removed it pulled outward with considerable force in a jerking fashion and reversed that force because there are signs of force reversal on the assembly."

Finally came medical examiner Michael Graham. Dark-haired, and of average height and build, he looked as pale as the bodies he worked on.

He explained the procedures by which he had determined that Julie had died by drowning. He described the injuries he had noted at the first autopsy.

The most significant were a large bruise on the back of her head and an abrasion on her right temple. In response to a question from Hoag, Graham said it was his opinion that the bruise on the back of her head did not result from a blow serious enough to cause her to lose consciousness. He said he based this on the fact that when he had opened her skull, he had found no traces of bleeding on the surface of the brain.

Under state law, he had been required to classify her death, he said. Because it was clearly not from natural causes, the choices were homicide, suicide, accidental, or undetermined.

He said he had chosen undetermined.

"I was not comfortable certifying the death as a homicide. I was also uncomfortable calling it an accident. I saw no evidence at all that it's suicide," he explained.

Even after the second autopsy, he remained unconvinced, he said.

Certainly, there were additional bruises, and the sheer number of the bruises would be hard to reconcile with a slip-and-fall accident, he said.

There was a cluster of bruising on the right arm that could have been caused by someone grabbing the arm.

"The one that gave me the most difficulty was the one low on the right side of the head," he said.

That bruise had been missed during the initial autopsy, Graham told the jurors, because the scalp had been peeled back farther in the second autopsy.

Hoag asked if that particular bruise could have been caused by the pressure of a hand holding Julie's head down in the tub.

"I couldn't say that's what caused it," he said.

"Could it have been caused by such an act?" Hoag prodded.

"It's consistent with that, but it's certainly not specific for that," Graham said.

"Did the results of the second autopsy alter your opinion one way or another as to your ultimate finding?" Hoag asked.

"Not substantially. She died of drowning. As far as the manner of death, it's still undetermined."

"Okay. That's all I have," Hoag said resignedly.

Whalen didn't want to do anything to denigrate Graham. It was damn near sensational that the state's own pathologist flatly refused to call Julie's death a homicide. The real problem would come with Dr. Death, the canny old pathologist from New Orleans whom Whalen knew from his days as a prosecutor.

Very tenderly, Whalen took Graham bruise by bruise through the second autopsy. Could this bruise have come from a slip and fall? How about this one?

Individually, sure, Graham said. But not all of them from one accident.

Whalen returned to safe ground.

"How many homicides do you think you've classified in your career?" Whalen asked.

"Hundreds," responded Graham.

"And do you have doubts about classifying this one as a homicide?"

Graham sighed.

"Obviously. Otherwise, I would have classified it as a homicide," he said.

"Thank you, Doctor," Whalen said.

When the trial recessed for the night, Post approached a newspaper reporter. He seemed concerned about something.

"Graham helped you," the reporter said.

Post nodded. "Yeah, but what do you think about Ashton?"

It seemed a strange question. Frankly, Phelps had seemed put out by the fact that this relatively minor figure in New Orleans had been nervy enough to call him about an obituary. Post seemed concerned about the slighting attitude of the publisher.

"Actually, it made you look a bit pretentious, that's all," the reporter said. "People don't call publishers about obituaries. Maybe if you're a big shot, you call an editor. Nobody calls the publisher."

Post thought about that for a second.

"If I'm going to go to a restaurant, I don't call the maître d' for a reservation. I call the owner. That's just me."

Indeed. Before Post had come to St. Louis for his convention, he had called the owner of the city's most exclusive restaurant to request a reservation.

He didn't get it.

Very early the next morning, Steve Moore's father died. The day's proceedings were canceled, and the jury was taken on an outing to the zoo.

Chapter Twenty-five

The trial resumed Friday morning with more expert testimony about the towel rings.

Frank DeRonja, a former FBI agent, and William Weins, the professor from Nebraska, both testified that they had studied the damage done to the towel ring assembly and had concluded that the deformation in the metal could not have been caused by a slip-and-fall accident. Torque had been applied. The assembly had been twisted and pulled off the wall plate.

Nevertheless, DeRonja was a big disappointment for the state.

During the long pretrial investigation, he had been the most impressive of the towel ring experts. A former member of the metallurgy department at Columbia University, he had spent twenty years in the lab with the FBI.

He retired in 1986 and started his own firm, Forensic Metallurgy Associates.

"Every piece of metal has a history," he had told Moore. "Through microscopic analysis, I can read that history, and tell you what forces caused the deformation you're talking about."

Indeed, his analysis had seemed crisp.

By pulling and twisting, one way and then another, he had managed to very nearly duplicate the deformation present on the towel ring.

So he promised to be a very good witness.

But he wasn't. He just couldn't connect with the jury.

A small man with gray hair and glasses, he seemed too eager to help the prosecution.

When Whalen asked about his fee, which had come to more than $11,000, DeRonja said, with perhaps too much pride, that as a former FBI agent, he always gave a discount to law enforcement agencies.

Eventually, his testimony seemed absurd.

"Had you been standing in an actual bathtub when you did these things that you did on the videotape," Whalen asked in cross-examination, "and that bathtub would have been filled with water, would you have soaked your feet, your shoes and your socks?"

Nobody had noticed Post's shoes or socks being wet.

DeRonja danced around the question. He had not been standing in a tub, he told Whalen.

"But had you been standing in a tub filled with water, would you have gotten your feet wet?" Whalen asked.

Again, DeRonja danced around the question.

Finally, in exasperation, the judge interrupted the proceedings.

"Let me try," he said.

"Please, Judge. Thank you," said Whalen.

A couple of the jurors were grinning.

"If the tub was filled with water, and you were standing in it, would you have gotten your feet wet?" Mummert asked the witness.

DeRonja seemed to sigh.

"If I were standing in water, obviously I would get my feet wet," he said.

That evening, at what had now become a nightly gathering in a deputy's room, Molina teased the three jurors who were present. "I hear the towel ring testimony is boring," he said.

"Shut up, Johnny!" said Janet Sullivan, the female deputy assigned to the trial.

Molina laughed and grabbed another beer from the trash can the deputies were using as a cooler.

Saturday was the day for Dr. Death.

Although the towel ring testimony had been boring, and DeRonja had been disappointing, Hoag and Moore both felt that the momentum had begun to swing in their favor.

From the beginning, it had been Hoag's contention that if the jury believed that the towel ring had been worked off the wall, the state would be more than halfway home.

But even if the jury believed that somebody had torn the ring from the wall and that Post was the one who had done it—despite the missing link in the chain of evidence—there was still nothing to show that Julie had been murdered.

Paul McGarry's job was to eliminate any doubts about an accident.

As he settled into the witness stand, he glanced briefly at Whalen, who gave him a slight nod.

"Let's go through, Doctor, the external examination that you made, detailing for the jury your observations," said Hoag.

"When I first saw the body," said McGarry, "I described a young woman, already embalmed, measuring five feet three inches long, enclosed in plastic containers, and having dark brown hair, having the eyes removed, having teeth in good condition, having the incision of a previous autopsy, plus incisions over her arms and legs where bones had been removed, and having numerous discolorations of the skin. These indicated blunt injuries."

He spoke in his deep, emotionless monotone.

"These I could see over the face, the forehead, around the right eye, over the temples, on the shoulders, on the back, on the chest, in the right groin area, over the hips, elbows, knees, back of the right hand, behind the thighs.

"I counted thirty-nine areas of blunt injury characterized by bruising of the tissue."

He then described how he cut into the areas of discoloration, so as to later observe, under a microscope, the internal aspects of the apparent injuries.

Hoag asked what such an examination could reveal.

The nature and age of the injury, replied McGarry.

"How are you able to determine the age of a bruise?" inquired Hoag.

"A person's body is bruised at the moment of impact. A bruise is a physical force going against tissue that causes breaking of the blood vessels. The small blood vessels break open and release blood into the tissue. That's what a bruise is, a disruption of tissue with no opening up of the area which would occur in a laceration," said McGarry.

Whalen looked at the jurors. They seemed to be paying rapt attention to McGarry.

"At the moment of the bruising, if the person dies, or within a few minutes of that time, that's all that is seen under the microscope—tissue with broken blood vessels and blood released into a red area of hemorrhage in the tissue.

"But if a person lives, sometime afterward then there is a reaction on the part of the body as it attempts to respond to that injury. And this is the process of inflammation, the process of repair that occurs after an injury. And what happens is the area becomes swollen. The blood in the tissue changes. Inflammatory cells come into the area, and all of that I can see under the microscope."

Hoag nodded.

"All right. Now let's go through your microscopic examination as it appears in your report. And, if you will, indicate what area we're talking about, what responses you noted, and the significance of what you noted."

Bruise by bruise, McGarry reported his findings. Starting with his examination of Julie's head, he noted the large bruise on the back of the head that had been evident at the first autopsy; the twin bruises at the lower back of the head he had uncovered during the second autopsy; a bruise over the bridge of the nose; another over the right eyelid; another on the right forehead; and two on the right temple, including one that appeared to be the result of scraping rather than blunt injury.

As he detailed each bruise, he reported finding no inflammatory reaction.

"Let me ask you, Doctor, the significance of that particular observation," Hoag asked.

"The significance is that the injury occurred very shortly before death. There was no time for the body to have any reaction to it. All there was is the bruise itself, the bleeding into the tissue," McGarry responded.

Down the body he continued. Bruising on the chest, the right shoulder, the right arm, the right forearm, the back of the right hand, the right hip, the right groin area, the right knee, the right leg.

Occasionally, he reported signs of inflammation, indicating that the bruise had not occurred in the moments before death.

Of the thirty-nine areas of discoloration, three showed signs of inflammation.

Then Hoag handed McGarry a photograph that McGarry had taken during the second autopsy and asked McGarry to identify it.

"This is a photograph of the right side of the head of Julie Post in which the areas of bruising and skin injury over the right forehead, right temple, right eye, and base of nose are evident."

Seven more photographs followed.

These photographs would be presented to the jury at the end of the state's case. They were morbid, graphic pictures of a body that had been buried for more than a month. The skin had started to shrivel. Rough stitching ran up and down Julie's arms and legs where the bones had been removed and replaced by wooden dowels. The same kind of stitching crisscrossed Julie's chest, where Dr. Graham had made his incisions to enter the body cavity during the first autopsy.

As the jurors looked at the photographs, they would be reminded that this was not a clinical courtroom exercise. This was what had become of a thirty-nine-year-old mother.

After McGarry identified the photographs, Hoag moved to the heart of his questioning.

"With respect to the bruises, do you view them separately or together in determining the cause and manner of death?"

"I look at each bruise separately as an individual area of abnormality, and examine and study each one by itself. And then I consider them all together," McGarry responded.

"Was the pattern, distribution, and arrangement of bruises and injuries that you observed consistent with Julie Post having fallen in the bathtub?" Hoag asked.

"No sir," said McGarry.

"Having fallen across or against a wall and then into the bathtub?" asked Hoag sarcastically, letting the jurors know—as if they didn't already—exactly what he thought of Whalen's contention, brought out in the cross-examination of the state's towel ring experts, that the distortion of the towel ring could be explained by Julie's falling one way and then another.

"No sir," said McGarry.

Almost finished, Hoag referred McGarry to the two bruises on the back of the head that had been discovered during the second autopsy.

"Where exactly are they located?"

"One is on the left at the lower part of the back of head where the rounded part of the head goes in and meets the neck. And it's the smaller of the two. One is on a sort of matching area on the back of the right side underneath the curve of the back of the head where the top of the neck reaches the head. And it's larger, two inches or so in diameter,'' McGarry said.

"Can you say what, if anything, those two bruises viewed in conjunction could be consistent with?" Hoag asked.

"They are indicative that injuries were inflicted on both sides of the back of the head in a forceful pressing of the head, either by some object pressed against the head or the head pressed against some other object. The configuration indicates that pressure was from both sides and did not cross the midline," McGarry said.

"As in someone holding someone underneath the water?" asked Hoag.

Whalen leaped to his feet.

"Objection as leading, your honor,"

"Sustained," said Mummert.

Hoag whirled to the judge.

"I think I can lead. He's an expert witness, your honor. I think the rules allow it."

"Overruled, overruled," said Mummert, correcting himself.

Hoag turned back to his witness, delighted he could ask the damning question a second time. And he did so, slowly.

"As in someone holding someone underneath the water?"

"That configuration could be the configuration of a thumb on one side and fingers on the other side, making a small and a large bruise," said McGarry.

"Doctor, were you able to form an opinion within a reasonable degree of medical certainty as to the manner of death of Julie Post?"

"Yes," said McGarry. "I think there are multiple injuries inflicted on several different parts of the body, most of them shortly before she died, or at the time that she was in the process of dying, and that they were not inflicted by her falling, but they were inflicted by another individual."

"The result of her death was a homicide?" Hoag asked.

"That's for you to decide. I decide only if this is the action of one person against another."

"And so she died at the hands of another?" Hoag asked.

"Yes," said McGarry.

"I have nothing further," said Hoag.

The judge called a ten-minute recess.

All in all, Whalen didn't think it had gone too badly. At least it hadn't gone any worse than he had expected. McGarry was a damn fine witness. If Dr. Death had a weakness, he was *too* favorable to the prosecution. In this case, he might have overstated things. As far as the defense was concerned, better that he found thirty-nine bruises rather than ten. At least some of the thirty-nine bruises could be attacked.

Which is what Whalen sought to do in cross-examination.

"Of the thirty-nine bruises that you've described, you would attribute *zero* to any medical procedure?" Whalen asked.

"I wouldn't attribute any of the ones that I described to medical procedures, no sir," said McGarry.

"And of the thirty-nine that you've described, you would attribute *zero* to any resuscitative efforts?"

"I didn't include the resuscitative injuries in those thirty-nine injuries," said McGarry.

"Is it fair to say, Doctor, that a number of these bruises that you've described are in the area of the long bone donations?"

McGarry resisted as well as he could, but several of the bruises were, in fact, in areas where the bones had been removed.

The bruise in the groin, for instance. The incision for the bone removal went right through the bruise.

"It just happens to be right over the incision, is that right?" asked Whalen incredulously.

The dowel inserted into the right elbow went directly through the bruise McGarry had identified in the elbow area.

"It has a dowel projecting through it?" Whalen asked in the same tone.

There was also a bruise on the chest that Graham, in his testimony, had suggested that he had caused in the course of the first autopsy.

"If the doctor who performed the original autopsy were of the opinion that he had caused that in the first autopsy, would you disagree with that?"

"Yes," said McGarry.

"If Dr. Graham testified before this jury that in his opinion the discoloration around the right eye was due to the removal of the eye for transplant purposes, would you disagree?"

"Yes," said McGarry.

And so it went for about fifteen minutes, with Whalen picking selected bruises and suggesting that explanations other than "the hands of another" could have caused them.

McGarry remained firm, as Whalen had known he would.

Finally, Whalen asked about the bruises on the lower back of Julie's head.

"As to the bruising on the back of the lower neck, I believe you told Mr. Hoag that that's consistent with someone being pushed from the back. Isn't it consistent with any number of other things, Doctor?"

"Not that I could easily come up with," shrugged McGarry.

"So the only thing you can think of to explain those bruises is someone pushing her head from the back?" Whalen asked. Again, he sounded incredulous.

"It could be a thumb and a hand pushing from behind," said McGarry. "It would not be the part of her head that would hit the floor as she fell. *If* she fell. Because it's in an indentation. Just like the eye injuries, some of the injuries are in naturally protected areas that don't hit the floor when a person falls.''

"Did you see any indication of four separate areas of bruising on the larger side?"

"No sir," said McGarry.

"Such as fingers might cause?"

"Well, it's an irregular configuration. It wasn't in four separate individual fingerlike imprints," said McGarry.

"So if Dr. Graham said that that was consistent with a number of other things, you'd disagree with that, too?" asked Whalen.

"I can't agree with that unless I know what that 'number of other things' is that he's thinking about. I think of something going into that area with great force at the same time or near the same time, smaller in size on the left, larger in size on the right. I would have a hard time thinking of any number of things that would do that," said McGarry.

"Did I just hear you say *great* force?"

"Well, great enough to injure tissue. Great is a little hard to define," said McGarry.

"I did hear you say *great* force, didn't I, Dr. McGarry?"

"I'm not sure whether I used that or not. If I used it, I guess you heard it," said McGarry, seemingly defensive for the first time.

"Do you have an opinion as to whether or not that blow was sufficient to cause unconsciousness?" asked Whalen.

"I don't think it did," said McGarry, finally realizing where Whalen was going.

"Okay. And how is it that pathologists normally determine whether or not a blow was sufficient to cause unconsciousness?"

"It depends on the location of the blow, how much damage it does to the tissue, whether it injures the brain in any way. Any unconsciousness would result from damage to the brain itself. Damage to the scalp does not cause unconsciousness.''

Whalen paused. He looked at the jury, and then back at McGarry.

''Dr. McGarry, were you able to see the brain of Julie Post?''

''No,'' said McGarry.

Whalen pretended to reflect on that for a minute. If unconsciousness depends on damage to the brain, and McGarry had been unable to see the brain because it had been removed in the first autopsy, then how could he have an opinion as to whether or not a particular blow could have caused unconsciousness?

''No further questions,'' said Whalen.

Dan Post was next.

Like the rest of the Post and Thigpen families, Dan and his wife, Martha, were staying at the swank Adam's Mark Hotel. To Dan, the mood of the entourage seemed curiously upbeat.

Because all the family members had been endorsed as witnesses, none was allowed to view the trial. Consequently, Ed gave them daily updates, which bordered on exultant. The state's case was not simply falling apart, it had never come together.

This interpretation was somewhat reinforced by the defense attorneys. Although they were more cautious than Ed, they seemed optimistic.

As a result, the group easily maintained a cheerful front. Their dinners, usually at the city's most expensive restaurants, were marked with laughter and much talk about the future.

The only discordant note was Ed's fixation that the state had bugged his hotel room. To a casual observer, it looked as if he and Toni had moved in. Their clothes overflowed from the closet onto a department-store rack. They had brought a CD and a VCR with them from New Orleans.

But it was uncomfortable visiting their room. Whenever a visitor asked anything about the trial, Ed would shake his head and point toward the ceiling.

"Somebody's listening," he would say.

Dan found that hard to believe, and he wondered if his brother's imagination could be coloring his opinion about the progress of the trial.

Prior to testifying, Dan had been told by the defense attorneys that Hoag seemed uninterested in any history of abuse between Ed and Julie. Neither of the Kreegers had been asked a single question about the incident to which they had testified before the grand jury.

Nevertheless, Dan was nervous as he took his seat on the witness stand. He nodded at his younger brother and then awaited Hoag.

The prosecutor asked him if he had taken photographs on the day of Julie's death, and he said he had.

The two men sparred briefly about the building the Post brothers partially owned, with Hoag pointing out that it didn't produce any income and Dan arguing that even without income it was valuable as a tax write-off.

Then Hoag sat down. Margulis asked Dan to describe his brother's state of mind since Julie's death.

"He's been heartbroken," said Dan.

Under questioning from Margulis, Dan explained that his law practice was in the probate field. He wrote wills.

"Did you ever prepare wills for Julie and Ed?"

"I prepared a draft of a will and I sent it to them to review, and invited them to review it and get back to me. They never did," said Dan.

"Did you ever talk with them about the advantages of having a will?"

"Yes," said Dan.

On redirect, Hoag asked if a will had anything to do with life insurance.

"A will has nothing to do with the proceeds of life insurance," Dan said.

With no court scheduled for Sunday, the deputies had their biggest party yet. Several deputies not assigned to the case came by. Amid the drinking, one of the alternate jurors put her room key in a deputy's pocket.

Later that night, he went to her room.

Chapter Twenty-six

Monday morning, as the Post trial moved into its final, crucial stage, the weather changed yet again. It was a cloudy, rainy day, with the temperature barely touching fifty.

Hollis Thigpen took the stand. He had already made his position clear. In an interview with a newspaper columnist, Thigpen had explained that he was an old construction man and he knew how the world worked. In this case, the Omni Hotel, fearful of a lawsuit, had put the arm on the St. Louis authorities, and a crooked cop and a bench-legged prosecutor were doing the hotel's work.

Despite such comments, Thigpen came across as a reluctant witness rather than a defiant one. An old man, still reeling from the death of his daughter, he looked weary. As always, he spoke slowly, and with a heavy drawl.

Hoag asked about the $15,000 he had lent Ed and Julie in 1983. "At the time of Julie's death, had they paid you back any of the loan?"

"No, they still owed me fifteen thousand," Thigpen said.

"One more area," said Hoag, consciously trying to be gentle. "What exactly did Ed tell you about the circumstances of his leaving Wagner-Truax?"

This was an important point to Hoag. Before the grand jury, Thigpen had testified that Ed had quit the company because Truax was refusing to expand. Better Homes and Gardens had offered the company an interest-free loan to

expand. Post had wanted to do it. Truax had balked. So
Post had quit.

The jury, of course, had already heard Truax. Hoag
wanted the jurors to see that Post had lied to his father-
in-law.

"Well, as I understood it, Better Homes and Gardens
had offered a good bit of money to expand and Dalton
Truax didn't want to do it, so that killed the deal," said
Thigpen.

"Thank you. I have no further questions," said Hoag.

Whalen, the close friend of Bill Bethea, the man who
was like a son to Thigpen, stood up to handle the cross-
examination.

"Mr. Thigpen, are you here willingly to testify for the
prosecution in this case?"

"No," said Thigpen, softly but firmly.

"Why is it you are here?"

"I came on my own to testify for Ed Post," Thigpen
said.

"What are your feelings today for Ed Post, Mr.
Thigpen?"

"Ed Post is my friend. Not only my son-in-law, but
he's my friend."

Whalen asked about the effect of Julie's death on Ed.

"It was a hard thing for our whole family," said Thigpen, talking even more softly than usual, almost as if he
were talking to himself. "It's unbelievable what the loss
of a daughter, or a wife, someone in your family, the
effect it will have. People that you love and cherish all
your life are gone. People telling you things that are not
true. Nobody in the world should have to go through it."

"Did some homicide detectives from St. Louis come to
your home?" Whalen asked.

"Yes," said Thigpen, as Hoag leaped to his feet.

"Judge, may we approach the bench on this please,"
Hoag said.

At the bench, Hoag turned challengingly to Whalen.

"I assume we're getting into an area of stuff that allegedly the police told him."

"Oh, yeah," said Whalen.

"Judge, I don't understand the relevance of what McCraw or Hollocher told Hollis Thigpen has to do with the guilt or innocence of this guy," Hoag said, appealing to Mummert.

"Let me explain it to you," said Whalen. "We are attacking the indictment. We are attacking the credibility of the police officers because these are the guys whose investigation led to this indictment. McCraw has looked at this report and has said that everything in there is valid. I think his credibility is at issue."

Hoag shrugged.

"Then I've got to put McCraw back on to impeach my own witness. We're going to put the whole report in. Do you want me to do that? That's okay with me."

The report, of course, was filled with allegations of which the jury knew nothing.

"No, we don't want that," said Whalen.

Mummert interrupted.

"I think he's got the right to impeach McCraw," the judge said. "Just try to stay away from hearsay."

Whalen, satisfied, nodded, and walked back to stand in front of the witness stand.

He asked if Hollocher and McCraw had told him that his son, Robert, was missing, and if they had suggested that Ed Post was responsible.

"Yes," said Thigpen.

"Were you offended by the actions of the police officers with regard to your son?"

"Yes, I knew it wasn't true," said Thigpen.

When asked about Julie's health, Thigpen said she had had fainting spells going back to high school. When asked about her life insurance, he said he had urged her to be well covered.

"On the issue of insurance, when the detectives told

you it had been increased a month before her death, did you express shock and anger?"

"No," said Thigpen.

He was excused.

The final witness for the state was Charles Fahrner, the IRS accountant who had worked with Hoag on Post's tax records and financial statements during the mail fraud investigation.

He talked about the large amounts of interest the Posts had paid—a total of more than $40,000 for 1985 and 1986.

"It tells me he has a lot of loans," the accountant said.

He talked about the manner in which Post had sold his assets, primarily stock in 1984 and 1985.

He talked about the amount of money that the Posts spent, and how far it exceeded their income. He said that from the beginning of 1986 to the date of Julie's death, they had spent $48,000. Had that pattern continued for the entire year, they would have spent more than $110,000, he said.

In cross-examination, Margulis asked Fahrner if he knew whether some of the 1986 expenses were nonrecurring expenses, such as school tuition.

Fahrner said he didn't know.

Before the state officially rested its case, a recess was called, and the lawyers met in the judge's chambers. Whalen objected to the photographs from the second autopsy and said the jurors should not be permitted to see them.

All those photographs would do is appeal to the jurors' passions, he argued.

Hoag said they were relevant, because they showed the bruises that McGarry had talked about.

The judge overruled Whalen's objection.

"I think those are gory photographs, but I believe they're relevant to the state's case," Mummert said.

Shortly before noon, the temporary recess ended, and

the jurors were allowed to view the exhibits. At 12:05, the state officially rested its case against Edward T. Post.

Whalen didn't like the expression on the faces of the jurors when they looked at the photographs from the second autopsy.

Chapter Twenty-seven

Ed Post was, by nature, a confident, optimistic man, and those traits were never more on display than in the moments following the conclusion of the state's case.

"I don't think they proved anything," he said, almost gleefully, to a reporter. "This whole thing has been absurd. They have nothing—unless you count McGarry, who struck me as ludicrous. Even the state's own pathologist doesn't agree with him."

The defense attorneys, although less high-spirited than their client, seemed hopeful. Nothing had occurred to alter the two-pronged defense strategy.

First, they would seek to muddy the state's case. To counter McGarry, they had their own pathologist, and his testimony would make the medical scorecard two against one in favor of the defense. How could a jury possibly convict Post of murder? After all, there would be reasonable doubt a murder had been committed.

To further that line of reasoning, Julie's physician would testify that she had a mild heart condition called mitral valve prolapse. One symptom is dizziness. In some cases, people faint. In extreme cases—rare but not unheard-of—people die. What's more, unless a pathologist is looking for it, it's difficult to diagnose in an autopsy.

Two metallurgists would muddy the towel ring testimony. In addition, nobody could say with certainty that the towel ring in Arbini's office was the towel ring from room 4063.

A banker would testify that Post had virtually unlimited credit. Besides, the mere fact that a man had financial problems was not proof that he had killed his wife.

The other part of the defense would be emotional. The families—Ed's and Julie's—would testify that Ed could not, and would not, have murdered his wife.

In a sense, that part of the defense case had already begun with Hollis Thigpen. The old man's defense of the man accused of murdering his daughter had been an emotional moment—and there would be more of those moments to come.

Of course, there was one great unknown. How would Ed Post do on the witness stand?

Neither of the defense attorneys had much confidence in him. They had even discussed hiring a speech teacher to give Post lessons. That idea was dismissed because of the fear it would only encourage him to talk more. All they could do, they decided, was to advise him to keep his answers short and hope for the best.

The defense began Monday afternoon. The first witness was Dr. Richard Mautner, who identified himself as Julie's cardiologist. He appeared to be in his early forties, and very self-assured.

He said that he had seen Julie twice, both times after she had complained of dizziness and irregular heartbeat. He had determined that she suffered from mitral valve prolapse.

"Would you explain to the ladies and gentlemen of the jury, in laymen's terms, what mitral valve prolapse is," Whalen requested.

"Mitral valve prolapse is a relatively common cardiological condition, frequently a hereditary condition, characterized by an abnormality in the leaflets of the mitral valve," the doctor said.

"This is a valve on the left side of the heart connecting two chambers of the heart. And basically, it's a disorder of connective tissue involving the valve. Patients with this condition frequently have symptoms related to irregular heartbeat palpitations. They frequently have episodes of dizziness and a lot of these individuals frequently have episodes where they pass out.''

"You've indicated that this condition is sometimes hereditary?'' Whalen asked.

"Very commonly.''

"In fact, have you treated either of Julie Post's daughters for this condition?'' Whalen asked.

"One of her daughters definitely has this condition. I've seen her for an episode at which time she also passed out, and we diagnosed mitral valve prolapse in her case.''

The doctor also said that persons with the condition have "loose connective tissue,'' and this could affect blood vessels in such a way as to make them more sensitive to injury.

"They bruise more easily?'' Whalen asked.

"Yes,'' said the doctor.

"Doctor, does mitral valve prolapse ever cause death?''

"Mitral valve patients are prone to irregular heartbeat rhythm disturbances and I would say about four thousand deaths in the United States are related to mitral valve prolapse and its complications a year,'' said the doctor.

"And in an autopsy, would you be able to diagnose mitral valve prolapse just by looking at the heart?'' Whalen asked.

"It's very difficult to diagnose it on an autopsy. Specifically, you have to do microscopic sections of the valve.''

"No further questions,'' said Whalen.

Hoag bounced out of his seat. Given his nature, he was at his best when on the attack.

"You indicated that four thousand a year die from mitral valve prolapse, is that right?''

"From mitral valve prolapse and its complications,'' said the doctor.

"Okay. And *then* you indicated that it is virtually impossible to diagnose that by virtue of an autopsy. Is that what you're telling the jury?"

The doctor hesitated.

"I'm telling this jury that a complete autopsy, yes, which includes—which would include microscopic examination of the valve," said the doctor.

"The four thousand you referred to. Do you know whether those complete autopsies are the way they were able to diagnose that?" Hoag asked.

"I don't know," said the doctor, his self-confidence visibly beginning to evaporate.

"Or do you know whether these were extreme cases of mitral valve prolapse as opposed to milder forms?"

"I would assume these would be the more severe cases," the doctor said.

"Isn't it a fact, doctor, that it is extremely rare for someone to die of a mild form of mitral valve prolapse? Isn't that true?"

"That's hard to—sometimes it's just—sometimes on a clinical basis it's difficult to assess mild versus severe mitral valve prolapse," said the doctor.

Then Hoag went into the history of when the doctor had seen Julie. The first time had been in 1977. The second, and last, time had been in May 1986, less than a month before her death.

"What prescription or what drugs did you prescribe for her to remedy this problem or assist in remedying it?" Hoag asked.

"I didn't prescribe any drugs at that particular time," the doctor said.

"So as a cardiologist, as her treating physician, you were not concerned enough to prescribe some sort of medication? Are some people on medication that have mitral valve prolapse?"

"There are some patients that are on medication with mitral valve prolapse," the doctor said.

"Now, would you say you were a close personal friend of the defendant in this case?" Hoag asked.

"Yes," said the doctor.

"Okay. Were you a pallbearer at the funeral?"

"Yes," said the doctor.

"During this period of time, from 1977 to 1986, did Julie at any time come to you and complain of any irregularities prior to May of 1986?"

"No," said the doctor.

"Did she ever complain to you of dizziness, or the like?"

"No."

"Did she ever tell you that she had passed out during this time period?"

"No," said the doctor.

"Okay. You indicated you have a log from her last visit. Could we get that?"

Whalen gave the doctor his notes from the May 1986 visit. The doctor handed them to Hoag.

"I can't read your handwriting, okay?" Hoag said, handing the notes back. "So maybe you can interpret it."

"I'll read you exactly what the page says," the doctor said. "Under complaints it says, 'Palpitations.' And then I wrote, 'Known history of mitral valve prolapse.' Electrocardiogram taken at that time was within normal limits. I wrote the diagnosis, 'Mitral valve prolapse.' And then I just recommend, 'Reassurance.' "

"Reassurance," said Hoag. "So there's no medical recommendation?"

"No medical recommendation," said the doctor.

"And the complaints did not include dizziness, fainting, passing out. Is that right?"

"Right," said the doctor.

"No further questions," said Hoag.

Dr. Roger Fossum, the pathologist, came next.
Hoag and Moore had been impressed with Fossum when

they visited him in New Hampshire earlier in the investigation. Hoag had even talked of calling Fossum for the state.

So he was unconcerned about Fossum's testimony. Fossum was going to be like Graham, unwilling to call it a murder, but skeptical about an accident scenario.

Two against one, the defense would argue, but Hoag was ready for that. It wasn't really two against one, he would say. It was one definite and two maybes.

Fossum was heavyset and balding, with unruly wisps of hair ringing his head. He was a smooth witness, deliberate and self-confident.

When asked how many times he had testified in criminal trials, Fossum shrugged and flashed a disarming grin.

"I quit counting at three hundred, and that was several years ago," he said.

"Doctor, are you a member of any boards that relate to your profession?" Whalen asked.

"I'm a member of the board of directors of the National Association of Medical Examiners," Fossum replied.

"Do you know of anyone else connected with this case who is also a member of the National Board of Medical Examiners?"

"Dr. Michael Graham," answered Fossum.

"Is Dr. McGarry a member of the national board?" asked Whalen.

"No," said Fossum.

Whalen paused, as if thinking that over.

"When you arrived in New Orleans, how did you find the facilities there in the coroner's office?" Whalen asked.

"Well, I remember my immediate thought was that it was like stepping back in time about fifty years, a bit primitive," said Fossum.

"Were you able to discuss Dr. McGarry's findings with him?"

"No," said Fossum.

"Why not?" Whalen asked, as if he were perplexed.

"He refused to discuss the case with Dr. Graham or myself."

After pausing again, Whalen moved to what Hoag figured was the heart of the questioning.

"Are you of the opinion that this offense should be classified a homicide?"

"No," replied Fossum. "From the information that I reviewed and from what I saw at the second autopsy, there is not enough medical information available to classify it as a homicide."

Up to this point, Hoag was not surprised. The testimony was going exactly as he'd thought it would.

But then Whalen began going bruise by bruise.

"There was a cluster of bruises on the inside of the right arm in the biceps area. Dr. Graham was unable to account for those bruises. Do you have an opinion as to how that cluster might have occurred?"

Hoag stiffened. These particular bruises were important. Hoag was certain that Ed Post had grabbed Julie's arm and squeezed it. Violently. Post was on top of her in the bathtub. Maybe he had sneaked in on her. Maybe he had volunteered to massage her back. At any rate, he was on top of her, holding her body down with his. One of her arms was pinned under her body. With the other arm she tried to fight him off, but he grabbed it, held it down, squeezed it, while his other hand forced her head under the water . . .

"I think a reasonable possibility would be that somehow in the movement of her body out of the bathtub and through the various resuscitation measures and things of that sort, that that area could have been grabbed or pulled on or something like that could have occurred," said Fossum. "A similar sort of grabbing or bruising could have occurred perhaps during the bone donation."

Hoag looked at Moore and mouthed the words "That son of a bitch."

Whalen, meanwhile, was moving on to another bruise.

"Dr. Graham also said that the other bruise that was not explained by the resuscitative efforts, the bone donation, and the fall backwards into a tub would have been the bruise in this area," and he touched his right temple.

The scraping bruise! There were three separate abrasions inside the bruise.

Again, Hoag felt this was an important bruise. As Julie struggled under the weight and force of her husband, his hand holding her head under the water, her right temple came in contact with the nonskid strip in the bottom of the tub. As she tried to move her head, she scraped her temple on the sandpaper-like substance. Three times.

"That could occur because as was indicated, her head was toward the back of the bathtub and the towel ring was also at the back of the bathtub, and if her head had impacted that towel ring, or had been lying on it, that perhaps could have left those marks," said Fossum.

Hoag leaned over and whispered a profanity to Moore.

Bruise by bruise, Whalen continued. Each time, Fossum found a way to dismiss the bruise. It was the result of the bone donations, or the resuscitative efforts, or the first autopsy, or was entirely consistent with a fall in a bathtub.

The double bruise on the back of the head where the neck joins the skull was airily dismissed. The large bruise could have been the result of a fall, and the smaller bruise could have been caused by any number of things, Fossum said.

"Do we have any areas of bruising that cannot be explained by the description of the fall that I've given you as well as the resuscitative techniques and the long bone donations?" Whalen asked.

"I think they all could be explained in some fashion or another by that scenario," said Fossum.

"Okay. Are the bruises that you found on Julie Post consistent or inconsistent with a theory that her face was held down underwater?" Whalen asked.

"In my opinion they are inconsistent," Fossum said.

Whalen then asked the pathologist how he would classify the death.

"I would classify the manner of death in this case as undetermined," said Fossum.

"And why would you not classify it as a homicide?" Whalen inquired.

"I don't believe there's anything here from an injury standpoint that points to this being a homicide," replied Fossum.

Whalen smiled, nodded, and sat down.

Hoag stood up. For a moment, he said nothing. In contrast to the dapper, sophisticated defense attorney, who always wore a pink rose in his lapel—in homage to his young daughter—Hoag was rumpled. Short and stocky and hunched over, his hands in his pockets, he shuffled slowly toward the witness.

Because he normally exuded so much energy, he seemed almost dangerous when he tried to act low-key.

"If there's 'nothing' in the injuries that would lead you to believe a homicide was involved, then why wouldn't you say it was an accident?" he quietly asked Fossum.

"Because there are some things here on this overall pattern that do not make that abundantly clear either, by itself," replied Fossum.

Hoag took his hands out of his pockets and threw his arms up in exasperation. When he next spoke, his voice was back to its normal level, loud and challenging.

"Well, you've just gotten trotted through each of the injuries and given a possible explanation for each of the thirty-nine injuries, and I heard you say there were a number of them that were blunt-force injuries . . ."

"Yes," said Fossum.

"And we're not talking about someone who lifted their head up. We're talking about more force than that, aren't we?"

"Yes," said Fossum.

"And we're not talking about someone who may have

lifted her arm up in the bone removal," said Hoag, now
speaking quickly, in a staccato fashion. "We're talking
about something more significant than that, aren't we?"

"Well, the bone removal can get a bit rough at times,
but basically I agree with you, yes," said Fossum, almost
good-naturedly.

"It's a surgical procedure, isn't it, Doctor?" asked
Hoag quickly.

"Yes," said Fossum.

"Have you ever done it?"

"Yes," said Fossum.

"Well, don't you treat it just like you would if the guy
was alive?"

"Well, not quite," said Fossum.

"No? You're a little rougher than that?"

"A bit, yes," said Fossum, still speaking deliberately,
in contrast to Hoag, who by now was standing in front of
the witness, firing the next question the moment the last
was answered.

"Geez, you don't intentionally bruise the body, do
you?"

"Not intentionally, no," said Fossum.

"Why would one want to perform an exhumation on a
body? Why would you do that?"

"The usual reason for performing an exhumation is to
answer previously unanswered questions," replied Fossum.

"Isn't it a fact, Doctor, that the body bruises, and it
takes some period of time before those bruises show up
on some people?"

"True," said Fossum.

Hoag then noted the difference between the number of
bruises evident in the first autopsy and the number evident
in the second.

"Significantly more, would you not say?" he asked
Fossum.

"Yes," said Fossum.

"And of particular significance were the ones in the back of the neck?"

"Yes," said Fossum.

"And why would you say those were significant?"

Again Fossum tried to slow the pace down.

"Well, the one in particular on the right. First of all, the one on the left is a very small area. So the one on the right has a particular significance. It is a pretty good-sized area of bruising of tissues," Fossum said.

While Fossum was answering, Hoag walked over to the table and picked up one of the photographs taken during the second autopsy. As he walked back to Fossum, he changed the pace of his questioning, becoming deliberate again, as if he were trying to make sense out of the doctor's testimony.

"How were you able to dismiss it as 'not significant'? I looked at this photograph here, which is the peeled-back portion—pardon me, but there's no other way to say it—and it doesn't look 'insignificant' to me. Are you saying that's an insignificant bruise?" he asked, handing Fossum the photograph.

Fossum looked at it for only a moment.

"The one on the left, that's a little bitty thing," he said.

"About an inch, is that what you're saying?"

"Perhaps," said Fossum.

Hoag was again directly in front of him, leaning into him.

"Big as my thumb?"

"Yes, about that," said Fossum.

"Big as my thumb. And yet you think it's insignificant?"

"Yes," said Fossum.

"And you're telling this jury then you think that the right temple, those areas of the right temple could have been caused by coming into contact with the towel ring?"

"Yes," said Fossum.

"How? Why don't you explain?"

"I believe that it's possible for this to have caused that injury in the fashion that if someone were lying on it, and caught the area where the setscrew is, it could leave a mark," said Fossum.

"That explains one of them, Doctor. Can you explain the other two?"

"The edges, if they were pressed hard enough, could do that," said Fossum, no longer sounding quite so self-assured.

Hoag paused, and walked over and picked up the towel ring.

"I see," he said. "Now if I slipped and fell, and I had this in my hand, and it wasn't in my hand when I was found, then it had to fall out of my hand at some point in time. So it would have to be in the water before my tail hit the water, and I'm going to have to land on top of it, right?"

"Yes," said Fossum.

Hoag shook his head.

"Okay. Now in the meantime, you've testified about these other bruises, these bruises that came as a result of BANG!"—and he clapped his hands. "Right?"

"Yes," said Fossum.

"Bang! Back here?" said Hoag, touching his back.

"Yes," said Fossum.

"And bang! On my butt," said Hoag, slapping his butt.

"Yes," said Fossum.

"Now, I'm landing in a tub, okay, Doc? Here's the tub, right?" Hoag asked, gesturing to the space between the witness chair and the jury box.

"Uh huh," said Fossum.

"And I'm landing in the tub, and after I've done all that banging, okay, somehow my body flips, okay? Not only does it flip, but I turn around because I'm found facing this way with the left side of my head facing down in the water," Hoag said, and as he talked he slapped his left shoulder, and his left buttocks, and spun around twice between Fossum and the jury.

"How is it, Doc, that we got these bruises on the right side of her face?"

"She was left side down?" Fossum asked weakly.

"Yes sir," said Hoag, once again standing directly in front of the witness.

"That would . . . that would make that a bit difficult then," said Fossum.

"It would, wouldn't it?"

"Yes, it would," replied Fossum.

"How is it, Doc, that I could BANG the top of my head, BANG the back of my neck, and wind up—after hitting those areas—wind up flipping over and turning on my left side with my feet stretched out as if I was taking a bath? Isn't it in fact very difficult in a bathtub to turn around on your stomach?"

"It can be difficult, yes," said Fossum.

"This was a small bathtub. No longer than five feet, and two feet wide. Would you expect then that the body would be able to do all those contortions all by itself?"

"I believe there is an explanation," said Fossum.

"Well, have you given us one?"

"No. You didn't let me," said Fossum.

Hoag stepped back, put out his arms, and said, with great enthusiasm, "Go ahead, Doc! I want you to tell us!"

Fossum managed a smile.

"I believe it's possible that in the scenario with the fall, striking the head, and then, but not being unconscious, getting up, or attempting to get up and moving around a bit, and I believe there was some indication that she had a cardiac irregularity problem, that then could have kicked in at that time and caused her to collapse facedown as she was attempting to get up and to turn in the bathtub."

Hoag scratched his head and moved toward the witness again.

"Well, I'm just wondering, Doc, how it is she bounced

on the side of her head three times, Doc, during your scenario, because aren't those bruises on the rounded portion of the head? They're not in a flat plane, are they, Doc?''

"No, they're not," said Fossum.

"Let me ask you this question, Doc. Would it be consistent with someone having grabbed her by the back of the neck and jammed her down into the tub as she turned her head to the right? Now, before you answer that, Doc, do you know whether or not there were safety strips in the bathtub? Do you know what I'm talking about?''

"Yes, uh huh," nodded Fossum, and to at least one courtroom observer, Fossum had the demeanor of a cobra giving in to a snake charmer.

"What kind of surface is that?" Hoag asked, speaking in a low voice.

"Very finely granular," said Fossum, just as softly.

"And that would cause what kind of an injury, Doctor?''

"Could cause a scraping injury," said Fossum.

"Could cause a scraping injury," Hoag repeated. "Consistent with this, Doctor, that is, the scrapes that you see here?" He handed Fossum the photograph of Julie's right temple.

Fossum looked at the photograph.

"It could do that, yes," he said.

"So that if I did three separate thrusts, three separate thrusts with the back of the head," and Hoag, still standing directly in front of Fossum, pantomimed a man thrusting something downward, "and forced someone's head down—one! two! three!—times on the safety strips, that would be consistent with this, wouldn't it, Doctor?''

"It could do that, yes," said Fossum.

Hoag turned away and walked along the jury box. Finally, he turned back to Fossum.

"Well, then your previous testimony that there is no

scenario or injuries that would be consistent with homicide, you might want to change that now, wouldn't you?''

Fossum nodded.

''Now that you've brought that one up, yes,'' he said.

Hoag knew that he could stop there, maybe even should stop. Burying a witness too deep can rouse sympathy in a jury. But there was still a little more ground to cover.

''How many of these wounds, bruises that you noticed, could be consistent, sir, with someone having murdered someone else?''

Fossum shrugged. ''I assume you are wanting to stay within the same scenario that we've been dealing with,'' he said. ''Then it could not be ruled out as to the side of the head, and the one in the back of the neck on the right is a possibility. The others I just have great difficulty with.''

''The top of the head?'' asked Hoag. ''I mean, if I came up to you in a bathtub and I shoved you like that and banged your head against the wall, that would not be consistent with a homicide?''

''Well, if that's the way you want to go with it, yes, that could happen that way, sure, sure,'' said Fossum.

Again, Hoag threw his arms out.

''Well, we're just trying to explore the possibilities,'' he said.

''Okay,'' said Fossum.

''Okay?'' said Hoag.

''All right,'' said Fossum.

''And what about the one on the rump? Could that be consistent with a homicide?''

Fossum nodded. That one, too, was consistent with a homicide.

Hoag sat down.

The rest of the afternoon was consumed by the defense's two metallurgists. Neither suggested that the distortion in the metal could have been caused by a slip-and-fall accident.

The first one had some mild criticism for the methodology used by one of the prosecutors' experts.

The second defense expert proposed the startling theory that the deformation in the metal had been caused by two simultaneous forces.

"And how many people were involved in this process?" asked Whalen.

"It could be done with two people. Not with one. One inside the tub, and one outside the tub," said David Colling.

Hoag and Moore had indeed decided not to call Colling. The state's reject testified for the defense.

Jurors were later to say they didn't understand what he was trying to say or how he had arrived at his conclusion.

When court adjourned for the day, Post agreed to meet two newspaper reporters for drinks. Whalen accompanied him, and said kiddingly to the journalists, "I'm just here to make sure he doesn't confess."

Despite prodding, Post talked little about the trial except to say that he thought it was going well. What he really wanted to talk about was his days in the Army. He'd once eaten snakes in Panama, he said.

Chapter Twenty-eight

The courthouse regulars all were in attendance on Tuesday. Some of them worked at the courthouse, and others were retired citizens who had discovered that a good trial has more drama than a soap opera. Closing arguments are usually good, and whenever a defendant testifies, the potential for high drama is increased.

In most cases, defendants don't testify. Some people assume that's because most defendants have criminal records that can be brought out in cross-examination, but the truth is otherwise. Most defendants are uneducated, and they're nervous, and they'd stand no chance against a prosecutor.

But Post was different. Bright, educated, and eager, he was going to testify.

In addition to being a "great white defendant," Post was already a media celebrity. During the trial, he had been chatting on a regular basis with a newspaper columnist, who had dubbed him "the Inappropriate Man" because he was so upbeat.

"I really like St. Louis," Post had said, and the columnist had wondered, in print, how a man in Post's situation could possibly like St. Louis.

"If you took your wife to a strange city, and she died in a horrible accident, and then the crooked police manufactured a case against you, which is what Post contends has happened to him, would you still like the city?" the columnist had written.

Now the public would get a chance to hear Post, and to see Hoag go after him.

Margulis, a veteran of dozens of high-profile cases, noted the crowded courtroom, but realized the spectators would have to wait. A big part of being a defense attorney is orchestrating the show. Before Post would testify, the proper mood had to be set—for the jury, if not the crowd.

The first witness was Jeffrey Buckner, a financial planner. Under questioning by Margulis, he explained that he had reviewed the same records and documents that the state's witness, the IRS agent, had studied. Not surprisingly, he had come to a very different conclusion.

Sure, the Posts had debts, but they were meeting all their obligations, Buckner pointed out. Ed had equity in the building he and his brother owned, and he had equity in his house. Plus, of course, the real estate industry was bound to come around.

In short, the Posts were weathering the bad economy very well.

Buckner also testified that the College of Financial Planning recommended a method for determining the amount of life insurance a person needed. According to its mathematical calculations, Julie Post should have been insured for approximately $600,000. So her insurance was not out of line.

Hoag tried to shake him in cross-examination, but for the most part, Buckner hung tough.

Only when Buckner tried to suggest that some of the expenses Fahrner had mentioned were probably nonrecurring did Hoag score.

"Which ones are you talking about?" Hoag asked. "Are you talking about the kids' education?"

"The educational costs are part of that," said Buckner.

"Would it surprise you to know that the tuition for Mercy Academy was paid on June 13th, that a check for fourteen hundred dollars was issued ten days after Julie died?" Hoag asked. "Would it surprise you to know that a check to Ursuline Academy in the sum of one thousand six hundred and sixty-three dollars was issued on the 19th of June?''

Hoag also asked Buckner if he was aware that Post had borrowed $2,000 on April 29.

''Yes,'' said Buckner.

''Did you know that the same day he purchased additional insurance?'' Hoag asked.

''No,'' said Buckner.

But he still maintained that Julie and Ed, while suffering a cash-flow problem, were not in any deep trouble.

The next witness was an insurance broker. He told Margulis that he had reviewed the Posts' insurance history and overall financial picture, and his recommendation would have been $500,000 for Julie.

So no, he said, $700,000 was not out of line.

He was unshakable on cross-examination.

James Ramsey Smith, a senior vice president of City National Bank in Louisiana, was next. He told Margulis that he was the Posts' personal banker.

''How was their borrowing power?'' Margulis asked.

''They had an excellent relationship with the bank. They had substantial borrowing power, and never actually reached the height of that,'' said Smith.

''Would you describe in early 1986 and the year or two before that Julie and Ed's financial situation in relation to the economy?''

Smith nodded.

''I would think they were better off than ninety percent of the state at this particular point, as far as being what we could classify as upscale or higher-income. No brand-new real estate investments. They were in much better shape than most,'' he said.

Under cross-examination, Smith said that Post had owed the bank $29,000 before Julie's death, and borrowed another $10,000 the week after she died.

Two real estate executives who had been at the meeting

in St. Louis testified. One was the jogger Post had seen as he was completing his morning run, and the other was a man who had been with Post after he returned from the hospital. Post was devastated, the witness said.

Mae Pelafigue, the elderly housekeeper, testified about the nights she had heard Post sobbing in his bedroom, unable to clean out his wife's closet.

The managing director of the Lake Lawn Metairie Cemetery and Funeral Home testified in the same vein. He said that Ed had broken down when he tried to select a casket for Julie. He also said he had often seen Ed visiting the gravesite.

In cross-examination, Hoag tried to pound away at the fact that 85 percent of the burials in New Orleans are above-ground, and wasn't this because of the high water level, but the director insisted that the real reason was the European tradition of the city.

Then came Dan's wife, Martha. She was followed by Ed's father, and then by Ed's mother. All testified that Ed had been devastated by the death of his wife.

Hoag asked Ed's father some financial questions about loans that he had made to Ed, loans that were never repaid.

Hoag declined to cross-examine Ed's mother.

And then it was time for Ed himself to take the stand. Court was recessed for lunch.

Ed Post wore a blue-striped suit and a solemn expression as he marched to the witness stand. He settled into the witness chair, adjusted his microphone, and looked expectantly at Margulis.

"For the record, would you tell the court and jury your name, please," the lawyer said.

"Edward T. Post."

Margulis led him through his life story. Married for almost twenty years, two children. Julie was a real estate agent with a "brilliant" future. Her problems at the office were behind her at the time of her death.

Her health was a source of some concern. Because of the mitral valve prolapse problem, she was prone to dizzy spells.

Were these dizzy spells unusual? Margulis asked.

These spells occurred on an almost weekly basis, Post testified.

Post described his financial situation as "comfortable."

Margulis handed Post a copy of the proposals Masson had presented in the spring of 1986 for Julie's life insurance. One proposal called for a $1 million policy on Julie. A second called for replacing her $400,000 policy with a $600,000 policy. The third called for buying a $300,000 policy to augment the existing $400,000 policy.

"We made a decision to buy the same amount that I bought for me, an additional three-hundred-thousand dollar policy," Post said. "We certainly didn't think that she needed a million dollars' worth of coverage."

Margulis led his client to the morning of Julie's death.

"Well, the first thing I did when I got up at six-twenty-five was call downstairs and cancel a wake-up call for six-thirty so the phone wouldn't ring and disturb my wife. Then I went into the bathroom and used the facilities and I cleaned up and put my contact lenses in, and put my jogging clothes on, and then I went in and woke Julie up."

As he spoke, Post seemed surprisingly calm.

"When I woke her up, she told me that her back was really giving her some problems, and it had some the night before because it was her menstrual period. I suggested that maybe I could rub her back and that might make it feel better, and she asked me to do that. After doing that, she asked me to prepare her bathwater and I went into the bathroom and stuck the stopper down in the tub and filled it up."

Margulis nodded. Go ahead, he said.

"I went back in and told her that it was ready and helped her get up, and we walked back into the bathroom together, and I kissed her goodbye and said, 'I'll see you in thirty minutes,' and turned and walked out of the bathroom door, and didn't close it completely, just almost closed, and went on out of the room and went off."

Margulis nodded. He was intent on keeping it slow.

"Do you remember, generally, where you went?" he asked.

"Well, of course, I came out of the hotel. I think I may have said something to the concierge on the way out. Went outside, and did some warm-up exercises and just started running down Market Street."

"What did you do when you got back to the hotel?" Margulis asked.

"I came on in and went back up to the room and used my key to enter the room. When I opened the door to the room, I didn't hear anything and called out Julie's name and I didn't get any answer. I then came on in and I noticed that the bathroom door was in the same position that it was in when I left.

"And I opened the bathroom door and as I was walking in, I slipped on some water that was on the floor and almost fell, but I caught hold of the doorknob to keep from falling. And I opened the door to the bathroom, and that's when I saw Julie."

He described his initial unsuccessful efforts to get her out of the tub—although he made no comment about "dead weight"—and he said that as he finally got her out of the tub, she slipped out of his arms and hit her head on the marble floor.

His story remained consistent with the story he had told from the first.

"How were you at the funeral?" Margulis asked.

"As controlled as I could be. I knew it was very important to help my daughters get through a terribly emotional experience, and I wanted to be a father figure. I knew that if I broke down, they would just completely melt at that point, so I tried to be some type of an inspiration to them.''

"How were the girls?" Margulis asked.

"They cried. It was very difficult. It was difficult for all of us," Post said.

Margulis walked over in front of the jury box. Post was doing well, and was keeping his attention riveted on his attorney. He had not yet even glanced at the jurors.

"Let me go in a different direction, Ed. You talked with Officer Kaelin?"

"Yes."

"And you also had a lengthy conversation by telephone with Detective Jacobsmeyer at a later time, didn't you?"

"Yes, I did," said Post.

"Were you talkative during that conversation?"

"Yeah," Post said.

"We've all heard the conversation," Margulis said gently.

"It appears that I was," said Post, and he forced a smile.

"Were you trying to cooperate?"

"Yes, I was," said Post.

"Were you trying to provide as much information as you possibly could?"

"That's absolutely right," said Post.

Hoag, who had been leaning back in his chair, stood up.

"May we approach the bench, your honor?" he said.

"We don't have to," said Margulis sternly.

"Yeah, we do," said Hoag, and he walked up to the side of the judge's bench away from the jury. He was joined by Margulis and Whalen.

"Judge, we're getting into an area where he's trying to lead the jury into believing that he was completely cooperative and that he did everything that the police asked him to do. And I know for a fact that he didn't, because they asked him to take a polygraph.''

"That's not coming in, no matter what," snapped Margulis.

Hoag turned to him.

"Now you keep this up, if we keep getting into this area, I'm going to ask him if there were some things that the police asked him that he didn't do.''

"Go ahead. Go ahead," said Margulis.

"I think that's looking for a mistrial," said Judge Mummert.

"You bet it is," said Margulis.

"We don't want to have to do this over again," warned the judge.

"I'm not going to ask him about the polygraph, but I'm going to ask him if they asked him to do some things he didn't do," persisted Hoag.

Mummert shook his head.

"The problem with that, Dean, is he can come back with—"

"Then restrict him from saying he cooperated," said Hoag.

"I'm not going to restrict him, but I am going to restrict you," said the judge.

Hoag shook his head in resignation, and with a disgusted look, walked back to his table.

"Ed, did you also have a conversation with Detective Hollocher?" Margulis asked. "Did you provide information?''

"Yes, I was very cooperative. I told him anything he wanted to know.''

"With regard to this conversation with Detective Hollocher at your house, Ed. In that conversation did he show you pictures of the towel ring and tell you that was the towel ring from room 4063? Did you make some comment about that?''

"I said there's no way my wife had bent that towel ring like that," said Post.

"Ed, did you kill Julie?"

"No, I did not," said Post emphatically.

"That's all, your honor."

Hoag had been looking forward to this encounter since he had first begun researching the case. He sincerely disliked Post. Yet, he was worried. Cross-examination was his forte, but he was at a distinct disadvantage in this instance.

He did not know what had really happened in room 4063.

Countless times he had tried to figure out how it had gone down. In a way, it made sense that Julie had voluntarily gotten into the tub. Maybe the water had soothed her aching back. Maybe Post had offered to massage her back, and then, once on top of her, had murdered her. In his statements, he had always claimed that he had massaged her back, and often in a lie there was a grain of truth.

On the other hand, the shower curtain had been found inside the tub. Would a woman as finicky and refined as Julie take a bath with the curtain inside the tub?

Hoag was fairly certain that the murder had occurred earlier than 6:30 or 7:00. Arbini had said that the water was cool to the touch when he picked up the towel ring, and yet the spigot had been all the way to hot.

Had she been murdered the night before?

Possibly, and yet the first autopsy had shown an empty stomach, which would indicate that she had eaten dinner several hours before her death. Maybe she had just picked at her food. Nobody from the dinner could remember.

So the how and when were a mystery. The why was easier. Post had been a troubled man in the spring of 1986. Financially he was facing ruin. Emotionally, he was lusting after another woman. If Julie were to die, all his dreams could come true. At least he would have believed so.

But Hoag had long ago decided not to use the other-woman theory. There were too many variables, too much chance something could go wrong. The money, the towel ring, and the bruises—they were his case.

Hoag got up and walked toward Post. From his seat in the witness chair, Post watched him advance. Just as Hoag had looked forward to this confrontation, so had Post. He had noticed the way the prosecutor would take the gory autopsy pictures and turn them toward him on the table. There was no doubt that these two men were adversaries.

"Mr. Post," Hoag said. "I'm going to ask you a number of questions. If there's any question you don't understand, or you don't hear, you ask me to repeat it. I'll be glad to do so, okay?"

Hoag said this in a tone that suggested a father lecturing a son, confronting the child over some moral lapse.

Post nodded.

"How would you characterize your wife's overall attitude at work?"

"She had a very positive attitude. She was a terrific salesperson. She could not have been successful with strangers and people without having a very positive attitude," Post replied firmly.

"What kind of a personality was she with you? Was she a strong personality? Was she a weak personality, kind of 'go along' with everything? What kind of a personality did she have?"

Post thought about the question for a second. Think before you answer, his lawyers had told him.

"She was pretty much 'go along with' in some respects. She certainly had her own opinions, and I respected her opinions. She was a very intelligent woman," he said.

Hoag asked a few questions about life insurance. Then he produced an application form and handed it to Post.

"Who filled that out? Is that your handwriting? Is that the doctor's, or do you know?"

Post looked at it.

"That is my handwriting right there. So this is apparently the policy that we purchased."

Hoag took it back.

"And I notice in here, sir, that one of the areas has to do with dizziness, fainting, convulsions, paralysis, stroke, mental or nervous disorder. And it's checked 'no.' Did you check it?"

Post looked at it again.

"I don't recall checking it. It's possible," he said.

"Now is there some reason why you would testify on direct examination that on a weekly basis Julie complained about dizziness, and you wouldn't fill this out and say dizziness was a part of her medical condition?"

"Could have been an oversight," Post said quickly.

"Were you attempting to deceive the insurance company?"

"Of course not," Post said.

"You weren't?"

"I would never do that!" Post said.

Hoag changed directions, and asked about Post's job status at the time of Julie's death.

"Dalton Truax testified here. He indicated that you and he had a deep philosophical difference in your management style. Do you recall that testimony?"

"I recall some . . ." Post said, and then stopped himself. "Yes, I recall the testimony."

"Well, he told us that he wanted somebody who'd get in the trenches and do more hands-on, and your approach was more up-above and hands-off, and he wasn't very happy with that. Did he ever express that to you, Mr. Post?"

"Not as strongly as you're expressing it to me, but he did express it to me that his management style would have been different. And two different managers will handle the same circumstances differently," Post replied.

Hoag turned to the phone calls Post had made following Julie's death.

"And the phone calls to Kim Autin. Where did you get her number?"

"Julie had it with her," Post said. "It was in her notes."

"You didn't contact Kim before you left to find out what the number was?"

Post stopped for a minute, as if to think about the question.

"Actually, I think Julie had it, and may have lost it, and at the last minute may have asked me to call back and get it again. It's possible I may have called back to get it for Julie."

"You seem to recall getting that information from Kim, do you?"

"I really wasn't paying attention to that at the time," Post replied.

Hoag walked over to the prosecution table and picked up the towel ring.

"When was the first time you ever saw this?" he asked.

"Probably in this courtroom," said Post.

Hoag ignored the comment and asked if the towel ring in room 4063 had been loose.

"I didn't pay any attention to it," replied Post.

"Well, I've noticed you're kind of a detail man," said Hoag. "I noticed that when I listened to your testimony and I heard you running down the street and you ran by Brooks Brothers, and you went down near Busch Stadium, and then you came up through the City Hall parking lot, and then you ran into a guy who was a police officer whose name was Gay."

"It was a fireman," said Post.

"Well, on the tape, though, you said you thought he was a policeman. Now that tells me that somebody has a great eye for detail. I suspect someone with that same great eye for detail, had there been some malfunction with that towel ring, would have pointed it out," said Hoag.

"If there had been one, I may have noticed it. I don't even know what color the towel was. I didn't pay any attention," Post said.

Hoag walked over to the table and put the towel ring down.

"The testimony shows your wife was a perfectionist. If she saw a towel ring bent, I would suspect that she would have brought that to the attention of the people at the Omni Hotel," Hoag said.

"Oh, I think she would have," Post said.

"You indicated that you had some CPR training. When did you have this CPR training?" Hoag asked.

"In the Army," Post said.

Hoag turned and moved away from the witness.

"Were you Regular Army, or were you National Guard?" he asked, his back to Post.

Post stiffened.

"If you're asking the question that limited, it would be National Guard, not Regular Army," he snapped.

"Six months training, and then you went on reserve status?"

Again, Post seemed offended.

"I spent a much longer time on active duty than six months. It was an unusual program. It was not the typical reserve program," he said.

"But you were in the National Guard. You were not in the Regular Army?"

"It was officially known as the National Guard, that's correct," Post said.

The questions turned to the morning of Julie's death.

"Now let me see here," said Hoag, looking at his notes. "You went in and filled her tub. Now did you say on direct examination that she asked you to? I must have missed it."

"She asked me to," Post replied.

"She asked you to?"

"Yes," said Post.

"Do you remember when Sergeant Jacobsmeyer asked you on June the 11th, okay, 'Did she ask you to fill the tub?' And your response was, 'No, I do that for her quite routinely at home when we're together. We're very close. So I went and filled the bathtub up for her.' Do you recall saying that?"

Post hesitated.

"At the point of that conversation, I was still very stunned," he said.

More questions followed concerning what Post had seen when he entered the bathroom and his efforts to get Julie out of the tub.

"Was there some reason why you didn't get inside the tub and get a better grip?" Hoag asked.

"It did not occur to me, and I probably would have slipped and fallen myself," replied Post.

Then Hoag posed more questions about finance and insurance.

"When was it, sir, that you decided that you were going to sue the Omni Hotel?"

"I have not made a decision to sue the Omni Hotel, Mr. Hoag," Post said.

"Let me hand you a check," said Hoag. "It's made out on June 11th of 1986. Made out to James P. Holloran. Wasn't that a check in anticipation of a lawsuit against the Omni Hotel?"

Post sighed.

"He's an attorney who does live here in St. Louis, yes. I asked him to check on certain things. In fact, my brother may have called him about some towel rings, something like that. I have not talked to this man in three years," said Post.

Hoag turned and walked away. He fired a question over his shoulder.

"Do you know Bobby Autin?"

"Sure, I know Bobby Autin. He was Kim Autin's husband at one time," said Post.

Margulis stood up.

"May we approach?" he asked the judge.

The four lawyers converged at the judge's bench.

"What's the intention here with reference to Bobby Autin? I'd like to know where we're going," Margulis said.

"I'm going to ask him whether he made a statement to Bobby Autin about Kim's sister," said Hoag.

Margulis shook his head.

"Judge, we had been assured by Mr. Hoag throughout the trial that we were not going to get into the marital relationship. We were not going to get into any of that! Now, the rules have suddenly changed."

"Hey, buddy, you're the one who put out all the evidence about how grieved Post was. I think I'm allowed to rebut that with any statement he may have made that shows he's not as grieved a widower as he'd like people to believe," responded Hoag.

The judge interceded.

"I think it's fair game," Mummert said.

As Margulis and Whalen sat down, Hoag walked back to Post.

"Do you recall, sir, a conversation with Bobby Autin after the funeral where you stated to him, 'Once this thing is over, maybe you can arrange a date with Kim's twin sister'? Do you remember saying anything like that?"

"I think that that's totally out of context, both in time frame and in implication," said Post calmly.

"Well, you tell me," said Hoag.

Post nodded.

"Could have been a few weeks after. A couple of weeks after, he met me for lunch and we were really not particularly on good terms at that point because I think he was showing some indifference to Julie's death, and if anything, could not understand why I was in such a grieved position. And he said, 'When do you plan on having a date or going out?' or something like that.

"And I recall my response was 'Sometime in the future.' Nothing in mind whatsoever. 'Maybe if Kathy's in town, maybe we could all go out to dinner or something like that.' It was a very innocent type of statement. And I've never done that, and never really had any interest in doing that since."

"And you've been under investigation since then, too, and under indictment, isn't that correct?" asked Hoag.

"Been under investigation apparently since the first day, Mr. Hoag," replied Post.

"No further questions," said Hoag.

The trial was over for the day. Post went into the hallway, where his family waited. Although they were barred from the courtroom, they had accompanied Ed to court to offer moral support.

Stephanie and Jennifer were with Julie's parents. Dan and his wife and parents were standing in another little cluster. As Ed came out, everyone huddled around him.

"How'd I do?" Ed called out to the newspaper columnist, the tone of his voice suggesting he already knew the answer.

"Hoag didn't lay a glove on you," the columnist said.

Ed grinned. Stephanie, the young woman who had all of her mother's mannerisms, hugged her father.

"Daddy, I love you," she said.

Chapter Twenty-nine

Hoag arrived at the courthouse for closing arguments at 7:00 A.M.

A deputy let him in without a word. Hoag was not the most approachable of men on a normal day, but this morning he seemed even more intense than usual. He took an elevator to an empty floor. Alone, he paced up and down the hallway, talking animatedly to himself, rehearsing his closing argument.

The night before, he had reread his closing argument from the Rothgeb case.

Before going to the courtroom, Deputy Kurt Steffen stopped on the first floor to visit some pals in the sheriff's office.

Guarding a sequestered jury was considered a good assignment because of all the overtime involved. Technically, it was considered a twenty-four-hour-a-day duty.

So Steffen was getting some good-natured kidding about the fact that the trial was coming to its conclusion. He grinned and then announced to a captain, and in front of several other deputies, that he would be *particularly* sorry to see this trial end.

"I'm making it with one of the jurors," he said.

"You're what?" said the captain.

"I'm making it with one of the jurors," Steffen repeated.

"You gotta be nuts, Steffen," laughed the captain.

As some of the other deputies shook their heads in amazement, and perhaps admiration, Steffen raised his eyebrows in Groucho Marx fashion.

"It's a dirty job, but somebody has to do it," he said.

Don Stock was one of the deputies who overheard the conversation. A muscular young man and a former professional wrestler whose *nom de guerre* had been the Mad Muscovite, he was perhaps the most gentlemanly of all the deputies. He was a born-again Christian who liked to visit with prisoners in the courthouse holding cells. During his visits, he would bear witness for Jesus.

He liked Steffen, and although he knew it was terribly wrong to have sex with jurors, Stock shrugged the whole thing off.

If the captain thought it was amusing, then so be it. Stock was not the sort who carried tales.

Post and his family arrived at the courthouse early. They broke into small groups and talked in the hallway outside the courtroom. At one point, Post was left alone, and he walked to a window facing west.

The more spectacular view was from the window at the east end of the hallway, where one could see the Old Courthouse, converted into a museum, where the Dred Scott case was heard, and beyond it, framing the green spire of the old building, the Gateway Arch.

But to Post, the view to the west must have been even more dramatic. From the west window, he could see Union Station, and the City Hall parking lot.

A reporter walked up to Post as he gazed out the window.

"A penny for your thoughts," the reporter said.

Post turned around with a smile.

"I was just thinking that your Chamber of Commerce must have ordered this weather," he said. "It's fantastic."

The courtroom was again crowded as the final day began. The defense was closing its case with family members. Stephanie was the first witness. She looked younger than her eighteen years, but she walked into the courtroom with a purposeful stride. She smiled at her father as she took her seat in the witness box.

She testified that her father had been sad and depressed in the weeks and months after her mother's death. She said the family had visited the gravesite frequently.

Margulis asked her if her mother had ever had any problems with dizziness or fainting.

"Yes, sir," Stephanie replied forcefully. "She frequently seemed to be dizzy, like when she would stand up from the dinner table or get up too quickly. Very frequently."

She spoke like a person who had rehearsed her lines.

"Stephanie, did you ever know of any situation in your family regarding money difficulties?"

"No, sir," she said.

Hoag did not cross-examine her.

Jennifer came next. She was less animated and less theatrical than her older sister, but she carried the same message.

"Do you recall your mother having any difficulty with balance or dizziness or fainting?"

"Well, on certain occasions, she would get up and she'd just look like she was unstable and she needed to hold on to something."

"Was it often when she was getting from a sitting to a rising position?" Margulis asked.

"Yes," said Jennifer.

Hoag had no questions.

Julie's younger sister, Joanne, was next. Joanne was attractive, with dark hair and fair skin. She testified that Julie bruised easily. So did she. Julie had problems with balance. So did she.

Hoag had no questions.

Etta Mae Thigpen was the final witness. As Whalen questioned her, she spoke softly but forcefully. She said that Julie had suffered from fainting spells. Once she had passed out at high school.

"Mrs. Thigpen, what are your feelings for Ed Post?" Whalen asked.

Hoag stood up and started to object.

"Never mind," he said, and sat back down.

"We love Ed," Etta Mae said softly.

Whalen pretended not to hear, and asked her to repeat it.

This time, she spoke a little louder.

"We love Ed."

That ended the defense case.

The final witnesses had taken less than half an hour, and by 10:00 A.M. the lawyers were ready to meet in the judge's chambers to discuss the instructions that would be given to the jury.

Moore and Hoag had a disagreement.

Although Post was charged with first-degree murder, Moore felt the state should tell the judge to include instructions for second-degree murder—that is, murder without premeditation.

Moore's argument was simple: the appellate court had ruled in another case that if the evidence could sustain a lesser charge, the state had to offer that option.

"We don't want this to get thrown out on a technicality," he argued.

Hoag strongly opposed the lesser charge. Conviction on first-degree murder brought life without parole. The sentence for second-degree murder could be as little as ten years. A person could be out in three years.

"Premeditation doesn't mean you have to plan for years. It means you act with cool deliberation. It takes a couple of minutes to drown somebody. That's plenty of time to deliberate on what you're doing," he said heatedly.

Unable to settle the matter, Hoag used the judge's phone to call George Peach, the circuit attorney.

"Include the second-degree option," Peach said.

Hoag hung up and grimaced.

"Include the second-degree instruction," he told the judge.

Margulis and Whalen had already discussed the possibility. The state's case was not strong. Still, Post was too cocky to be likable, and the jurors were aware that if he got off, he would become a wealthy man. Despite the weaknesses in the state's case, if the jurors were given a compromise choice, they would surely grab it.

Neither man wanted to give the jurors that easy out.

"Give us a minute, Judge," Margulis said. "We want to confer with our client."

"Gonna let lead counsel make the choice?" asked Hoag sarcastically. With considerable disgust, he had noted during the trial the way Post would scribble notes and confer with his lawyers.

Margulis and Whalen talked with Post. "You've been here just like us. Do you think the evidence has been strong enough to convince all twelve jurors, beyond a reasonable doubt, that you should go to prison for the rest of your life?"

Post felt very strongly that the state had not proved its case. Accepting a second-degree instruction would be almost akin to pleading guilty. He agreed with his lawyers. Don't give the jury a chance to compromise.

Margulis and Whalen came back in. They turned down the second-degree option.

Before closing argument could begin, Hoag had a announcement for the defense lawyers. Although the state's case was closed, he was going to call a rebuttal witness— Bobby Autin, who would testify about the conversation he had had with Post on the day of the funeral.

Whalen and Margulis immediately objected to the judge.

As the term implies, a rebuttal witness can only be called to rebut testimony. In this instance, Post had admitted under cross-examination that he had talked to Autin about the possibility of dating his sister-in-law.

Hoag argued that Post had denied approaching Autin on the day of the funeral, and that therefore Autin was a proper rebuttal witness.

The judge overruled the objection from the defense.

"Is Autin here, Dean?" the judge asked.

"On his way, Judge," Hoag said.

"We won't wait forever," said the judge.

A squad car picked Bobby Autin up at the airport. Siren wailing and lights flashing, the squad roared down Interstate 70 toward St. Louis.

At 10:55, Autin arrived in court. His eyes were bloodshot and his shirt was open at the collar.

With a glance at Post, Hoag approached the witness box.

"State your name for the record, please."

"My name is Bobby Autin."

"Did you have the occasion to attend the funeral of Julie Post?"

"Yes, I did."

"Did you have occasion to have a conversation with the defendant at any point in time during or after the funeral?"

"Yes, I did."

"What, if anything, did he say to you?"

"He said. 'When this is over, maybe I could date your sister-in-law.' "

Hoag hesitated for a second.

"Who was he referring to?" he finally asked.

"My ex-wife's sister."

"What's her name?"

"Kathy."

"Kathy," repeated Hoag, and then he turned to the defense table.

"Your witness," he said.

As soon as the defense had learned that Bobby was coming, Margulis and Whalen had struggled with a question. Should he be cross-examined?

Margulis thought no. The guy was an absolute loose cannon. There was no telling what he'd say, except whatever it might be, it would be harmful, maybe devastating. If all he said was that Ed wanted to get fixed up with his sister-in-law, Margulis felt it was best to let the matter rest there.

Whalen, of course, thought otherwise. All during the preparation for the trial, he had relished the thought of going after Bobby.

"Let's wait and see what he says," Margulis suggested.

While Hoag walked back to his seat, Whalen asked for the go-ahead. As Bobby sat in the stand with bloodshot eyes an hour shy of noon, Whalen knew the first question he would ask—"How many drinks have you had so far today?"

Margulis voted no, and Post cast the deciding vote not to cross-examine him.

Whalen stood up.

"No questions," he said.

Bobby walked out of the courtroom.

Hoag felt as if he were a catcher again and had just called for the fastball in on the hands. It had whistled into his mitt, completely freezing the hitter.

For the final arguments, the judge had reserved the first two rows behind the defense table for Post's family. As witnesses, they had been excluded from the trial, but they would be permitted to hear the closing arguments.

The Posts came in with the Thigpens. To the courthouse

regulars, it seemed an odd arrangement. Usually a murder trial resembles an unhappy wedding, with the victim's family on one side of the aisle and the defendant's family on the other.

Hoag had argued for a two-hour time limit, or at the very least an hour and a half. Margulis had said one hour would be sufficient. The judge had decided to split the difference. Each side would get an hour and fifteen minutes.

In a criminal case, the state gets to split its time. It goes first to present its case, and then, after the defense presents its argument, the state, because it has the burden of proof, gets the final word.

Hoag stood up to face the jury.

He said he had to prove three elements. First, that Post had killed his wife. Second, that he had meant to kill her. Third, that he had acted with cool deliberation.

Now I've got to prove those three elements beyond a reasonable doubt, he said.

"And when you're looking at the evidence, ladies and gentlemen, and you're talking about a reasonable doubt, keep in mind my burden is not beyond a shadow of a doubt. I can't prove to you beyond any and all doubt that I'm the same lawyer that's been here for two weeks," he said, and he stood there for a minute, short and stocky and rumpled, bristling with energy, a one-of-a-kind lawyer.

"I can't prove this case to you beyond any and all doubt. You see, in order to meet that kind of burden, all of you would have to be transported back in time, and somehow witness the events that took place in room 4063. We don't have that burden. We have beyond a reasonable doubt."

He looked briefly at the defense table.

"Be careful when you're talking about two people who take the stand and take two different approaches. Like for instance, if I had a pot of boiling water on that table right there and I put my hand in it, and Mr. Margulis put his hand in it, and I took the witness stand and said it's hot, and he took the stand and said it's cold, what do you do? Do you throw your hands up in the air, and say, 'I don't know. That's reasonable doubt'?

"You do what the Court says. You bring to bear your common sense."

Then Hoag began reciting the evidence and the testimony of the various witnesses.

Arbini had taken the towel ring to his office and his secretary had said nobody came in and got it until Tim Kaelin did.

The towel ring experts said that the ring would not have come off the wall in a slip-and-fall accident, and more important, that the distortion in the metal of this particular towel ring showed it had been twisted and pulled and worked from the wall.

Hoag talked about the Posts' financial situation, their increased debt, their selling off of assets. According to the tax records, Julie's real income, after expenses, was only about $10,000 a year.

"You see a man who in 1983 went into business and then the bottom fell out. And here is a man who continued to spend at a rapid rate. They're making at best sixty thousand, and he's spending a hundred and fourteen thousand a year," Hoag said.

And what did he do then? Hoag asked, pointing his finger at Post.

"He's cash-poor, and he's in debt, and he's borrowing money, and what does he do then? He buys more life insurance."

That wouldn't be a big deal, Hoag said, except that Julie already had $400,000 worth of life insurance.

"The financial people say, 'You got to take care of your debts. You got to take care of your kids' education, got to replace your wife's income.'

"Well, let's do it, ladies and gentlemen. Let's take four hundred thousand dollars. He had a debt of two hundred thirty thousand dollars on June 3, 1986. Now we've got a hundred and seventy thousand, don't we? And we've got his house paid off, and all his debts cleared. And let's take care of the funeral, say ten thousand dollars. And we've got a hundred and sixty thousand now, don't we?

"And if we put that in a CD and we get ten percent, don't we get sixteen thousand dollars a year? And that's replaced her income. And we haven't touched the hundred and sixty thousand dollars, which we can use for the girls' education."

Hoag turned back to Post.

"They had sufficient insurance," he said.

He then asked the jurors to remember the medical testimony.

Graham said Julie hadn't died as a result of mitral valve prolapse. He said none of the bruises would have rendered her unconscious. He said the totality of the bruises were not consistent with a slip-and-fall accident.

"And in substance, he walks up to the diving board, and he springs and he doesn't jump in. He tells you 'undetermined.' "

Hoag briefly outlined McGarry's findings and then spoke of Fossum.

"In an effort to be fair to Dr. Fossum, I had his transcript for cross-examination typed up, and I'm going to read a couple excerpts."

He read Fossum's testimony leading up to and including the dramatic point at which Fossum admitted that the scraping bruise was consistent with somebody's holding Julie's head down against the safety strips in the tub.

So Julie was murdered, Hoag said. The medical evidence tells us that. And somebody pulled the towel ring off the wall. The scientific evidence tells us that, he said.

He asked the female jurors how many had husbands who drew their bathwater, and he asked the male jurors how often they drew their wives' baths.

"And then he goes out on his jog," Hoag said, putting

all the distaste he felt for Post into the word "jog." "And let me tell you something. This was not an ordinary jog, ladies and gentlemen. This was an alibi jog. He made it a point to say something to the concierge, to say something to the bellhop, and he went down the street, noting all the signs, the Brooks Brothers, the stadium, City Hall parking lot, and he saw Officer Gay."

Hoag shook his head in disbelief, and then talked about Post's story about finding his wife in the tub.

"And how does he pull her out? He grabs her by the arms and he slips three times in trying to pull her out—several times, not three—and then finally, I guess, he had to turn her over and pull her facedown and when he pulls her, she slips and bangs her head.

"Now that's one bang on the head, okay? But, of course, he knows it's there, so he's got to account for it. Fortunately, we know that the three bangs on the head are on rounded portions of the head so one bang can't cause all three bruises.

"Now you got to ask yourself another question. When you come upon your wife or spouse in the bathtub, what's your immediate reaction?

"You're going to jump in there and get her out!"

Let's talk about the defense theories, Hoag suggested.

The towel ring is not the same towel ring, Hoag said sarcastically. Why would everybody lie?

How about mitral valve prolapse? Hoag asked. Or maybe a slip and fall?

Neither theory accounts for the towel ring, or the bruises, Hoag said.

"She can't flip around, ladies and gentlemen. She can't levitate her body and then bang three times on the right side of her head and wind up on the left side. It can't happen. Those are absurd theories."

What about the theory that the towel ring was already damaged? Hoag asked.

"You've got the best evidence going that there wasn't

any preexisting damage. He's sitting right over there," Hoag said, pointing again at Post.

"He didn't see it. He was there three days. He didn't complain about it, and his wife, who was also a detail person, didn't see it and didn't complain."

A final theory, Hoag said. The one-armed man theory, the phantom killer like the one in the television show *The Fugitive*.

"You know what eliminates the phantom killer in this, ladies and gentlemen? The defendant himself. Because the door, the door to the bathroom, was open one inch when he left, and one inch when he came back. And there are no signs of forced entry, no signs of a burglary, no sexual assault. People don't go around thrill-killing by drowning.

"Just as importantly, if she had a split second to recognize someone in her bathroom that shouldn't be there, she'd have screamed bloody murder. And you know what that tells you when you heard from those people in the adjoining rooms? She knew her attacker and she didn't expect it."

Gesturing toward the family members, Hoag said he felt sorry for them. They don't want to believe he did it, Hoag said.

Quickly, Hoag ran over the case again. Julie was difficult to get along with and was causing problems at work. Post was in financial trouble. He decided to kill her for the insurance money, but then decided to go after even bigger bucks and sue the Omni, which is why he tore the ring from the wall.

"But you know what—and this is the sheer irony of it—details convict him. Details convict the Detail Man. Because he didn't count on the details in the examination of the towel ring, and he didn't count on the exhumation, and the details that would bring to light. He made two critical mistakes, small but critical, and that's the way people get caught," Hoag said.

"Details and greed, that's what caught him."

Hoag sat down.

The judge called a ten-minute recess.

Post's relatives seemed numb as they went into the hallway.

"I hate Dean Hoag," said Stephanie.

A reporter asked Hollis Thigpen what he thought. The old man began talking about the Marine Corps and World War II.

As in all his trials, Art Margulis had begun writing his closing argument during jury selection. He kept a notebook exclusively for his final argument, and as the trial proceeded, he made notes to himself. He went over the notes constantly, formulating and updating his closing statement. Although he outlined his argument the night before, he was so familiar with it that he seldom had to refer to his notes.

He had the outline in his hand as he stood to face the jury. Impeccably dressed, he seemed to have more dignity, if less energy, than his adversary, who was sitting in his chair, hunched over the table.

"Ladies and gentlemen, it's been a very long trial, and on behalf of myself and Mr. Whalen, I want to tell you how much we appreciate your attention and your courtesy and your sense of humor after all this time. And most important, I want to thank you all for Mr. Post, who obviously has more at stake here than anyone else in the room.

"The charge here is murder in the first degree. And the punishment for that offense is life in the penitentiary. No probation, no parole. That's what we're dealing with. We're dealing with the rest of a man's life in the Missouri state penitentiary. And that's what we're going to have to work with, and that's what you all are going to have to consider."

Margulis reminded the jury of the state's burden. Instruction number four, he said, would be about reasonable doubt. The state had to prove, beyond a reasonable doubt, that Ed Post had killed his wife, and that he had done so after deliberating upon the matter.

"In other words, he thought about it, planned it, premeditated it," Margulis said.

You have to believe that the state proved every element of its case, beyond a reasonable doubt, in order to convict, he said.

Then he talked about the evidence.

First, Michael Graham.

"He tells us that he has ruled hundreds of deaths homicides in St. Louis, and on this one what does he say? Not only that he's uncomfortable calling it a homicide, but he has doubts, and that's why he can't do it.

"And that's why I just read to you instruction number four. The medical examiner himself had doubts and consequently could not classify it as a homicide."

McGarry?

"More than a month later, the body is exhumed and Dr. McGarry conducts a second autopsy. He conducts it after there have been bone donations and eye donations. He conducts it after there's been an exhumation, after the body's been embalmed, and after the body's been buried, and in so doing disagrees with everything that Dr. Graham says."

Margulis reminded the jury that the third pathologist, Roger Fossum, preferred accident to homicide.

"So we have three expert opinions—one who says undetermined, one who says homicide, one who says accident. And I am asking you, where does that line up with the concept of the law which you must follow that says reasonable doubt? Three opinions. Two of them cannot call it a homicide."

Referring to Hoag's argument and his reading of a transcript of part of Fossum's cross-examination, Margulis pointed out that Hoag had not read the part in which Fossum accounted for the bruises around the head.

"But let me tell you what else the prosecutor said to Dr. Fossum when he was on the stand, and I made a note of it when it happened. Mr. Hoag said, 'Well, Doc, we're just trying to explore the possibilities.'"

Margulis paused for a moment, and then continued.

"And I'm saying to you that that is what this whole case has been about, and that's what is wrong with this whole case. The state has taken whatever they think they've got, and they've just tried to explore the possibilities," he said.

"You can't speculate, and you can't 'explore the possibilities.' You have got to deal with facts, and you've got to deal with evidence, and you've got to deal with those things keeping in mind the guideline—beyond a reasonable doubt."

One of these theories the state has concocted, Margulis said, is that Ed Post chose an in-ground plot to somehow speed the decomposition process.

"Not only did Julie and Ed talk about bone donations and decide to leave the decision to the survivor, but they talked about cremation and also left the decision to the survivor, and Ed Post didn't want to do that. How could he have better covered up than to have followed that course? And he didn't do it!"

Then Margulis talked about the towel ring, and the chain of evidence. He reminded the jury that nobody could say with any certainty that the towel ring Kaelin had picked up in Arbini's office was the towel ring from room 4063.

He had a chart set up on an easel, and each page listed points of difference among the experts.

"Let me run through these. I don't even know what some of these things mean," he said.

For the direction of the primary force applied to the ring, one expert had said counterclockwise, another had said left, relatively horizontal, another had said five directions minimum.

"Force of magnitude," Margulis said, flipping the page. "Doesn't know, doesn't know, thirty to seventy-five pounds, one hundred twenty-five to two fifty, three hundred and eighty-five.

"We're talking about proving something beyond a reasonable doubt, to send a man to the penitentiary for the rest of his life!"

He ran through the other pages, listing the differences among the experts. Finally, he stopped.

"I just wanted to illustrate the point, ladies and gentlemen. I hope I have. This towel ring story, if it was a game, maybe would be fun. But it's not a game because there's too much at stake," Margulis said.

He ridiculed the idea that Post's jog had been an alibi.

"How did Ed Post know that a fire inspector named Gay would be on his route? How did Ed Post know that a fellow he knew from the organization would be out for a jog? And what's so unusual about going out for a jog at six-thirty or seven in the morning?"

And if there was such a big fight, a fight that would have caused thirty-nine different bruises, how come nobody heard anything? Margulis asked. If Julie had been engaged in that kind of life-and-death fight, wouldn't she have screamed?

Again, Margulis paused, to let the jury think about that point.

"Ladies and gentlemen, there is absolutely no motive in this case. There is no reason in the world for Ed to have done this, except for the imagination of the prosecutors."

Margulis said the state started out with one theory—Julie is difficult, Julie causes problems at work.

When the people from New Orleans didn't substantiate that one well enough, the state trotted out another motive, Margulis said.

Finances.

"Julie Post was approved for one million dollars in life insurance, and she and Ed elected to take only seven hundred thousand."

His brother's a probate lawyer, Margulis said. If Ed had planned to kill Julie for money—and Margulis reminded the jurors that if they were to convict for first-degree murder, they would have to believe that Ed had planned to kill her—wouldn't he have made sure she had a will?

Ed Post cooperated with this investigation, Margulis said. He talked to Kaelin, and he talked to Hollocher and Jacobsmeyer, and he agreed to the exhumation.

"Where did it get him?"

Finally, as his time was running out, Margulis talked about the family.

"What did Hollis Thigpen, Julie's father, tell you about Ed Post? 'He's not only my son-in-law, he's my friend.' Julie's mother says. 'We love Ed.'

"If you set aside the emotions that the prosecutor is trying to engender in you, you'll end this nightmare. You'll put this family back together. And you'll find Ed Post innocent. He is innocent. Thank you."

Hoag got up and shook his head. He had spent almost an hour of his time on the first half of his argument. He had eighteen minutes left.

"I must be missing what the words 'speculation' and 'conjecture' mean because I heard him call the state's case speculation and conjecture about fifteen times," Hoag said.

The only speculation and conjecture comes from them, Hoag said, as they try to figure out a way to account for the twisted towel ring and the bruises.

"But you know what? They can't account for all the bruises. No matter how much they speculate, no matter how much Dr. Fossum wants to give you his Disneyland scenario, he still can't account for the three bruises on the side of her head."

They're trying to play the reasonable doubt game, Hoag said, but there are obvious answers to all the little questions they pose. Why didn't anybody hear the fight?

"Nobody heard the struggle because that woman got surprised. She wasn't expecting this. She was not prepared for what happened. She got a black eye as a result of it. She got a large bump on the back of her head, and another large bump on the back of her neck.

"And she got another one, the size of a thumb, on the back of her neck. And three different times, three different times, someone put her head in contact with something that scraped it. Three different times.

"And he says, 'What's the motive?' Well, I heard the instructions. And I've heard instructions for many years. And I've never seen one that said the state has to prove motive.

"I could speculate about motive, but see, we're talking about facts."

Hoag turned and glowered in the direction of the defense table, and then turned back to the jury.

"He says to put the family back together. He says the state has built this case on speculation. Well, I think you know better. You got enough to convict him beyond a reasonable doubt, not even taking into consideration the insurance, not even taking into consideration his efforts to aid in his lawsuit, not even taking into consideration how much money he spent and how dry the well was.

"Forget all of that. And not even taking into consideration all those little bitty factors, all those little bitty incidents which tell you something, don't they?"

Hoag walked over and picked up several of the photographs from the second autopsy.

"When you go back there, and you say, 'Boy, the punishment in this case is life without parole, wow, isn't that something?' Well, that's a hell of a burden, but I haven't heard anybody talk about how long this is," he said, and he held the photographs up for the jurors to see.

"This is forever, ladies and gentlemen. Any man that can do this to a woman deserves to go to jail for life. He did it," Hoag said, and he walked over toward the defense table and pointed at Post.

"It's time to pull the curtain down on his act. His theatrics will go no more. He tried to fool the citizens of St. Louis, and he can't do it. He fooled them in New Orleans and he's fooled his family. It's time to look at the objective facts. Thank you."

The jurors were led out of the courtroom. Margulis stood up and extended his hand to Hoag.

Hoag looked at the extended hand, and then turned and walked out of the courtroom.

Chapter Thirty

Deliberations begin at 1:45 P.M. when the nine women and three men were led to the jury room.

"I guess we need a foreman," somebody said. "Anybody want to volunteer?"

All of the women shook their heads. One of the men, an older man who had been on a jury before, agreed to serve.

"First let's take a vote, and see where we stand," he said. One of the women distributed pieces of paper, and the jurors voted.

Six guilty, three not guilty, three undecided.

The foreman then read aloud the instructions concerning burden of proof and reasonable doubt.

"Now let's open the discussion," he said.

Everybody started talking at once. For two and a half weeks, the jurors had been listening to the case, wanting to talk about it. The foreman waved his arms to get everybody's attention.

"Let's do it this way. We'll go around the table. When it's your turn, you say how you vote and bring up whatever point you want to make. No interruptions until somebody makes their point and then we'll discuss it."

The foreman led off.

"I'm voting guilty, and one thing that really got me was the insurance," he said. The foreman, not incidentally, had reported in voir dire that he had $7,000 of life insurance and his wife had $5,000.

Several people nodded assent. No one spoke on Post's behalf.

Next, one of the other men said he was voting guilty. He couldn't believe that a man would not jump in the tub to pull his wife out.

Again, nods of assent.

Then came one of the undecideds, a woman. She said she had worked in an office filled with women, and knew how catty women in an office could be, and therefore she was discounting the stories about Julie being a problem at work.

Several of the guiltys immediately challenged her. Even if she didn't think Julie was a problem at work, there's plenty of other evidence, they said.

It was clear that the guiltys held their opinions more strongly, or at least were more vociferous, than the not guiltys and the undecideds.

Another juror spoke. The medical evidence and the conversation with Bobby Autin had convinced her that Post was guilty, she said.

Again, the points were discussed, and again, the guiltys did the talking. Two jurors remarked on the fact that the defense had not even tried to cross-examine Autin.

"I'm just not sure," said one of the not guiltys when it was her turn to speak.

"If Dr. Graham isn't sure it's a homicide, I just don't know," said another not guilty when it was her turn.

He's not saying it wasn't a homicide, said one of the guiltys. He didn't do a very good autopsy, said another guilty. Bruises don't show up until later, said yet another.

After two go-arounds, the jurors buzzed the judge. They wanted to see some evidence.

They asked for the insurance policies, the autopsy reports, the towel ring, and the photographs from the second autopsy.

The evidence was reviewed and discussed in the same round-table fashion.

After every circuit, another vote was held.

The guilty voters continued to be the most vociferous, but the others held firm.

By eight o'clock when the jurors were taken back to their hotel for the night, only one vote had changed. One of the not guilty votes had gone into the undecided column.

The next morning, as one of the undecideds was freshening up in her hotel room, she looked at the bathtub. It was about the same size as the tub in room 4063 at the Omni. She tried to imagine how a person could drown in such a tub. She decided to change her vote to guilty.

She had been, perhaps, the strongest of the undecideds.

The jurors opened their deliberations by taking another secret vote. Three of the undecideds had changed overnight to guilty, and one of the not guilty votes had changed to undecided. It was suddenly nine guilty, two undecided, and one not guilty.

The jurors called for another piece of evidence—the tape of the Jacobsmeyer-Post conversation.

More discussions followed. Then another vote. The two undecideds swung over to guilty. Eleven to one.

"I just can't send somebody to prison for life unless I'm absolutely sure," said the one holdout. Before long, she was crying.

Everybody was trying to persuade her.

"Maybe it's not the same towel ring," she said.

Among the evidence the jurors had was the batch of photographs the police technician had taken when police were first summoned to the scene.

One of the jurors laid the towel ring on the floor and put the photograph of the towel ring in the tub next to it.

"Doesn't that look the same?" she asked.

Other jurors tried other tactics.

"You explain this, then," they'd say, and bring up

something like the insurance, or the Bobby Autin conversation.

After a couple of hours, the holdout folded. Shortly after noon, the jurors had reached a unanimous verdict.

The courtroom was only half filled when they returned. The Post family were in the two front rows.

"Have you reached a verdict in this case?" the judge asked the foreman.

"We have, your honor."

The judge turned back to the spectators.

"Before I have the clerk read the verdict, let me say that I know there's a lot of emotion involved, but the Court will not tolerate any outbursts in the courtroom. If you don't think you can handle that, if you think you're going to get extremely emotional, I suggest you leave."

Seeing that no one was leaving, the judge instructed the sheriff to bring the verdict to him. He looked at it and then handed it to the clerk for reading.

"We, the jury, in the aforementioned case, find the defendant, Edward T. Post, guilty of first-degree murder."

At the word "guilty," Stephanie began to wail. Al Post, Ed's father, gasped and clutched his throat with his right hand.

"He didn't do it!" screamed Stephanie. "He didn't do it! Oh God!"

Family members, clutching each other for support, stumbled out of the courtroom.

Only Post himself had remained calm.

In the hallway, Stephanie spotted Dee Vossmeyer, who had come to hear the verdict. Family members had to restrain her.

"I hate you!" she screamed. "You've taken my father! My life is over!"

Inside the courtroom, the jurors heard the screaming and were unnerved. The judge sent them back upstairs to the jury room. He asked McCraw to go speak to them.

"You did the right thing," the detective told them. "There are things you don't even know about."

City Jail, a blocky six-story structure, had been built near the turn of the century and had a medieval feel to it. It was more a dungeon than a jail, and the prisoners went up and down the staircases shackled together in groups of eight.

A visitor allowed to stand in a stairwell as these manacled prisoners filed by would have been struck by the fact that almost all of them were young black men, tough and sullen-looking.

Into this milieu was cast Edward Post, a forty-six-year-old, slightly overweight wine connoisseur from New Orleans.

Several days after his conviction, a newspaper columnist visited him.

Post seemed surprisingly chipper.

"I played eighteen holes of golf today," he said.

"You did what?" the visitor asked.

"In my mind, I mean," Post said. "It's the only way to get through a time like this. You have to play games with your mind. It's something I learned in the Green Berets. Thank God we had good prisoner-of-war training."

At about the same time, a public defender went to the jail to visit one of her clients. When she noticed that the usual madhouse around the telephone on the cellblock seemed to be organized for a change, she asked her client, a young black man, what had caused the change.

"Mr. Post has taken charge," he said.

An appeal bond was set at $700,000, with $500,000 of it required in cash.

As soon as Dan returned to New Orleans, he began trying to raise the money.

The insurance company had refused to pay on the $300,000 policy Ed had purchased shortly before Julie's death, but did pay on the original $400,000 policy. The payment was made to the daughters. Because Jennifer was only fifteen, her money went into a trust, but Stephanie, who was eighteen, was able to pledge her share toward the cost of her father's bond.

Al and Ann Post had already spent all of their available cash. The trial had been a tremendous financial drain—legal fees, experts' fees, and travel costs for all the participants. In fact, the hotel bill at the Adam's Mark, where the family and the experts had stayed during the trial, came to $10,000.

But with the last of their reserves—certificates of deposit for which they gladly accepted the early-withdrawal penalties—Al and Ann were able to raise most of the remaining $300,000.

Dan's fund-raising campaign took care of the rest. He ignored his law practice to beg and borrow. He told people about the deplorable conditions at City Jail. He talked about a jury that couldn't understand the concept of reasonable doubt. And, mostly, he talked about his brother's innocence.

After only two weeks, the money was raised. Dan and Toni went to St. Louis to free Ed.

When Ed walked out of City Jail, he noticed a small group of reporters clustered around Dan. The reporters marveled at the fact that a man who was supposedly financially strapped—at least that's what the state had claimed during the trial—had friends and family who could raise $500,000 in cash. They wanted to know where the money had come from.

Ed stood for a moment, ignored by the press, while his brother answered questions. Later, Ed would say of his jealous feelings as he watched his brother take center stage, "I wanted to puke."

Before leaving St. Louis, Ed and Dan and Toni went to a French restaurant. Ed ordered for Toni. Twice, he informed the waiter that the food had been inadequately prepared and sent it back to the kitchen.

Normally, an appeal bond is valid until the appeal is exhausted. But for first-degree murder, the bond is revoked at the time of sentencing. Post would have only three weeks of freedom.

After Post's conviction, Jennifer had moved in with Dan and Martha and their three daughters. During his three weeks in New Orleans, Ed spent almost all his time with Toni. He saw Jennifer only three times. One occasion was for the taping of a television news show about his conviction. A second was when one of Martha and Dan's daughters had a baby; he visited the hospital and, by chance, saw his younger daughter. Only once did he come by the house to see her.

This inattention bothered Martha. In her anger, she felt the first stirrings of doubt. She remembered the times Julie had said that Ed beat her.

Dan continued to organize a letter-writing campaign to Judge Mummert. Dan urged people to plea for leniency. Dozens of people wrote letters.

Ed confided to close friends that there was a chance Mummert might set him free. Simply by returning for his sentencing he would be demonstrating his innocence, he said.

On the morning that Ed was to return to St. Louis, the entire Post family gathered at Dan and Martha's house.

"Toni is my spiritual wife," he said. "She will be my ears and eyes in New Orleans while I'm gone."

Then he flew to St. Louis, where he was sentenced to life without the possibility of parole.

The prison at Potosi was opened in January 1989, and in some ways it was state-of-the-art.

Unlike old-fashioned prisons, it did not have cellblocks

stacked on top of each other. Each prisoner had his own room—without bars.

The rooms were narrow, and along the length of the door ran an unbreakable plastic window. A guard, walking by, could look through the window and see the inmate.

The prison was designed to house people who would never be released, people doing life without parole, as well as troublemakers from other prisons. It also housed death row.

Although it could hold seven hundred inmates, at the time Post was sent there fewer than three hundred prisoners in the state qualified for Potosi. Because the inmates would never be released, the prison offered little in the way of rehabilitation. An inmate's time was his own.

Post chose to spend his evenings watching television in his room—inmates were allowed to purchase televisions—and most of the rest of his time in the law library. He concocted a number of ideas for ways to win his freedom. Some were farfetched. He had heard that trumpeter Al Hirt was friends with a man who was politically influential in Missouri. He wrote Dan and suggested Hirt be recruited to help.

He also came across a statute allowing a judge to order a prisoner's release after 120 days of incarceration—the so-called shock statute, because it is intended to shock the prisoner with the reality of prison. Although it is almost always used for people convicted of minor crimes, it gave Ed new hope. He wrote Dan and asked him to pursue this avenue.

Dan did, and in August, a contingent of supporters from New Orleans came to St. Louis to visit Mummert and to ask that Ed be released. Mummert politely refused.

Most of the group went home. Dan Post and Harby Kreeger rented a car and drove to Potosi to visit Ed. On this trip, their relationship began to evolve from acquaintance to friendship.

When a reporter visited Ed Post in the fall of 1989, he

seemed remarkably upbeat. He said he was confident that his appeal would be successful.

He acknowledged that Potosi was a dangerous place—with no one having a release date, prison authorities had little with which to threaten the inmates—but he insisted that he was having no problems. Authorities confirmed his statement.

He said the food was nutritious, if not the gourmet fare of which he was so fond. His legal studies had confirmed, he said, that the state's towel ring testimony should not have been allowed.

Likening his case to a Kafka novel, he maintained his innocence.

He had been particularly distressed, he said, to read a newspaper story in which Hollocher had pointed to his little feet as a sure sign of guilt.

In that same story, Hollocher had claimed that one evening he had parked in front of Post's house and Post had come out and taunted the detective.

"He came out to my car and said, 'You're not smart enough to catch me,' " Hollocher had said.

Post shook his head.

"Anybody who knows me would know I'd never do anything like that," he said.

His family still believed in him, he said, and he showed the visitor a heartrending letter from Stephanie.

"We all know your innocence will be the winner in the end. I love you, Daddy. I am proud to be a Post!"

She signed it, "Your First and Most Faithful Daughter."

Chapter Thirty-one

One evening in the winter of 1989, Deputy Johnny Molina fell on the courthouse steps and injured his back.

It happened on a very cold night when the steps were icy and hazardous. There were two versions of how the accident occurred.

There was Molina's version. A homeless drunk, realizing that it was too late to get into one of the nearby shelters, had come to the courthouse to seek refuge from the cold and, as he climbed the stairs, he fell. Molina went to help him, and as he tried to lift the drunk, he wrenched his back and also fell.

Another version had it that there was no drunk—except perhaps Molina—and that the deputy, in charge of guarding the empty courthouse, had fallen as he trudged up the steps to work.

At any rate, Molina was injured.

He later claimed that he called his lieutenant to report that he would have to miss work to see a doctor, but the lieutenant claimed not to have received such a call.

Three facts were never in dispute. Molina missed a day of work because of his injury. He was docked a day's pay. The loss came to $60.

Then in the spring of 1990, the sheriff announced that he was transferring Molina from the empty courthouse to City Jail.

Molina was outraged.

Twice now, he had been wrong. Actually, he had never

recovered from the first outrage. He carried in his wallet the stub for the paycheck in which he had been docked. Sometimes he pulled it out of his wallet and simply stared at it.

The transfer was an even greater insult. To work at the jail meant actually having to work.

In St. Louis the sheriff's department was a patronage office. A job-seeker needed the endorsement of a ward organization or a political boss to be hired. Under Sheriff Jim Murphy, a deputy could go as far as his connections could take him.

For instance, Scotty Lammert, who had headed the deputies in charge of Post's sequestered jury, was the son of a Democratic ward committeewoman.

Molina had equally strong credentials. His family had owned a saloon that was a hangout for politicians. So Molina had come on board directly from Sheriff Gordon Schweitzer, Murphy's predecessor. When Schweitzer retired, Molina supported Murphy, a former legislator who had lost a reelection bid after a minor scandal involving an attempt to sell insurance to city employees on city time. Murphy's campaign headquarters had been provided courtesy of the Molina family.

No wonder, then, that Molina felt betrayed.

Molina remembered Ralph Whalen's name. He had once known a bartender with the same last name.

So in March 1990, filled with the resolve of the persecuted, Molina called information in New Orleans and asked for an attorney named Whalen. He got the number and called.

"Would you be interested in hearing about misconduct with the deputies and the jurors in the Ed Post case?" he asked.

"What kind of misconduct?" asked Whalen.

"Getting drunk, having sex, that sort of thing," Molina responded.

Whalen took Molina's number and called Margulis. Within minutes, Margulis was talking to Molina.

"Yes, I'd be willing to give an affidavit," said Molina. "I'll be happy to testify if it comes to that."

Molina went to Margulis's office and told Margulis that the sequestered jury duty for the Post trial had been one long party. He said he remembered a night when he had to carry a drunken juror back to his room. The jurors often discussed the case with the deputies and with each other. And that was saying nothing about the sex that went on.

As Molina talked, Margulis tried to size him up. Although he claimed to be acting for altruistic reasons—everybody deserves a fair trial—it was clear that he had his own agenda.

"Be honest with me, John. Are you having troubles at work? Believe me, everything is going to come out in the end," Margulis said.

"Some troubles," Molina admitted, "but mainly I'm doing this because I think it's the right thing to do."

Molina made a taped statement, and Margulis sent a private investigator to search for witnesses who could substantiate Molina's allegations.

One such witness was Kathy Maddux, a cocktail waitress and part-time bartender at the Holiday Inn on Market Street, the hotel where the jurors had been sequestered.

A bleached blonde, she told Margulis that the jury had been drunk every night. In fact, she said, there had been nights when she had to ask them to hold it down with talk about the murder trial for fear they would chase her other customers away.

If only her story weren't quite so bizarre, thought Margulis. If she claimed to have overheard only one conversation, that would be better. One discussion among the deputies and the jurors might be believable. But wild conversations every night?

Meanwhile, his private investigator was interviewing the jurors. All denied any knowledge of heavy drinking or sex, but one told the investigator that Deputy Lammert's girlfriend, a St. Louis police officer, had visited with and talked to the jurors on several occasions.

A cop visiting and drinking with the jurors during the trial!

That by itself might be enough, thought Margulis. After all, the cornerstone of any criminal defense is ''The state cannot be trusted. The cops are lying.''

Was it fair that while the defense made that argument, the jurors were allowed to socialize with cops? Of course not.

Molina had also supplied Margulis with a list of the deputies who had visited the sequestered jurors.

Margulis filed the affidavits with the court, and the media went wild. Molina became a star. When rumors began to shoot around the courthouse that somebody was paying Molina to do this, he contacted a newspaper columnist to set the story straight.

''Let me tell you what happened,'' he told the columnist. ''I'm from the old school. I'm no snitch, and I'm sick of people saying I got paid to do this. I didn't.''

And then he explained about the transfer, and the docking of a day's pay.

The columnist came to Molina's defense.

''There are only two pure motives in the world. Love and revenge. Molina is fueled by the second,'' the columnist wrote.

Meanwhile, the jurors felt humiliated and puzzled. Most of them had been completely unaware of the activities in the deputies' rooms. One such juror, an alternate named Mary Rempe who had not attended a single party, told a reporter that the allegations were ridiculous.

The day that story appeared, another man contacted Margulis. His name was Ray Simon, and he identified himself as a concerned citizen who was interested only in justice.

''I'm friends with Mary Rempe's husband,'' he said.

"She's lying. Her husband talked to her every night and used to go to the hotel to visit. He even went with the jury when they took a field trip to the zoo. He told me all along that the jury thought Post was guilty."

Margulis filed a third affidavit with the court.

The affidavits were filed in April with the Missouri Court of Appeals. The court ordered Judge Mummert to hold a hearing to determine whether the allegations were true.

Stephanie Post had moved to Mobile, Alabama, in the spring of 1990 for a job. She had accomplished something most teenagers could only dream of doing—she had spent more than $200,000 in less than a year. She had splurged on trips, and clothes, and cars, and more trips and more clothes. She had spent her half of the proceeds from her mother's life insurance.

In Mobile, though, she was trying to get her life together. She began dating a doctor who attended meetings of Alcoholics Anonymous. Stephanie began attending Al-Anon, a support group for families of alcoholics. She heard a lot of talk about denial and about the need to face reality.

Her boyfriend weighed in with his opinion about the autopsies. He suggested her mother's death might not have been an accident.

Stephanie thought about the fights her parents had had. She thought about the night her father had told Kim Autin he loved her. She thought about an incident, after her mother's death, when her father had kicked her.

But still, when her father would call from prison, she was his loving daughter.

The doubts that were building she shared with no one.

The hearing, held in June, fell somewhere between a circus and a reunion.

Post's parents and his daughters were there along with

the jurors, the lawyers, and the deputies. Also present, of course, were the new stars—Molina, Maddux, and Raymond Simon, the "concerned citizen" who had contacted Margulis about the juror's husband.

Molina, wearing black slacks, a yellow T-shirt, and a red baseball cap, paced the hall prior to the hearing. He was introduced to the Post family, and Post's father eagerly extended his hand.

"It took real guts to do what you did. Real guts," he said.

When Al Post turned away, Molina rolled his eyes.

"I don't know if I'm a hero or an antihero," he said.

Stephanie Post seemed much older and much more composed than she had just a year earlier. She told a reporter she had quit school and was working and making a real good living.

Dee Vossmeyer-Hayes walked past. Stephanie said nothing.

"Hey, you've really grown up," said the reporter. "A year ago, you would have tried to attack her."

"Oh, I have grown up," Stephanie said. "Plus, I'm not judgmental anymore." Then she motioned toward the courtroom in which her father was sitting. "I don't even judge Ed."

It seemed a strange thing to say.

Sheriff Murphy, whose department was being blasted in the media, was also in the hallway. He seemed less concerned about the alleged improprieties by his deputies than by the fact that some of the deputies had admitted the improprieties.

If people had known enough to keep their mouths shut, this wouldn't have happened, he said.

Molina was the first witness. He said that deputies not assigned to the case, including himself, had mingled with certain jurors, and that rumors were rampant about sex between the deputies and jurors. He talked about jurors and deputies getting drunk, and he testified that he had heard jurors discussing the case among themselves.

Hoag was scathing in his cross-examination, and while Molina admitted that he had come forward partly for personal reasons, he clung doggedly to his story.

Kathy Maddux, on the other hand, was pretty well demolished in cross-examination. She stuck to her story about drunkenness and loud talk—Molina was the worst offender, she said—but Hoag thoroughly discredited her.

Not only had she been written up by the hotel for being drunk on duty during the trial, but she testified to things that were proved to be false. For instance, she claimed that the jurors ate dinner every night at the hotel, and that was shown not to be the case. When confronted with records indicating that most of the meals were at a nearby restaurant, she hesitated—and then hung with her story.

The "concerned citizen" was even worse. Simon testified that the juror's husband had told him the day before the trip to the zoo that he would be accompanying the jurors.

As Hoag pointed out in a rhetorical question, the jurors were taken to the zoo only when the trial was postponed for a day because of the death of Steve Moore's father. Since nobody knew that he was going to die, how could the juror's husband have known a day in advance?

Simon turned hostile. Further questioning revealed that Simon had been sued by the juror's husband, and was an enemy rather than a friend.

To top it off, Hoag produced a criminal record indicating that Simon had been arrested with Paul Leisure, a mobster who was doing time with Post in the prison at Potosi. Furthermore, Simon had been convicted three years earlier for tampering with a witness.

Although Hoag had brought two guards from the prison who were prepared to testify that Leisure and Post were friends and spent a lot of time together, so thoroughly was

Simon discredited that Hoag didn't bother to have the guards testify.

Hoag's problem, however, had to do with the deputies.

In they marched, one after another, reluctantly testifying that although they hadn't been assigned to the case, they used to hang out in Deputy Lammert's room and in the hallway outside his room.

They drank, played cards, threw Frisbees, and socialized with the jurors. They made it sound as if the trial had been *Perry Mason* by day, *Animal House* by night.

Lammert testified that he didn't know what his duties were as deputy in charge of a sequestered jury. And yes, his girlfriend, the police officer, had meals with the sequestered jury, and had come to his room to socialize with the jury. He didn't know that was wrong, he said.

She testified, too, and said she had not known that was wrong.

Stock testified about Steffen's boast that he had been having sex with a juror. A lieutenant also testified about Steffen's boast.

Steffen took the stand and denied having made the statement. To Steffen, the denial was a point of honor, although it opened him to charges of perjury. He was being loyal to the sheriff. He was also, to his thinking, being chivalrous to the juror.

He had already called her.

"I want you to hear it from me," he said. "This is going to sound awful, but during the trial, I pretended we were having sex."

The juror, of course, was aghast.

"The worse news is it's going to go public," he told her.

Murphy himself took the stand and testified that the deputies should have known how to conduct themselves with a sequestered jury because the proper procedures were listed in the rule book.

Under cross-examination, he admitted that he had not

yet finished writing his rule book, so of course it had not yet been distributed.

As a columnist wrote, "If Sheriff Murphy were trying to play the part of a dumb sheriff, you'd have to say he overacted."

Finally the jurors themselves testified. To the jurors, this whole ordeal had been humiliating. It was bad enough to have to serve on a jury in a murder trial; to see the entire proceedings held up to ridicule because of misconduct by the deputies was even worse.

Most of the jurors, of course, had not been aware of the drinking and the misconduct. Most had chosen to spend the evenings reading in their rooms. The few who had accepted Lammert's invitation to attend the nightly parties had not known anything was wrong. To them, the deputies represented officialdom.

But one by one, the jurors were called to the stand. In front of a crowded courtroom, they had to answer questions as to whether they got drunk with the deputies and/or had sex with them.

No, and no, everybody said.

Had they ever discussed the case with the deputies or with each other?

No, and no, they said.

Had the deputies ever discussed the case in their presence?

No, most of them said. Only Molina with a casual remark about the towel ring testimony, others said.

Most of them also said they had not been aware that Lammert's girlfriend was a police officer.

One of the jurors testified, however, that on one occasion Lammert's girlfriend had come upstairs in her police uniform.

When Hoag heard that, he said nothing. He had the demeanor of a doctor who is looking at a dark spot on an X-ray.

"Did that affect your ability to judge this case fairly and impartially?" he asked.

No, it did not, said the juror.

Still, the overall impression was not a good one.

And if the overall impression had been bad as far as the spectators were concerned, Hoag knew the truth was even worse.

Of all the talk about sex, the allegation that seemed to have the most substance concerned the young juror who had supposedly put her room key in a deputy's pocket. Like Mary Rempe, who had been falsely accused of socializing with her husband, this juror had been an alternate. But while Hoag had been sure that Rempe would be vindicated, he was not so sure about this second alternate.

She presented a problem for Mummert, too. The judge wanted to learn the truth, and he was afraid the circuslike atmosphere in the courtroom would intimidate the young woman. Hopeful that he was more likely to get a truthful response if the young woman was spared the humiliation of testifying in the open courtroom, Mummert had brought her into his chambers.

With only the attorneys present, Mummert had asked her about the allegation.

Yes, the deputy came to her room, she said. Yes, there was sexual contact, she said. Kissing and touching, but no intercourse.

Hoag listened and closed his eyes.

"Judge, she was only an alternate," he finally said. "She took no part in the deliberations. The other jurors didn't even know it happened."

Margulis tried to suppress a smile.

While both sides waited for the judge to make his recommendation to the appellate court, Kathy Maddux was arrested.

After her testimony, she had been interviewed by the

television reporters. With her stories about an "endless party," she was a wonderful interviewee.

Unfortunately for Maddux, one of her neighbors recognized the pearls she was wearing. They had been stolen from the neighbor's apartment. The neighbor called the police, and Maddux was arrested.

Her arrest occurred on Bastille Day, the day that commemorates another effort to set prisoners free.

Mummert filed a recommendation with the appellate court that Post be given a new trial.

In February 1991, the appellate court, citing "outrageous behavior on the part of the deputies that had poisoned the deliberate atmosphere a jury requires," ruled that Post had been denied a fair trial. His conviction was reversed.

The ruling was handed down the same day that Hollocher resigned under pressure from the police department. The official reason was that he had violated the police department's residency requirement because he lived outside the city in an adjoining county.

But inside the department, everybody knew that internal affairs was looking into allegations of more serious misconduct. None had to do with the Post case.

As soon as the appellate court reversed Post's conviction, Margulis went to a judge and argued that Post should be released on bond. Hoag insisted that the proper remedy would be a speedy retrial.

The judge ruled in favor of Margulis. After all, the conviction had been reversed. Legally, Post was merely accused of a crime. Furthermore, his history was in his favor. He had been on bond prior to his first trial and he had not fled. Then he had been on bond prior to his sentencing and he had returned to St. Louis fully aware that he was to be sentenced to life without parole.

Post was transferred from Potosi to City Jail in March

1991. A formal bond hearing was scheduled for the second week in April. Post was going to get out of jail.

Hoag was devastated. He knew that once Post got out, the defense lawyers would do everything in their power to delay the new trial.

Delays always hurt the prosecution. Witnesses die, or forget things. Evidence gets lost. Unanticipated events occur.

On March 22, as Post awaited his bond hearing, a career criminal named Adolph Archie murdered a policeman in New Orleans.

In the course of his arrest, Archie was slightly injured. His trip to the hospital was delayed, however, and he was taken to the district police station at St. Louis and Basin streets, just west of the French Quarter. He remained there for forty minutes, in the custody of the slain officer's partner.

Archie died that night at the hospital.

Dr. Paul McGarry performed the autopsy. He found a skull fracture, and he determined that the injury was consistent with a fall.

A pathologist who performed a subsequent autopsy on behalf of Archie's family alleged that McGarry had missed a second skull fracture, a fractured larnyx, extensive internal bleeding, and a mass of clotted blood in the right testicle. Federal and local authorities began immediate investigations.

When Post heard of McGarry's problems, he became exuberant. He predicted that the state would be forced to drop its case against him.

Chapter Thirty-two

For almost two years, Post had been trying to head his family from a jail cell, and he was looking forward to assuming his familial duties in person.

There had been problems.

The most significant one had to do with the sale of his house on the West Bank. He had given Dan the power of attorney to handle the negotiations. The sale Dan arranged included some of the paintings that hung on the walls.

Ed had gone totally berserk. Those were paintings he and Julie had bought together! You can't sell paintings like that to strangers, he had shouted over the phone. He even accused Dan of trying to engineer a quick sale just so the family could begin to recoup from the financial disaster of the legal costs.

That outburst had hurt Dan badly. In truth, a real estate agent who knew Ed had handled the sale, and the house had fetched a remarkably good price. What's more, Dan's legal practice had been on hold while he took care of Ed's affairs. To then be accused of working against Ed's interests was almost more than Dan could bear.

Besides, Dan was hardly convinced of his brother's innocence.

Sometimes Dan would see Stephanie and Jennifer and think about the emotional turmoil in their lives. Their mother was dead; their father was serving life in prison. The girls were convinced he was innocent, and this notion of their father's unjust imprisonment was tearing them apart.

The same sort of emotional trauma was being visited upon Dan's parents. In addition, the family had spent so much money that Al had returned to work.

Dan was becoming increasingly bitter. But still, he said nothing to his nieces or his parents, and he continued to be supportive toward his younger brother.

Only once did he do anything remotely spiteful. When the news had broken about the deputies' misconduct and Ed had begun writing and talking about the lawsuit he would eventually file and the book and movie contracts that were going to come his way, Dan had sent him a promissory note to sign. According to the note, Ed owed their parents $500,000. That figure was supposed to include the cost of supporting Ed while he was unemployed and awaiting trial, as well as the cost of the trial and the appeal.

Naturally, Ed had not signed it, and the matter had been dropped. As far as Ed knew as he sat in City Jail awaiting his bond hearing and his subsequent release, his friends and family were still strongly behind him.

The only possible exception was Stephanie. She was sounding increasingly distant when he called her, and in his final month at Potosi she had not sent his monthly allowance to his commissary account. When he called to remind her, she had been flippant.

"So sue me," she said.

Ed was not too concerned, however. In a few days he would be out, and whatever was troubling his older daughter could be dealt with then.

Although Dan did not share his doubts with his parents or his nieces, he had become very friendly with Harby Kreeger, and to each man's surprise, neither was truly sure of Ed's innocence. Dan's suspicions had to do with what he knew of the violence in Ed's household. Harby's doubts were fed more by what he knew of Ed's interest in other women.

But the real doubters among Ed's circle of supporters were the women. Martha Post, Dianne Kreeger, and another friend had been sharing stories and pooling information. Dianne told how Julie had talked about a divorce. Martha talked about the times Julie had said that Ed beat her. There had been times, too, Martha said, when Julie had called Dan and had asked him to intervene. Dianne said that the reason Julie had wanted a divorce was that the abuse was beginning to veer toward the girls.

Incidentally, this was one story that Harby just couldn't believe. Maybe Ed had flipped out and had killed Julie, but even so, Ed was simply incapable of abusing his own daughters, as far as Harby was concerned.

Meanwhile, in an effort to sort out her conflicting emotions, Stephanie was undergoing counseling. As part of her therapy, she was hypnotized. She was able to recall what the hypnotist said were long-suppressed memories. She remembered her father locking her in a closet. She remembered him being violent toward her mother.

Two days before Post's bond hearing, Stephanie called Harby to talk about something totally unrelated to her father. Harby tried to listen, but he kept thinking of Dianne's story.

Right out of the blue, he said, "Steph, I've got to ask you this. Did Ed ever beat you up?"

She told Harby about a time, after Julie's death, when Ed had knocked her down and kicked her, and she wanted to know, of course, why he had asked.

He put Dianne on the phone.

When she finished talking to Diane, Stephanie called Dan.

"I think my father killed my mother. What do you know?" she asked.

"Your mother used to call me," Dan said.

Stephanie hung up and called the Thigpens.

"Do you know anything about my father beating my mother?" she asked Hollis. He handed the phone to Etta Mae.

"We know about one time," she said.

Stephanie poured out her story to the Thigpens. She told them her father had been in love with another woman. The Thigpens didn't need much convincing.

When she was finished with the Thigpens, Stephanie called Dean Hoag. "You've got to keep my father in jail," she said. "He killed my mother, and if he gets out, I'm afraid he'll kill me."

Hoag could hardly believe what he was hearing.

Minutes later, he received a call from Hollis Thigpen.

"That boy is where he belongs. You keep him there," said Hollis.

In the course of an hour, the equation had changed. Unbeknownst to Post as he sat in City Jail, much of his support had just washed away.

The next day, Ed called Stephanie to talk about his imminent return.

"You killed my mother," she said and hung up.

She then called Art Margulis and told him she had undergone hypnosis and was now able to remember many things.

The next night, Ed called his mother to find out what travel arrangements had been made for his release the following day. She told him everything was on hold. Stephanie had called Hoag.

Hoag filed a motion to delay the bond hearing while Stephanie's allegations were investigated. After all, she was now going to be a witness for the state, and she was claiming her life would be endangered if Post were released. The judge granted the delay. Margulis notified Post, who was absolutely devastated.

Jennifer, meanwhile, was at a private boarding school in San Antonio, unaware of the evolving situation. More than Stephanie, she had always been Daddy's little girl. She got a call from her older sister.

"I just want you to know that I'm not letting Ed come home," Stephanie said.

Jennifer thought it was silly the way Stephanie called their father Ed all the time, as if she were so grown-up. But as far as any talk about murder, Jennifer simply didn't want to hear it. She hung up on her sister and went back to her studies. She was due to graduate from high school in a month.

The next night Toni called.

"Stephanie is crazy. Unless we do something, she's going to keep your father in prison. She says she's afraid he's going to kill her if he gets out. You've got to call Margulis."

Jennifer felt pulled in fifty different directions. She was closer to her sister than to anybody else in the world, but she knew Stephanie's fears were a joke. Even if she believed that their father had murdered their mother—and Jennifer refused to even think about that—it was ludicrous to think that Stephanie's life was in danger.

Actually, Jennifer thought the whole thing had to do with a family power play. Stephanie felt she was the new head of the family. She didn't want to yield her authority to their father.

Jennifer called Margulis and made a taped statement in which she did not recall any of the abuse that Stephanie was alleging.

Hoag, Moore, and Jacobsmeyer flew to Mobile, taped a statement from Stephanie, and then flew to New Orleans to get statements from Kim Autin and Dianne Kreeger. Both women backed Stephanie.

The bond hearing was held in early May. Margulis argued for the $50,000 bond that had been tentatively set and that would require only $5,000 cash. Hoag argued for no bond.

The judge set the bond at $750,000, with the stipulation that $500,000 had to be in cash.

This time, it was out of reach.

Post remained in City Jail to await his second trial.

After Stephanie turned on her father, Ann Post sent her a letter warning her of what would happen to her reputation if she testified against her father. All your psychiatric and emotional problems, your attempted suicide, your abortion, the ridiculous way you spent over $200,000, the sleeping around—all these things will come out, the letter warned.

Stephanie showed the letter to Dan, and he wrote to his parents, informing them that he and Martha were convinced that Stephanie was telling the truth and had decided not to let her stand alone.

Do what is best for Ed in the long run, he wrote. Dan urged his parents to encourage Ed to plea-bargain. Only then could the family find peace, Dan insisted. He also suggested that a new trial would almost certainly result in another life sentence.

Al and Ann responded that they would never encourage Ed to plea-bargain.

Later that summer, Hoag went to New Orleans to talk to his witnesses. When he visited Harby Kreeger, Dan Post was present. The three men talked about the possibility of a plea bargain. Hoag explained that he would have to clear any such deal with George Peach, the circuit attorney, but added that he thought a plea to second-degree murder and a twenty-five-year sentence would be possible. In Missouri, a person generally must serve a third of the sentence before being paroled, so under such a plea agreement, Ed would have to serve a total of approximately eight years.

Dan agreed that he would testify against his brother if the case went to trial.

In St. Louis, Ed refused to discuss a plea bargain. He maintained his innocence.

Upset about the delays and the lack of communication with his attorney, he fired Margulis and hired Richard Sindel. Among Sindel's former clients was Paul Leisure, Ed's friend from Potosi.

The relationship between the Post brothers was by now irrevocably broken. So dramatic was Dan's turnaround that he offered to send Hoag the long and detailed rebuttal Ed had written of the police report back in '86. Concerned that it could contain confidential defense information—use of which by the prosecution could cause another mistrial— Hoag told Dan not to send it.

But Dan did package the letters he had received from his brother in prison and sent those to the prosecutor. Hoag threw them out.

Chapter Thirty-three

Richard Sindel was in his early forties, and he cut a dashing figure around the courthouse. He was handsome, with dark hair and a mustache, and except when he was in court, he was usually smiling. Despite his relative youth, he was near the top in the informal hierarchy of defense attorneys, only a rung below Margulis, and the Post case presented him with a no-lose situation. The lawyer with the biggest reputation in town had lost this case already—and that was before Post's family and friends had come over to the side of the state.

Few observers expected Sindel to win. But he had a chance, he thought, of surprising everybody.

He was knowledgeable about forensic medicine, and from the time of his first reading of the transcripts and the autopsy reports he was convinced he could disprove most of McGarry's findings.

He didn't believe a pathologist could pinpoint the age of a bruise, as McGarry had done at the first trial. The testimony about the bruises occurring "at or near the time of death" was nonsense. Although the judge had ruled that the Adolph Archie case could not be used to discredit Paul McGarry, Sindel was unperturbed.

He had hired the pathologist who had done the second autopsy on Archie. That would mean four pathologists would testify. It would be three undetermined to one homicide. It would also be three to one about the impossibility of pinpointing the age of a bruise relative to time of death.

Furthermore, the nurse in charge of the bone harvesting had remarked about the perfect condition of Julie's body. Even though bruises grew more pronounced with time, there was no way Julie could have received the severe beating McGarry's testimony indicated—thirty-nine areas of bruising—if virtually none of the bruises were visible hours after her death.

Sindel also had noticed something about the so-called fingerprint bruises on the back of the head. Whatever forces had caused them had been unevenly applied. The "thumbprint" bruise was much fainter than the other one. Sindel had taken a grapefruit and squeezed it. His thumb had exerted as much pressure as his fingers.

The new dramatic allegations of abuse were more of a problem, but hardly insurmountable. Even the state's witnesses had seen Julie stand up to Ed. She did not fit the profile of a woman who would have stayed with an abusive husband for almost twenty years. Furthermore, the person who should know best, the family psychologist, would testify that there had been no indications of abuse.

The only thing that could not be explained away was the twisted towel ring. Sindel had to convince the jurors that Officer Kaelin had picked up the wrong towel ring from the hotel security chief's office.

If he could do that, his client might walk out of the courtroom.

What a boon that would be to Sindel's résumé. But the funny thing was, Sindel wasn't thinking much about his reputation. He really believed that Edward Post might be innocent.

In February 1992, almost three years after the first trial and almost six years after the death of Julie Post, the second trial began, with Judge Anna Forder presiding.

The courtroom was crowded. The stories of drinking and sex during the first trial had captured the media's attention and had focused attention on the case. But there were no clusters of supporters waiting in the hall for Post as there had been during the first trial. Only his parents talked to him during breaks. His spiritual wife had not made the trip.

Gerald Arbini, the former security chief for the Omni Hotel, testified on the second day of trial. He repeated his testimony from the first trial. Kaelin had picked up the only towel ring that had ever been in his office, he said. It was the ring from room 4063.

In cross-examination, Sindel produced the report that Arbini had written for the hotel.

" 'The towel ring was brought to my office,' " Sindel read. " 'Officer Kaelin picked up a towel ring from my desk.' "

The attorney tried to make a point about the difference between "the" ring that had been brought to Arbini's office, and "a" ring that Kaelin had picked up.

"Unintentional wording," said Arbini.

Stephanie and Dan waited together in the witness room as the second week of trial commenced. When Stephanie was summoned, she rolled her eyes at her uncle.

"Chin up," he said.

"This is for my mother," she said.

She marched into the crowded courtroom, stared briefly at her father, and then focused on Hoag.

"There has been testimony that there were problems in the marriage," he said. Sindel immediately objected, and the judge called the lawyers to the bench for a conference.

Stephanie began to cry.

When the trial resumed, Hoag asked her if she had been aware of problems in the marriage. Struggling, often unsuccessfully, to maintain her composure, Stephanie described a household from hell. Her parents fought often, she said, and used terrible, vulgar language during their fights. She said she sometimes heard her parents fighting in their bedroom, and then her mother would come into her room to sleep. Most often, the fights occurred after her parents had been drinking.

Hoag asked if she had been honest in her previous testimony.

She said she had not been, that she had been coached by her father.

When asked if her father had ever been abusive to her, she said that after her mother had died, she had been in an accident in a new car her father had bought her. He had struck her, knocking her down, then had kicked her while she lay on the ground.

The cross-examination was brutal. Sindel knew he risked looking like a bully, but he felt he had no choice. He led her through a laundry list of her past problems.

Had she ever tried to commit suicide? Had she ever been hospitalized for psychiatric problems? Had she ever been kicked out of high school? Had she ever had a substance-abuse problem? Had she ever been arrested for shoplifting?

At one point, she rolled her eyes and looked at her boyfriend in the courtroom.

"You can just answer questions. You don't need to look out there," Sindel snapped.

Hoag flew out of his chair. "He can just ask questions, judge. He doesn't need to give a lecture!"

The judge sustained the objection, and Sindel continued.

"These fights you talk about. Would Jennifer have heard them?"

"She was asleep probably," replied Stephanie.

Now it was Sindel's turn to roll his eyes. Then, in an effort to show she had been close to her father even since her mother's death, Sindel asked Stephanie if she had ever confided to her dad that she had had an abortion.

"Yes," she said, and then broke into hysterics.

After a recess, Hoag stood up for redirect. He asked Stephanie why she had lied in previous testimony.

"I was afraid. I had been lied to about the evidence

and I didn't want my father to go to jail at that time," she almost shouted.

As she left the witness stand, she glared hatefully at her father.

When Dan found out about the cross-examination, he was furious. His mother's warning to Stephanie had been acted upon. He called his parents at their hotel room.

"I didn't really believe you'd destroy your granddaughter," he said.

"Don't talk to your mother this way," Ann Post said.

Dan hung up on her.

Ed told a reporter that this had been the worst day of the entire ordeal. "But what were we supposed to do?" he asked.

The next day, Dan testified about the times Julie had called him to intervene in fights. He recalled a history of abuse that stretched from right after Ed and Julie were married to shortly before Julie's death. He didn't look at his brother as he testified.

Harby Kreeger testified about the violent incident he remembered from 1976.

Kim Autin testified that the day after Ed returned from the fateful trip to St. Louis, he had complained to her and Bobby that his thumb hurt. She testified about the bruises she had seen in San Francisco and Julie's comment that Ed had caused them. She told the jurors about the fight at Lenfant's and how Ed had come to her house and kissed her. She said he had sent her flowers the next morning.

McGarry was, as before, a very strong witness. He was unshakable in his conviction that he could determine the time of a bruise in relation to a person's death. When Sindel read a passage from a medical book stating that such a determination was impossible, McGarry calmly announced that he disagreed with the author.

"That's a bad translation," he said.

Nevertheless, Ed remained upbeat. When a real estate

friend from St. Louis visited him in the courtroom during a break, Ed assured his friend that things were going well.

"Don't believe the newspaper," Ed said.

Graham and the two defense pathologists, Roger Fossum and Kris Sperry, were in general agreement. It was impossible to tell when most of the bruises had occurred. There was, however, enough inflammation with the head bruises to determine that they had been caused shortly before death. All three doctors agreed that the manner of death was undetermined.

Sperry said he had inspected the bathtub in room 4063 and was of the opinion that the safety strips were not coarse enough to have caused the abrasions on the forehead. He said those were most likely caused by Julie's forehead coming in contact with the baseboard during the efforts to revive her.

"You don't know what condition those strips were in six years ago, do you?" Hoag asked in cross-examination.

"No," said Sperry.

Jennifer told the jurors that she did not recall the abuse about which her older sister had testified. She could recall only one loud argument, she said. Most of the bickering between her parents had been about Stephanie, she said.

During her testimony, she was soft-spoken and composed. Occasionally she smiled at her father. Once, looking at her father, she had to fight back tears.

The final defense witness was a financial consultant who testified that the Posts were not in financial trouble in the spring of 1986. Ed Post did not testify.

Circuit Attorney George Peach attended the trial that day. That evening, he went to a hotel in the county, registered under an assumed name, and, according to a prearranged plan, met a woman whom he believed was a prostitute.

* * *

With only minor revisions, Hoag delivered the same closing argument he had used at the end of the first trial.

He ridiculed the two defense pathologists. Of Fossum, he said, "That guy don't need a medical license. He needs a Ouija board." Of Sperry, he said, "There was no evidence to back him up, but that don't bother Doc Sperry."

Sindel tried to stress the medical evidence. "We've had a parade of experts in here. Don't you think that if they could have found one pathologist in the whole country who agreed with Dr. McGarry, he would have been here?"

He suggested that somebody at the hotel had pulled a towel ring off the wall in a second room just to see how easy it would come off, and then Kaelin had picked up that second ring.

"At the time, this was just about a lawsuit, but once you get on the roller coaster, you can't get off," he said.

After explaining Stephanie as a troubled young woman who simply wanted attention, Sindel turned to Dan Post's testimony.

"Dan Post slithered into this courtroom and he left it the same way. Brothers might sometimes turn against brothers, but I have never seen anybody do it with such enthusiasm. He searched through his brother's computer looking for defense notes—"

Hoag leaped out of his chair. Without bothering to formally register an objection with the judge, he advanced on Sindel.

"Let me tell you what the truth is," he said. Sindel turned to meet him.

"Don't tell me anything. You've had your argument. I know the truth."

"Then tell them the truth!" Hoag shouted.

Pounding her gravel, the judge demanded order. Hoag sat down.

Sindel returned to his argument. He pointed out that

both sets of parents were wealthy, and therefore the insurance angle made no sense.

"If that was the plan, why didn't he give himself a little more time, or why didn't he spend an extra ten bucks and get a million?"

Finally, Sindel asked why Julie, if she had wanted a divorce, would have signed the new insurance policy?

In Hoag's final statement, he called Sindel's theories a house of mirrors.

Deliberations began Wednesday afternoon and continued until the jurors were sent to the hotel for the night. The defense was somewhat heartened by the fact that the jury had requested to visit room 4063. Apparently, somebody wanted to feel the safety strips and test Sperry's observation that they were not granular enough to have caused the abrasions on Julie's face. The judge ruled, however, that because six years had elapsed, the condition of the strips could have changed. The jurors were not allowed to test Sperry's contention.

Thursday morning, the lead story in the newspaper said that Circuit Attorney George Peach had been arrested for soliciting a prostitute. Peach announced that he would read a statement to the media that afternoon.

To the superstitious, it seemed like a positive omen for Post.

Exactly one year earlier, the appellate court had granted Post a new trial. On that same day, George Hollocher had resigned under pressure from the police department.

Now, one year later, another of Post's adversaries was in trouble. At 3:00, in the courtroom across the hall from the Post trial, a grim-faced and haggard Peach admitted that the story was true. Although he declared his intention to remain in office, it was clear that his political career was over.

Twenty minutes later, the buzzer in Division Seventeen rang twice. The jury had reached a verdict.

As the jurors filed in, Post turned in his chair and scanned the crowded courtroom for Stephanie.

"I love you," he mouthed.

The verdict was read. Post was found guilty of first-degree murder. Mike Tully, an investigator for the circuit attorney's office who had assisted Hoag through both trials, led Stephanie out of the courtroom. Post sat impassively in his chair.

During routine rounds in the early hours of Friday morning, guards discovered Post lying unconscious on the floor of his one-man cell. He was rushed to the hospital. Doctors said he was comatose and unresponsive to stimuli, but his vital signs were stable.

In the outgoing mail that day, he had posted letters to family members. He restated his innocence and he said he forgave the people who had testified against him.

After seven hours, he regained consciousness. Toxicology reports indicated he had overdosed on two antidepressants—Elavil and Pamelor.

In May, he was formally sentenced and was sent back to the Potosi Correctional Center to serve life without the possibility of parole.

Epilogue

Two days after Ed Post was convicted of murder for the second time, his brother, his older daughter, and his best friend, all of whom had testified against him, sat in a backyard near Lake Pontchartrain and tried to sort out their emotions.

" 'Angst' is a good word," said Dan Post. "There is no way anybody can be happy about any of this."

"I'll never have another friend like Ed," said Harby Kreeger.

"I hate what he did, but he's still my father," said Stephanie Post. "You know, people probably get the wrong impression, like living with Ed was constant hell or something. It wasn't like that. Sometimes he could be a great father. He'd climb in bed and read to me. I remember that."

She also wanted to set the record straight about her abortion. She had been in the hospital for minor surgery, not knowing she was pregnant. She had been given drugs. When she learned she was pregnant, the doctors advised her to have the abortion.

Later that day, Jennifer reflected on the events of the preceding six years.

"I was twelve when Mom died, so you can imagine how rough this has been. For a long time, I just didn't want to think about it. I even went through a period when I didn't want to talk to him.

"I was always Daddy's girl, much more than Steph. It's like she'd hold herself back. Now my relationship with him is not like that anymore. It's person-to-person. We're friends."

A visitor wondered about her relationship with Stephanie.

"Oh, it's fine. We live in the same apartment building. I see her every day. We just don't talk about Dad, that's all."

The visitor asked if she thought her father was guilty. She hesitated for a moment.

"Even if he did it—in a fit of passion—he's forgotten. He doesn't believe he did it. So when he swears he's innocent, he's telling the truth.

"Besides, this might sound too legal, but I don't think they proved he did it."

She hesitated again, searching for words.

"Some of the things my dad says are a little ridiculous, I'll admit, but I just don't think he could have done it. I just don't know. If he did kill her—which I don't like to think is true—he deserves to be in jail. But I don't think he did."

Jennifer eventually changed her mind. A month after her father's conviction, she sought counseling. She is now convinced that her father murdered her mother. She is living with Dan and Martha and attending college.

In July 1992, a reporter met with Ed Post at Potosi. Ed said he was off all medication and was thinking clearly. He said he was optimistic about another appeal.

"I've been spending all my time in the law library here and I've found dozens of cases that impact directly on mine. In that sense, I'm very lucky."

After Ed recited a few of the cases his research had turned up, the reporter mentioned certain photographs that he was returning to Ed.

"I'm glad you're going to use that Mother's Day picture," Ed said. "Because that's the way it really was. I wouldn't try to tell you that Julie and I had a perfect marriage. There is no such thing. But most of the time, it was good. We had some wonderful times together."

Eventually, the discussion turned to Post's case.

"If you had cremated Julie's body, you wouldn't be here," the reporter said.

Post nodded. "Those thirty-nine bruises that McGarry made such a big deal of, they were from the long bone donations. Those bruises simply gave him an opportunity to say whatever the state wanted him to stay. If I hadn't consented to the long bone donations, I wouldn't be here. I think about that a lot."

As the months went by, life began to regain a sense of normalcy. The lawyers moved on to new cases, the girls, with the resiliency of youth, began to put their double-tragedy behind them and Dan Post began the process of reconciling with his parents.

"I'm a father myself," he said, "and I have to understand how parents are. Sometimes your love gets in the way of reason. Really, everybody in the whole family was trying to do what they thought was right. Me included."

Remembrances of Julie come less often. The daily humdrum of life sees to that. But when the remembrances come, they come with startling clarity.

Martha Post, who once shared an interest in extra sensory perception with Julie, remembers something that happened on the fifth anniversary of Julie's death.

"A white dove flew into the yard. You don't see many white doves around here. It just hung around, watching me. It was the strangest thing. Finally, it flew away, but it swooped down and almost brushed against me.

"Even aside from her death, the worst thing about this is the way they made Julie look. Like some kind of evil witch. She was really a good person."